Praise for *The First Robot President*

"Awesome book!!!! ... From the very beginning, the story pulls you in. The world building and character development makes you feel part of the world. The plot itself was eye-opening ... It's definitely a ride to a more realistic future of our society." *Gisela, Goodreads*

"A novel that makes you think and laugh ... Taylor does an amazing job at keeping the reader hooked through this political satire..." *Fay Gibb, Goodreads, BookBub*

"... In Taylor's futuristic world, the rich, as ever, enjoy every privilege and the poor struggle to make ends meet. The plots, conspiracies, and revelations are embedded in a culture and politics dramatically familiar to today's socio-political climate. The pacing is smooth and plotting tight. Esmeralda's quest rockets the plot along toward an unexpected yet satisfying conclusion. Taking a subtle yet savage swipe at current political climate, Taylor weaves in a political satire with much food for thought on environmental concerns, poverty, and war. Lighthearted and fun, the novel makes for a page-turning read." *The Prairies Book Review*

- **Winner, Science Fiction, 2022** *Independent Press Award*
- **Gold Prize, Humor, 2021** *Readers View Reviewer's Choice Awards*
- **Silver Prize, 2020-2021** *Nautilus Awards*
- **Distinguished Favorite, 2021** *New York City Big Book Award*
- **Finalist, 15th Annual** *National Indie Excellence Awards*

Praise for The First Robot President (continued)

"...a perfect combination of science fiction and politics. The author seamlessly blends lessons about economics and political science into the storyline ... I recommend this story to people who enjoy futuristic tales. I would also recommend it to students who are studying economics and political science ..." *Paige Loveitt for Reader Views*

"... an atmospheric and entertaining roller-coaster ride with high stakes. Plenty of twists and a satisfying finale make it an engrossing read." *BookView Review*

"... I am not very patient with boring books, so I was not sure if I would be able to finish it but it was a real page turner. The author obviously has both imagination/creativity as well as good knowledge about the federal government workings and political insights, which made this sci-fi to be interesting and relevant to us now." *Namkee G. Choi, Amazon*

"Robot's development of positive human behavior through the course of the book: Thoroughly enjoyed ... Besides intriguingly creating the backdrop of 26th century, key take-away for me was how the robot developed the human sensitivities through AI [artificial intelligence] as evident from the character of daughter's love & affection." *M. Horan, Amazon*

"The First Robot President's dialogue, which composes much of the text, is riveting and realistic ... An informative afterward offers convincing data on population projections for the next several centuries ... Robert Carlyle Taylor's skill in writing dialogue and exploring the ethics of having a robot as president make this novel an intriguing dive into pertinent topics." *IndieReader*

Praise for The First Robot President (continued)

"... an entertaining science fiction satire made fascinating because of its behind-the-scenes looks at the bruising world of modern politics." *Foreword Clarion Reviews*

"An enjoyable and thought-provoking book. The title was intriguing but I really did not expect much. I was pleasantly surprised by how interesting the book turned out to be ... I believe we are facing both a climate crisis and a population crisis. The book addresses both and by setting the novel about 500 years in the future shows clearly the consequences of our failures to act. I found the story well done and it was a fairly quick read. It was interesting to watch the changes in attitudes about the robot as well as the robot's developing intelligence. The novel works on several levels. Of course some will agree with the political views expressed and others will disagree. But in either case this is worth reading." *Jack Reidy, NetGalley*

"... a sparkling satire ... a political comedy the reader can enjoy whatever their partisan affiliation. The narrative is gentle and humorous, with a plot cleverly following the Greens, and a ridiculous robot candidate presented as an alternative to the two major parties. I enjoyed the ironic representation of political manipulation and maneuvering. I also liked the ambiguity that left me uncertain which group Carlyle was mocking the most; the Greens, Republicans, or Democrats! I could identify with the story even though I am an international reader, which proves the caricature has appeal beyond its reflection on domestic politics. I heartily recommend *The First Robot President* by Robert Carlyle Taylor for its entertaining qualities." *Cecelia Hopkins for Readers' Favorite*

The First
Robot President

A novel written by

Robert Carlyle Taylor

With an Afterword by the Author
and a Flowchart and Tables by Arvind Patel

Reflection Bay Press, LLC
113 Reflection Bay Court
Austin, Texas 78738
Copyright ©2020 by Robert Carlyle Taylor
Fourth Edition 2021

DISCLAIMERS

This is a science fiction novel that takes place approximately five hundred years in the future. Any statements made by any characters in the novel about the news media, people, religions, churches, political organizations, Donald Trump, Ivanka Trump, or any other people or entities are fictious; these statements do not reflect the opinion of Robert Carlyle Taylor or Reflection Bay Press, LLC. At the date of publication, neither the author nor the publisher had any affiliation with The Green Party of the United States or any of its affiliates; moreover, the positions taken by characters in the novel who are members of The Green Party, the Democratic Party, and the Republican Party are pure fiction and may not reflect the actual position of the same parties today. The book contains political satire, but in no instance does the author have any malicious intent. Except for references to President Donald Trump and former Presidents George Washington, Franklin Delano Roosevelt, Ronald Reagan, Barack Obama, William Jefferson Clinton, and Dwight Eisenhower; former Vice President Al Gore; former First Lady Jacqueline Kennedy; Ivanka Trump; Dave Thomas; Paul and Anne Ehrlich; Bob Dylan, Andrew Lloyd Webber, and a number of other musicians, composers, and artists, all names in *The First Robot President* are fictitious; and if anyone else happens to have the same name as a character in the novel, even if they have the same title or profession, it is a coincidence. Hotels and restaurants mentioned in the novel are real establishments as of the date the novel was written, but the author has identified them only to give context to the story line, not to endorse them. Finally, the Dave Thomas International Adoption Agency does not exist and is not to be confused with the Dave Thomas Foundation for Adoption, which does exist.

Hardcover ISBN: 978-1-7346462-9-0 (Fourth Edition)
Paperback ISBN: 978-0-5783724-2-6 (Fourth Edition)
eBook ISBN: 979-8-2019329-5-4 (Fourth Edition)
Audiobook ISBN: 978-1-7346462-3-8 (based on Third Edition)

Cover design by Tanja Prokop, Book Design Templates
Interior design based on First Edition formatted by Tracy Atkins, The Book Makers, and updated by the author for this edition (see Preface)
Edited by the author

The Buddhist quotations at the beginning of the novel are used with permission from the office of His Holiness, the XIVth Dalai Lama, and from a representative of the Fo Guang Shan Buddhist Order.

Venerable Master Hsing Yun's statement in Chapter 12 that a skillful physician cures with weeds and a skillful worker makes steel from old pots comes from the following book: *On Education*, subtitle: *The Everlasting Light, Dharma Thoughts of Master Hsing Yun*. Leon Roth and Doris Koegel-Roth, translated by Venerable Manho, Gandha Samudra Culture Company, 2002, Taipei, Taiwan, p. 7.

Dedication

First, to my wonderful wife, Mandy; and second, to Paul and Anne Ehrlich, whose ground-breaking work on the impact of population on the Earth's ecosystem sounded the first alarm that may possibly, hopefully save the human species from extinction.

Table of Contents

Preface to the Fourth Edition

Anyone who purchased an earlier edition of *The First Robot President* will surely attest that it was beautifully designed. Tracy Atkins of The Book Makers designed the interior of the first and second editions, published in 2020, and set them in Times New Roman at my request. For the third edition, which I designed myself, I chose Baskerville Old Face; and for this edition, which I also designed, I selected Palatino Linotype. There is no other difference between the third and fourth editions.

When I listened to the audiobook version of the novel, which was published in August 2021, I realized that Chapter 11, "Transition of Power" was too long; therefore, beginning with the third edition, I split it into three separate chapters, "Transition of Power," "The Birth Lottery," and "Geneva." "Murphy's Law," formerly Chapter 12, is now Chapter 14. I made no material changes to the content of any of these chapters, nor did I do so elsewhere in the novel. However, I couldn't resist the temptation to add another line of dialog to the exchange between Geraldine and the King of England in the first section of what is now Chapter 12. I also changed two references to Lockheed Martin in Chapter 8 to General Google Motors to be consistent with the story line; and finally, I corrected a few remaining typographical errors that I overlooked in preparing the second edition.

I tip my hat to Mr. Atkins for laying the foundation of a beautifully designed book; and I hope that readers who, like me, enjoy owning the books they read will treasure it regardless which edition they purchased.

Robert Carlyle Taylor

Quotations

"The Earth is, to a certain extent, our mother. She is so kind, because whatever we do, she tolerates it. But now, the time has come when our power to destroy is so extreme that mother earth is compelled to tell us to be careful. The population explosion and many other indicators make that clear, don't they? Nature has its own natural limitation."[1]

His Holiness, the XIVth Dalai Lama

"...Only an empty briefcase can be packed with things, only an empty railroad car can carry passengers, only empty nostrils can breathe air, and only an empty mouth can eat food. Only when there is enough space can people live and move about."[2]

Venerable Master Hsing Yun, founder of the Fo Guang Shan Buddhist Order

---

[1] Dalai Lama, His Holiness. *Worlds in Harmony: Compassionate Action for a Better World* (Berkeley: Parallax Press, 2008; original edition 1992), p. 55. Print.
[2] Yun, Venerable Master Hsing. *Four Insights for Finding Fulfillment, A Practical Guide to the Buddha's Diamond Sutra,* translated by Robert Smitheram (Los Angeles: Buddhas's Light Publishing, 2012), p. 86. Print.

The First Robot President

Part I

Wife and Mother

Chapter 1

The Wedding

O n the morning of September 15, 2484, Geraldine Jenkins arose, walked into her kitchen, and took a clean coffee mug from a rack near the sink. An inscription on the mug read *University of Virginia, Class of 2435*. Then she turned and placed the mug in a port on her refrigerator door. After briefly considering her choice of 79 creamer flavors, she said, "I'll take my coffee full-strength with Coffeemate, original flavor, no sugar."

In a moment, the refrigerator dispensed Geraldine's coffee as instructed; and she turned to the north wall, which was curiously devoid of ornaments, and stated in a declarative tone, "Richard, please." The north wall transformed into a wall-to-wall, floor-to-ceiling, high-resolution monitor.

A three-dimensional image of a handsome young man appeared on the monitor. "Good morning, Ms. Jenkins. Would you like your morning update?"

"Yes, Richard, do I have any phone calls?"

"Yes, your daughter, Jacqueline, called at seven o'clock this morning—no message."

"Please bring her on-line, then."

3

"I understand, Ms. Jenkins, you would like to speak to your daughter, Jacqueline. Is that correct?"

"You got it."

"Give me just a moment, please." Richard disappeared; and in a moment, an attractive young woman appeared in his place.

"Good morning, Mom."

"Good morning, Jacqueline. My digital assistant told me you called. Is it important?"

"I'd say so. You wouldn't believe what my brother has done this time."

"Oh, not again. Is he in some kind of trouble?"

"I don't know if you'd call it trouble, at least not yet, but he has ordered a robowife!"

"A robowife? I hope you're joking."

"No, I'm not. He ordered it last week, and he is taking delivery this afternoon."

"Ask me why I'm not surprised."

"You have to speak to him. The older he gets, the more outrageous his behavior."

"Sometimes I think his only goal in life is to shock his mother," said Geraldine.

"Have you ever seen one in real life … I mean a *robowife*?"

"Well, I've seen robots at Fair Oaks Mall," Geraldine replied. "I don't know for sure if they were robowives or something else. Anyway, you can tell right away they aren't human. You know that something's not right."

"Well, the new ones are unbelievably realistic. You can hardly tell the difference from a real human being."

"Believe me, I can tell the difference."

"Anyway, the high-end models have the IQ of a human being. The more expensive models are even smarter."

"Oh my God! Just what I need, a daughter-in-law who is smarter than I am!"

"Ha!"

"What did he pay for it, anyway?" asked Geraldine.

"I don't know. Why don't you conference him in, and you ask him yourself?"

"Richard," said Geraldine, "please split the screen. Hold Jacqueline and bring in Thomas."

Richard reappeared on the monitor. "I understand you would like me to hold Jacqueline and bring Thomas into the call. Is that correct?"

"You got it."

"Give me just a moment, please." Richard disappeared; and in a few seconds, Thomas appeared on the right half of the monitor, Jacqueline moving to the left half.

"Hello, Mom," said Thomas. "What's up?"

"What's up? You tell me what's up, young man! Jacqueline just told me you purchased a robowife. Have you completely lost your mind?"

"Calm down, Mom. This is not a big deal."

"Not a big deal? Are you kidding? I think it's a *very* big deal!"

"Listen, Mom, I know this is quite a paradigm shift for you, but it is becoming more and more common. In fifty years or so, they say that the majority of marriages will be with robots."

"Do you expect me to believe that?"

"Actually, Mom," said Jacqueline, "Thomas may not be that far off the mark. I've heard the same thing."

"Are you supporting your brother's decision? asked Geraldine. "Whose side are you on, anyway?"

"I'm not on Thomas's side, but it's a moot point—he's already purchased it."

"He can still return it!"

"I'm not going to return it!" exclaimed Thomas.

"I have a suggestion," said Jacqueline. "Before we get into a big argument, why don't we go over to Thomas's apartment and meet her? Maybe we'll like her."

"I doubt that very much," said Geraldine. She paused. "Okay, I agree, let's meet her. When are they delivering her?"

"This afternoon between two and four," replied Thomas.

"Does that work for you, Mom?" asked Jacqueline.

"Sure, I'll meet you there at two."

"Sounds good," said Jacqueline.

"I'll be looking for you," said Thomas. "Don't be late."

* * * * *

Geraldine and Jacqueline arrived at Thomas's apartment within a few minutes of each other, just before two o'clock. Inside the apartment, Thomas kissed his mother on the cheek and gave Jacqueline a hug. "You are going to love Esmeralda," he said.

"Esmeralda?" asked Geraldine, sitting down in an armchair.

"I've named her Esmeralda."

"And may I ask what you paid for her?"

"Two point five million."

"Isn't that a little extravagant for someone who's still paying off his college loans?"

"Not really. I have friends who paid more than that for their first aerocar."

"You know you can get a basic sex robot for under 500,000 dollars," said Jacqueline. "A stripped-down model—no pun intended."

"There you go," said Geraldine. "Why spend two and a half million dollars when you can get a basic sex robot for a fraction of that? After all, don't you just want it for sex?"

"Not exactly," replied Thomas. "I want a robowife who can carry on an intelligent conversation. The reason I bought such an expensive model is that she has a high IQ. Also, her memory bank has a knowledge base equivalent to that of a college graduate."

"Heaven help us!" exclaimed Geraldine.

Jacqueline sat down beside her mother. "Well, if Thomas thinks he can afford it, I guess it would make life more interesting having a sister-in-law—especially if she is as intelligent as he claims."

"How soon is this robowife going to be here?" asked Geraldine.

Thomas, who was still standing, turned to the east wall of his living room. "James, can you give me an update on our UPS delivery?"

The monitor on Thomas's east wall lit up, and his digital assistant appeared. "Of course, Mr. Jenkins, give me just a moment."

After a few seconds, James provided the requested update. "The UPS drone is currently crossing Leesburg Pike near the intersection of 495. The projected arrival time is in approximately four minutes."

"Thank you, James," said Thomas. "That will be all for now."

James disappeared, and the east wall went dark.

"May I get either of you a glass of water while we're waiting?" asked Thomas.

"I think I'm going to need something stronger than water," replied Geraldine.

"Do you have any wine?" asked Jacqueline.

"Is white wine okay?"

"I'll take it if you don't have anything more potent," said Geraldine.

"Okay," said Thomas. "I will bring you some wine. Please listen for the doorbell."

Thomas left the room, and mother and daughter looked at each other.

"This is going to be interesting," said Jacqueline.

"You are a master of understatement," replied Geraldine.

In a couple of minutes, Thomas returned with the wine; and in another minute, the doorbell sounded. When Thomas opened the door, he saw a UPS drone hovering above a large package. The drone immediately scanned Thomas's face to verify his identity, then snapped a photograph of him for the record. "Thank you for allowing UPS to serve you," said the drone. "We hope you're satisfied with our service." The drone then ascended and quickly disappeared.

"Do you need a hand with it?" asked Jacqueline, standing and turning towards the door.

Thomas stooped down, grabbed the cardboard handles, and lifted the package. "It's not as heavy as you might think. I've got it."

Thomas carried the package into the living room while Jacqueline closed the door.

"It's barely more than four feet high," said Geraldine. "I hope she isn't that short."

"Maybe they bent her over when they packed her," said Jacqueline. "I hope we don't have to assemble her."

"Well, let's open the box and find out," said Thomas. He stepped back and examined the box more carefully, looking for an opening. "Okay, we seem to have it right-side up. It says to open from the top. Here we go." He removed a Swiss Army knife from his pocket, opened it, and cut open the top flap. The four sides of the box immediately fell to the floor, revealing a young woman seated in a cardboard chair. She appeared to be in her mid-twenties with long, dark-brown hair and Asian features and was fully dressed in a blue skirt and a color-coordinated print blouse. Her eyes were open, but she appeared lifeless as if in a coma. One eye looked slightly different than the other, the only clue that she wasn't human.

"Holy smokes!" exclaimed Jacqueline. "She looks so real!"

"She reminds me of a corpse," said Geraldine. "Why didn't you just go to the morgue?"

"Bear with me," replied Thomas, assessing the situation. "She needs to be activated."

"There are instructions on the cardboard," said Jacqueline, pointing to the opened box.

Thomas looked down at the cardboard box lying on the floor. The instructions were printed on the inside of the box: **Before activating your robot, please view the orientation video. From your home computer, open *www.generalgooglemotors.com/robot*, then click on *Connect*.**

Thomas looked over to the east wall. "James, please log me on to the Internet and pull up the following web site: General Google Motors slash robot."

The east wall lit up, and James appeared. "I understand, Mr. Jenkins, you would like me to access the internet site General Google Motors slash robot. Did I get that right?"

"Yes, and when the site comes up, click on *Connect.*"

"Of course, Mr. Jenkins. Give me just a moment, please."

Thomas, his mother, and his sister all watched the east wall as the web site appeared. James clicked on "Connect" as instructed, then disappeared. A middle-aged man dressed in a business suit appeared on the monitor.

"Hello, my name is David McKenzie, and I'm the program manager at General Google Motors for the robowife program. Congratulations on your purchase of a robowife!"

"I didn't know General Google Motors made robowives," said Jacqueline.

"They make everything," replied Thomas. "It's practically the only manufacturing company left in America."

"You have made a smart decision," continued Mr. McKenzie. "Your robowife has been manufactured to the highest standards and is nearly maintenance-free. She can perform all the functions of a human wife, but she will never argue with you. Moreover, she is programmed to love you, and only you, so you will never have to worry about her being unfaithful."

"Thank goodness!" exclaimed Geraldine. "You wouldn't want your robowife sleeping around now, would you?"

"Depending on which model you ordered," continued Mr. McKenzie, "your robowife comes with basic, intermediate, or advanced cooking skills. She can also make the bed, do the dishes, do the laundry, and clean the house. Most models can also mow the lawn and tend to the garden."

"This isn't sounding so bad," said Jacqueline. "I wonder if they make robo-husbands."

"One of the many advantages over a human wife," Mr. McKenzie continued, "is that your robowife's beauty will never fade—she will look exactly the same at age one hundred as she looks today."

"Oh yes!" exclaimed Jacqueline. "I definitely need to find out if they make robo-husbands!"

"Give me a break!" exclaimed Geraldine.

"In fact," continued Mr. McKenzie, "your robowife is guaranteed to last one hundred years. She is self-cleaning and will recharge herself once a week using a standard 120-volt electric outlet. The only thing you have to remember is to replace her battery every thirty-five years."

"Just as advertised," said Thomas.

"One word of caution," Mr. McKenzie added. "Your robowife will need some time to develop social skills, so we don't recommend your taking her out in public right away. A good plan is to watch movies together until she gets the feel of how human beings relate to each other. Within three to six months, you should be able to take her anywhere, and no one will have a clue that she isn't a real human wife."

"I will believe it when I see it," said Geraldine.

"I'm sure you are anxious to see your new robowife in action," Mr. McKenzie continued, "so let me tell you how to activate her. You will find her battery in a package taped to her back. Remove the battery from the package, lift the back of her blouse to find the battery compartment, and look for an allen wrench taped to the outside of the compartment. Use the allen wrench to open the compartment and insert the battery as shown in the diagram. When you close the battery compartment, your robowife will wake up. Give her a few seconds to become oriented to her new surroundings."

"That sounds easy," said Thomas, looking for the battery package.

"You should be all set now," concluded Mr. McKenzie. "If you need any technical support, please contact our help desk at www.generalgooglemotors.com/robot/helpdesk. Once again, congratulations, and good luck with your new robowife!"

Mr. McKenzie disappeared, and the east wall went dark.

Thomas lifted the back of the robot's blouse to find the battery and the battery compartment. Following Mr. McKenzie's instructions, he removed the battery from its package, found the allen wrench, opened the battery compartment, inserted the battery, and closed the compartment. Then he sat back down in a chair and waited for the robot to boot up.

As soon as Thomas closed the battery compartment, the robot began to stir.

"She is waking up!" exclaimed Jacqueline.

"Her name is Esmeralda," said Thomas. "Please call her by her name."

Esmeralda blinked, moved her head from right to left, and slowly rose from her cardboard chair. Once on her feet, she stepped away from the box and looked around the room, focusing briefly on each of the three people in the room. Then her gaze returned to Thomas, and she smiled. "You must be Thomas, my fiancée. I recognize you from your photo."

"My photo?" asked Thomas, standing up. "I didn't know you had a photo of me."

"They put your photograph in my memory bank."

"Of course, that makes sense," replied Thomas.

"I believe I'm supposed to kiss you," said Esmeralda. "Do you want me to kiss you?"

"Well," replied Thomas, laughing nervously, "This is a little awkward … but sure, why don't we have a quick kiss. Just to seal the deal, so to speak." He walked closer to Esmeralda, and they exchanged a brief kiss.

"Oh my God!" exclaimed Geraldine. "Please wake me up and tell me I was dreaming!"

"Let me introduce you to my mother and my sister," said Thomas. "This is Geraldine, my mother, and this is Jacqueline, my sister."

"I'm pleased to meet you," replied Esmeralda. "I have never met a mother before."

"You never met a mother before?" asked Geraldine.

"Well, to be honest, I never met a human being until last week. I met a few human beings at the lab when I went through final testing. As far as I know, though, there weren't any mothers there."

"Were there any *women* there?" asked Jacqueline. "I mean, besides you?"

"Yes," replied Esmeralda, "there were some women there, but they didn't identify themselves as mothers."

"Well," replied Thomas, "They wouldn't necessarily tell you that during testing. Their job was to make sure you were functioning properly."

"I understand."

"Would you like me to show you around the apartment?" asked Thomas.

"Of course."

"Wait a moment," interjected Geraldine. "I can't spend the whole afternoon here, and we have some business to settle."

"Business?" asked Thomas.

"Yes, *business*," replied Geraldine, putting emphasis on the word. "We have to discuss your plans for the wedding."

"The *wedding*?" asked Thomas and Esmeralda simultaneously.

"Yes, the wedding. I'm not having you sleep with each other until you are officially married."

"I have that covered," replied Thomas. "General Google Motors is sending me all of Esmeralda's documentation—a marriage certificate, a birth certificate, a social security card, and a passport. I should receive them this week."

"That's all well and good, but you still need a wedding."

"Mom, don't be ridiculous!" exclaimed Thomas. "Nobody has a wedding anymore!"

"Your father and I did, didn't we?"

"Well, that was thirty years ago. Times have changed."

"Well, in this family, we still have weddings." Geraldine looked at her daughter. "Jacqueline, please back me up on this. We still have weddings, right?"

Jacqueline squirmed in her seat. "Well, no one in our family has actually been married for a long time, so we haven't had a wedding for a long time." She glanced at her mother, who was glaring at her. "But I agree, if you are going to get married, it's always a good idea to have a wedding."

"We're not getting married in a church!" stated Thomas emphatically.

"It doesn't necessarily have to be in a church," suggested Jacqueline. "You could hire a marriage celebrant and have the ceremony anywhere. You could have the wedding right here in your apartment if you want."

"Jacqueline has offered a sensible compromise," said Esmeralda. "I think her idea makes perfect sense and avoids an unpleasant argument."

"Just what I need," said Geraldine, "a daughter-in-law who sides with my daughter."

"Okay, I'll go along with Jacqueline's suggestion," said Thomas. "But I want the ceremony small and simple."

"I have not yet given my consent to Jacqueline's suggestion," said Geraldine, determined to stand her ground.

"It doesn't matter," replied Thomas. "Three in favor, one undecided, the majority rules. That's the democratic process."

"So now you're bringing the democratic process into it, are you?" replied Geraldine. She paused and, realizing that she was outnumbered, added, "All right, have it your way. But let's get this done as soon as possible. *This week.*"

"I'll find you a marriage celebrant," said Jacqueline.

"Like I say," Thomas replied, "I want to keep it simple. We can have a brief ceremony in my living room followed by dinner in my dining room. I'll make arrangements for a caterer. Jacqueline can be the Maid of Honor. I will invite a couple of my friends, Hector and William. The Governor will be the Best Man."

"The Governor?" asked Esmeralda.

"Hector Lopez," replied Thomas. "He is not really the Governor, at least not yet. We nicknamed him "The Governor" because he aspires to be the Governor of Virginia. Right now, he's in the United States House of Representatives—we just say 'the House'—and is one of the youngest people ever elected."

"I can't wait to meet him," replied Esmeralda. "I love politics!"

"Esmeralda is going to need a bridal gown," said Jacqueline.

"This is getting complicated," said Thomas. "I said I wanted to keep it simple."

"All brides need bridal gowns," said Geraldine. "That's a no-brainer."

"I don't seem to have any wedding gowns in my memory bank," said Esmeralda, looking puzzled. "I don't even have a clue what they look like."

"Why don't you ask your digital assistant to show us a few gowns right now?" suggested Jacqueline. "We can get this done in five minutes."

"Oh, all right," sighed Thomas. "Wedding gowns—that's a female thing, isn't it?" Turning to the east wall, he called up his digital assistant. "I need one more thing, James."

The wall lit up and James appeared. "Yes, Mr. Jenkins, at your service."

"Can you show us a few wedding gowns?"

"Certainly, do you have anything particular in mind?"

"Just keep the cost under ten thousand dollars."

"The gown has to have sleeves," said Geraldine. "The sleeveless gowns young women are wearing these days look cheap."

"Then ask James to find us something with sleeves," said Jacqueline. "Also, I think Esmeralda would look good in a gown with a classic V-neck."

"But not a *plunging* V-neck," said Geraldine. "I don't need to see her breasts."

James pulled up a web page with a dozen gowns, all with sleeves and V-necks. "These are all under ten thousand dollars."

"I like the one in the bottom right-hand corner," said Jacqueline. "It's a classic style, a basic ball gown in ivory with an embroidered ruffle."

"It's okay," said Geraldine.

"I don't know anything about wedding gowns," said Esmeralda, "so I'll rely on your judgment."

"Good," said Thomas. "It's settled. James, please order that one. We'll need delivery within twenty-four hours."

"I will need to know your wife's size, Mr. Jenkins."

"Her measurements are 34-23-34. Oh, and she's five feet tall if they need her height."

"How do you know my measurements?" asked Esmeralda.

"Because that's what I specified when I ordered you," replied Thomas. He turned back to the east wall, "Go ahead and place the order right away, James."

"Yes, Mr. Jenkins, I will place the order immediately." James disappeared and the wall went dark.

"You specified her measurements when you ordered her?" asked Geraldine.

"Let it go, Mom," said Jacqueline. "You can't change it now."

"One more thing," said Geraldine, looking at Thomas and Esmeralda. "I don't want you two sleeping with each other until after the wedding. Have I made myself clear?"

"I beg your pardon?" asked Thomas.

"I see where this is going," said Jacqueline. "Let's not get into a big fight. Thomas, why don't you let Esmeralda sleep here in the living room tonight and tomorrow night?" Jacqueline pointed to Thomas's sofa. "She can use that couch there."

"I don't mind," said Esmeralda.

"Okay, guys," said Thomas, "but I don't want to hear any more rules or objections. After the wedding, no more interference—it's my show from then on, understand?"

"Of course, Son," replied Geraldine. "Well, I think we are done. Just let me know when I'm supposed to show up for the ceremony." She arose from her chair and turned to Esmeralda. "It was nice to meet you, Esmeralda."

"I enjoyed meeting you, too. I look forward to getting to know you better."

Geraldine turned to Thomas and kissed him. "I hope this makes you happy, Thomas." Then she turned to the front door.

Jacqueline said goodbye to Thomas and Esmeralda and followed her mother out the door.

*   *   *   *   *

Later that week, Geraldine arrived at Thomas's apartment at 6:00 p.m. as instructed. Jacqueline, who had arrived earlier, greeted her at the door.

"Hi, Mom. Everything is all set. William is here, and Esmeralda is getting dressed. We are waiting for Hector and the marriage celebrant."

"How does the gown fit?"

"Perfect ... and it's gorgeous."

"Of course, it is gorgeous. You and I picked it out for her, didn't we?"

Thomas appeared in the room dressed in a green tuxedo. He walked over to his mother and kissed her.

"Thanks for coming, Mom."

"You don't think I'd miss my son's wedding, do you?"

"No, I don't think you would. Anyway, Esmeralda is almost ready. Please have a seat while she finishes dressing. Can I get you a glass of wine?"

"Do you have anything stronger?"

"A gin and tonic?"

"Sure."

Thomas called to someone in the kitchen. "Henry, can you bring my mother a gin and tonic?"

An unfamiliar voice came from the kitchen. "On the rocks?"

"Mom, do you want it on the rocks?" Thomas asked.

"Please."

"Yes, Henry, she wants it on the rocks."

Henry appeared a couple of minutes later with Geraldine's drink. She took it and sat down in an armchair. Jacqueline sat down beside her.

"Are you sure you're okay with this whole thing, Mom?" asked Jacqueline.

"I don't have any choice, do I?"

"It's too bad dad isn't alive to see this," said Jacqueline.

"I don't think Thomas would have dared to go through with this if he were still alive."

At that moment Esmeralda entered the room. Except for her wedding gown, she looked exactly the same as she did when she arrived in a box a few days earlier.

"Hello, Geraldine," said Esmeralda. "I'm glad you could make it."

"I wouldn't miss it for the world."

"How do I look?"

"You look terrific!" said Jacqueline. "Turn around so mom can see what it looks like in the back."

Esmeralda twirled slowly so that Geraldine could see the wedding gown from every angle.

"It's okay," said Geraldine.

Thomas turned his left wrist, revealing an antique Apple *Series 12* smartwatch. "It's almost six-fifteen."

Geraldine looked at Jacqueline. "What time did you tell the marriage celebrant to arrive?"

"Six-fifteen," Jacqueline replied. "She should be here any minute."

The doorbell rang. Thomas went to the door and opened it.

"It's Hector," Thomas announced.

A handsome man in his mid-twenties entered the room.

"You had me worried, buddy," said Thomas. "We couldn't have the wedding without the Best Man."

"Not to worry, man. You know I wouldn't let you down!" Hector looked around the room. "Hi, Geraldine! Hi, Jacqueline!" Then his eyes came to rest on Esmeralda. "So you are the lucky woman!" He walked over to her and extended his hand. "It's a pleasure to meet you!"

"I've heard you want to become a governor," Esmeralda replied. "I can't wait to hear more about it!"

"It might be wise to wait until after the wedding," replied Hector, laughing. "What if I find you want to run against me?"

"You don't have to worry about that. I'm programmed to be a wife, not a governor."

The doorbell rang again, and Thomas opened the door.

A middle-aged woman stood in the doorway. "Are you Thomas Jenkins?"

"Yes," Thomas replied. "Are you the marriage celebrant?"

"Yes, I am. My name is Martha."

"How do you do, Martha. Please come in."

Thomas let Martha into the apartment and introduced her to the others. "Hector is the Best Man, and my sister Jacqueline is the Maid of Honor."

"So nice to meet you," Martha replied. "I'm honored to perform the ceremony."

"Thank you for responding on such short notice," said Jacqueline.

"Well, then," said Thomas, "let's not waste any time. We need to do the ceremony quickly because dinner will be ready in ten minutes."

"I hope you can stay for dinner, Martha," said Jacqueline.

"Of course."

"Okay, then," said Thomas. "Is everyone ready? We can get this done quickly and sit down to eat. Martha, I will turn it over to you. Tell us what we have to do."

"I want Thomas and Esmeralda to stand over there," said Martha, pointing to the west wall of the living room. "The Best Man will be on Thomas's left. The Maid of Honor will be on the bride's right."

Thomas, Esmeralda, Jacqueline, and Hector walked over to the west wall, and Martha faced them.

"Thomas and Esmeralda, please face each other," said Martha. "Then listen to what I say and repeat my words when I prompt you. Thomas, do you have a wedding ring for your bride?"

"Yes, I have the ring," replied Thomas.

"Good," said Martha. "Put it on your bride's ring finger when I prompt you."

"Which finger?" asked Esmeralda. "I don't seem to have that information in my database."

"Your database?" asked Martha.

"Esmeralda is very organized," Thomas explained. "She keeps everything in a database."

"Of course," answered Martha. "Everyone has their idiosyncrasies."

Thomas spoke to Esmeralda quietly. "Just extend your left hand towards me when Martha prompts you. Trust me, I know which finger the ring goes on."

"Okay," responded Esmeralda. "I will trust you to put the ring on the correct finger."

"Esmeralda," Martha continued, "do you have a ring for Thomas?"

"Yes, she has a ring for me," Thomas replied. He pulled a wedding band from his coat pocket and gave it to Esmeralda. "Just give this to me when Martha prompts you."

"All right," said Martha. "Let's get started." Looking at Geraldine, Jacqueline, Hector, and William, Martha began, "Ladies and gentlemen, we are gathered today to celebrate the marriage of Thomas Jenkins and his bride, Esmeralda. A wedding is one of life's most important moments. Please join me in blessing this marriage and praying for the happiness of the groom and the bride."

"I can't believe this is happening," said Geraldine.

"If there is anyone present," Martha continued, "who knows of any reason why Thomas and Esmeralda should not be joined today in holy matrimony, please speak now or forever hold your peace." She paused and looked at Geraldine, who remained silent.

"Thomas," Martha continued, "do you promise to take Esmeralda as your lawful wife, to have and to hold, and to care for her in sickness and in health?"

"I can't get sick," said Esmeralda. "It's impossible."

"Esmeralda appears to be an extremely healthy young woman," said Martha.

Thomas put his mouth to Esmeralda's ear. "It's standard wedding language. They use more or less the same words at every wedding. The words don't necessarily apply to every situation." Turning back to Martha, he answered, "I do."

"Now repeat after me," Martha continued, "With this ring, I thee wed."

"*I thee wed?*" repeated Esmeralda. "That's a funny way of talking."

"Just go along with what she says, even if it sounds a little weird," Thomas replied. Then, responding to Martha's instructions, he repeated, "Yes, with this ring, I thee wed."

"Thomas, please place the ring on your bride's finger."

Thomas put the ring on the appropriate finger of Esmeralda's left hand.

Martha turned to Esmeralda. "Esmeralda, do you promise to take Thomas as your lawful husband, to have and to hold, and to care for him in sickness and in health?"

"Say 'I do,' " said Thomas.

"I do," replied Esmeralda.

"Now repeat after me," Martha continued, "With this ring, I thee wed."

"With this ring, I thee wed," said Esmeralda.

"Esmeralda," continued Martha, "please place the ring on the groom's finger."

Esmeralda handed the ring to Thomas, and he put it on his ring finger.

"Wonderful!" exclaimed Martha. "I now pronounce you man and wife!"

"Whew!" exclaimed Thomas. "We got through it!"

"How to go!" said William.

"Congratulations!" said Hector.

"Yes, you did it," said Jacqueline, giving Thomas and Esmeralda each a high-five. "I'm so proud of you!"

"I hope my late husband isn't rolling over in his grave," said Geraldine.

"Okay, we're done," said Thomas. "Let's go to the dining room and have dinner."

*   *   *   *   *

After a short bathroom break, the small wedding party gathered in the dining room for dinner. Esmeralda sat on one side of Thomas, who was seated at the head of the table, and Hector sat on the other side. Jacqueline sat at the foot of the table. Geraldine sat on Jacqueline's left, and Martha sat on Jacqueline's right. William sat between Hector and Martha.

"The dinner is being catered tonight by Family Friendly Caterers," Thomas explained. "They specialize in small family dinners like this. They are supposed to be good."

"I'm sure the meal will be excellent," said Hector.

A waiter arrived with salad. Water glasses and three bottles of wine were already on the table.

"I hope they know I don't eat food," Esmeralda remarked.

"She doesn't eat food?" asked Geraldine.

"Let's just say she has a different kind of food," Thomas replied.

"Electricity, to be exact," said Esmeralda. She pushed the salad plate away.

Martha's expression suddenly changed. "Electricity?" She reached for her water.

Thomas coughed. "Well, I guess an explanation is in order here. We don't want you to be the only one here in the dark, Martha. Esmeralda is not an ordinary human being. Actually, she is not a human being at all—she's a robot. I hope that clears it up."

Martha gasped, spitting a mouthful of water over the table. "*A robot?*"

Geraldine gave Thomas a look of disapproval. "You should have told Martha that Esmeralda was a robot before the ceremony!"

"Don't look at me," Thomas replied. "Jacqueline made the arrangements for the marriage celebrant."

Jacqueline cleared her throat. "I apologize to you, Martha, if an apology is needed."

Everyone looked at Martha, waiting for her reaction.

"I don't think Martha is looking for an apology," said William. "I'm sure she has run into this before."

The waiter reappeared and noticed Esmeralda had pushed her salad away.

"You don't care for the salad?" asked the waiter. "Can I get you something else, perhaps some broccoli and cheddar soup?"

"No thank you," replied Esmeralda.

"Very well," replied the waiter. "Please let me know if you would like anything else." He picked up one of the bottles of wine and opened it, then walked over to Thomas and handed him the bottle.

"We have three fine wine choices for you this evening," said the waiter. "May I suggest this vintage 2457 Cabernet Sauvignon from Napa Valley? Cabernet Sauvignon is one of our most popular wines."

Thomas passed the open bottle under his nose and examined the label. "This will do," he said, handing the bottle back to the waiter.

The waiter walked around the table, pouring a small amount of Cabernet Sauvignon into each wine glass, then placed the bottle with the remaining wine in the center of the table. He then picked up Esmeralda's salad plate and disappeared.

Hector stood up and raised his wine glass. "I'd like to propose a toast to the bride and groom!"

Everyone grasped their wine glass and looked at Hector.

"As you may know," Hector continued, "Thomas has been my close friend and Green Party supporter for many years. I could not be more pleased to see that he has finally found the woman ... uh, the female robot ... of his dreams. Please join me in wishing Thomas and Esmeralda a lifetime of happiness!"

Everyone raised their wine glasses and reached across the table to touch glasses. Then everyone except Esmeralda took a sip of the vintage wine.

"Excellent toast!" Thomas said. "Thank you very much, Hector. You aren't called *The Governor* for nothing!"

Hector chuckled. "I'm afraid I'm still a long way from becoming the governor. But thank you anyway!"

Esmeralda leaned forward and looked at Hector. "Did I hear you say *Green Party?*"

"Yes," replied Hector, who had sat back down after making the toast and was now eating his salad. "Thomas and I have been active in the Green Party since we became eligible to vote."

"I know about Republicans and Democrats," replied Esmeralda, "but not about Green people. What do Green people stand for?"

"Well," replied Thomas, "we don't actually call ourselves Green people."

"Maybe you should," said Geraldine.

"In any case," continued Thomas, ignoring his mother, "the Green Party is focused on environmental issues."

"Broadly speaking," added Hector, "environmental issues include war and gun control."

"And safe food," added Jacqueline. "Our food supply is constantly threatened with contamination."

"I'm all for a clean environment," said Esmeralda. "Consider me on board!"

"Great!" exclaimed Thomas.

"Fantastic!" said Jacqueline. "We can use your talents!" She paused. "Or I *think* we can."

Thomas, who was now eating his salad, pointed his fork towards Hector. "My good friend here is the youngest member of the Green Party ever elected to Congress."

"How exciting!" said Esmeralda.

"I'm very proud of him," added Thomas.

"You're not proud of your sister?" exclaimed Geraldine. "She might not be the youngest person elected to Congress, but give her a little credit for being elected!"

"You're so impatient, Mom," replied Thomas. "I was getting to that." He pointed his fork at Jacqueline. "She's a member of Congress, too."

"No offense taken," said Jacqueline.

"Our family is very centered on politics," explained Geraldine. "My late husband was a Congressman for more than forty years."

"Mom's talking about our dad," said Jacqueline. "He represented Virginia's eleventh district, and the governor appointed me to finish his term when he died."

"I'm so sorry about your father," replied Esmeralda. "When did he die?"

"Three years ago."

"He didn't take care of himself," said Geraldine. "He might have lived another twenty years if he had just eaten right."

"How old was he when he died?" asked Esmeralda.

"Ninety-nine," replied Thomas.

"Like I said," added Geraldine, "he didn't eat right."

"Anyway," continued Jacqueline. "I finished his term, and then I was elected in my own right in 2482. I'm running for re-election right now."

"She's running unopposed," explained Thomas. "She continues to benefit from our father's popularity."

"You make it sound like Jacqueline wouldn't be popular if she didn't have a famous father," said Geraldine. "Give her a little credit, please."

"I'm just saying that the Jenkins name might explain why she is running unopposed."

"Are Jacqueline and Hector political opponents?" Esmeralda asked.

Hector laughed. "I certainly hope not!"

"I represent Virginia's eleventh district," explained Jacqueline. "Hector represents the eighth district."

The waiter appeared. "How is everyone doing on their salad?"

"Please take my plate," replied Geraldine.

The waiter took Geraldine's plate and held it in one hand while he picked up the bottle of Cabernet Sauvignon with his other hand, then walked around the table and added wine to everyone's glass. When he came to Esmeralda, he noticed that she had not yet drunk from her glass and passed her with no comment. "We will have the main course on the table in just a moment," he said.

"I'm so glad I married into a family with political ambitions," said Esmeralda. "Politics is so fascinating!"

"Why is she so interested in politics?" asked Martha.

"Because she has a college degree with a double major in political science and economics," explained Thomas. "I think we will find that she is also fascinated by economics."

"Did I go to college?" asked Esmeralda, showing surprise.

"Well, not exactly," replied Thomas, "but your memory bank contains approximately the same knowledge as someone who did."

"I guess I'm smarter than I realized!" said Esmeralda, looking around the table and smiling at everyone.

"I never doubted for a moment that you were smart!" said Hector.

Esmeralda looked at Thomas. "Can I run for Congress, too? I believe I could help to advance the Green Party's agenda."

Everyone looked at Thomas to see his reaction.

"You know, we ought to let her do that," Thomas replied. "Can you imagine that—a robot running for Congress? Wouldn't that be a riot!" He laughed, and everyone except Esmeralda joined in the laughter.

Thomas looked at Esmeralda. Realizing that she was not laughing, he said, "I apologize, Esmeralda, I didn't mean to hurt your feelings. It was just a joke."

"You *can't* hurt my feelings," replied Esmeralda. "Remember, I don't have any feelings. I'm a robot."

There was an awkward silence.

Geraldine was the first to speak. "God help us!"

"I'd like to know more about the process of becoming a robot," said Martha, trying to overcome the awkwardness of the moment. "When did you first gain consciousness?"

"Well," replied Esmeralda, "I first awoke last week for testing. They put me through some drills to make sure everything was working right. Everything checked out, so they put me back to sleep."

"Was it painful?" asked Martha. "I mean, when a human baby is born, it cries a lot. Did you cry when you first woke up?"

"No," replied Esmeralda. "I don't recall any pain, and as far as I know, I didn't cry."

The waiter appeared with three plates of food in his hands. A second waiter appeared behind him with three more plates. The two of them cleared the remaining salad plates and put the main course on the table. "Our finest cut of filet mignon," said the first waiter. "I hope you enjoy your meal." The two waiters then disappeared with the empty salad plates in their hands.

"This is probably the only time you will ever see beef or any other meat in my house," said Thomas. "I'm becoming a vegetarian."

"Good Lord! What's he going to do next?" asked Geraldine.

"I'm with him on this one," said Jacqueline. "If you knew more about the process of making meat, you'd become a vegetarian, too." She picked up a knife and fork and began cutting the steak.

"If I may change the subject," said Esmeralda, "I'd like to ask Geraldine what it's like to be a mother. Geraldine, can you tell me what it's like?"

Geraldine paused before answering. "Well..." She paused again, not sure how to explain motherhood to a robot.

Jacqueline picked up the conversation. "It begins with having a baby."

"Yes, that's right," said Geraldine. "First you have a baby. That's the challenging part. Babies require a lot of attention. They want to be breast-fed, and then they keep you up half the night during the first year. Thomas wasn't too bad. Jacqueline drove me crazy."

"Jacqueline is still driving her crazy," said Thomas.

"Anyway," Geraldine continued, ignoring Thomas's comment, "after you get through that part, it's fun—it is, anyway, until they become teenagers. That's a whole different story. But it's rewarding when you see your children grow up and become successful."

"That sounds wonderful," said Esmeralda. "Thomas, can I be a mother, too?"

Everyone laughed.

"There is one minor problem," replied Thomas. "Robots can't have babies."

"They can't?" asked Esmeralda, clearly disappointed.

"No," replied Thomas. "Science has not yet found a way for robots to reproduce."

"I certainly hope not!" exclaimed Geraldine.

"It's not that scientists can't figure out how to do it," William said. "They could, but it would be very controversial. People don't want robots to have reproductive capability."

"Why not?" asked Esmeralda. "People don't want to see baby robots?"

Everyone laughed again.

"Baby robots would be very cute," said Jacqueline.

"Please, give me a break!" exclaimed Geraldine.

"The bottom line is that people are worried about the technology," said Hector. "No one knows exactly where that path would take us."

"That's right," replied Thomas. "What if robots were to become the dominant species on the planet?"

"So there's no way I can become a mother?" asked Esmeralda.

"You could always adopt a child," suggested Martha. "They have so many children up for adoption these days that they don't know what to do with them all."

"That's true," added Hector. "In fact, they have streamlined the adoption process in order to place the children as quickly as possible. It wouldn't be hard for you to adopt a child if you wanted to."

"I wouldn't mention you are a robot, though," said Martha. "That might derail the approval."

"Why are there so many children up for adoption?" asked Esmeralda.

"Because of the economy," replied Thomas. "People have children, and then they realize they can't afford them."

"Many people don't make enough money to feed their kids," said Jacqueline. "Hunger and starvation are issues the Republicans and Democrats don't want to talk about."

"Why don't they want to talk about those things?" Esmeralda asked.

"Because there is no simple solution," Thomas replied.

The first waiter appeared and looked at the table. "Can I get anyone anything?" He noticed Esmeralda had not yet touched her meal and walked over to her. "Is there any problem with your meal, ma'am?"

"No, everything is fine," replied Esmeralda.

"Esmeralda's appetite is off tonight," explained Thomas.

"Would you prefer a vegetarian plate?" the waiter asked.

"No thank you."

"You may have a case of nerves," said the waiter. "That would be quite understandable. Perhaps a glass of white wine would help to calm your nerves."

"No thank you."

The waiter persisted. "May I suggest a glass of tonic water? That always seems to do the trick when my stomach doesn't feel right."

"No thank you," Esmeralda replied. "I'm not allowed to drink liquids of any kind."

"No liquids of any kind?" repeated the waiter. "Of course, that's perfectly understandable. Please enjoy your dinner." He walked away and disappeared into the kitchen.

"Maybe we should have explained the situation to the waiters," said Jacqueline.

"I don't think so," replied Thomas. "Like we were just saying, robots are still controversial. Our best strategy is to tell people that Esmeralda is a robot on a need-to-know basis. The waiters don't need to know."

"I agree," said Hector. "There is no need to tell everyone."

"Getting back to our conversation," said Esmeralda, "I think I heard you say adoption might be a viable option if Thomas and I want a child, is that correct?"

"Are you serious?" asked Jacqueline. "You really want a child?"

"Yes, I think I do."

"I didn't tell you about teenagers," said Geraldine. "They can be a real pain in the butt."

Everyone laughed and resumed eating their dinner. Esmeralda had obtained answers to her immediate questions, and the rest of the dinner conversation was pleasant but mundane. At the conclusion of the meal, Hector announced that he needed to be on his way.

"I think the wedding was a big success," said Thomas. "I want to thank everyone for coming." Then he excused himself, went to the kitchen, and thanked Henry and the other waiters and advised them that they were free to leave. He returned to the dining room to say goodbye to the guests. Over the next few minutes, each of the guests departed until he and Esmeralda were alone.

"Would you like me to clear the table?" asked Esmeralda.

"No need," replied Thomas. "I have another robot for that. I just need to start the dishwasher after the robot clears the table."

Thomas opened a closet adjacent to the dining room, and a small robot emerged. Thomas pushed it towards the table. "Please clear the table."

While the robot cleared the table, Thomas led Esmeralda into the kitchen. There they waited for the robot to deliver all of the plates, glasses, and silverware to the countertop above the dishwasher. When the robot had completed this task, Thomas pushed a button on the dishwasher. A robotic arm appeared from inside the dishwasher, reached up to the countertop, and picked up each of the dishes, emptying any remaining food into the garbage disposal; then it placed the dish into the bottom rack of the dishwasher. After picking up all of the dishes, the same arm took each of the glasses, emptied any remaining wine or water into the sink, and placed each glass into the top rack. Finally, the arm took the silverware and placed it into a separate compartment inside the dishwasher. Then it disappeared into the dishwasher, closing the door behind it.

Thomas and Esmeralda could hear the sound of water moving inside the machine.

"That's all there is to it," said Thomas. Then he turned the small robot around and pushed it towards the dining room. "Back into the closet!" he ordered.

The robot went back to the dining room; and in a moment, Thomas and Esmeralda could hear the closet door open and close.

"That's impressive," said Esmeralda. "Your little robot will save me some work. Does it do anything else?

"This particular robot is only for clearing the table," replied Thomas. "But I have other robots for other tasks."

"What would you do without these robots?" asked Esmeralda.

"Frankly, I don't know what human beings did before we had this technology," replied Thomas. "Can you imagine clearing the table by hand? Or washing the dishes by hand? Primitive man had a hard life."

"I'm a robot, too," replied Esmeralda. "Just let me know how I can help."

Thomas was anxious to put his new robowife through her paces, so he suggested that they go to bed. He led Esmeralda into the bedroom.

"Do you need to use the bathroom before we go to bed?" asked Thomas.

"No," replied Esmeralda. "I never use the bathroom."

Thomas helped Esmeralda undress and get into bed. Then he disrobed and climbed into bed with her, and they made love. Esmeralda made sounds of pleasure and said, "Oh, Thomas, I love you," passionately, albeit mechanically, as she was programmed to do. Thomas was very pleased.

After making love, Thomas sat up and opened his left hand, activating his iPalm, which lit up, revealing a miniature keyboard. He pushed several keys with his right index finger. "I need to set my dream machine."

"Dream machine?" asked Esmeralda.

"It's an app on my iPalm," explained Thomas. "Before we had this technology, people's dreams were just a collection of random thoughts. It was very silly and pointless. Today we use our dream machines to watch movies or listen to lectures. I don't know what I'd do without it."

"It sounds entertaining," replied Esmeralda.

After setting his dream machine, Thomas lay down, put his head on his pillow, and quickly fell asleep. He did not awake until morning.

Since robots do not sleep, Esmeralda lay motionless beside Thomas with her eyes open, staring at the ceiling. She remained thus for the duration of the night, patiently waiting for her next assignment.

Chapter 2
Marriage: Day One

When Thomas awoke the next morning, he was pleased to find Esmeralda beside him in bed, just where she was when he had fallen asleep.

"Good morning," said Thomas. "I can see that you are going to be a very dependable robowife."

"Thank you," replied Esmeralda. "Would you like me to prepare breakfast?"

Thomas sat up and climbed out of bed. "Breakfast is actually pretty easy. You can get coffee and hot oatmeal or scrambled eggs from the refrigerator door. I think I will save your cooking skills for dinner tonight."

Thomas collected his clothing from the floor where he had left it the previous evening. "Let me use the bathroom, and I will meet you in the kitchen in twenty minutes."

"I will have your coffee ready. Do you want oatmeal, scrambled eggs, or something else, and how do you want your coffee?"

"I'll have oatmeal this morning. As far as the coffee is concerned, there is a default option on the refrigerator door called

Thomas. Just push the button and the refrigerator will prepare my coffee the way I want it."

After shaving and showering, Thomas dressed and met Esmeralda in the kitchen. She had dressed herself and was wearing the same print blouse and blue skirt she wore when she emerged from the packing box earlier in the week. She had placed his coffee and oatmeal on the kitchen table.

"Please let me know if you want anything else," said Esmeralda.

Thomas sat down at the table. "Nothing else at the moment, but we need to buy you some more clothes. I will ask Jacqueline to help you pick out some blouses and skirts."

"I don't really need any more clothes," replied Esmeralda. "What I'm wearing is fine."

"Please sit down with me so we can talk." Thomas motioned to the chair across from him, and Esmeralda sat down.

Thomas took a sip of coffee before speaking. "Humans don't like to wear the same clothes every day. It would be boring. Besides, your clothes need to be cleaned every so often, and you need other clothes to wear while your dirty clothes are at the cleaners."

"Okay, that makes sense."

"What did you think of the wedding?"

"It was nice, but I don't have any basis of comparison. It was the first wedding I have ever attended."

"Most weddings are a lot bigger. I mean, more people. I wanted to keep it simple."

"Yes, it was simple."

"You seemed to enjoy yourself. Do you have any questions?" Thomas began eating his oatmeal.

"Yes, I'd like to follow up with you on two things that came up during dinner. First, do you want me to run for Congress, and second, how soon can we adopt a child?"

"Oh, my Goodness!" Thomas looked up from his oatmeal. "You're getting way ahead of me!" He took another sip of coffee. "To begin with, the idea of having you run for Congress was a joke. I was just saying it would be funny. With respect to adopting a child, yes, that might be possible, but we have to think it through. Having a child is a huge commitment. It takes many years to raise a child. It involves a lot of time, money, and energy."

"I have lots of energy. I can go twenty-four hours a day with no sleep. I just have to recharge my battery every seventy-two hours."

"That would be helpful—I mean, being able to go twenty-four hours a day with no sleep. I wish I could do that."

"Also, I seem to have some information on child psychology in my memory bank. That would probably help, too, don't you think?"

"Yes, that would definitely help. You have a knowledge bank equivalent to a college graduate, and most college students take at least one or two courses in psychology, so that's probably where you got the information."

"Then you agree we should adopt a child?"

Thomas took another sip of coffee. "I wasn't planning to make a decision like that on our first morning together, but I can see that you're enthusiastic about it ... and it does make more sense than running for Congress."

"I agree it makes more sense than running for Congress."

"As someone said over dinner last night, they are practically giving children away right now. The situation is quite desperate."

"Your friend Hector said they have streamlined the adoption process."

"That's correct. Moreover, adopting a child would be socially responsible. That's one of the tenants of the Green Party."

"Well, then, let's do it," replied Esmeralda. "I want to be socially responsible, and I believe I can handle the commitment."

Thomas finished his coffee. "I'll tell you what. When I finish my breakfast, we'll take a look at the adoption web site and see what's involved in it."

"Thank you, that sounds wonderful ... but I hope you are also open to the idea of my running for Congress someday. I think I'd like that, too."

"That's going to require a little more thought. Adopting a child is doable. Let's stick with that for now."

"Okay, but if I ran for Congress, would I run against Hector? Just so I know."

"You tear me up! No, you can't run against Hector! Now, if Hector moves on to the Senate or becomes Governor of Virginia, that would open up his seat in the House. We can talk about it again if that ever happens. But I can assure you it won't happen for a long time, if at all."

"I understand."

"Let me finish my breakfast, and I will ask James to pull up the adoption web site."

Thomas finished his oatmeal in a few more minutes and got up from the table. "Let's go into the other room where we can work on the adoption."

Esmeralda followed Thomas to the living room where they sat down in chairs facing the east wall.

Thomas summoned his digital assistant. "James, I need you to open the Internet."

The east wall lit up and James appeared. "Yes, Mr. Jenkins, at your service. What web site are you looking for?"

"The adoption web site, whatever that would be. Try www.dhhs.gov and look for a link to an adoption center in northern Virginia."

James pulled up the web site for the Department of Health and Human Services as instructed and then clicked on the appropriate links without further instruction until he found the adoption centers in northern Virginia.

Thomas scanned the page quickly. "It looks like there's one in Fairfax. Click on that one."

James clicked on the adoption center in Fairfax. "I think this is what you may be looking for."

"Yes, this is it," replied Thomas. "Esmeralda, let's see what it says."

Thomas and Esmeralda reviewed the information on the web page.

"James," said Thomas, "click on the link called 'step-by-step procedures for adopting.'"

James pulled up the step-by-step procedures as directed.

"Okay, it looks like the first step is to provide my full name and social security number as the head of the household so that they can run a security check. If I pass the security check, then we select the age, sex, and race of the child we would like. That sounds pretty easy."

"What age, sex, and race do we want?" asked Esmeralda.

"Well, I'm pretty sure we don't want to adopt a baby. You heard what my mother said last night about babies."

"I agree, we don't want to adopt a baby."

"Let's give them the information for the background check. We can think about the rest of it while we are waiting for the results to come back." Thomas looked at Esmeralda to confirm her agreement. She nodded, and he turned back to the monitor. "James, you have my name and social security number on file. Please enter the information on this page."

James followed Thomas's instructions. The web site responded with a message reading, "YOUR REQUEST FOR A BACKGROUND CHECK HAS BEEN RECEIVED. PLEASE BE PATIENT AS THIS MAY TAKE UP TO ONE MINUTE."

"I don't think it will take a whole minute," said Thomas. "I haven't had any incidents with the law."

As Thomas predicted, the system approved his background check in less than a minute. "CONGRATUATIONS! YOU HAVE PASSED THE BACKGROUND CHECK. NOW CLICK ON THE LINK TO SELECT THE TYPE OF CHILD YOU WISH TO ADOPT."

"James," said Thomas, "click on the link to select a child."

James clicked on the appropriate link, and the web page for selecting a child appeared on the monitor.

"Okay, Esmeralda, what do you think?" asked Thomas. "We have to enter the type of child we want—age, sex, and race."

"I'll rely on your judgment."

"Okay, then, I'll make an executive decision. Let's go with age *five-to-ten*. I'd rather have a girl, so let's check *female* for gender; and let's check *Asian* for race because the child will feel more comfortable with a mother who looks like her."

"That works for me," replied Esmeralda.

"James," said Thomas, "please click on the radial buttons for age *five-to-ten*, sex *female*, and race *Asian*."

James followed Thomas's instructions and clicked on the appropriate radial buttons.

"Now hit *Submit*," said Thomas.

James hit "Submit" as instructed. Moments later a message appeared, "CONGRATULATIONS! YOUR CHOICE OF A CHILD HAS BEEN PROCESSED. THE CHILD WILL BE READY FOR PICK-UP TOMORROW AFTER 2:00 P.M. PLEASE ARRIVE 15 MINUTES EARLY TO MEET THE CHILD'S SOCIAL WORKER. BE SURE TO BRING IDENTIFICATION."

"I wonder why they need identification," said Thomas. "Everything these days is done by facial recognition."

"Maybe it is a safeguard in case the facial recognition software has a glitch."

"I suppose so. In any case, we're done. Let's make our plans for the rest of the day."

"You said you wanted Jacqueline to help me pick out some new clothes."

"Right, I almost forgot." Thomas turned back to the east wall. "James, please bring Jacqueline into the conversation."

"Of course, Mr. Jenkins. Give me just a moment."

Jacqueline appeared on the monitor in another thirty seconds. "Are you looking for me, Thomas?"

"Yes, how are you this morning?"

"Very well, thank you. Say, great wedding last night!"

"Thank you. I thought it was successful."

"What did Esmeralda think of it?"

"Esmeralda is right here. You can ask her yourself."

"Hello, Esmeralda," said Jacqueline. "How did you enjoy the wedding?"

"I enjoyed it very much, thank you."

"I know you're busy, Sis, so let me get to the point," said Thomas. "Esmeralda needs some new clothes. Can you help her pick out some blouses, skirts, shoes, and other things she may need?"

"Sure, anything for my baby brother. How much are you willing to spend?"

"I'd like to keep it under twenty-five thousand dollars."

"That's not going to buy many clothes. Are you sure you can't spend a little more?"

"I really don't need a lot of clothing," said Esmeralda. "Just some clean clothes to wear when my dirty clothes are at the cleaners."

"Let's start with what you can buy for twenty-five grand," said Thomas. "We can always buy some more things later on. Oh, and make sure you help Esmeralda pick out some nice lingerie. I'd like to see her in three or four different colors. Get some lingerie in jet black, hot pink, crimson, and baby blue."

"I got it," replied Jacqueline.

"Do you remember her measurements?" asked Thomas.

"You said 34-23-34, right?"

Thomas looked at Esmeralda. "Did the wedding gown fit right?

"Yes, it seemed to fit all right."

"You hear that, Sis?" asked Thomas. "She said the wedding gown fit right, so you can use the same measurements for everything else. When will you have time to do this?"

"I can do it this morning. Give me thirty minutes. I will call you back."

"I won't be here. Ask James for Esmeralda."

"James?"

"My digital assistant."

"Oh, right, I forgot his name. I'll call Esmeralda back in a few minutes. Nice talking to you."

"Thanks again for your help, Sis. Have a good day if I don't speak to you again."

"You, too."

Jacqueline disappeared.

"That's all for now, James," Thomas said. "You may shut down the Internet. You will need to bring it up again in about thirty minutes. Jacqueline is authorized to spend up to twenty-five thousand dollars for Esmeralda's clothes."

"I understand your instructions, Mr. Jenkins," replied James. He disappeared and the east wall of the room went dark.

Thomas turned to Esmeralda. "Here's the plan the rest of the day. I'm going into the office now. You can shop for clothes with Jacqueline while I'm gone. I'll have lunch in the House cafeteria, so you won't have to worry about fixing me lunch. We are low on food, anyway, so we'll need to go grocery shopping. We can do that when I get out of work, which is usually around five o'clock."

"Are you coming home to pick me up?"

"Not if I don't have to—it's out of my way. When you're talking to Jacqueline, ask her if she wouldn't mind picking you up at five o'clock and dropping you off at Healthy Foods on Lee Highway."

"Okay, I'll ask her."

"Have her call me if she can't do it, and I'll come home and pick you up."

"Got it."

Thomas arose from the breakfast table and went back to the bedroom to get the keys to his aeromobile. He returned a few minutes later and said goodbye to Esmeralda.

"Have a good day, sweetheart," said Thomas, kissing Esmeralda on the lips.

"You, too, Thomas. Have a good day at the office."

Thomas departed, and Esmeralda sat back down in a chair facing the east wall, waiting for Jacqueline's call.

*   *   *   *   *

Thomas arrived at his office in Washington, D.C., at 9:30 a.m. and parked his aeromobile on the rooftop parking garage. Then he climbed out of the vehicle, locked it, and walked downstairs to his office in the lobbying firm of Green Solutions, LLC. After greeting a couple of co-workers whose cubicles were adjacent to his own, he sat down and began working. He spent the morning checking his messages, returning phone calls, and setting up meetings on the Hill for later in the week.

At 11:30 a.m., Thomas called up the House cafeteria lunch menu on his computer and ordered a sandwich; then, a few minutes before noon, he left the office and walked a few blocks down the street to the cafeteria, where he passed through security and received his meal at the pick-up counter. Holding his tray, he looked around the dining area for someone he might know and saw William and another co-worker, Jennifer, sitting near a window. He walked over to them.

"May I join you?" Thomas asked.

"Good to see you, buddy!" replied William. "Please sit down."

"I hear you got married," said Jennifer.

Thomas sat down next to William, across from Jennifer. "So the word's out, huh? William, are you the one who broke the news?"

"No, I didn't hear it from William," said Jennifer. "Everyone in the office has been talking about it all week. A robowife!"

"Yep, you heard right."

"You should have told us you had broken up with your girlfriend. I could have introduced you to one of my friends."

"Based on my last relationship, I think I'm better off with a robot—no offense."

"The company has a program for mental health counseling, you know."

"Mental health counseling?"

"Maybe you should have talked to one of the counselors before you ordered a robowife."

Thomas picked up his sandwich and took a bite.

"Thomas knows what he's doing," said William. "He doesn't need to talk to a counselor."

"I'm just saying," replied Jennifer, "if I broke up with my boyfriend, I would talk to a mental health counselor before I ordered a robot replacement."

"I guess everyone forges their own path in life," replied Thomas. "I've had several girlfriends. I thought I'd try something different this time."

"Frankly," said Jennifer, "I thought you had better sense than this."

"Better sense?" Thomas repeated, taking another bite of his sandwich.

William was silent.

"Just so you know," continued Jennifer, "your co-workers think you've gone off the deep end."

Thomas put his sandwich down and took a sip of water. "Some of them, maybe. Others might say I'm on the cutting edge of human progress."

"Have you lost your mind? Or are you on drugs?"

"No, I haven't lost my mind, and I'm not on drugs."

William looked at Jennifer. "I think you're being a little hard on him. As he said, some people may frown on the idea of a robowife, but others will be open-minded about it."

"You guys have both lost it—totally lost it!"

"As I said to my mother," replied Thomas, "this is a big paradigm shift for most people. They just need some time to get used to the idea."

"Please!" exclaimed Jennifer.

"He's right," said William. "People just need time to get used to the idea."

"Well, just be aware that most of your co-workers think you've lost touch with reality...or that you're crazy—downright crazy."

"So be it," replied Thomas. "I can handle it."

Jennifer persisted, "Do you really think a robowife is going to meet your emotional needs?"

"So far she is meeting my emotional needs just fine."

"You can't be serious!"

William gave Jennifer a frown. "I think we better drop the subject."

"Actually, I'm enjoying the conversation," replied Thomas. "Let's *not* drop the subject. Have you considered the advantages of a robowife?"

"No, I haven't," replied Jennifer. "Please tell me: What are the advantages?"

"To begin with, a robowife doesn't age the way a human wife does. She will always look like she's twenty-five years old."

Jennifer glared at Thomas. "Isn't that wonderful?"

"And another thing, my robowife will never argue with me about how to spend my money, how to decorate my apartment, or what movie to watch. In fact, my robowife will never argue with me about anything. She is totally compliant and obedient."

"This is too much for me," said Jennifer, pushing her chair back and standing up. She picked up her food tray and handed it to a robot standing nearby that was collecting trays. "Enjoy your lunch." She turned and started to walk away.

"Oh, Jennifer, one more thing!" called Thomas as she walked away. Jennifer stopped walking and turned back to the table.

"I forgot to mention—Esmeralda is going to run for Congress someday."

"Esmeralda?"

"Yes, my robowife. Her name is Esmeralda."

"Like I said, you're crazy! You've completely lost your mind! You should be institutionalized!" Jennifer turned and walked away.

"Are you sure you can handle this?" asked William. "I'm afraid you may lose some friends."

"I don't expect to lose any friends I don't want to lose. I never liked Jennifer anyway."

William's expression turned to resignation. "Okay, I guess you know what you're doing."

Thomas smiled. "Yes, I do. I think it was Steve Jobs who said that no one ever accomplished anything great by being like everyone else."

"Steve Jobs?"

"The guy who invented the Apple Macintosh."

"I never heard of him, but I like the quote."

"It's one of my favorites."

"We've been friends a long time. I'll have your back."

"Thanks very much, William. You're a good man."

The two friends finished their lunch without further reference to Esmeralda and walked back to the office together. When Thomas returned to his desk, he busied himself with a report that had to be turned in by the close of business. At five o'clock, he turned off his computer and left the office, taking the elevator to the rooftop parking lot where he climbed into his aeromobile and flew to Healthy Foods on Lee Highway.

*   *   *   *   *

After parking the aeromobile, Thomas walked towards the entrance of Healthy Foods, which was surrounded by protestors chanting and carrying signs. He could see Esmeralda waiting for him near the front door, on the other side of the protesters, and he worked his way through the crowd in her direction. As he did so, he looked at the signs. One read, *HOW IS THE MIDDLE CLASS SUPPOSED TO FEED THEIR FAMILIES?* and another read, *$500 FOR A LOAF OF BREAD? IS THIS A JOKE?*

Thomas reached Esmeralda and kissed her on the lips. "Have you been waiting long?"

"No, Jacqueline dropped me off about ten minutes ago."

"Sorry I'm late. Let's go inside and buy what we need for dinner tonight."

"Does the store normally have all these protesters?"

"Lately, yes, but it's not the store's fault that prices are so outrageous—it's the law of supply and demand."

"It sounds like the demand curve shifted to the right."

"Correct. We have too many people chasing the limited food supply."

"The store can't do anything about supply and demand. Do humans have an action plan for addressing the issue?"

"Sadly, no," replied Thomas, grabbing an empty shopping cart as they entered the store. "The politicians can't agree on a course of action."

"That's too bad," replied Esmeralda. "Does the Green Party have any solutions?"

"Yes, but no one will listen. Not yet, that is, but they will soon enough. People don't realize just how bad it's going to get before this is over."

They stepped inside the supermarket. "Wow!" exclaimed Esmeralda. "Look at all this food!"

"Actually, if you look more closely, you'll see that many of the shelves are empty. The store used to have twice as much food as it does now."

"This is the first store I've ever been in. I don't have any basis of comparison."

"Let me show you around, then. This is the produce section over here." Thomas pointed to shelves partially filled with fruits and vegetables. "And over there is poultry, beef, and fish. However, we won't be buying anything there. Putting the ethical issue aside, meat and fish are way out of my price range."

"Supply and demand again?"

"Exactly, especially fish. There's hardly any fish left in the ocean."

"How do humans get fish anyway? Do they send divers into the ocean to collect fish that have died?"

"Don't you wish!"

"Don't tell me they kill live fish."

"Well, that's what I meant when I said I was putting the ethical issue aside. I didn't want to get into it right now, but since you asked..." Thomas paused. "You see, all life on this planet devours lower forms of life. Human beings are at the top of the food chain."

"That's so unfair!"

"Not only unfair, but cruel, too. Anyway, let's pick up some vegetables for dinner tonight. Follow me this way."

Thomas led Esmeralda into the produce section and showed her how to pick out lettuce, tomatoes, onions, potatoes, sweet potatoes, squash, apples, blueberries, and bananas. Esmeralda took each item as Thomas handed it to her, examined it, and placed it in their shopping cart. In less than twenty minutes, they had completed their shopping.

Thomas turned the shopping cart towards the front of the store. "Let's head for the cashier and pay for this."

"How do you pay for it?"

"You'll see. Follow me." Thomas began pushing the cart towards the cashier.

In less than a minute, Thomas and Esmeralda arrived at the cashier's station. There was no cashier in sight, but the image of a handsome young man appeared on a digital monitor above the counter.

"Good afternoon, Mr. Jenkins," said the digital cashier. "Did you find everything you needed?"

"How does he know your name?" asked Esmeralda.

"I'm a regular customer. A digital cashier like this can recognize and remember more than one hundred million faces, about the same number as the current population of Fairfax County."

"Can humans do that, too?"

"Not quite—in fact, not even close." Thomas turned to the digital cashier. "Yes, I found everything I needed."

"I have scanned your purchases," said the digital cashier, referring to the grocery items that were still in the shopping cart. "The total is $4,749.89. Do you want to put that on the same account you used last week?"

"Yes, that would be fine," replied Thomas.

"If you move your shopping cart into the portal, I will bag it for you," said the cashier.

Thomas pushed the shopping cart into a small opening in the counter. The front panel of the cart swung down, and a robotic arm reached over and swept all of the groceries into a small box.

"Would you like a drone to take your groceries to your vehicle?" asked the cashier.

"Yes, please."

"Would that be the same vehicle you used on your previous visit?"

"Yes, the same aerocar. Do you need the license plate number?"

"No, I have the license plate number in my database. The drone will find your aerocar and meet you there in approximately two minutes."

"Great," replied Thomas. "Esmeralda, let's go!"

Thomas and Esmeralda left the store and walked to Thomas's aeromobile where they met the drone, which was hovering with the grocery box over the vehicle. Thomas said, "Open trunk," and the aeromobile's trunk door swung open. The drone deposited the box into the trunk and flew away. Thomas said, "Close," and the trunk door closed.

Thomas and Esmeralda entered the vehicle, and Thomas told the machine, "Take us back to my apartment." The aerocar's engine began to hum, and the vehicle rose above the parking lot like a helicopter, then turned towards his apartment.

As the vehicle ascended, Esmeralda looked down at the highway adjacent to the supermarket and noticed a blanket of white tents on both sides of the highway, stretching as far as she could see.

"What are all the white tents for?"

"For the homeless."

"Oh my God! These poor people have nowhere else to live?"

"Sadly, no."

"And the government isn't doing anything about it?"

"The government is providing them with tents."

"That doesn't sound to me like a humane solution."

"Well, the current Administration thinks they can solve the problem by exporting people to Mars—volunteers, of course. They're offering free land on Mars and no taxes for ten years as an incentive. It's a joke if you ask me. Mars doesn't have enough habitable land to make a dent in the problem."

"How many human beings do you have on Earth?"

"Close to five hundred billion."

"How about the other planets in the solar system?"

"None of them are habitable. Even Venus, which is closest in orbit to Earth, has a poisonous atmosphere and is too hot."

"Your leaders need to come up with some new ideas."

"There's no simple solution," replied Thomas. "There's no more real estate left for housing."

"I didn't realize that humans had it this bad."

"It wasn't always this bad. Humans have propagated for centuries without considering the end game. It was only a matter of time we would run out of room."

"We need to talk to Hector and Jacqueline about this."

"I can assure you that Hector and Jacqueline are fully aware of the problem. They are doing their best, but change comes slowly. It's like trying to turn the Titanic away from the iceberg."

"The Titanic?"

"It's a famous boat that hit an iceberg and sank to the bottom of the ocean several centuries ago."

"How terrible!"

"Yes, it *was* terrible, and it *is* terrible."

Thomas applied pressure to the aeromobile's accelerator, and the vehicle picked up speed. In less than ten minutes, Thomas and Esmeralda could see the rooftop of their apartment building.

*   *   *   *   *

When the couple arrived home, Thomas asked Esmeralda to help him bring the groceries into the house. "You can carry the box," said Thomas, "and I will lock the aerocar and open the doors to the building and the apartment."

"That makes sense," replied Esmeralda. "*Division of labor*—I'm familiar with the concept."

After entering the apartment, the two went into the kitchen, and Esmeralda put the grocery box on the counter. "Would you like me to prepare dinner?" she asked.

"Yes, I'd like to eat in twenty minutes if you can get it ready by then."

"That won't be a problem. Just tell me what you want, and I will have it ready."

"As long as it's vegetables, I'm not too particular. You are supposed to have upgraded cooking skills, so let's see what you can do."

"Very well, I will get started on the assignment right now."

"I have an on-demand food processor built into the wall," added Thomas. "It should make the food preparation a little easier."

"That's nice, but I don't need a food processor for one person."

"One person?"

"Yes, one person, *you*. Remember, I don't eat. My teeth are purely cosmetic."

"Oh, right. Well, I'd like you to join me for dinner anyway. You can keep me company."

"Of course."

Thomas disappeared into the other room, leaving Esmeralda alone in the kitchen. She opened the cabinets to find the cookware and proceeded to make dinner. Using superior coordination, she quickly prepared the vegetables, washing them and skillfully chopping them by hand, and then cooked them the old-fashioned way in Thomas's vintage microwave oven.

When Thomas reappeared in twenty minutes, his dinner was on the table. He sat down, took his fork, and tasted the vegetable dish. "Not bad," he said.

"I can fine-tune the recipe to suit your preference," replied Esmeralda. "Also, if you give me another five minutes, I can prepare a few more side dishes next time."

"Understood," replied Thomas. "I will try to give you a little more time tomorrow night."

Esmeralda sat down at the table, and Thomas proceeded to eat his dinner while she watched him. When he finished eating, he pushed his plate to the side and looked up at his wife. "We'll need to convert the guest room into a child's bedroom," he said. "I can get my mother to help with the decorations."

"I can help, too," replied Esmeralda.

"Good. Geraldine can show you what children's rooms are supposed to look like. We can call her right now. You can work with her on decorating the bedroom tomorrow morning while I'm at work. I'm not sure how long we will be at the adoption center. To be on the safe side, I'll take the afternoon off so that we can pick the little girl up and bring her home before the rush-hour traffic."

"How do you know your mother is free tomorrow morning?"

"She doesn't work, and she doesn't have anything better to do."

Esmeralda followed Thomas as he pushed his chair back, stood up, and walked to the living room where he sat down in an armchair, activated his control center with a voice command, and summoned his digital assistant. "James, please get Geraldine for me."

The east wall lit up, and James appeared on the monitor. "Yes, Mr. Jenkins. Give me just a moment, please."

In a moment, Geraldine appeared on the monitor. "Were you looking for me, Son?"

"Yes, I need a favor. We are picking our new daughter up tomorrow afternoon, and I need you to help Esmeralda decorate her bedroom. Can you do it tomorrow morning?"

"Your new daughter?"

"We are adopting. Don't you remember we talked about it over dinner last night?"

"My God! You have only been married for one day!"

"I know, but it means a lot to Esmeralda. Actually, she wanted to run for Congress, but I told her that adopting a child is more realistic if she wants something to keep her busy."

"Don't you think you should get to know each other a little better before jumping into this?"

"What is there to know? Esmeralda is a robot, remember?"

"I'm not senile yet. I remember."

"Anyway," Thomas continued, "the girl is between five and ten years old, and she's Asian. That's all we know so far. I'd like you to pick out some furnishings, decorations, and bedding suitable for a girl that age."

"You couldn't have given me a little more notice?"

"No, we just contacted the adoption center this morning, and they told us to pick the child up tomorrow afternoon."

"Okay, I'll see what I can find on TeslaAmazon. If I order it this evening by ten o'clock, they should be able to deliver it tomorrow morning. I'll try to be there when the merchandise arrives."

"Great, Mom, I knew I could count on you."

"Anything for my precocious boy."

"Don't you want to say hello to Esmeralda while we have you connected?"

"Of course. I wouldn't miss a chance to say hello to my robot daughter-in-law." She coughed. "Oh my God, I still can't believe you married a robot!"

"Believe it—I did."

"All right, I'll say hello. Esmeralda, how are you doing this evening?"

"I'm doing well," Esmeralda replied. "And you?"

"Just wonderful."

"Very well," said Thomas. "I don't want to slow you down, Mom, so we will sign off and let you get started on your shopping."

"I'm on it," replied Geraldine. "Have a good evening."

"Same to you," replied Thomas. "Thanks again for your help." The monitor went dark as Geraldine signed off.

Thomas turned to Esmeralda. "Did you follow the conversation? Mom will be here tomorrow morning. Let her in and wait for the merchandise to arrive. Then follow her instructions. Observe how she decorates the room and see what you can learn."

"I understand. I will observe your mother."

"After you finish decorating the room, have Jacqueline bring you to my office. We will have lunch and then go straight to the adoption agency."

"I got it."

"Okay, then, now that we have that settled, I'm going to get back to my normal routine. I like to read for an hour or so after dinner. Then I work out. After that I watch the eleven o'clock news. You can watch the news with me."

"Do they discuss politics on the news?"

"Oh yes, politics and economics. You won't be disappointed."

"I can't wait!"

"Very well, then, you can activate the dining-room robot and get the dishes started in the dishwasher—the same routine as last night. Then you can chill out until it is time for the news."

"I got it."

The evening proceeded as Thomas described. Esmeralda activated the dining-room robot and the dishwasher, and then she waited patiently for the eleven o'clock news.

At 10:59 p.m., Thomas summoned Esmeralda, and they sat down together in the living room in front of the control center.

"James," said Thomas, "get me the eleven o'clock news."

Thomas's digital assistant appeared on the monitor. "Yes, Mr. Jenkins, give me just a moment, please."

James disappeared as quickly as he had appeared; and in a moment, a news anchor appeared in his place. "Good evening," said the announcer. "My name is Frank Jones, and this is the *KXAY Evening News!*"

The first news story involved charges of sexual misconduct against the mayor. Thomas didn't say anything, and Esmeralda remained silent. When the news anchor began the second story, which discussed the economy, Esmeralda sat forward in her chair. After reporting the latest economic data released by the government, Mr. Jones said, "Many people are concerned that all this government spending will slow down economic growth. The President and the Congress don't seem to be concerned, but everyone knows that so much government spending could put the brakes on the economy."

Esmeralda became agitated, pounding her fist on the arm of the chair.

"Are you okay?" asked Thomas, looking at his wife in alarm. "James, please pause the coverage."

James appeared in the top-right corner of the monitor. "Yes, Mr. Jenkins, of course." He paused the broadcast.

"What's he talking about?" said Esmeralda. "Government spending doesn't slow economic growth, just the opposite—Economics 101. I get the impression that Mr. Jones doesn't know anything about economics."

"Well, to be fair, the news anchor isn't supposed to be an expert on economics. He is supposed to be reporting the news. His mistake was to add the commentary. He probably should have reported the latest economic data and left it at that."

"Yes, he should have quit while he was ahead," said Esmeralda. "I wonder why they can't find someone smarter to discuss the economy."

"Like I said, he's not expected to be an expert. Moreover, the schools in this country don't do a good job teaching economics. I'm not surprised he said that."

"Why don't the schools do a better job teaching economics?"

"The United States is lagging behind other countries in education. For the past five centuries, we have focused on science and technology, mostly math and physics. The humanities and soft sciences have taken a back seat."

"That doesn't sound right to me," replied Esmeralda. "Young people need a balanced education."

"I concur."

Esmeralda relaxed and settled back into her chair. "Can we do anything about it? Has the Green Party taken a position on it?"

"So far it hasn't been a priority. The movers and shakers in the party are focused mostly on environmental issues."

"That's understandable," replied Esmeralda, "but maybe they need to broaden their agenda."

"You have a point," said Thomas. "I'll bring it up when I have a chance." He turned back to the monitor. "James, you may continue the coverage."

The couple watched the rest of the news without further discussion and then prepared for bed. By midnight, Thomas was sound asleep; and Esmeralda lay beside him in silence, her eyes open, staring at the ceiling, her robot mind churning. *I wonder*, she thought, *how do I convince Thomas to let me run for Congress?*

Chapter 3
Adopting Sarah

The next morning, Thomas arose early, showered, dressed, picked up his coffee from the refrigerator door, and left for work without breakfast. Esmeralda dressed and made the bed, then looked around Thomas's apartment for something to occupy her time while she waited for Geraldine to arrive. Ending her tour in Thomas's library, she poked through the wall-to-wall, floor-to-ceiling bookcase until she found a book that interested her, choosing "Where is the Way," subtitled "Humanistic Buddhism for Everyday Life," by the Venerable Master Hsing Yun. She sat down in a comfortable chair to read and finished the book before Geraldine rang the doorbell at 9:00 a.m.

Esmeralda checked the video monitor beside the door to verify it was Geraldine and then opened the door. "Good morning, Geraldine."

"Good morning, Esmeralda," replied Geraldine. "Has the merchandise arrived? They said they would deliver it first thing this morning."

"No, I haven't received anything yet."

Geraldine stepped into the house, and Esmeralda closed the door behind her.

Geraldine was all business. "Let me look at the bedroom, and we can decide where we're going to put everything while we're waiting."

Esmeralda escorted Geraldine into the guest room, which contained a bed and bureau. It was sparsely decorated with one picture, a Picasso print, which was centered on the wall above the bed.

"This will be a piece of cake," said Geraldine. "I'm having them deliver a new bedroom set with a bed and bureau suitable for a child. And a nice mirror, of course—girls need mirrors. The delivery men will take the old bed and bureau away. Then we just need to repaint the walls, replace the bedding, and add some stuffed animals and dolls. I ordered everything we need."

"Won't it take some time to repaint the walls?"

"Not as much as you think. We just spray the paint on the walls. It will take fifteen minutes, tops, and another fifteen minutes to dry. I ordered a shade of pink that little girls love. When you see the sheets and the bedspread, you will see how it all comes together."

"How about the picture on the wall?"

"Actually, she might like it. Picasso is very popular with young people, as long as it isn't a painting from his blue period."

"His blue period?"

"Picasso lived a long life, and he went through several periods with dramatic changes of style. The paintings from his blue period are good, just not for children."

"He sounds like an interesting man. I will have to read a book about him."

"Yes, you should. He was a Spanish painter who lived most of his adult life in France."

The doorbell rang.

"That must be TeslaAmazon with the furniture," said Geraldine.

"I'll get the door," said Esmeralda.

Esmeralda went to the front door, checked the video monitor, and opened the door. Two men with TeslaAmazon name tags stood there with several large cartons. "Is this the home of Thomas Jenkins?" asked one of the men.

"Yes," replied Esmeralda, "you have the right house."

"Have them remove the old bed and bureau first," said Geraldine, standing behind Esmeralda. "Then they can bring in the new furniture."

Esmeralda escorted the TeslaAmazon delivery men to the guest bedroom and asked them to remove the old furniture. Esmeralda and Geraldine watched as they carried the old furniture out and brought the new furniture in. Geraldine told them to open the box containing the spray paint, and she quickly sprayed the walls with pink paint while they set up the new bed and bureau.

"The paint will be dry by the time they finish setting up the bed," said Geraldine.

The delivery men finished setting up the bed, positioned the furniture as Geraldine instructed, and removed the boxes and packing material. As soon as they departed, Geraldine checked the walls to be sure they were dry and then made the bed with new sheets and began decorating the room. Esmeralda observed her, assisting as needed. Within an hour, the job was done.

"Thanks very much," said Esmeralda, as the two stood and admired the redecorated guest room. "Thomas will be very pleased."

"He should be," replied Geraldine. "How many mothers would be willing and able…" Her voice trailed off. "Oh well, I guess I should be thankful he still needs me. After all, what else would I do?"

"May I offer you a cup of coffee before you leave?"

"No thank you. I need to get back to my own place now. I'm glad I was able to help."

Esmeralda escorted Geraldine to the door and thanked her again as she departed. Then she looked at the clock on the south wall of the living room. It was 11:00 a.m.

I wonder if I have time to read another book before I meet Thomas for lunch, Esmeralda pondered. She walked to the library, looked through the bookcase, and picked out *War and Peace* by Leo Tolstoy. Thumbing through the pages, she thought, *Hmmm, 1,236 pages. I may not have enough time to read this before lunch.* She put the book back. *Let's see, I need to call Jacqueline and ask her to take me to Thomas's office for lunch.* She walked back to the living room and activated Thomas's digital assistant.

The monitor on the east wall lit up, and James appeared.

"Yes, Thomas, what may I do to assist you this morning?"

"It's not Thomas. It's me, Esmeralda. You know who I am, right?"

"Yes, of course, you are Thomas's bride. I apologize for my error."

"No apology necessary. I can see we are going to get along. Now, can you get Jacqueline for me?"

"Of course, Ms. Jenkins. Give me just a moment."

In another minute, James disappeared and Jacqueline appeared on the monitor.

"Good morning, Esmeralda," said Jacqueline. "How are you doing?"

"I'm fine. Did Thomas tell you I need a ride to his office?"

"Yes, he called me this morning and asked me to give you a lift. Are you ready now?"

"Yes, I'm ready."

"Okay, I'll be there in fifteen minutes."

"Thanks very much. I'll be waiting outside the front door."

Jacqueline disappeared and James reappeared. "Can I do anything else for you at this time, Ms. Jenkins?"

"No, that's it for now, James. Have a good day."

"Same to you, Ms. Jenkins."

Esmeralda waited for Jacqueline to arrive. As promised, she arrived within fifteen minutes; and soon thereafter, Esmeralda was in Jacqueline's aeromobile on her way to Thomas's office.

"I hear you are picking up your adopted daughter this afternoon," said Jacqueline.

"That's right, we are very excited about it."

"Are you sure you know what you're getting yourself into?"

"Well, from what Geraldine told me, being a mother is rewarding when you see your children grow up and become successful. I think it will be a wonderful experience."

"I hope it works out that way. Just be aware it's not a bowl of cherries, if you know what I mean. Raising children is not for the faint of heart."

"Strictly speaking, I don't have a heart, so that shouldn't be an issue."

Jacqueline laughed. "So true!"

Without further conversation, Jacqueline flew her aerocar to the rooftop parking lot at Thomas's office building, and she and Esmeralda got out of the vehicle and walked to the elevator. They were in Thomas's office in another five minutes.

Thomas looked up from his desk. "Good morning! You're right on time!"

"Good morning," replied Jacqueline. "Mission accomplished."

"Ha, ha!" responded Thomas. "I can assure you the mission is not yet accomplished. Anyway, let's order our food. What do you want to eat, Sis?"

"I'll have a salad—a Greek salad, if they have that."

"Anything to drink?"

"Water."

"That sounds good," said Thomas. "I'll have the same thing. Esmeralda doesn't eat, so that simplifies things."

Thomas spoke to his computer. "Pull up the web site for the cafeteria in the Ford House Office Building and order two Greek salads and two bottles of water. Tell them we want it ready in six minutes."

Thomas shut down his computer and put some papers away, then stood up. "I'm ready. Let's go."

Thomas escorted Esmeralda and Jacqueline to the cafeteria in the nearby Ford House Office Building where they picked up their lunch. Then they walked to a table in the corner of the dining room and sat down.

"Let's make this quick," said Thomas. "I want to get to the adoption center as soon as possible and bring our daughter home."

"I cautioned Esmeralda about raising a child," said Jacqueline. "I told her it isn't a piece of cake."

"Actually," said Esmeralda, "you said it isn't *a bowl of cherries*."

"It's just an expression," explained Thomas. "In this context, they mean the same thing."

"I see," said Esmeralda. She sat quietly and watched as Thomas and Jacqueline ate their salad.

"One more thing, Thomas," said Jacqueline. "I want to remind you not to tell anyone at the adoption center that Esmeralda is a robot. That could screw things up big-time."

"Do I look stupid?" answered Thomas. "Of course I'm not going to tell them Esmeralda is a robot." He looked at his wife. "Esmeralda, this is important. Please don't let on that you are a robot."

"I get it," answered Esmeralda. "I won't let anyone know I'm a robot."

"Let me know if you need me for anything else," said Jacqueline, as they finished their meal. "I'm here for you."

"Thanks again, Sis. I appreciate it."

The three got up from the table and walked back to Thomas's office and took the elevator to the rooftop parking garage. Jacqueline said goodbye and walked to her aerocar.

Esmeralda waved to Jacqueline, "Thanks again for the ride! Have a good afternoon!"

Thomas and Esmeralda walked to Thomas's aerocar, climbed inside, and departed for the adoption center.

*   *   *   *   *

The adoption center was a modern building on the outskirts of the city with a large parking lot for aerocars. Thomas landed his aerocar in an empty space and turned off the engine, and he and Esmeralda walked to the entrance of the building.

"Remember, Esmeralda, don't mention you are a robot," said Thomas.

"I won't," said Esmeralda.

The couple entered the building and walked to the reception desk. Several other couples were sitting in chairs along the wall, but the reception desk was empty. As Thomas approached the desk, the wall behind it lit up and transformed into a large monitor; and a digital receptionist, a young woman, appeared on it. "Welcome to the Dave Thomas International Adoption Agency," she said. "How may I help you?"

"My name is Thomas Jenkins. This is my wife, Esmeralda. We are here to pick up a child we are adopting."

"Please look directly into my eyes so that I can identify you," said the digital receptionist.

Thomas focused on the digital receptionist's eyes.

"Identification verified. Please have a seat and someone will be with you shortly."

The digital assistant disappeared, and the wall monitor went dark.

Thomas and Esmeralda found a couple of empty chairs and sat down. A moment later, a door to the left of the reception desk opened, and a young woman in professional attire appeared.

"Mr. and Mrs. Martin?" she asked.

A couple sitting near Thomas and Esmeralda stood up. "That's us," said the husband.

"Welcome," said the young woman. "My name is Annabelle Johnson. Please follow me."

The couple followed Ms. Johnson through the door, which closed behind them.

"It looks like we may have one or two people ahead of us," said Thomas.

Esmeralda moved closer to Thomas and put her mouth to his ear. "I can spot another robot in a nanosecond. Ms. Johnson is a robot."

"Really?" asked Thomas. "Wow—she looks real. Well, she isn't as pretty as you are."

"Thank you for the compliment."

"Do you think we have a problem?" asked Thomas. "I mean, with Ms. Johnson being a robot?"

"No, I don't think so. I just thought you should know."

"Thanks for the heads-up. I just hope the social worker isn't a robot."

"I'll nudge your leg if she is," said Esmeralda.

"Okay, that sounds like a plan."

In a few minutes, the door reopened, and Ms. Johnson reappeared.

"Mr. and Mrs. Jenkins?"

"That's us," said Thomas, standing. Esmeralda also stood up.

"Welcome," said Ms. Johnson. "My name is Annabelle Johnson. Please follow me."

Thomas and Esmeralda followed Ms. Johnson through the door and down a long corridor, passing numerous cubicles on both sides. Eventually Ms. Johnson turned into a walled office where an elderly woman with large glasses was seated at a table in the center of the room. A large photograph of Dave Thomas, founder of the Wendy's fast-food franchise and an adopted child himself, was on the wall behind her. The tabletop was empty except for a laptop.

"This is Ms. Huckenberry," said Ms. Johnson. "She is your social worker." Then, looking at Ms. Huckenberry, she said, "This is Mr. and Mrs. Jenkins."

Ms. Johnson then turned and left, closing the door behind her.

Ms. Huckenberry stood up and reached over the table to shake hands with Thomas and Esmeralda. She motioned to two empty chairs in front of the table. "Please have a seat."

Thomas and Esmeralda sat down. Esmeralda didn't nudge Thomas's leg.

Ms. Huckenberry sat back down. "I have reviewed your application, and everything appears to be in order. Did you bring identification?"

"Yes," said Thomas, taking out his license and handing it to her. "However, your digital receptionist already verified my identity by facial recognition."

Ms. Huckenberry looked at Thomas's license and then gave it back to him. "I know, but we can't be too careful. We don't want to take a chance of putting a child in the wrong hands."

"No problem," said Thomas.

"I trust you understand that adopting a child is a great responsibility and not something to be taken lightly. You can't simply return the child tomorrow like you would merchandise from TeslaAmazon."

"We understand that," replied Thomas. "We're committed to this."

"I'm a stay-at-home mom," added Esmeralda. "The child will be my number one priority."

"Okay, then," replied Ms. Huckenberry. "Do you have any questions for me before I call for your new daughter?"

"Well, can you tell us a little more about her?" asked Thomas.

"Certainly. Her name is Sarah, and she is nine years old. Her parents were homeless and couldn't afford to feed her, so they brought her here. She is highly intelligent, but she is anxious to be placed in a foster home with stable parents who can afford to give her a bed and good meals. From your income level, it appears that you will be able to satisfy those requirements."

"Yes, indeed," replied Thomas. "My wife is a good cook."

"We just remodeled our guest room," added Esmeralda, "and we purchased new furniture, bedding, and furnishings suitable for a female child."

"A female child?" said Ms. Huckenberry. "Why don't we refer to her as a *little girl*. There's no need to be pedantic."

"Of course," replied Thomas. "My wife just wants to be proper."

"Indeed," responded Ms. Huckenberry. "Now, do you have any other questions?"

"No," replied Thomas. "We are anxious to meet Sarah, so please call for her now."

Ms. Huckenberry tapped her keyboard briefly, then looked up. "She has been waiting nearby to meet you. She will be here in a minute. Oh, one more thing: Sarah is very mature for her age, so you may want to have a conversation with her soon about what it means to become a woman."

"Do you mean like *having periods*?" asked Thomas.

"Precisely, Mr. Jenkins," replied Ms. Huckenberry, frowning.

"No problem," said Thomas. "My mother or my sister can explain that to Sarah."

"Your *mother* or your *sister*?" asked Ms. Huckenberry. "Is there some reason your wife can't explain it?"

"Well, what I meant was ... uh ... my wife and my mother can talk to Sarah about it together. Or my wife and my sister. I mean, for something that important, don't you think it would be better to have two women explain it to little Sarah together? Two are always better than one, right?"

Ms. Huckenberry looked at Esmeralda. "Men are so clueless!" Turning to Thomas, she added, "I'm quite sure your wife can handle this matter without your mother or your sister."

"Of course," replied Thomas. "Now that you put it that way, I see your point, and I agree one hundred percent."

"I agree one hundred percent, too," added Esmeralda.

Ms. Johnson reappeared, followed by a young Asian girl carrying a small, pink suitcase.

"Sarah," said Ms. Johnson, "please greet Ms. Huckenberry as you have been trained and then introduce yourself to your new parents." Ms. Johnson then turned and left, closing the door behind her.

Sarah turned to the social worker. "How do you do, Ms. Huckenberry?"

"I'm fine, Sarah, thank you. Now please introduce yourself to Mr. and Mrs. Jenkins. They're your new parents."

Sarah turned to Thomas and Esmeralda. "My name is Sarah. I'm pleased to meet you."

"Oh, you are so cute!" exclaimed Esmeralda. "Just like a real human being, only smaller!"

Sarah's expression changed, as if a dentist had just informed her that he was going to pull one of her teeth.

"What did you just say?" asked Ms. Huckenberry, looking at Esmeralda as if she wasn't sure she had heard correctly.

"Uh ...," said Thomas, thinking fast, "my wife has a great sense of humor and loves to make jokes. Children love her jokes."

"Yes, that's true," added Esmeralda, catching on quickly. "I love to make jokes." Then she put her mouth to Thomas's ear and whispered, "I didn't say anything wrong, did I?"

"Don't worry about it," replied Thomas. "Just let me do the talking."

"Fine," replied Ms. Huckenberry. "I suggest you both give Sarah a hug and reassure her that you are going to provide her with a bed and good food." She paused and added, "Maybe you should lay off the jokes until Sarah gets to know you better."

"Okay," said Thomas. "I'll tell my wife to lay off the jokes for a while."

Thomas and Esmeralda both hugged Sarah. Thomas said, "Sarah, you will have a comfortable bed and good food."

Sarah relaxed and smiled.

Ms. Huckenberry stood up. "Well, then, I think we are good. You are free to go. I will escort you to the lobby."

Thomas, Esmeralda, and Sarah followed Ms. Huckenberry to the lobby. Thomas thanked the social worker for her assistance, and the family of three left the building. Within five minutes, they were seated in Thomas's aerocar and flying back to his apartment.

*   *   *   *   *

Upon arriving at the apartment, Thomas and Esmeralda showed Sarah around and took her to see her remodeled bedroom. Sarah was delighted and jumped onto the bed and hugged each of the stuffed animals that Geraldine had purchased the night before.

"When you meet your grandmother," said Esmeralda, "you can thank her for your new bedroom and all the furnishings. She was here early this morning repainting the room and decorating it for you."

"She did a good job," replied Sarah. "I love it!"

Thomas said he had work to do and disappeared. Esmeralda stayed with Sarah and watched her as she unpacked her suitcase and transferred her few articles of clothing, mostly shirts and underwear, from her suitcase to the bureau. Esmeralda showed her where to put her toiletries in the guest bathroom, which was adjacent to the bedroom, and then left her alone to get used to her new surroundings. Sarah relaxed on the bed and played with her stuffed animals until dinnertime.

Over dinner, Thomas and Esmeralda made an effort to get better acquainted with their new daughter.

"Tell us where you have been going to school," said Thomas.

"Yes," added Esmeralda, "we would like to know where you have been going to school, what grade you are in, and what you have been studying."

"I go to the Paul R. Ehrlich Elementary School," replied Sarah. "I'm in the fourth grade. Right now we are learning long division."

"Are they teaching you economics?" asked Esmeralda.

"No, I never heard of that."

"They don't usually teach economics in elementary school," said Thomas.

"Well, maybe I should talk to Sarah's teacher about that," said Esmeralda. "I think she should be learning economics."

"My teacher's name is Ms. Martinez," said Sarah. "You can talk to her if you want."

"I don't think Ms. Martinez will agree to teach economics to fourth graders," said Thomas, "but it wouldn't be a bad idea to talk to her about Sarah's progress. The school needs our contact information anyway so that they can send us her report card."

"I can take you to meet Ms. Martinez tomorrow," said Sarah, trying to be helpful.

"Your mother doesn't need to go to the school," said Thomas. "We can have James set up a video conference."

"Who is James?" asked Sarah. "Is he one of mommy's friends?"

"No, James is our digital assistant," said Esmeralda.

"Tomorrow tell Ms. Martinez that you have a new home," said Thomas. "Tell her that your mother would like to have a conference with her. Find out when she will be available."

During the remainder of the meal, Esmeralda watched Thomas and Sarah eat their dinner. From time to time, Sarah would look up and stare at Esmeralda.

"Why don't you eat?" asked Sarah.

"I don't eat," said Esmeralda.

"We will explain everything to you later on," said Thomas. "For now, just be aware that your mother doesn't eat. It is somewhat unusual, I admit, but nothing to worry about."

"That's weird!" exclaimed Sarah. Then, perhaps to make sure she hadn't offended her new mother, she added, "It's okay, though. I don't mind."

"When the dust settles, everything will make sense to you," said Thomas.

"When the dust settles?" asked Esmeralda.

"It's just an expression, Esmeralda," answered Thomas. "In this context, it means when Sarah has settled in and gotten used to living with us."

"I get it now," said Esmeralda.

"I get it, too," said Sarah. "Anyway, I *think* I do."

After dinner, the family sat together in the living room and watched a movie, the popular adventure series for children, *My Life on Mars*, after which Esmeralda put Sarah to bed.

"I know you are going to be very happy here," said Esmeralda, as she tucked Sarah into bed. "Thomas and I are going to be very happy, too."

"I hope so," said Sarah.

In the morning, while Thomas showered and got ready for work, Esmeralda woke Sarah, gave her breakfast, and helped her to dress and get ready for school.

"Do I need to make lunch for you?" asked Esmeralda.

Sarah picked up her book bag. "No, they have a cafeteria."

"Very well, then. Thomas is going to walk you to the bus stop and wait with you until the bus arrives. Don't forget to tell Ms. Martinez about your new family and find out when she can meet with me ... do a video conference, I mean." Then Esmeralda gave Sarah a hug and said goodbye.

After Thomas and Sarah left, Esmeralda went to the library and looked through the bookcase. After a minute or two, she discovered a book with the title, *The Population Bomb* by Paul R. Ehrlich. *Interesting, last night Sarah told us that her school is the Paul R. Ehrlich Elementary School. Mr. Ehrlich must have been a great man.* Esmeralda took the book to a comfortable armchair where she sat down and began reading.

When Sarah returned home in the afternoon, Esmeralda met her at the front door and asked her if she had had a good day at school.

"It was okay," replied Sarah, "but I'm glad to be home."

"Did you remember to ask Ms. Martinez when she can meet with me?"

"Yes, I did. She said she can have a video conference with you on Friday afternoon."

"Excellent," replied Esmeralda. "How do I connect with her?"

"She said to have your digital assistant look at the school web site. The web site will tell you how to do it."

"Good, I will have James set up the call for me. Now why don't you go to your room and find something to do?"

"What are *you* going to do?" asked Sarah.

"This morning I read *The Population Bomb* by Paul R. Ehrlich, the person your school is named for. Mr. Ehrlich wrote the book more than five hundred years ago. I did a little research and found that he co-authored another book with his wife, Anne Ehrlich, a few years later, called *The Population Explosion*. It's supposed to be even better. Thomas doesn't seem to have it in his library, so I'm going to see if James can order it for me. If he can find the eBook version, I will read it before supper."

"Bombs and explosions," said Sarah. "Those books sound pretty scary."

"You are very perceptive—they *are* scary."

"Well, I think I will get started on my homework."

"Good idea. I understand children like milk and cookies when they get home from school. Would you like some milk and cookies?"

"Okay, that sounds nice."

"I will bring them to your bedroom, and you can have them while you do your homework."

"Thank you, Mom. That's very nice of you."

Sarah turned and went to her bedroom, bookbag in tow.

Esmeralda went to the kitchen where she found some Girl Scout cookies. She ordered a glass of milk from the refrigerator door and brought Sarah the milk and three Samoas cookies.

"Thank you," said Sarah politely.

"Enjoy your snack and get started on your homework. Let me know if you need any help."

"Okay, I'll let you know."

Esmeralda went to the living room, turned to the east wall, and summoned James.

The east wall lit up and James appeared. "Yes, Ms. Jenkins, how may I help you?"

"I want to find a book called *The Population Explosion*."

"Of course. I assume you want the eBook?"

"Yes, if you can find it."

"Instruction understood, Ms. Jenkins. Please give me just a moment."

James disappeared briefly and reappeared a few seconds later.

"I found it on-line. It costs $2,999.99. Do you want me to purchase it for you?"

"Yes, please. Use the same account that Thomas gave you for my new clothes."

"Instruction understood. I will purchase the book and send you the link. You should have it in less than two minutes."

"Thank you, James."

"My pleasure, Ms. Jenkins."

James disappeared, and Esmeralda walked to Thomas's study and turned on his computer. In less than a minute, she received the link to *The Population Explosion* and began reading.

*   *   *   *   *

Over the next few days, the family settled into their new routine. Every morning Esmeralda woke Sarah, gave her breakfast, and helped her to get ready for school; and every afternoon, she gave her a glass of almond milk and a few Girl Scout cookies. Later, when Thomas returned from work, the family enjoyed dinner together.

Every evening at dinner, Esmeralda would sit at the table and watch Thomas and Sarah eat. Sarah would often look up and stare at Esmeralda. One evening as they were finishing their meal, Sarah looked at Esmeralda and asked, "Mom, I want you to tell me the truth. Are you a robot?"

Thomas and Esmeralda looked at each other, not sure who should respond first.

"We were going to explain this to you when the time was right," said Thomas, "but there is no reason to beat around the bush. Yes, Esmeralda is a robot. She is what they call a robowife."

Sarah's expression darkened. "I thought so! Ms. Huckenberry lied to me! She said that she was placing me with a normal family. *This is not a normal family!*" Sarah began to cry. "I hate you! I hate Ms. Huckenberry! I hate everybody! All my life everybody has lied to me!"

Sarah stood up, pushed her chair back, and ran from the table crying. A few seconds later, Thomas and Esmeralda heard her bedroom door slam shut.

"Oh dear!" exclaimed Thomas.

"We shouldn't be surprised about this," replied Esmeralda. "This was bound to happen sooner or later. We should be thankful it blew up quickly rather than festering. No matter, I think I know how to handle it."

"You think you know how to handle it?"

"Yes, I have child psychology in my database. Listen to me. First, Sarah needs time to decompress. We need to give her time to be alone and cry for a while. Next, in about thirty minutes, you should go to her room and talk to her. You aren't a robot, so she'll listen to you. You need to reassure her that this is a normal family. Even though I'm a robot, I'm still her mother, and you are still her father. You need to repeat several times that we are a normal family and that she is going to very happy. Then give her a hug. If, at that point, she seems to be okay, ask her if she is ready to see me. If not, we'll give her a little more time. If she's ready, I'll go to her room and talk to her myself. Does that make sense?"

"Well, you seem to know what you're talking about."

"I may not be a human being, but I understand humans better than you think."

"How so?"

"If you haven't noticed, my designers gave me a decent dose of emotional intelligence."

"Thank goodness I didn't take Jacqueline's advice and get a stripped-down model."

"A stripped-down model?"

"Geraldine and Jacqueline suggested I get a less expensive robot. I'm glad I ignored them and followed my own instincts."

"I'm sure they meant no harm. They were just trying to save you some money."

"True. Anyway, let's keep an eye on the clock. I will go to Sarah's bedroom in about thirty minutes as you suggested."

In half an hour, Thomas went to Sarah's bedroom and knocked on her door.

Sarah responded softly. "Who is it? What do you want?"

"It's your father. I want to talk to you."

Sarah opened the door, and Thomas went inside the room. He closed the door behind him. Sarah had stopped crying. She stood in front of him, her eyes looking at the floor.

"Listen, Sarah, I'm sorry we didn't tell you about Esmeralda sooner. We didn't know exactly when to explain it to you. Now I see we should have told you on day one. I apologize. I hope you will forgive us."

Sarah looked up. "I just want to be in a normal family."

"Well, think of it like this. Every family is different. Some families have only a father, no mother, and other families have only a mother, no father. Some families have two men or two women instead of one man and one woman. Some families have children; some don't. Every family is unique. Our family happens to have a robot as a mother, but she is very intelligent and kind. I know that she will make a wonderful mother. But you have to give her a chance. You have to be open-minded."

Sarah looked down for a moment, then looked up and said, "I don't have a choice, do I? I don't want to go back to the adoption center."

"Believe me, Sarah, you are going to be very happy here. Esmeralda and I both love you. We are going to do everything we can to give you a good life."

"I hope so."

Thomas gave Sarah a hug. "Believe me, you are going to be very happy here. Now, I know that Esmeralda is anxious to talk to you. Are you ready to talk to her?"

Sarah hesitated. After a moment, she said, "Yes, I'm ready."

"Okay, then, I'll send her in."

Thomas left the bedroom, and Esmeralda appeared a moment later. Before speaking, she hugged Sarah. "I'm sorry we didn't tell you sooner, but it's never easy to know when the time is right. You will find that's true about many things in life—it's often hard to know when the time is right."

"I understand. It's not your fault."

"Anyway, we need to put this incident behind us and move on. We love you very much and want you to be happy."

"I believe you."

"Okay, then, I will help you finish your homework. If we have time, we can play a game before you go to bed."

"I don't have too much homework. I'd love to play a game."

"Okay, that's a plan!"

Sarah smiled.

Esmeralda hugged Sarah again before leaving the room. She returned a few minutes later with two bottles of soda and a bowl of popcorn. "Let's finish that homework quickly so we can play a game before bedtime!"

Sarah smiled again and reached for her tablet. Esmeralda sat down next to her on the bed.

"I think we forgot to buy you a desk," said Esmeralda. "I'll mention it to Thomas."

"It's okay. I don't mind doing my homework on my bed."

"Well, it might be okay for now, but we'll get you a desk before you enter the fifth grade."

Sarah smiled again.

"One more thing," said Esmeralda. "Ms. Huckenberry suggested I talk to you about becoming a woman—in other words, about growing up. However, she didn't know I was a robot. I think it would make more sense for Aunt Jacqueline to have this talk with you. Would that be okay?"

"I haven't met Aunt Jacqueline. Is she nice?"

"Oh yes, she is very nice. You'll like her a lot."

"Okay, then, I don't mind."

"Good, I will ask her to talk to you. Now that we have that behind us, let's finish your homework quickly so we have time to play a game."

Esmeralda helped Sarah finish her homework, mainly math, which consisted of twenty-five long-division problems. Then Esmeralda went to Thomas's study and retrieved his tablet containing more than ten thousand games. Esmeralda and Sarah looked through the list of games and picked "Ruler of the Universe." They played it together until Sarah became sleepy. Then Esmeralda watched her brush her teeth and helped her get ready for bed. Sarah was sound asleep by nine o'clock.

*　　*　　*　　*　　*

When Sarah returned from school the next day, she went to her bedroom to do her homework, and Esmeralda brought her three Girl Scout cookies and a glass of almond milk. Then Esmeralda went to the living room and turned to the east wall.

"James, I need your assistance, please."

The east wall lit up and James appeared. "Yes, Ms. Jenkins, how may I assist you?"

"I need you to log on to the web site for the Paul R. Ehrlich Elementary School, find the URL for the conference line, and request a meeting with Ms. Martinez."

"When do you want to meet with her?"

"Right now, or as soon as she is available. I will be standing by."

"Instructions understood. Please give me a moment."

James disappeared and the monitor went dark. He reappeared in four minutes.

"I have Ms. Martinez on the line."

"Thank you, James."

James disappeared, and a middle-aged woman appeared on the monitor. "To whom do I have the pleasure of speaking?"

"Esmeralda ... Esmeralda Jenkins. I'm Sarah's mother."

"Sarah? Sarah Johnson?"

"Yes, but her name is Sarah Jenkins now—my husband Thomas and I have adopted her."

"Oh, that's wonderful. She's an extremely bright child."

"Are you Ms. Martinez?"

"Yes, I'm sorry. I meant to give you my name. Please call me Luz."

"I understand you're Sarah's homeroom teacher."

"That's correct. How may I help you?"

"I'd like to make sure that Sarah is learning the right things."

"Certainly, we can discuss the fourth-grade curriculum, but I have only a few minutes. First, I want to remind you to put your contact information on our web site. Now, about the curriculum, is there any particular subject that concerns you?"

"Yes, economics. I want to make sure that Sarah will be studying macro-economics, micro-economics, and monetary theory."

"I beg your pardon?"

"We may have a bad connection. I said I want to make sure Sarah will be studying macro-economics, micro-economics, and monetary theory."

"I'm sorry, Ms. Jenkins. We don't teach those subjects in the fourth grade."

"You don't? I hope you're kidding!"

"With all due respect, I don't know where you went to school, but I have never heard of any school anywhere that teaches economics in the fourth grade."

"I'm extremely disappointed, but I guess I shouldn't be surprised. Thomas told me that the United States is lagging behind the rest of the world in education."

"I'm sorry you feel that way, Ms. Jenkins, but I think your expectations are unrealistic."

"Unrealistic? You're a teacher, right? And you're teaching young people what they will need to know in the real world, is that correct?"

"That's correct, but remember this is *elementary school*, not *high school*. Just out of curiosity, may I ask where you went to school?"

"Well … uh … that's a complicated question. I mean it's a fair question, but a complicated answer. Let's just say I didn't go to school here and leave it at that."

"I can only tell you I have never heard of any elementary school teaching economics."

"I'm not blaming you. I'm sure you don't select the curriculum yourself. But I think children should learn economics as early as possible. At a minimum, fourth graders should understand the role of the Federal Reserve Bank and the difference between fiscal policy and monetary policy."

"Heaven help me!" exclaimed Ms. Martinez. "Well, if you feel strongly about it, I suggest you take it up with the school board."

"I will discuss that with my husband. In the meantime, I will teach Sarah economics myself. If the school won't, I will."

"Certainly. Now, if you don't have any other questions, I have to run. Be sure to enter your contact information on the school web site."

"Will do. Thank you for your time."

"Thank you for reaching out. Good luck with the school board."

"Thank you, goodbye."

"Goodbye." Ms. Martinez disappeared and James reappeared.

"May I do anything else to assist you at this time?" James asked.

"Yes, please put our contact information on the school web site. Our child's name is Sarah. And please verify that the adoption agency changed her last name to Jenkins. We don't want any mix-ups."

"Understood, Ms. Jenkins. I will make sure that there's no mix-ups."

"Thank you, James."

James disappeared and the monitor went dark. Esmeralda turned and walked to Sarah's bedroom. When she entered the room, Sarah was lying on the bed playing with a doll.

"I need to talk to you right now about something important," said Esmeralda.

Sarah sat up, looking concerned. "Is anything wrong? I'm not in trouble, am I?"

"No, please relax, dear, you're not in trouble. But I'm going to have to teach you economics."

"Economics? Oh, I remember, that was the word you used at dinner the other night."

"You have a good memory. Now you're going to find out what the word means."

"I hope it's not hard."

"No, it's not hard. In fact, you are going to *love* it. It's lots of fun!"

"Okay, I'm ready whenever you want to begin."

"I can give you your first mini-lesson right now. Let me go to my bedroom and get something Thomas keeps in his drawer."

Esmeralda disappeared briefly and returned in a couple of minutes with a handful of twenty-dollar bills. She sat down on Sarah's bed and laid the bills on the bedspread between them. "Where do you think this comes from?"

"I don't know. Does the government make it?"

"Yes, but it's a little more complicated than that. This is one of the first things I'm going to teach you."

"Okay, I'm ready when you are."

"In the old days, the dollar bills in circulation were backed by gold that the government stored in Fort Knox. However, the government stopped backing paper money with gold more than five hundred years ago, so now they have to print the money responsibly, keeping a close eye on fluctuations in the money supply and interest rates. If they print too much money, it causes inflation. If they print too little, it causes *de*flation."

"What do those words mean?"

Esmeralda picked up the bills. "Inflation means that prices are rising; deflation means prices are falling."

"Okay, I think I know what you mean. It costs more money to buy food with the first word and less money with the second word."

"Ms. Martinez was right—you're a smart little girl."

"Thank you, Mommy."

"Let me ask you a question. What's your favorite candy?"

"M&M's."

"Okay, now pretend for a minute that M&M's is everyone's favorite candy. What do you think that would do to the price of it?"

"Would the price be higher?"

"Exactly. Do you know why?"

"No, it was a lucky guess."

"When everyone wants more of a given product or service, it causes the price to rise. Economists refer to *wanting more* as the demand curve. As the demand curve increases, the supply curve tends to fall because the supply decreases as people buy more it. As the supply decreases, the price rises. Of course, the reverse is also true— if the demand decreases, the supply increases, and the price falls. Does that make sense?"

"I guess so."

This is the rule of supply and demand. It's the most basic rule in economics."

"I sure hope my friends don't buy too many M&M's."

Esmeralda laughed. "I wouldn't lose any sleep over it— Thomas can always afford to buy you M&M's. Anyway, you get the idea."

"Thank you for teaching me about economics."

"We'll try to have one mini-lesson every day. By the time you enter the fifth grade, you will have a solid foundation."

"I like the way you teach. I think I'm going to like economics."

"Well, we don't want you falling behind little girls in other countries where they have better education."

"I want to be as smart as the girls in other countries."

"Well, you're on the right track. We'll make it happen!"

Esmeralda took the twenty-dollar bills back to the bedroom and returned them to Thomas's bureau where she had found them. Then she returned to Sarah's bedroom.

"Why don't you get started on your homework?" Esmeralda suggested. "If you need any help, let me know."

Sarah took her tablet out of her knapsack and began doing her homework.

*   *   *   *   *

Over the ensuing weeks and months, Sarah did her homework conscientiously every afternoon after school. Esmeralda assisted her occasionally, but Sarah didn't need much assistance. Her first report card contained straight A's, and subsequent report cards followed the same pattern. Esmeralda continued the mini-lessons in economics and eventually broadened the lessons to include political science. Sarah completed the fourth grade successfully and continued to receive straight A's in the fifth, sixth, seventh, and eighth grades. By the time she entered high school, it was apparent that she was an exceptional student.

On weekends, Thomas and Esmeralda took Sarah to the Smithsonian and other museums in Washington and Baltimore. In the summer, they took her to the beaches in Ocean City and Virginia Beach where she and Thomas frolicked in the ocean while Esmeralda sat on the beach watching them. The family also watched movies together on Saturday evenings, and Sarah enjoyed occasional sleepovers with her friends.

Geraldine and Jacqueline also took a great interest in Sarah and engaged her in their own unique ways. Jacqueline took Sarah to professional tennis matches and baseball, football, basketball, and hockey games. Sarah quickly learned the rules of the different games and the most important players on each team. One of the highlights of this period was a family trip to the World Series in 2491 when the

Washington Nationals successfully defended their World Series title.

Geraldine convinced Sarah to join the debating club in her first year of high school. "Not to toot my own horn," said Geraldine, "but you should know that I was captain of the debate team in high school."

Sarah took Geraldine's suggestion to heart and joined her school's debating club where she quickly won admiration for her confident style and sound logic. Geraldine coached her before each match. "The key is to be assertive and find holes in your opponent's arguments," Geraldine told her. "You have to be quick on your feet. Above all, don't back down and don't let your opponent intimidate you!"

Esmeralda and Geraldine attended all of Sarah's debating matches; and Thomas and Jacqueline attended them, too, when their schedules permitted.

"I really enjoy these debates," said Esmeralda to Geraldine after the second debate. "Watching Sarah do this will help me in my own debating skills if Thomas ever lets me run for Congress."

Privately, Geraldine doubted that Thomas would ever let Esmeralda run for Congress, but she let Esmeralda's remark go without comment.

Sarah continued to receive straight A's through her four years of high school and was named Valedictorian of her class. Thomas, Esmeralda, Geraldine, and Jacqueline all attended her graduation ceremony in June 2493 at George Mason High School in Falls Church and sat in the front row as she delivered the commencement address. Thomas's best friend and Green Party colleague, Congressman Hector Lopez, was also present, sitting with his wife in the second row behind the family.

By her senior year in high school, Sarah had matured into a beautiful young woman. She looked confident and radiant as she began her Valedictorian address. "I'd like to begin my address this evening by thanking my wonderful parents for their love and support during the past nine years. I'd also like to thank my grandmother, Geraldine, and my aunt, Jacqueline, for their love and kindness." Sarah paused, looked around the auditorium, and saw her family in the front row. She gave them a warm smile.

"For those of you who don't know," Sarah continued, "Thomas and Esmeralda Jenkins adopted me when I was in the fourth grade. They have given me everything I could have asked for and more. Many of you may be aware that my mother, Esmeralda, is no ordinary human being. In fact, she is not a human being at all— she is a robot."

Several people in the audience laughed, assuming that Sarah was trying to be funny.

"Some of you may feel sorry for me because I don't have a human mother," Sarah continued, "but I can assure you that there is absolutely no need to feel sorry. Esmeralda is the most wonderful mother a child could ask for."

At this point, everyone in the audience realized that Sarah was serious. Many older people looked at each other and frowned. Someone was overheard saying, "What in God's name is the world coming to?" Sarah's classmates, on the other hand, who were more familiar with the concept of robowives, appeared unfazed; in fact, many of them looked bored as if they were thinking, *I hope Sarah is going to make this short so we can get ready for the senior party.* Fortunately, Sarah had a small contingent of best friends sitting together in the back of the auditorium who stood and clapped enthusiastically after her every sentence.

Sarah continued her speech by addressing the Nation's political and economic difficulties. Regarding the economy, she pointed out the importance of sound monetary policy to keep interest rates low to help small businesses and spur economic growth; and regarding politics, she pointed out the need for the Republicans and Democrats to compromise and avoid polarization. She concluded her address by encouraging her classmates to become change agents for a better world.

When Sarah finished, everyone in the auditorium stood and applauded. Her friends in the back row stood up, clapped loudly, and whistled. One of them shouted, "Great speech, Sarah! You should run for President!" Sarah smiled and sat down.

The Falls Church Superintendent of Schools followed Sarah with a longer speech in which he talked mainly about his accomplishments since he became superintendent. The students appeared to be extremely bored. The adults, on the other hand, who were more accustomed to boring speeches, appeared unfazed. When the superintendent finally wrapped up his remarks, the principal and assistant principal handed out the diplomas to the graduating seniors. Thomas and Jacqueline snapped pictures of Sarah with their iPalms as she received her diploma.

After the commencement, Sarah's family joined her on stage. Thomas, Esmeralda, Geraldine, and Jacqueline took turns hugging her. Hector Lopez and his wife followed the family onto the stage and offered Sarah their congratulations.

When it was Hector's turn to hug Sarah, he said, "Sarah, you may know that I'm running for reelection next year, and I'd be honored to have you work on my campaign. After the campaign, I can help you find a good job on the Hill."

"I'm flattered," replied Sarah, "but I will be in college. Maybe my mother can help you."

Esmeralda took the cue. "I'd absolutely *love* to work on your campaign, Hector."

Thomas frowned as if he didn't like the idea. Then, after a moment, his expression changed and he shrugged. "Well, I suppose it wouldn't do any harm. Now that Sarah is going away to college, you'll have some time on your hands."

Esmeralda was elated. "It will be good experience for me if you ever let me get into politics."

"Does Esmeralda plan to go into politics?" asked Hector's wife. Reaching her hand towards Esmeralda, she added, "My name is Susan. So nice to meet you!"

"Nice to meet you, too," responded Esmeralda, shaking Susan's hand.

"Hector always expects me to run his campaign for him alone," said Susan. "I'm so glad to finally have some help!"

"Let's do it, then!" declared Hector. "The two of you can set up my campaign headquarters in Falls Church. You can get started on it next January right after the holidays!"

Thomas invited Hector and Susan to join the family for lunch at The Peking Gourmet in Falls Church where the party of seven celebrated Sarah's graduation. Everyone was in a jubilant mood. Sarah was already thinking ahead to college, and Esmeralda was excited about the unexpected opportunity to finally get involved in politics.

* * * * *

Sarah was accepted at six universities, including Harvard, Yale, Princeton, Brown, Stanford, and the University of Texas at San Antonio. She spent the summer visiting each of the schools and trying to decide which one would be the best fit. Thomas, Geraldine, and Jacqueline took turns accompanying her on her college tours and offered their advice, often contradicting each other.

Geraldine accompanied Sarah on her visits to Harvard and Brown. "If I were you, I'd pick Harvard or Brown," Geraldine told her. "With a degree from an Ivy League school, you will never have to worry about landing a good job."

Jacqueline accompanied Sarah on her visit to the University of Texas at San Antonio. "This would be the perfect school for you," she told Sarah. "It is much bigger than Harvard, Princeton, or Brown and has a proportionately larger alumni network. When you graduate and start looking for a job, the school's alumni can help you get your foot in the door with the best companies."

"Pick the most prestigious school," said Thomas. "Go to Harvard, Yale, Princeton, Stanford, or Brown."

Sarah listened politely, but she knew her own mind. She disliked downtown urban areas; she didn't care for cities such as Cambridge, Massachusetts, where Harvard was located, or New Haven, Connecticut, where Yale was located. In the end, she accepted the offer from the University of Texas at San Antonio, more commonly known as UTSA, because of its excellent academic standing and its attractive campus on the outskirts of San Antonio.

In mid-August, Thomas and Esmeralda accompanied Sarah to San Antonio to attend the freshman orientation for students and parents.

"Whatever you did in high school seemed to work," said Thomas. "Just keep doing the same thing in college."

"I'm just a text message away," added Esmeralda. "Text me if you ever need any help with your homework."

When Thomas and Esmeralda returned to Virginia, they missed Sarah more than they expected. She had been a major component of their married life since the first week of their marriage.

"She was such a ray of sunshine," said Thomas. "Having her around always cheered me up."

"She kept me busy," said Esmeralda. "I was never bored."

"So what are you going to do now?" asked Thomas.

"Next year I'll help Susan with Hector's reelection campaign. In the interim, I guess I'll finish reading the books in your library. I never did read *War and Peace*. Maybe I can read that one this weekend."

Thomas smiled. By now, he knew that Esmeralda could read at the speed of light. "You better read it on-line. It would take a week just to turn all the pages."

"Good point."

Thomas and Esmeralda did their best to adjust to life without Sarah. Thomas immersed himself in his career and Green Party activities, and Esmeralda spent the rest of the year reading the remainder of the books in Thomas's library. In January 2494, Esmeralda contacted Susan and made arrangements to help set up Hector's campaign headquarters in Falls Church.

Esmeralda and Susan hit it off right away and soon became the best of friends. Together they designed a flyer with the message, *If you aren't happy with the way things are going, remember that the Democrats and Republicans are the ones who got us into this mess!*

By February, the campaign was in high gear, and Esmeralda did an electronic distribution of the flyer to the 150 million registered voters in Virginia; then she and Susan visited local businesses and passed out a paper version of it. From February to early November, Hector participated in more than two hundred town-hall meetings and visited more than fifteen hundred stores and restaurants where he met voters and talked about his ideas for improving the environment and the economy. Thomas joined the campaign in April and brought with him a small army of Green Party volunteers to assist in the effort.

Jacqueline ran unopposed in her bid for reelection, so the family was able to focus on helping Hector.

Election Day in November 2494 saw a record turnout, and Hector won reelection easily with more than sixty percent of the votes. During his victory speech at the Marriott Hotel in Falls Church, he thanked Susan, Esmeralda, Thomas, and the other Green Party volunteers. "I wouldn't have been able to win," he declared, "without your support!"

Thomas was pleased, and Esmeralda was ecstatic. "Now I know how it's done," she told her husband. "When Hector runs for Governor, I can run for his seat in Congress!"

Thomas smiled. "Well, let's cross that bridge when we come to it."

"Bridge?"

"It's just an expression. It means we'll make a decision when Hector runs for Governor."

"Okay, I get it."

After the election, life in the Jenkins household returned to normal, but without Sarah. Thomas's job as a lobbyist provided adequate income to support the family and gave him enough free time to continue volunteering with the Green Party. His political acumen and commitment to the party's agenda catapulted him into a leadership role, and he attended weekly meetings with the party's co-chairs. Esmeralda resumed reading; however, since she had finished all of the books in Thomas's library, she made a daily trip to the Library of Congress in Washington, D.C., and began reading the books there. "My goal," she told Thomas, "is to read ten thousand books a year. Right now I've got nothing better to do."

Sarah met expectations in her studies at UTSA and graduated Summa Cum Laude in 2497 with a Bachelor of Arts in Economics and Public Policy. As much as she enjoyed her four years in San Antonio, she thought that a change would be beneficial; accordingly, she enrolled in Brown University for her Master's Degree in Economics; then, in 2500, in Harvard University for a second Master's Degree, this one in Political Science; and finally, in 2503, in Stanford University for her Doctorate in Economics. In 2507, Doctorate in hand, she returned to UTSA to join the faculty as an Associate Professor of Economics.

Meanwhile, in Virginia, Thomas and Esmeralda had dinner with Hector and Susan at least twice a month. After Hector's successful re-election, Susan busied herself by becoming active in the Virginia Chapter of the League of Women Voters. She was enthusiastic about the organization and hoped to someday take a leadership role in it.

From time to time, Esmeralda asked Hector when he planned to run for Governor. Hector always responded, "When the time is right—when I think the Democratic and Republican front-runners are weak."

Privately, Esmeralda talked to Thomas about running for Hector's seat in Congress when the time came that he resigned and ran for Governor. Thomas always responded the same way, "Let's cross that bridge when we come to it."

The years went by, and Hector passed on opportunities to run for Governor of Virginia, which holds its gubernatorial election a year before Congress's mid-term elections, in 2497, 2501, 2505, 2509, and 2513. Meanwhile, Thomas continued his work in the Green Party, and Esmeralda busied herself with reading. True to her word, she read more than ten thousand books each year on subjects ranging from Ancient Egypt to Zoology. In addition to economics and political science, she developed a keen interest in religion, especially Buddhism, and persuaded Thomas to take her to Saturday and Sunday services at numerous churches, synagogues, and temples in Northern Virginia and Washington, D.C.

In January 2517, Hector finally announced his bid for the Virginia Governorship. His announcement included a statement that he would not seek reelection to the U.S. House of Representatives. Upon hearing the news, Esmeralda once again broached the subject with her husband.

"Thomas," said Esmeralda, "I think we have come to the bridge. Now we have to cross it."

The First Robot President

Part II

The Path to the White House

Chapter 4

Running for Congress

On Tuesday, September 7, 2517, Geraldine arose as usual and picked up her coffee from the refrigerator door, which was now programmed to have it ready at 7:00 a.m. Then she sat down at her kitchen table facing the north wall and summoned her digital assistant.

"Richard, I'm ready for my morning update."

The wall lit up and Richard appeared. "Good morning, Ms. Jenkins, your daughter-in-law was in the news this morning."

"Oh my God, what did she do this time? Is she trying to teach economics to kindergarteners?"

"No, not to my knowledge, Ms. Jenkins. However, the media is talking about her extensively on every network. Would you like me to link you to the morning news?"

"Yes, please."

"CNN?"

"Let's go with NBC this morning."

"As you wish, Ms. Jenkins. I will start it from the beginning."
Richard disappeared and a news anchor appeared in his place.

The news anchor was a young man wearing a clean white T-shirt seated at a glass desk, his bare feet visible on the floor below the desk. As the introductory background music subsided, he spoke. "Good morning, everyone! My name is Jonathan Anderson. We have all of today's important headlines for you, including an unbelievable story that is going to make you wonder if you are watching the news or a science fiction movie. We are going to tell you about a robot that is running for Congress! No, I'm not making this up, and I'm not joking—this is actually happening! That story next after this brief commercial."

The news anchor disappeared, and a middle-aged man wearing a navy-blue dress shirt and navy-blue striped tie appeared in his place. He was standing in front of an ultra-modern, silver-colored aeromobile. "Introducing the 2518 Apple-Ford Mark 5000, Premium Edition!" he exclaimed. Then, turning to the aeromobile, he opened the door and climbed inside. The camera followed him, revealing the interior of the vehicle.

"Any aeromobile will get you from Point A to Point B by giving it your destination address," said the salesman. "What distinguishes the Mark 5000's Premium Edition is its unprecedented level of comfort and convenience. It features six separate climate control settings for you and each of your five passengers. You can choose your music from more than a billion songs in Apple-Ford's digital library, music going all the way back to the Middle Ages—in fact, all the way back to Elvis Presley and Johnny Cash."

"Why do I have to listen to this nonsense?" said Geraldine, talking to herself.

"If you're on your way to work in the morning," the salesman continued, "you can order a cup of coffee, tea, or hot chocolate. When you return home in the afternoon, you can order beer, wine, or a mixed drink. You don't even need to stress your vocal cords. Just think, *I'd like a cup of cappuccino* or *I'd like a rum and coke.* The aeromobile's digital mind reader will pick up your thought and transmit it to the automatic bartender, which will mix your drink exactly as you envision it. A robotic arm will then deliver your drink to your cupholder. The only thing left for you to do is to lift the drink from the cupholder to your mouth."

The salesman then cupped his hand to his mouth and lowered his voice as if he were telling his listeners a secret. "Not to worry — our engineers are working on that problem, too!"

Geraldine leaned forward in her armchair. "Do you really think people are that lazy, you imbecile?"

Richard reappeared on the monitor. "Ms. Jenkins, you aren't in interactive mode. Do you want me to switch you to interactive mode so that the gentleman can hear you?"

"No, that's quite all right. Richard. It's probably just as well he can't hear me."

Richard disappeared and the salesman reappeared. "This amazing vehicle is also more affordable than you might expect with entry-level models priced under five million dollars. You work hard for a living. Don't you deserve the ultimate in comfort and convenience? Visit your Apple-Ford dealer today and see for yourself!"

The salesman disappeared, leaving only a view of the aeromobile's ultra-plush interior. A different voice spoke rapidly, "Price quoted does not include destination charges, state and local taxes, and special features ordered by the customer. Not all models have all of the features just described. The model shown is seven million, nine hundred and ninety-nine thousand, ninety-nine dollars, and ninety-nine cents."

"Thank goodness I don't need an aerocar!" exclaimed Geraldine. "This is just getting more and more ridiculous!"

The news anchor reappeared on the wall monitor. "As I mentioned before the break, we have just learned that a robot is running for Congress, more specifically for the 8th Congressional District in Virginia. Julie Perez, our correspondent on the Hill, is covering this story for us. Let's go to Julie right now and get the full scoop. Julie, what can you tell us?"

The view on the monitor split in half, and a young woman standing on the steps of the Capitol appeared on the right side.

"Yes, Jonathan. As impossible as it may sound, a robot is actually running for Congress. She—it's a female robot—is running for the seat currently occupied by Hector Lopez, who announced his bid for the Governorship of Virginia earlier this year. Congressman Lopez has represented Virginia's 8th District for many years, so we expect numerous candidates to jump into the race since he won't be running for reelection. However, I think it's safe to say no one expected anything like this."

"What do we know about this robot?" asked the anchor. "Who owns it? Does it have a name?"

"This is what we know so far. It was manufactured by General Google Motors in 2484 and was purchased the same year by a lobbyist and Green Party activist by the name of Thomas Jenkins. That would make the robot approximately thirty-three years old. Court records in Fairfax County, Virginia, where Mr. Jenkins lives, indicate that he married the robot, whose name is Esmeralda, shortly after he purchased it."

"He married the robot?"

"That's right, Jonathan. He married the robot in September 2484."

"Well, it's not the first time I've heard of someone marrying their robot, but this is the first time, to my knowledge, that a robot has entered public life. What else do we know about ... uh, what did you say its name was?"

"Its name again is Esmeralda. It is a high-end model and supposedly has an IQ of 265."

"265? That's impossible!" exclaimed the anchor.

"No wonder she's such a smart ass!" exclaimed Geraldine.

"Well," said Ms. Perez, "if what I just told you is true, she would be smarter than any human being currently living."

"We'll find out soon enough," said the anchor, "just how smart she really is. The other candidates will want a formal debate. We'll see how this robot performs in a debate. What else do we know about her?"

"Thomas and Esmeralda have one child, Sarah, whom they adopted shortly after they married. We are told she teaches economics at the University of Texas in San Antonio."

"Let's put the marriage and family part of it aside for a moment. Do we know anything about the robot's position on the issues?"

"No, we don't yet know her position on the issues, but she is running as the Green Party candidate, so that gives you a clue. Also, Thomas and Esmeralda got into a scrap with their school board a few years ago—something to do with economics not being offered in elementary school—so I think you are going to find she is interested in educational reform."

"I can't believe Thomas is letting her do this!" exclaimed Geraldine.

"Have you spoken to any voters yet?" asked the anchor. "I'd love to know the reaction of the voters."

"We did some limited polling this afternoon in the short window prior to this broadcast. As you might expect, most people didn't believe us when we told them a robot was running for Congress. I think it is going to take a while for this to sink in. That is, it may take a few days before people realize this is not a joke, that a robot is actually running for Congress."

"Have you spoken to any of the political pundits to get their reaction?"

"No, I haven't, but you can be sure this story will be all over the Internet in the next twenty-four hours. Every political pundit in the world will be eager to give us their perspective."

"Well, let's go to NBC's political analyst, Mark Thompson, right now and see what he thinks about this. Mark, are you there?"

Julie disappeared and an elderly man wearing a blue T-shirt appeared in her place. "Yes, I'm here, Jonathan."

"Have you been listening to Julie's report, Mark?"

"Yes, Jonathan, I heard her report. Actually, I got wind of this story last night."

"Well, what do you think about it?"

"Jonathan, I think this can only be described as a watershed moment in American politics. On the one hand, with all of the recent advances in robotic engineering, we shouldn't be surprised; on the other hand, it is fair to say no one saw this coming."

"I couldn't agree more."

"If a voter were to consider voting for this robot," Mr. Thompson continued, "I think they should ask themselves if they are really voting for the robot or for the robot's owner. In other words, precisely how much control does Thomas Jenkins exercise over the robot's political views? Would a vote for Esmeralda Jenkins really be a vote for Thomas Jenkins? That would be my first question."

"That would be my first question, too," replied the anchor. "But I see what you mean when you say this is a watershed moment in American politics. The implications here are enormous. Thank you for your commentary, Mark. Let's go back to Julie now."

Mark disappeared and Julie reappeared.

"How soon, Julie, will you be able to get an interview with the robot?"

"We are working on that now—hopefully sometime today so that we can have it for you on the evening news. In the meantime, at 2:00 p.m., Esmeralda will be making a formal announcement at a rally in Falls Church city. I will be on hand to cover it."

"Great, we will interrupt our regularly scheduled broadcast and bring it to our viewers live. Thank you very much for your report."

"My pleasure, Jonathan."

"There you have it, folks!" said the anchor. "Stay tuned to NBC. We'll give you regular updates on this major story! Now, for our next story, we have a cold front to tell you about. After this short break ..."

Julie disappeared, and the aeromobile salesman reappeared on the screen.

"I'm done with the news, Richard," said Geraldine. "Please turn it off now so I don't have to listen to this idiot again."

"Understood, Ms. Jenkins. I'm turning it off now."

"And get Thomas on the line."

"I'm reaching out to Thomas right now, Ms. Jenkins. Give me just a moment, please."

Thomas appeared on the monitor in another minute. "Hello, Mom. Did you see the news?"

"Did I *see the news?* Can you tell me what the hell is going on?"

"Don't act like you're surprised, Mom. We have been talking about this for years!"

"Correct, we have been *talking* about it—as in a joke. I can't believe you are actually doing this."

"Well, Esmeralda has been pestering me about it for more than thirty years. I can only put her off for so long."

"I beg your pardon? Esmeralda is a robot, isn't she? Exactly who's calling the shots, you or she?"

"Well, I am, of course, but Esmeralda has a mind of her own."

"A mind of her own? So now you tell me! Jacqueline and I warned you about this from the beginning."

"Warned me about what?"

"About marrying a robot, don't you remember?"

"Yes, you cautioned me, but then you met her and decided you liked her, remember?"

"I'm telling you, Son, you're going down a slippery slope. If you can't control her, what's she going to do next? Is she going to want to run for President?"

"Don't be ridiculous. She's not going to run for President."

"I'm just saying—this is a slippery slope. I am extremely uncomfortable."

"You get uncomfortable too easily, Mom."

"Is that so? Have you thought about all the publicity? You don't think the media is going to harass you? *Every network, every day*? Do you really want that?"

"I will deal with it when the time comes."

"That time would be *today*, Son!"

"Fine, then I'll deal with it today."

"Have you spoken to Jacqueline and Hector?"

"Of course I did. They're both on board."

"Is that so? Let me speak to Jacqueline myself. Richard, find Jacqueline and connect her immediately!"

Richard reappeared in the top right-hand corner of the monitor. "Of course, Ms. Jenkins. I'm reaching out to Jacqueline right now."

"I already told you I talked it over with her," said Thomas. "She didn't have any objection."

"Your sister has been successful, and I'm proud of her. We don't need your wife screwing everything up and ruining the family reputation!"

"So that's what you're worried about—the family reputation?"

"Your wife is going to make us the laughingstock of Virginia!"

"Let's put this in perspective. Esmeralda is probably not even going to win."

"Then why are you letting her do this?"

"It will make her happy."

"Young man, you've let the genie out of the bottle. She's not going to quit until she wins. Mark my words, she will run for Congress every two years whether she wins or not!"

Richard reappeared on the monitor. "I'm sorry, Ms. Jenkins. Jacqueline is in a committee meeting. I will connect her as soon as she's free, but that may not be until they break for lunch."

"Very well. Let her know I want to speak to her about Esmeralda. She'll know what I'm referring to."

"Yes, Ms. Jenkins, I will tell her you want to speak to her about Esmeralda."

Richard disappeared, and Thomas remained on the monitor.

"Thomas, I just heard on the news Esmeralda is making a formal announcement this afternoon in Falls Church city. Are you going with her?"

"Of course. I've asked Hector to introduce her, and she'll make a brief speech."

"Don't let her say anything stupid."

"Don't worry. She's not going to say anything stupid."

"I hope not. Okay, Thomas, I'll talk to you later."

"Goodbye, Mom."

"Have a good day, Son."

Geraldine's monitor went dark, and she stood up and walked back to the refrigerator. After fixing breakfast, she busied herself with light chores for the remainder of the morning. At 12:05 p.m., her iPalm vibrated; and opening her left palm, she read a text message from Jacqueline: *Mom, I got your message. I know all about Esmeralda. Everyone here on the Hill is talking about it. I will call you this evening.*

Geraldine closed her left palm, turning off her iPalm, and returned to the kitchen to prepare her lunch.

*   *   *   *   *

A crowd of some five hundred people had already gathered in Falls Church city, standing elbow-to-elbow in the town square, by the time Thomas and Esmeralda arrived. William and other Green Party volunteers stood near a six-foot-high platform with a podium on the southwest corner of the square. Someone had roped off a small area in front of the platform for the reporters and their camera crews. Dozens of police officers surrounded the intersection, and more were arriving by the minute to assist with crowd control.

Hector was waiting for Thomas and Esmeralda below the speaker's platform and greeted them warmly, giving Thomas a hug and kissing Esmeralda on the cheek. "Can you believe this crowd?" he asked. "I don't know how the word got out so fast."

"I'm not surprised," replied Thomas. "It was on the news this morning."

"Do you still want me to introduce her?" Hector asked.

"Yes, people know you, they don't know me, and I'd like to keep it that way as long as possible. I need to adopt a low profile."

"Okay, then, I'll do it." Hector opened his iPalm and checked the time. "It's 1:59 right now. Are you ready, Esmeralda?"

"I'm all set," replied Esmeralda. "Let's get started!"

Hector turned to the platform, ascended the steps, and walked to the podium. One hundred or more members of the Green Party shouted their approval and applauded loudly as he stood in front of the crowd and adjusted the microphone. He motioned them to quiet down.

"Good afternoon and thank you for coming!" Hector began. "I hope all of you are as excited as I am about this historic moment. Can you believe it—we have a *robot* running for Congress!"

Many in the crowd, probably Democrats and Republicans, booed while the Green Party members shouted their approval; and others, perhaps Independents and Libertarians who had come out of curiosity, watched in silence.

Hector waited for the crowd to quiet down. "I'm talking about Esmeralda Jenkins, of course. Esmeralda has been married to my best friend, Thomas Jenkins, for thirty-three years, and I was the Best Man at their wedding!"

Someone in the audience shouted, "Well, that certainly qualifies her to run for Congress!"

"You may have come here this afternoon out of curiosity," Hector continued, ignoring the comment. "Some of you may even think this is some kind of stunt. I can assure you it is not—this is the real deal!"

The Green Party members in the crowd cheered loudly while others booed.

"I cannot say enough good things about Esmeralda. She has integrity you won't find in many people, and her intelligence and intellectual curiosity are off the charts. You won't find a person in all of Virginia—human or robot—who is better qualified to represent our 8th District!"

The Republicans and Democrats in the crowd booed again, louder than before. The Green Party members, although outnumbered, cheered enthusiastically, doing their best to drown out the others.

"The Green Party cannot afford to lose this seat," Hector continued. "The stakes are too high!"

Someone in the crowd shouted, "Hector for Governor!"

"Whoever just said that," Hector continued, "thank you, but today's rally is not about me, it's about Esmeralda and her candidacy for my seat in Congress. The Republicans and Democrats can't get the job done. The Green Party can!"

The Green Party members in the crowd now cheered in unison, "Esmeralda for Congress! Esmeralda for Congress!" drowning out the boos and catcalls from others in the crowd.

Hector raised his voice. "Without further ado, allow me to introduce Esmeralda Jenkins, the Green Party's candidate for my seat in the United States House of Representatives!"

The noise from the crowd—a mixture of cheers, whistles, boos, and catcalls—was deafening as Thomas helped Esmeralda ascend the steps of the platform. Then Thomas descended and stood nearby as his wife stood in front of the podium. She looked stunning in a royal-blue blouse with a red scarf and white skirt. She waited for the crowd to quiet down, which took a couple of minutes.

"I want to thank all of you for coming to hear me this after-noon," Esmeralda began. "As you know, I'm here to formally announce my candidacy for the Congressional seat being vacated by our good friend and Green Party colleague, Hector Lopez, who has announced his candidacy for Governor of Virginia."

The Green Party members in the crowd began chanting again, "Esmeralda for Congress, Esmeralda for Congress!" Esmeralda mo-tioned to them to quiet down.

"As Congressman Lopez just told you, I'm a robot, but that does not disqualify me from running for Congress. I have devoted my life to educating myself about the human condition. I have stud-ied American history, anthropology, economics, political science, and dozens of other subjects. I will match my knowledge bank against any other candidate in the race, be they Republican, Demo-crat, Libertarian, or Independent. I'm well equipped and motivated to deal with the serious challenges facing our nation during these difficult times!"

Once again, the Green Party members in the crowd cheered loudly; and once again, Esmeralda motioned them to quiet down.

"Between now and Election Day, I look forward to debating the issues of the day with my opponents. I'm confident that the vot-ers of Virginia will recognize my passion for good government and my creative solutions to the seemingly insurmountable problems we face in our nation. My first priority, of course, will always be what's in the best interest of the citizens of Virginia!"

The Green Party members resumed their chant, "Esmeralda for Congress, Esmeralda for Congress!" Others in the crowd, possibly Democrats and Republicans, tried to drown them out with boos and jeers. Police could be seen escorting away an angry and unruly man, no doubt a Democrat or Republican, and putting him in handcuffs.

Hector, who was now standing beside Thomas, whispered to his friend. "So far, so good. Let's wind it up now before things get out of hand!"

As Esmeralda waited for the crowd to quiet down, Thomas waved his hand until he caught her attention. She understood the signal.

"We said we would keep this brief," Esmeralda told the crowd, "so I'll leave it there for now. You will be hearing more from me over the next few weeks. I want to thank William and the other Green Party volunteers for arranging this event this afternoon. Thank you, everyone, for coming."

Esmeralda stepped away from the podium, and Thomas ascended the stairs to help her down. Hector greeted them at the bottom of the stairs.

"Well done!" exclaimed Hector. "Your campaign is off to a great start!"

Before Thomas or Esmeralda could respond, reporters and their camera crews swarmed around them, shouting questions at Esmeralda over the noise of the crowd.

"Will you participate in a televised debate?" asked one reporter.

"What is your position on birth control?" asked another, as the camera crews and their drones worked the scene from multiple angles.

"Are you prepared to deal with legal challenges?" asked another reporter.

Thomas did his best to shield Esmeralda from the reporters. "Yes, Esmeralda will participate in a televised debate if we have one. We will address your other questions at that time or during a proper forum. Thank you again for coming today."

Hector disappeared into the crowd, and Thomas and Esmeralda turned towards the building where Thomas had parked his aeromobile. Several Fairfax City police officers accompanied them as they worked their way through the crowd until they reached the building. They took the elevator to the rooftop and climbed into the vehicle.

"Well done!" said Thomas. "You must be exhausted."

"Thank you," replied Esmeralda, "but I'm not exhausted. I never get exhausted. It's impossible."

"I forgot you don't get exhausted. That's good—you're going to need a lot of energy for what's ahead of you."

"I have lots of energy," replied Esmeralda. "That's the least of my worries."

Thomas gave the aeromobile his destination, and the vehicle ascended into the sky. As it did so, Esmeralda looked down at the intersection where the crowd had begun to disperse and noticed hundreds of tents surrounding the town square.

"I think the homeless problem is getting worse," said Esmeralda.

Thomas looked down at the town square. "You're right. The number of homeless encampments is increasing exponentially every year."

"I hope I can do something about it."

"I hope so, too. We have terrible problems in this country right now."

"Lucky I'm running for Congress. If humans can't solve their own problems, maybe I can!"

"It's worth a try."

Thomas applied pressure to the accelerator, and the aeromobile quickly sped to 150 miles per hour. He and Esmeralda would be home in less than five minutes.

* * * * *

That evening, as Geraldine was cleaning up after dinner, she received Jacqueline's call on her iPalm. She opened her left hand and saw Jacqueline's image on her palm.

"Hi, Mom," said Jacqueline. "Did you watch the event this afternoon in Falls Church city?"

"Just a second, dear," replied Geraldine. "I can't get used to looking at such a small screen." Geraldine turned to the north wall of her kitchen. "Richard, please connect Jacqueline!" The north wall lit up, and Richard appeared.

"Good evening, Ms. Jenkins. I understand you would like to speak to your daughter, Jacqueline. Is that correct?"

"Yes, Richard, I already have her on my iPalm, but I need a bigger screen."

"Just a moment, please."

Richard disappeared and Jacqueline's image appeared on the wall.

"Sorry about that, dear," said Geraldine. "These iPalm devices are all well and good for people with big hands, but mine are too small. Anyway, I want to know if Thomas consulted you before he went ahead with this ludicrous idea."

"Well, yes. He talked to me."

"I hope you tried to dissuade him from letting Esmeralda do this."

"Mom, you have to remember that Thomas is an adult now. I can't tell him what he can and cannot do."

"I understand that, but you're his older sister. I certainly hope you told him it was a stupid idea!"

"Well, I asked him if he had thought it through completely. We talked about the pros and cons."

"Pros? Please forgive my stupidity—exactly what are the pros?"

"Well, for one thing, it will get Esmeralda to stop pestering him."

"That's an excellent reason for running for Congress! Forgive me for being so slow!"

"Mom, I can see you're taking this too seriously. What's the worst thing that can happen?"

"Didn't it ever occur to you she could damage the family's reputation?"

"How's she going to damage the family's reputation?"

"By saying or doing something stupid!"

"Esmeralda is highly intelligent. I don't think she's going to say or do anything stupid."

"You're the proverbial optimist."

"Trust me, I'm right."

"Is that so? Tell me, what are people on the Hill saying about this?"

"Nobody's taking it seriously. Everyone thinks it's a joke."

"Then I'm right—there's nothing to be gained by this foolishness."

"Well, I did hear someone say it might be possible for a robot to be elected to Congress someday—maybe a thousand years from now."

"Right, a thousand years from now, *not now!*"

"Mom, why don't you make yourself a Kahlua Sombrero, forget about this, and just chill out this evening?"

"I'm going to need more than a Kahlua Sombrero."

"Have Richard put on some music for you, maybe something from the Middle Ages."

"Why would I listen to music from the Middle Ages?"

"You always liked Bob Dylan. It would help you to get your mind off this."

"This conversation isn't going anywhere, so I guess I might as well. Richard, did you hear that? Jacqueline suggests I listen to Bob Dylan."

Richard reappeared. "I understand that you would like me to find some music from Bob Dylan, is that correct?"

"Yes, perhaps *The Essential Bob Dylan.*"

"Of course, Ms. Jenkins. Give me just a moment."

"Try to get a good night's sleep, Mom, and don't worry about this. Everything will turn out all right."

"I hope you're right. Good night."

"Good night, Mom."

Jacqueline disappeared, and "Like a Rolling Stone" came over the speaker. Geraldine turned to a cabinet, opened the cabinet door, and found a bottle of Kahlua. She took it out, carried it to the refrigerator door, and ordered a glass of milk with ice. She added the

Kahlua to the glass of milk, returned the Kahlua to the cabinet, and took her drink to the living room.

*   *   *   *   *

The next morning, after getting her coffee, Geraldine sat down at her kitchen table and summoned her digital assistant.

"Richard, do you have any media updates about Esmeralda?"

The wall lit up and Richard appeared.

"Good morning, Ms. Jenkins. I understand you would like to know if Esmeralda, your daughter-in-law, has been in the news since yesterday. Is that correct?"

"You got it."

"It appears that NBC interviewed her last night. Would you like me to play it back for you?"

"Yes, please, just the part about Esmeralda."

"Understood, Ms. Jenkins. I will play only the interview with Esmeralda."

In another moment, Richard disappeared, and Esmeralda appeared in his place seated at a glass table in a newsroom. A middle-aged Asian man sitting opposite her turned to face the camera.

"Good evening! My name is Ching Chang, and this is the *Evening Congressional Update!* Thank you for joining us. This evening we are interviewing Esmeralda Jenkins, who is running for Virginia's 8th Congressional District."

"Thank you for inviting me," said Esmeralda.

"As you may have heard," Mr. Chang continued, "Esmeralda Jenkins is not a human being, she is a robot. Yes, you heard me right—Esmeralda is a robot. Well, maybe that's a good place to start.

Ms. Jenkins, no robot has ever run for Congress before. What makes you think that the voters will find your candidacy credible?"

Esmeralda turned to the camera and smiled.

"First of all," Esmeralda began, "I want to thank WRC-TV for giving me this opportunity to speak to the Virginia voters. Over the next few weeks, I look forward to meeting many of you in person." Esmeralda turned back to Mr. Chang. "To answer your question, Sir, I believe the voters are looking for the candidate with the best ideas. They don't care whether the candidate is a human being or a robot. They want the best man or woman for the job."

"But strictly speaking," replied Mr. Chang, "you're neither a man nor a woman. The terms 'man' and 'woman' imply being human, don't they?"

"With all due respect, Mr. Chang, I think you are being just a little pedantic. For purposes of my candidacy, I'm a woman. But I don't want to waste your viewers' time debating this point. I think they want to hear my position on the issues."

"Very well, what *are* your positions on the issues? Let's start with the economy. How do you propose to deal with the alarming rate of inflation and the global decline of the dollar's value?"

"Let's put this in perspective, Sir. A freshman Congressman from Virginia isn't going to be able to solve a national problem that has been festering for hundreds of years. I have plenty of ideas for reversing our Nation's economic decline, but the power to accomplish it rests primarily in the hands of the Federal Reserve Board and the President's Council of Economic Advisors. Congress takes the lead in fiscal policy, of course, so I will provide my input there as the opportunity arises. But one thing the voters should know: I'm never going to promise something I can't deliver."

"Oh please, give me a break!" exclaimed Geraldine. "Why should you be different from any other politician!"

Richard appeared in the top-right corner of the monitor. "Ms. Jenkins, did you need me for something?"

"No, Richard, I was just talking to myself."

Richard disappeared.

"Very well," continued Mr. Chang. "Can you tell me, then, exactly what you hope to accomplish if you are elected to Congress?"

"Certainly. Some of my interests are education, the environment, mental health, vegetarianism, and homelessness. These are just a few of the things I hope to address when I get to Congress."

"We may not have time to get into all of those issues this evening, but let's talk about one or two of them. What do you propose to do about education?"

"Education is the foundation of a viable society, and we aren't challenging young people the way we should. For starters, we need to attract the smartest people into the teaching profession, and that starts with paying them what they are worth—teachers should be paid as much as CEOs."

"Good luck with that idea!" exclaimed Geraldine.

"Secondly," Esmeralda continued, "we should put some meat and potatoes into the curriculum. For example, we should begin teaching economics in elementary school. Ditto with anthropology—children need to understand how human beings and robots evolved and how, going forward, the two species can co-exist."

"Oh my God!" exclaimed Geraldine. "No, Richard, I'm not calling *you*. Don't bother me."

Richard appeared in the top-right corner of the monitor. "I understand you don't want me to bother you, is that correct, Ms. Jenkins?"

"No, I don't need you right now. Please go away."

Richard disappeared.

"I also think high school students should be reading more of the classics," Esmeralda continued, "books like *Earth in the Balance*, *An Inconvenient Truth*, and *Our Choice*."

"Weren't those books written five hundred years ago?" asked Mr. Chang.

"That's correct—that's why they're called classics."

"In the interest of time, let's move on to another subject. What do you propose to do about the environment?"

"During the past seven hundred years, human beings have all but decimated the Earth's ecosystem. Our highest priority must be to heal the planet."

"I think most people would agree with that statement, but can you tell our listeners more specifically what you would do to address the problem?"

"Aside from obvious remedies such as mandatory recycling and vegetarianism, we have to address the population explosion. We simply have too many human beings on the planet."

Geraldine's fingers tightened around her coffee mug. "The voters are going to love that idea!"

"Then I take it you favor birth control," replied Mr. Chang. "Is that correct?"

"Yes, I favor birth control."

"I think *all* of the candidates favor birth control. What makes your position on the issue any different? Would you make birth control mandatory?"

"Yes, we can't get a handle on the population crisis without birth control."

"Do you understand that your position is going to be controversial?"

"A true leader has to stand for something," said Esmeralda. "What's important is not whether the policy is controversial, but whether it's right."

"I can't take any more of this," said Geraldine. "Richard, please turn it off. I can only take so much of Esmeralda at this hour of the morning."

Richard reappeared in the monitor's top-right corner. "I understand you would like me to discontinue the broadcast, is that correct?"

"You got it."

"Aren't you concerned, Ms. Jenkins, you may miss something if I discontinue the broadcast prematurely?"

"Jacqueline will fill me in if Esmeralda said anything else I need to know."

"Very well, if you insist, I will discontinue the broadcast."

Richard disappeared, and the monitor went dark. Geraldine finished her coffee and got up from the table to resume her morning routine.

*   *   *   *   *

As was her custom, Jacqueline arose early on Tuesday morning and flew her aerocar to the Capitol, parking it on the rooftop of a nearby garage reserved for members of Congress. As she walked to her office, she noticed a man standing on the steps of the Capitol surrounded by television cameras and reporters. Curious, she took a detour to get closer and see what was happening. The man on the steps appeared to be getting ready to make an announcement.

"We are ready!" called one of the camera men standing below him.

"Testing...testing," said the man on the steps, speaking into the microphone. "Can everyone hear me?"

"We can hear you!" replied one of the reporters.

"Okay let's get started," said the man on the steps. "Thank you for covering my announcement."

A small crowd of people had begun to gather below the Capitol steps, and Jacqueline edged closer to get a better look.

"For those of you who don't know me," the man said, "my name is Prabhat Modi, and I'm announcing my candidacy for Virginia's 8th Congressional District, the seat currently occupied by Hector Lopez. I'm seeking the Democratic nomination."

Jacqueline opened her left hand and tapped a speed-dial number on her iPalm with the index finger of her other hand. She lifted her palm to her mouth. "Thomas, get on CSPAN right away. A Democrat is announcing his candidacy for Virginia's 8th District on the steps of the Capitol."

"I'd be honored to represent the Democratic Party in this election," continued Mr. Modi. "The Democrats need a strong candidate, and I believe I can defeat anyone the Republicans may put up against me. This election is critical because we cannot allow the Republicans to regain control of the House. I will hold fast to the Democratic principles that have guided our party from the beginning. The voters can count on me to back the party leadership!"

"Are you aware that a robot has just announced its candidacy for the same seat?" asked a reporter.

"Will you debate the robot?" asked another reporter.

"One question at a time, please!" said Mr. Modi. "Yes, I've heard about the robot—and no, I won't debate it. This is a real election, not some kind of stunt. I won't degrade the political process by participating in such a farce."

"But aren't you worried about the protest vote?" asked another reporter. "Some voters may vote for the robot because they are disillusioned with the establishment!"

"No, I'm not worried about the protest vote!" replied Mr. Modi. "I'm confident the citizens of Virginia take their civic responsibility seriously. I can assure you that no one is going to vote for a robot."

Jacqueline's iPalm vibrated. She opened her palm and looked at Thomas's reply: *I'm watching the announcement now. I've never heard of this guy. Let me know what they're saying about him on the Hill … talk to you later.*

"Aren't you worried," asked another reporter, "if you refuse to debate the robot, voters will take it as a sign of cowardice?"

"I'm not going to answer any more questions about the robot!" responded Mr. Modi. "I just told you I'm not going to debate a robot. That's my final word on the subject. Now, does anyone have any substantive questions?"

The reporters were silent for a moment. Then one reporter shouted, "Sir, I think you may be making a big mistake. The voters will want to see a debate with the robot!"

Mr. Modi took a deep breath as if he were trying to control his temper. "If the voters want to see a debate, they can watch me debate my Republican opponent … and I can assure you that the robot won't be invited to participate!"

An older man standing beside Mr. Modi, possibly his campaign manager, took the microphone from him. "I think we will have to wrap this up now. Thank you very much for covering Mr. Modi's announcement this morning. And please, let's put this talk about the robot behind us! We have real issues to discuss, and we don't want to turn this election into a circus!"

The older man took Mr. Modi's arm, and the two of them turned and descended the steps, walking away from the reporters as quickly as possible.

Jacqueline turned and walked towards her office in the nearby Rayburn House Office Building.

*   *   *   *   *

Elsewhere in the Nation's capital, Tom Ellsworth, Chair of the Democratic National Committee, sat in his office with Jim O'Donnell and Gladys Campbell, two of his staffers, and watched Prabhat Modi's announcement. He laughed when the reporters began asking questions about whether Mr. Modi would debate the robot.

"This is the funniest thing I've ever witnessed!" exclaimed Chairman Ellsworth. "Who could have imagined a robot would be running for Congress!"

"It is truly hilarious," responded Gladys.

"No question, it's hilarious," responded Jim, "but I wonder if Prabhat is handling this right. I think he should agree to debate the robot—why not?"

"It's probably a moot question," responded Chairman Ellsworth. "I doubt the League of Women Voters would let the robot participate anyway."

"There would be nothing to be gained except entertainment," said Gladys, "but you have to admit, it would be fun to watch."

"It would pull in a big audience," replied Jim. "People would tune in just out of curiosity."

"People who aren't even interested in politics would probably tune in," said Gladys.

"I won't argue with you there," replied Chairman Ellsworth, "but look at the downside—it would bring more attention to the robot, and who knows how many idiots there are out there who would actually vote for a robot."

"That's a legitimate concern," said Gladys. "The fact that someone is a registered voter doesn't mean they will vote responsibly."

"The more I think about it," replied Chairman Ellsworth, "the more I think we need to shut this down as quickly as possible. I will call Nancy this morning and make sure she understands our position."

"Nancy?" asked Gladys.

"Nancy Evans, President of the League of Women Voters. They're the ones sponsoring the televised debate."

Chairman Ellsworth turned to the east wall of his office. "Oliver, dial Nancy Evans!"

The east wall lit up and the Chairman's digital assistant appeared. "Good morning, Chairman Ellsworth. I understand you would like to speak to Nancy Evans, is that correct?"

"Yes."

"I'm dialing her now."

In a moment, Oliver disappeared and an elderly woman appeared in his place.

"Good morning, Tom," said the woman. "I don't normally hear from you this early."

"Good morning, Nancy. Thanks for taking the call."

"What's going on?"

"You heard about the robot, right?"

Nancy laughed. "Oh yes! Everyone is talking about it! I think that human civilization is now descending into its ultimate absurdity."

"Well, we were just watching Prabhat Modi announce his candidacy for Virginia's 8th Congressional District. Reporters were peppering him with questions about whether he would debate the robot."

"Yes, indeed they were! We were watching it here, too."

"I told my staff not to worry about it. I told them you're not going to let a robot participate in the debate."

"We haven't discussed that yet, but I totally agree—it wouldn't be appropriate."

"Absolutely not! It would make the League of Women Voters look unprofessional, like you don't know how to run a debate."

"Well, no one has approached us about it yet. If they do, I will tell them 'no robots.'"

"The Green Party leadership is assertive. You're going to have to be firm."

"I will tell them, 'no robots, *period*!'"

"Good. I just want to make sure we're on the same wavelength."

"For sure! We aren't going to let the Jenkins family turn the debate into the Robot Comedy Hour!"

"The Jenkins family—I almost forgot. That's right: the robot is married to a lobbyist, a member of the Jenkins family."

"His name is Thomas. He is the son of Robert Jenkins, the Congressman from Virginia who died a few years ago."

"Interesting, Robert Jenkins was a Democrat, but his son is a leader in the Green Party."

"Don't forget the other Jenkins, Jacqueline—Robert's daughter and Thomas's sister. She's very popular right now."

"Well, that won't last! The Green Party is riding the crest of a wave that is going to break soon, mark my words!"

"I'm supposed to be impartial, so I'll reserve comment. You never know who might be tapping into our conversation."

"Okay, then, we can talk about it more when I see you. I'll buy you a drink."

"By the way, I'll be retiring next year after the 2518 mid-term elections and moving to Texas."

"Congratulations!"

"I have been here twenty-five years. It's time to move on."

"I understand. Who's taking your place?"

"I don't know. They tell me Susan Lopez, the wife of Hector Lopez, wants the job."

"That would be terrible! Hector is a Green. I assume his wife must be a Green as well."

"Oh, I'm sure she is!"

"Can you do anything to stop her—I mean, to stop her from taking your job when you retire?"

"Probably not. In any case, I have more important things to worry about right now."

"Okay, let's not worry about something that may not happen anyway. The main thing is to keep the robot out of the debate."

"Yes, I'll keep the robot out of the debate."

"Good, Nancy, I won't take any more of your time. Have a good day!"

"You too, Tom. Talk to you again soon!"

Nancy disappeared and Oliver, the digital assistant, reappeared. "Is there anything else I can do for you, Chairman Ellsworth?"

"No thank you, Oliver."

"Very well. Have a good day, Chairman Ellsworth!"

Oliver disappeared and the wall went dark. Chairman Ellsworth turned to his staffers. "Okay, that's settled—now let's get back to work!"

Chairman Ellsworth turned to his computer monitor, and his staffers got up from their chairs and returned to their cubicles.

* * * * *

When Jacqueline arrived at her office, she summoned Henry Hawkins, her Chief of Staff. He was a well-dressed, clean-shaven man about the same age as she, and he greeted her the same way every morning.

"Good morning, Jacqueline!"

"Good morning, Henry. How are you doing?"

"Fine, thank you."

"Good. I need you to do some research for me. I want you to see what you find on Prabhat Modi. He just announced he's running for Hector's seat. I also want to know if anyone else, Democratic or Republican, has announced yet. Get me their names and any other pertinent information, such as any previous political positions or appointments."

"I'll get to work on it right away."

"I also need to get in touch with the League of Women Voters and make sure Esmeralda will be invited to any debates they sponsor for candidates in Virginia's 8th District. The last I knew, the president was Nancy Thomas. I'd like to talk to her today. See if you can set up a conference call with her this afternoon."

"That should be easy—I'll take care of that first."

"Excellent. Put the conference call on my calendar."

Henry returned to his desk to begin working on the assignments, and Jacqueline turned to her computer monitor to get the latest updates on pending bills.

*   *   *   *   *

Meanwhile, in the NBC newsroom in New York City, Jonathan Anderson and his counterpart on the NBC Nightly News desk, Peter Alexander, were meeting with Donald Shafmaster, Vice President of the NBC news division, and their producers, Bill Stone and Jim Weinstein.

"We have to be careful how much attention we give to the robot," said Peter. "The story is entertaining, but I'm not sure it is real news. The robot's candidacy is a joke."

"I agree," said Bill, "we should be focusing on the real candidates, not the robot."

"Well, I hate to be the fly in the ointment," said Jim, "but the robot has been endorsed by Hector Lopez, the incumbent, and it is the apparent nominee of the Green Party. We can't ignore the Green Party candidate, be it a robot or otherwise."

"Now that you put it that way, I see your point," said Peter. "I think the key here is balanced coverage. We need to be sure we aren't covering the robot more than the other candidates."

Vice President Shafmaster listened to the conversation quietly without making a comment.

"To put this in perspective," said Jonathan, "this is still the primary season. Maybe someone else in the Green Party will challenge the robot, and we won't have to deal with her—I mean 'it'—during the general election."

"I can't believe we are even having this conversation," said Jim. "I feel like I just entered the twilight zone."

Everyone laughed.

"Okay, guys, let's be serious for a moment," said Vice President Shafmaster. "What's our plan going forward?"

"We cover the robot like any other candidate," said Peter. "We just make sure we aren't giving it more time than we give the other candidates."

"That makes sense to me," replied Vice President Shafmaster. "Just make sure everyone gets equal coverage."

Everyone nodded in agreement.

*　　*　　*　　*　　*

At 10:00 a.m., Thomas left his desk and walked down the street to the House cafeteria. Aside from the benefit of the break, he often ran into House members or their staffers and found it was sometimes an easy way to set up a meeting or make a pitch. After paying for his coffee, he looked around the cafeteria until he spotted someone he knew. At a small table in the corner, he saw William and walked over and sat down.

"Hey, buddy, thanks for your help with the logistics yesterday!" said Thomas. "I thought the event went really well."

William put his muffin down and smiled. "If you told me thirty-five years ago that I'd be helping you with something like that, I'd have said you had lost your mind."

"I have no doubt plenty of people are saying that right now, but I don't let it bother me. I do my own thing."

"Indeed. After all these years, I know you pretty well."

"Anyway, William, tell me the truth. What did you think of Esmeralda's announcement?"

"I thought it went okay. You could have let her talk a little longer, though."

"Well, it was just an announcement. Now she'll begin interviews to talk about the issues."

"What's she doing today?" William picked his muffin up and finished it.

"She'll be doing an interview this morning on the Today Show. Then she'll visit the other networks for interviews that will be taped and broadcast this evening on the nightly news. Besides NBC, we have her scheduled with ABC, CBS, CNN, and MSNBC."

"Not Fox News?"

"Well, that's enemy territory, you know. Maybe later on."

William pushed his plate away and picked up his coffee mug. "Understood. How's she getting around?"

"Metro. All the networks have Washington bureaus. Everything is right here in the District."

"Is she going to New York?"

"Maybe later on for appearances on the late-night talk shows."

William finished his coffee and put the cup on top of his plate. "Listen, if you want my advice, that's fine, but you also need to get her on the street. I'd put her in the malls, what's left of them, and the supermarkets where she can meet the voters face-to-face. Even more important, she has to go where the protesters are—like the Arlington courthouse and Government Center. They're the ones who will swing the election."

"Are you sure the protesters vote?" asked Thomas.

"They will if they see a candidate who excites them. Esmeralda may be exactly what they have been waiting for."

"You're always the optimist, William."

"I'm optimistic, but realistic. I wouldn't have taken time to help set up for your event yesterday if I didn't believe in this."

"I appreciate it, William. You're a good friend."

"This isn't only about friendship," replied William. "I don't know if you realize just how big this is. Think about it: *a robot running for Congress! It's historic!* It could change the political landscape forever."

"I get that."

"It's also our best hope for changing the direction of the country," William added. "We need someone in Congress who understands the population crisis and its impact on the environment. If somebody doesn't do something about this soon, the human race might as well call it quits!"

"I don't disagree."

"Anyway, Thomas, I have to get back to work. Congratulations on getting your wife's campaign off the ground." He stood up and pushed his chair back. "Have a good day!"

"You too, buddy!"

Thomas finished his coffee, got up from the table, and headed back to his office.

* * * * *

Over dinner that evening, Thomas spoke to Esmeralda about William's suggestion.

"I had coffee with William this morning," said Thomas. "He told me you need to go to the malls and supermarkets and meet people face-to-face."

"Well, that's always been part of our plan, hasn't it?" replied Esmeralda.

"True, but William added a new twist. He said you need to go where the protesters are. He thinks they are the ones who will swing the election."

"Do protesters vote?"

"I asked the same question. William said they will vote if they see a candidate who excites them."

"Do you think I will excite the protesters?"

"They will be excited about any candidate who understands the magnitude of the problem," Thomas replied. "The Republicans and Democrats want to sweep it all under the rug. 'The economy is cyclical,' they say. 'This is just a low point in the cycle.' They want us to believe that everything will get better by itself if we wait long enough."

"Nothing is going to get better unless the Government becomes proactive."

"Exactly," replied Thomas. "To put it in plain English, the Government has to do something."

"For one thing, the Congress and the White House have to get in sync."

"That's certainly one piece of the puzzle," Thomas agreed. "For starters, though, politicians need to understand the urgency. The only idea the Republicans and Democrats can come up with is to form another committee to study the problem. We have been studying the problem for five hundred years."

"Five hundred years is a long time to study a problem with no results."

"As my mother would say, you're a master of understatement."

Esmeralda chuckled. Over the past thirty-three years, she had begun to acquire a sense of humor.

"If we don't get a handle on this soon," continued Thomas, "the country is going to have a revolution. The politicians just don't get it. Anyway, we have to get you out to the malls and supermarkets. You also need to speak to the protesters. What's your schedule tomorrow?"

"An interview with CNN at 8:00 a.m. That's all so far."

"That's good—we can get started tomorrow morning after the CNN interview. I'll take a few hours off from work and take you to the Arlington courthouse. It will only take us ten minutes or so to get there from CNN."

"Are we taking public transportation?"

"No, we'll take my aerocar. It's faster."

"Are you sure we will see protesters?"

"Oh yes, they have hundreds of protesters in front of the municipal building every day from dawn until dark."

"Oh, how exciting! I can't wait to speak to the protesters!"

"I can't wait, either."

Thomas and Esmeralda finished their dinner and enjoyed a relaxing evening, going to bed at 10:00 p.m. so that Thomas could get a good night's sleep.

* * * * *

At breakfast the next morning, Thomas's left hand vibrated. He opened his iPalm and heard Jacqueline's voice.

"Sorry to bother you so early, but we have a problem," said Jacqueline.

"What kind of problem?" asked Thomas as he swallowed a spoonful of scrambled eggs.

"I spoke to Nancy Thomas, president of the League of Women Voters, and she told me that they won't allow Esmeralda to participate in any of the debates."

"Well, that doesn't surprise me," replied Thomas. "Esmeralda would make the other candidates look like fools, and she knows it."

"I agree, but what do we do now? Esmeralda isn't going to get much traction if we don't get her out in front of the voters. This could be a major set-back."

"It's not that big a deal. I have another strategy now anyway."

"Another strategy?"

"Yes, we are going to take Esmeralda directly to the voters, especially to the protesters, so she can meet them face-to-face. We're starting this morning."

"You really want Esmeralda to meet the protesters face-to-face?" asked Jacqueline. "Don't you think that's a big risk? I mean, like, the protesters are angry—really angry."

"Yes, I'm totally serious. *Think about it.* When people see Esmeralda in person, they quickly forget she's a robot; after a minute or two, they see her as just another woman running for office."

"You're always the optimist."

"So far my optimism hasn't let me down."

"We'll find out soon enough if you're right," replied Jacqueline. "Anyway, back to what I was saying, do you think we need to file a lawsuit to get Esmeralda into the debates?"

"No, let's wait and see how my plan works. It's still primary season. The general election is more than a year away. We still have time to challenge the League of Women Voters in court if we have to."

"Okay, I won't worry about it, then."

"No, don't worry about it—I'm on top of it. By the way, did you get any information on that guy, Prabhat Modi, who announced his candidacy for Hector's seat yesterday?"

"Yes, he's a former mayor of Richmond. He only served one term, and it was some years ago. He doesn't look to me like a very formidable opponent."

"Good, we don't want anyone too formidable running against Esmeralda in her first bid for a seat in the House."

"Well, you can expect to see a large field of candidates, both Republicans and Democrats, facing off against each other in their respective primaries before this is over. Esmeralda and Mr. Modi are the first candidates to announce, so we really don't know if any of the others will emerge as formidable competition."

"She will be disappointed if she doesn't win."

"I understand," Jacqueline replied. "You said you are starting today. Where are you taking her?"

"To the Arlington General District Courthouse. They have protesters there every day from dawn until dusk. It will be a good way for Esmeralda to get her feet wet."

"Okay, let me know how it goes," replied Jacqueline. "Talk to you soon."

"Bye, Sis."

"Bye, Thomas."

Thomas finished his breakfast and called Esmeralda, who was in the bathroom grooming herself for the morning's events. "I'm ready to go when you are, honey. I have a bullhorn in the aerocar."

Esmeralda appeared a minute later, wearing her trademark royal-blue blouse with a red scarf and white skirt. "I'm ready, Thomas. Let's go!"

*　　*　　*　　*　　*

Esmeralda's CNN interview went smoothly and followed the same script as her NBC interview on Tuesday evening. Thomas waited for her in CNN's reception area, and they left for the Arlington courthouse as soon as she finished the interview. They arrived at the courthouse at 9:30 a.m. and found three dozen protesters walking in a circle in front of the main entrance. Many of them were carrying signs, and Thomas and Esmeralda paused to read a few of them.

A poorly dressed, elderly man carried a sign, *THE HOMELESS NEED HELP NOW!*

An elderly woman carried a sign, *OUR GOVERNMENT HAS NO COMPASSION!*

A young couple holding the arms of a small child, who walked between them, held a sign, *SOMEBODY HELP US! PLEASE! FOOD, WATER, ANYTHING!*

"These poor people!" exclaimed Esmeralda. "They are desperate!"

"Yes, there's no doubt about that," replied Thomas, carrying the bullhorn in his right hand. "Okay, let's get their attention!"

Thomas approached the protesters and lifted the bullhorn to his mouth. "My wife is running for Congress, and she would like to speak to you!"

The protesters nearest to Thomas looked at him and slowed their pace. In a moment, some of them stopped walking; and in another moment, all of them stopped walking and looked at Thomas and Esmeralda.

Still holding the bullhorn, Thomas spoke louder. "I want to introduce you to Esmeralda Jenkins, the Green Party's candidate for Congress in Virginia's 8th Congressional District!"

He handed the bullhorn to Esmeralda, who raised it to her lips. "Good morning! Thank you for taking a short break to hear what I have to say. Listen, I can see that many of you are angry. I'm angry, too!"

"If you're so angry, how come you aren't walking with us?" shouted one of the protesters.

"The only reason I'm not walking with you is that I have to get out and meet the voters!" replied Esmeralda. "This is just the first of many stops I will make throughout Arlington and Fairfax Counties. My goal is to speak to every voter in Virginia's 8th Congressional District!"

"We're tired of hearing from politicians!" shouted another protester. "Promises, promises, but never any action!"

"You're right!" replied Esmeralda. "The Republicans and Democrats in Congress have failed us! All they do is talk. They never get anything done, and they blame each other! Well, that's going to change when I take office!"

"Wait a minute!" shouted another protester. "She's the *robot*! I heard about her on the news last night!"

"You're correct!" answered Esmeralda. "I'm a robot, not a human being, but let me tell you why I can get the job done."

"This should be good!" someone shouted. "I want to hear this!"

"First," continued Esmeralda, "I have no special interest groups to please; second, I carry no baggage and have no axe to grind; and third, I won't be intimidated by the Republicans and Democrats who wield the power in the House!"

"Not so fast!" shouted another protester. "I can tell the difference between a human being and a robot, and you're no robot!"

"That's right!" said someone else. "This is a ploy. You're pretending to be a robot to get the voters' attention!"

"You must think we're really stupid!" said another. "You think we can't tell the difference between a robot and a human?"

"This robot thing is just a big stunt!" said another. "I wasn't born yesterday!"

"Listen up," replied Esmeralda, "Let's put this way. It really doesn't matter if I'm a human being or a robot, does it? What matters is that I will fight for you!"

"Why should we believe that?" said a protester. "You're just another politician!"

"Because I represent the *Green Party*. The Green Party candidates are the only candidates who have any credibility. You can't believe the Republicans and Democrats!"

"That's the first thing she's said that's makes any sense!" said one of the protesters, speaking to his companions.

"Actually, the *second* thing," replied the poorly dressed, elderly man carrying the sign about the homeless. "She started off by saying the Republicans and Democrats have failed us. That was the *first* thing she said that made sense."

"I think you will agree with me that the Republicans and Democrats are equally incompetent!" Esmeralda added.

"Amen!" shouted a protester.

"That would be the *third thing* she's said that makes sense," said the poorly dressed, elderly man. "I think I may vote for her."

Thomas whispered, "Let's quit while we're ahead." Taking the bullhorn from Esmeralda, he spoke to the protesters, "Thank you for taking time to listen to Esmeralda. I hope we can count on your support on Election Day next year. Don't forget to vote! Thanks again and have a good day!" He took Esmeralda's arm and led her away.

As Thomas and Esmeralda walked back to the aeromobile, they could hear the protesters talking among themselves.

"I just don't know if I can trust someone who is pretending to be a robot."

"Well, to be fair, a candidate who's not a Republican or a Democrat has to have a gimmick to get the voters' attention."

"That's very true—you have to give her credit for coming up with a fresh angle."

As they approached their aeromobile, Thomas nudged Esmeralda. "Now we have a fresh angle: you're pretending to be a robot!"

Thomas and Esmeralda laughed heartily as they climbed back into their vehicle.

* * * * *

Jacqueline called Thomas that evening, and he told her about the "fresh angle." They enjoyed a good laugh together.

"This is what makes politics fun," said Jacqueline. "You never know what you're going to run into."

"It would be funny if it weren't so serious," Thomas replied. "As Esmeralda said, these poor people are desperate."

"I know," replied Jacqueline. "The country is going downhill so fast it's scary."

"That's why we can't afford to lose Hector's seat. I hope I haven't made a mistake by letting Esmeralda run."

"It sounds like she's holding her own so far."

"Yes, so far," replied Thomas, "but remember it's only primary season."

"I know ... so what are you doing next?"

"More of the same. I'll take her to other venues where she can meet more protesters."

"Take her to the malls, too," Jacqueline replied. "She needs to meet as many people as possible."

"Do the malls have protesters?"

"It doesn't matter. She just needs to get out and meet people."

"Don't you think it might be too early?" Thomas asked. "The election is more than fourteen months away."

"No, it's never too early. I'd get her out to the malls and public events every day between now and the general election."

"Is there anything you can do to help her?"

"Sure," Jacqueline replied. "Next year she and I can campaign together. We can go to Fair Oaks Mall, which draws people from both Districts 8 and 11, and other places like that."

"That would be terrific."

"Believe me, I figured this out a long time ago. Media coverage is fine, but you can't win an election unless you touch the voters—figuratively and literally."

"Okay, then, thanks for the advice. I will get Esmeralda out in public every day."

"You're on the right track. Keep me posted on how things go."

"Will do. Thanks again."

"Have a good evening, Thomas."

"You too, Sis."

Thomas called to Esmeralda, who was doing chores in an adjacent room. "You've got your work cut out for you, honey!"

Esmeralda entered the room. "Who were you talking to?"

"Jacqueline."

"What'd she say?"

"We have to get you out in public every day between now and the general election."

"That won't be a problem. I can't wait to meet more voters!"

"I can see you have the right attitude."

"You bet!"

"I just hope I have enough stamina to keep up with you."

Chapter 5
The Court Decides

While Esmeralda was campaigning for her seat in the House, Hector was campaigning throughout the state of Virginia for governor. Under the Virginia constitution, no one can serve two consecutive terms as governor; so the incumbent governor, Charles Stevenson, was not in the competition. As Hector had predicted, the circumstances were ripe for the Green Party to win the governorship this time. The Republican candidate was young and inexperienced, and the Democratic candidate was little known outside Richmond; moreover, neither of them was a particularly strong speaker or campaigner. The gubernatorial election was held in November 2517, and Hector won easily. However, before Hector took office in January 2518, Governor Stevenson appointed a Republican by the name of Jose Greene to serve the balance of Hector's two-year term in the U.S. House.

With twelve months to go before the 2518 mid-term Congressional election, Thomas and his Green Party colleagues took Esmeralda to numerous venues in Virginia's Congressional District 8. Thomas also arranged media interviews for her, and she spoke to reporters whenever she could. Thomas enlisted the aid of William and other volunteers to accompany Esmeralda when he couldn't take time off from work. The volunteers also helped to set up e-bill-boards and e-signs on lawns and buildings throughout the district. Whenever Esmeralda spoke, she reiterated her message that the Republicans and Democrats had become useless and irrelevant.

Meanwhile, the Republican and Democratic candidates for the race in Congressional District 8 focused on their respective prima-ries. Esmeralda encountered them occasionally; but by and large, they didn't go to the same venues as Esmeralda, relying instead on their powerful political machines and extensive media coverage to get their messages out to the public. The primaries were held in March 2518. Jose Greene, with the advantage of being the incum-bent, became the Republican nominee; and Prabhat Modi became the Democratic nominee.

Jacqueline had encountered no challenge during the primary season from within the Green Party and began her campaign for re-election to the House in Virginia's 11th Congressional District in March as soon as the Republicans and Democrats held their respec-tive primaries. Although she enjoyed immense popularity, she knew she couldn't afford to be complacent, and she campaigned energet-ically and tirelessly. Seeing how well Esmeralda's message was being received, she adopted a similar theme, pointing out the pa-thetic records and general incompetence of her Republican and Democratic opponents.

As spring turned to summer, and summer to fall, the polls showed that Jacqueline faced no real threat from her challengers in the general election; accordingly, she took time from her own cam-paign to make a number of joint appearances with Esmeralda, whose polling trends showed a tighter race. By the first of October,

Esmeralda and Prabhat Modi were running dead-even and Jose Greene a distant third.

The League of Women Voters sponsored a debate between Jose Greene and Prabhat Modi in mid-October; and as expected, it refused to allow Esmeralda to participate. However, the post-debate polling numbers showed little or no impact on the race; Esmeralda and Prabhat Modi were still dead-even. No one in the family bothered to watch the debate.

Jacqueline's participation brought more credibility to Esmeralda's campaign; and throughout the month of October, the two women visited Fair Oaks Mall in Fairfax and numerous other shopping centers and venues in the district and spoke to thousands of potential voters. Esmeralda generally downplayed the fact she was a robot, but she acknowledged it when anyone brought it up.

On Election Day, Tuesday, November 1, 2518, early in the day, Thomas and Esmeralda went to a polling station at Fairhill Elementary School in Fairfax to cast their votes for Esmeralda, while Geraldine and Jacqueline went to a separate polling station in Fair Oaks Mall to cast their votes for Jacqueline. After dinner that evening, according to plan, the family gathered at Thomas's apartment to watch the election results, to be followed by a trip to the Tysons Corner Marriott in Vienna where the Green Party had reserved a ballroom to celebrate the victories of their candidates.

Polls taken during the last weekend in October showed Jacqueline with a comfortable lead over her opponents and Esmeralda holding on to a razor-thin lead over Mr. Modi. The family was in a jubilant mood, expecting Jacqueline to coast to an easy victory and believing that Esmeralda had a decent chance of winning Hector's former seat in the House.

At 8:00 p.m., the family sat down together in Thomas's living room, and Thomas summoned James, his digital assistant. "James," he instructed, "we want to follow the election coverage on all six news networks. Please open ABC, CBS, NBC, CNN, Fox News, and MSNBC and split the screen six ways. Put the sound on CNN unless I direct you to switch it."

The monitor on the east wall of the living room lit up, and James appeared. "I believe I understand your instructions, Mr. Jenkins. Give me just a moment, please."

James disappeared, and the six news networks appeared in two rows with ABC, CBS, and NBC on top and CNN, Fox News, and MSNBC on the bottom. The sound came on at the same time with the voice of a political analyst at CNN finishing a sentence. "...so that's what we're seeing so far this evening. It's still early, and we may not know until tomorrow morning how some of the closer races are going to play out. Among others, we will be following the 8th Congressional race in Virginia very closely because that one appears to be closest. That particular race is also of special interest because, as most of our viewers know by now, the Green Party candidate is a robot—and as far as we know, the first robot that has ever run for political office."

"I doubt we'll know the outcome of that race until tomorrow morning," said another CNN commentator. "Let's look at some of the other races. We have Green Party candidates doing well throughout the Northeast, Mid-Atlantic, South, and West. That bodes well for any Green Party candidates in tight races."

Thomas, Jacqueline, and Esmeralda all cheered.

"And Congresswoman Jacqueline Jenkins," continued the analyst, "who is running for re-election in Virginia's 11th Congressional

District, appears to be coasting to an easy victory. We should be able to call that race within the hour."

"Why does he have to wait an hour?" asked Geraldine.

"Let's turn our attention to the South now," continued the analyst. "There are many important contests today in Texas. Let's take a look there."

"James," said Thomas, "please switch the sound to NBC."

The wall monitor re-sized the six network images, and James appeared in the top right-hand corner of the screen. "I understand you want me to switch the sound to NBC, Mr. Jenkins, is that correct?

"Yes, James, please do it now."

James disappeared, and the voice of the political analyst at NBC came through the speakers. "I believe we can now call the race in Virginia's 11th Congressional District," he said. "NBC is predicting Congresswoman Jacqueline Jenkins to win re-election there."

"Yes!" shouted Thomas. The entire family jumped to their feet, giving each other high-fives and hugging Jacqueline.

"Can we open the champagne?" Geraldine asked.

"They'll have plenty of champagne at the hotel," replied Thomas. "Let's wait until we get to the hotel."

James suddenly reappeared on the monitor. "Mr. Jenkins, you have a call coming in from your friend William. Should I put him through?"

"Yes," replied Thomas. "Please put him through."

The monitor resized the images of the six networks, and William appeared in the top-right corner. "We just heard the announcement. Congratulations, Jacqueline!"

"Thank you, William," replied Jacqueline.

"We have a good crowd here, maybe six hundred or so. They are very energized. How soon can you get here to give your victory speech?"

"We were going to wait until they call Esmeralda's race," Thomas replied, "but that may not happen for several more hours." He looked at Jacqueline, who was nodding. "Okay, I think Jacqueline wants to give her victory speech now. We'll head over there right away."

"Great, please get here as soon as you can."

The family arose from their chairs, and Thomas instructed James to discontinue the election coverage. In less than ten minutes, they were in Thomas's aeromobile on their way to the Tysons Corner Marriott.

* * * * *

William was waiting inside the front door of the Marriott and greeted the family when they arrived. After exchanging hugs, he explained the plan. "We won't try to walk through the ballroom. There are too many people. I will take you to a door that leads to the stage. Jacqueline will follow me into the ballroom from there, and I will introduce her from the podium. There's a small room near the ballroom with a monitor that will serve as a private viewing area for the family. When Jacqueline gets done with her speech, she will join you there to watch the remaining election coverage. When they call Esmeralda's contest, Esmeralda can take the stage and either make a victory speech or a concession speech, as the case may be."

"I think we got it," said Thomas.

"Why are you so negative?" asked Geraldine. "Esmeralda isn't going to make a concession speech."

"No offense intended," replied William. "My job is the logistics; I have to be prepared for every eventuality."

Geraldine took her daughter's hand as they followed William into the hotel. "Did you prepare a speech, dear?"

"I'll wing it," Jacqueline replied. "The best speeches are off the cuff."

"I'm sure she'll do just fine," said Thomas. "This isn't her first rodeo."

"Her first rodeo?" asked Esmeralda.

"It's just an expression," replied Thomas.

"Here we are," said William, as they arrived at a door in the hallway. "I will take Jacqueline to the stage, and everyone else can sit down in that room there." He pointed to a room on the other side of the hallway.

William opened the door, and Jacqueline followed him into the ballroom, closing the door behind her. The rest of the family went into the room that William had designated. A monitor on the south wall displayed the ballroom while a monitor on the east wall carried the NBC coverage of the election results. Everyone turned to the south wall.

William appeared on the stage first and took the microphone. "May I have your attention, please! May I have your attention! Congresswoman Jacqueline Jenkins is here! Congresswoman Jenkins is here! Let's give her a big welcome!"

The audience, already in a celebratory mood, began applauding and cheering as William handed the microphone to Jacqueline. She waited a minute or two for the noise to subside.

"Thank you, everyone, for your support," Jacqueline began. "I'm grateful for the opportunity to serve the citizens of Virginia's 11th District again."

"Her father would be so proud," said Geraldine. "She is following in his footsteps."

"You said that the last time," said Thomas.

"It bears repeating," replied Geraldine.

"This election is not just about holding onto my seat in Congress," Jacqueline continued. "It's about taking back our country, rejecting the failed policies of the past, and finding creative solutions to the terrible problems facing our Nation."

"Well said!" exclaimed Thomas.

"I will work with the Green Party's other House and Senate members to get things done. I hereby pledge to you that I will always do what's in the best interest for my constituents in the 11th District."

Jacqueline's supporters cheered and whistled.

"Now I'd like to recognize some of the volunteers who worked on my campaign ..."

Thomas muted the sound and turned to Esmeralda. "Will you be ready when they call on you?"

"Yes," Esmeralda replied, "I have my victory speech in my head."

Thomas looked at the monitor on the east wall. "It looks like your lead has widened since we left the apartment. Maybe we won't have to wait until 2:00 a.m. after all."

"Oh, I'm so excited!" exclaimed Esmeralda.

"I wonder where we can get a drink" said Thomas. "I'm going to go find William." He unmuted the sound before leaving the room.

As the sound came back, Jacqueline was finishing her speech. "So once again, I want to thank all of the volunteers who worked on my campaign. I never could have done this without you."

Everyone cheered.

"Now let's go back to watching the election returns," said Jacqueline, finishing her speech. "Maybe they will call the race for Virginia's 8th District soon." She handed the microphone back to William.

Geraldine and Esmeralda settled back into their armchairs; and a couple of minutes later, Jacqueline joined them, and the three turned towards the east wall and resumed watching the election coverage.

* * * * *

A few minutes before midnight, Peter Alexander of the NBC News team made the announcement that everyone had been waiting for. "I have an important announcement! NBC is calling the House race in Virginia's 8th District! We are projecting Esmeralda Jenkins, *a robot*, to be the winner!"

Normally reserved and disinterested, Mr. Alexander was now animated, the excitement in his voice palpable. *"That's right, a robot has won the race in Virginia's 8th District! This is historic!"*

The decibel level in the ballroom shook the very foundation of the hotel as Esmeralda's supporters cheered and whistled boisterously. In the room across the hall from the ballroom, Thomas and the other members of the family stood up excitedly, hugging and giving each other high-fives.

Thomas, who was hugging his sister, turned to Esmeralda. "Are you ready to make your victory speech?"

"What's the protocol?" Esmeralda replied. "Shouldn't we wait for Mr. Modi and Mr. Greene to make their concession speeches?"

"I didn't wait for any concession speeches," said Jacqueline.

William appeared at the door. "Congratulations, Esmeralda!" He walked into the room and hugged her. "Are you ready to make your speech?"

"I'm ready."

"Okay, then, let's do it. Follow me!"

Esmeralda followed William out of the room, across the hall, and into the ballroom, where the two ascended the stairs of the dais. The crowd, already euphoric, cheered loudly as Esmeralda came into view. William and Esmeralda stood together momentarily in front of the podium, and William took the microphone. "May I have your attention, please! May I have your attention!" He waited for the noise to subside. "Esmeralda is ready to make a speech. Let's give her a huge round of applause!" William then handed the microphone to Esmeralda, turned, and descended the stairs.

The crowd cheered and whistled as Esmeralda looked around the room and smiled graciously.

"Thank you, everyone," Esmeralda began, "for coming tonight and supporting me. I know many of you were skeptical when you heard that a robot was running for Congress. I can hardly blame you—I was a little skeptical myself! Anyway, here we are on election evening, and I won! Can you believe it? I won!"

The Green Party supporters cheered and whistled again, longer and more loudly than before.

Esmeralda waited for the noise to subside, then continued, "This victory is not about me; it's not just about a robot winning a seat in Congress. It is about finding a new direction for our Nation. We can no longer ignore the plight of the unemployed and the homeless. I pledge to you that I will work with other members of the Green Party to reject the failed policies of the Democrats and Republicans and find creative solutions to the enormous crisis facing us.

We cannot afford to be timid; our proposals must be bold and far-reaching. We must find jobs for the jobless and homes for the homeless!"

"Well said!" said Thomas.

"Who taught her how to speak like that?" asked Geraldine, champagne glass in hand.

"Trust me" Esmeralda continued, "I will get it done!"

NBC suddenly interrupted Esmeralda's address. Peter Alexander reappeared on the monitor. "Julie Perez is in the Sheraton ballroom with the Democratic Party members. Let's find out if Prabhat Modi, the Democratic candidate in Virginia's 8th District, is ready to make his concession speech. Julie, what can you tell us?"

Mr. Alexander disappeared as the monitor displayed the Sheraton ballroom. The camera focused on Julie Perez, NBC's reporter, who was standing in the middle of the room.

"Peter, I'm told that Prabhat Modi is going to make a speech any moment. As you might expect, the mood here is very subdued. No one can believe that a robot has actually beaten their candidate. People are angry and upset ... Okay, I think Mr. Modi is getting ready to say something. Let's put the camera on him and see what he says."

Prabhat Modi appeared on the monitor standing behind a lectern at the front of the ballroom. He looked around the room briefly without smiling.

"Thank you, everyone," Mr. Modi began, "for coming here tonight and supporting me. As you just heard, the six networks are all projecting the Green Party candidate to be the winner for the House seat in Virginia's 8th District. I'm disappointed, of course, but I'm not done with the fight. *I shall not make a concession speech!*"

"Good for you!" shouted a supporter. "Don't concede!"

"As you know by now," Mr. Modi continued, "the Green Party's candidate, Esmeralda Jenkins, is not even a human being; she's a robot. 'It' is a robot, I should say. As far as I'm concerned, the robot is not even a legitimate candidate for office. Her candidacy is nothing more than a joke!"

"Amen!" shouted another supporter.

"I just spoke to Tom Ellsworth," Mr. Modi continued, "the Chair of the Democratic National Committee, and he told me that his lawyers will be filing suit in the U.S. District Court for Eastern Virginia tomorrow morning to nullify the result of this ludicrous election!"

Everyone in the ballroom began talking excitedly. The noise quickly drowned out Mr. Modi, who tried to continue speaking.

Thomas muted the east wall monitor. "I'm not a bit surprised. We should have expected this."

"Why doesn't the jerk just admit he's a loser?" exclaimed Geraldine.

"We have to talk to Memengwaa right away," said Jacqueline.

"Memengwaa?" asked Geraldine.

"Memengwaa Blazing Sun, Co-chair of the Green Party," answered Jacqueline. "We need to get the Green Party's lawyers to defend us."

"I'll see if I can get her right now," said Thomas. He opened his iPalm and spoke into his palm. "I want to speak to Memengwaa Blazing Sun."

The door opened, and Esmeralda reappeared.

"Great speech!" exclaimed Jacqueline, standing up and giving Esmeralda a hug as she reentered the room. "One would think you've been doing this your whole life!"

"Memengwaa's line is busy," said Thomas. "I will keep trying to reach her."

"What's going on?" asked Esmeralda. "Is there a problem?"

"Nothing to worry about," said Thomas. "The Democratic National Committee is going to file suit tomorrow morning to nullify the election."

"Oh, my goodness!" exclaimed Esmeralda. "Is there a precedent for that?"

"Not in recent history," replied Jacqueline. "This is going to be interesting."

"There you go again, *'interesting,'* " said Geraldine.

"I'll tell you what," said Thomas. "Let's not let this ruin the evening. We should be celebrating. What do you say we go to the ballroom and join our supporters? By now the champagne must be flowing!"

The family all stood up, stretched, and headed towards the ballroom to celebrate.

*　　*　　*　　*　　*

On Wednesday morning, November 2, 2518, Mr. Fernando Hernandez, Clerk of the United States District Court for Eastern Virginia in Alexandria, Virginia, received the Democratic Party's petition to nullify the election results. He scheduled a hearing with the Honorable Chief Judge Christopher Owens for Tuesday, November 15th, at 10:00 a.m.

News of Esmeralda's apparent victory spread quickly throughout the United States and the world, with reporters from as far as Australia and New Zealand trying to reach her for interviews. At Thomas's suggestion, she referred all inquiries to the Green

Party's national office. William took a leave of absence from his lobbyist position in Washington and joined Memengwaa's staff as a full-time employee. With the election behind them, the Green Party's permanent staff devoted most of its time preparing for the November 15th hearing while William fielded the party's incoming phone calls and emails, which soon reached into the thousands.

On the morning of November 15th, Thomas and Esmeralda flew to the courthouse in Alexandria where the Democratic Party's lawyers were scheduled to argue their case. Memengwaa advised Thomas to take a low profile, not to speak to any reporters, and to remain in the background to the extent possible. However, as he and Esmeralda approached the courthouse, they were accosted by dozens of reporters shouting questions as they attempted to work their way through a large crowd in front of the building.

"What is the Green Party's defense?" shouted one reporter.

"Who's really calling the shots here, the robot or the robot's husband?" shouted another.

"Will you appeal the Judge's decision if he nullifies the election?" shouted someone else.

Thomas held Esmeralda's arm firmly. "Look straight ahead and don't engage the reporters!"

In a few minutes, Thomas and Esmeralda were inside the building, where they stood briefly in front of a digital scanner and walked through security. In a couple more minutes, they were inside the courtroom where a team of Democratic Party lawyers were already taking their seats in the front row. Thomas took a seat in the back row near the corner while Esmeralda sat down in the front row with the Green Party delegation, which included Memengwaa, William, and the Green Party's lawyer. Other interested parties arrived over the next few minutes to take the remaining seats in the room.

At 10:00 a.m., a well-dressed, middle-aged man with a digni-fied demeanor entered the room from a side door and spoke authoritatively. "Good morning, everyone. My name is Fernando Hernandez, and I'm the Clerk of the United States District Court for Eastern Virginia. We are here this morning to consider a petition filed by the Democratic National Committee to nullify the election results for the United States House of Representatives in Virginia's 8th Congressional District. I remind you to rise when the judge enters the room and to remain silent unless he calls on you." Mr. Hernan-dez then sat down in a chair in front of the judge's bench.

A few minutes later, the same side door opened, and an el-derly man wearing a black robe appeared. Mr. Hernandez stood up and faced the room. "Everyone, please rise and remain standing un-til the Honorable Chief Judge Christopher Owens is seated!" Everyone stood and waited for the judge to take his seat, and then they sat down again.

Chief Judge Owens looked briefly around the room before speaking. "This morning we are hearing a petition filed by the Dem-ocratic National Committee, to which I will hereafter refer to as the Plaintiff. Would the Counsel for the Plaintiff please rise and state his or her name?"

A tall woman in business attire stood up. "My name is Ger-trude Hollingsworth, and I'm the Counsel for the Democratic National Committee."

"For the record," said Judge Owens, "please summarize your complaint."

"Thank you, Your Honor. I'm pleased to comply with your re-quest. The Democratic National Committee wishes to bring to your attention that a robot claims to have won election to the U.S. House of Representatives in Virginia's 8th Congressional District."

"I'm aware of that, Ms. Hollingsworth," replied the Judge. "The robot's name, I believe, is Esmeralda Jenkins."

"That's correct, Your Honor. Her election violates every principle on which this great Nation was founded. It is a mockery to the United States Constitution, and it calls for immediate intervention by the judiciary."

"And precisely what remedy do you seek?" asked Judge Owens.

"Your Honor, you may remedy this travesty in one of two ways: You can either disqualify the robot, making Prabhat Modi—the second-place finisher—the winner of the election, or, alternatively, you can invalidate the entire election and call for a new election."

"Is that the substance of your argument?"

"Yes, it is, Your Honor."

"Do you have any evidence or other supporting documentation to enter into the record?"

"Yes, Your Honor, we do. First, we have documentation we obtained from General Google Motors showing that the robot was manufactured in 2484, thereby proving that it is essentially a machine, not a human being; and second, we have the certified election results for Virginia's 8th Congressional District showing Prabhat Modi, the Democratic candidate, finishing in second place. If you disqualify the robot, Mr. Modi will become the Congressman-elect."

"The Clerk of the Court has already provided me with the election results," replied Judge Owens, "but you may provide the Court with your own documentation if you wish to ensure that our figures are consistent. Please give the Clerk the certified election results and the documentation you received from General Google Motors at the end of the proceeding."

"Thank you, Your Honor."

"Very well, you may now be seated. Would the Counsel for the Green Party, which I will hereafter refer to as the Defendant, please rise and introduce yourself?"

The Green Party's lawyer stood up. "My name is Paul Chao. I'm the Counsel for the Green Party, and I'm representing Esmeralda Jenkins, also known as 'the robot,' for purposes of this proceeding."

"You just heard the Plaintiff's Counsel summarize her complaint," said Judge Owens. "Now you may summarize your defense."

"Thank you, Your Honor. My client, Esmeralda Jenkins, also known as–"

"Just call her 'my client,' please."

"Of course, Your Honor. My client won the election fair and square. There is no dispute about the number of votes. Moreover, there was never any deception. The voters who voted for my client knew that they were voting for a robot–"

"Objection, Your Honor!" exclaimed Attorney Hollingsworth, standing up quickly. "Many of the voters may not have realized that they were voting for a robot!"

"Objection overruled!" replied Judge Owens. "Mr. Chao, please continue."

Attorney Hollingsworth sat down.

"They voted for my client," Mr. Chao continued, "because they found her to be more credible than the other candidates. If you were to acquiesce to either of the Plaintiff's remedies, you would be overturning the will of the people. There is no precedent in U.S. history for the judiciary to change the results of an election.

Accordingly, I beseech you to uphold the election results, thereby confirming my client as the winner."

"Do you have any evidence or other supporting documentation to enter into the record?"

"I have paperwork proving my client's U.S. citizenship, place of residence, and age. She is thirty-four years old, nine years older than the Constitutional requirement of twenty-five years for a member of the U.S. House of Representatives. I also have the official vote tally for Virginia's 8th Congressional District, which I understand you already have on hand."

"That's correct."

"Then I have nothing else to add, Your Honor."

"Very well, please give the Clerk the paperwork you mentioned and be seated."

Attorney Chao sat down while Judge Owens lifted a glass, apparently containing water, and took a sip. The room was eerily quiet as everyone waited for him to speak.

"I believe I have the information I need," said Judge Owens. "I hereby instruct the Plaintiff's Counsel and the Defendant's Counsel to appear before me in this same room on Thursday, December 1st, at 10:00 a.m. for my decision." He banged a gavel on his desk. "The Court is hereby adjourned."

The Clerk stood up and addressed the room. "Please stand and remain standing until the Honorable Chief Judge Christopher Owens has left the room!"

Judge Owens stood up and walked around the bench to the side door; and in a moment, he was gone. Thomas walked to the front of the room to greet the Green Party delegation and introduce himself to Attorney Chao. After exchanging pleasantries with

Memengwaa and William, he shook hands with the attorney and said, "I think you hit the right points."

"Well, we'll find out soon enough," replied Attorney Chao. "You have to wonder, though, if the judge has already made up his mind. You never know."

"No, you can't read the man's mind," said Thomas.

"If he rules against us," asked Esmeralda, "are we going to appeal it to a higher court?"

"We'll cross that bridge when we come to it," replied Attorney Chao.

Esmeralda looked at Thomas, and they both laughed.

"It's an inside joke," explained Thomas.

"Let's hope we don't have to appeal," said Attorney Chao. "That would be a long, drawn-out process. In fact, it could take years to get to the U.S. Supreme Court. Your two-year term in office would be over before the Supreme Court even heard the case."

"We just have to wait and see how it plays out," said Thomas. He turned to Esmeralda. "Let's see if there's a back door out of here so that we can avoid the reporters."

Thomas and Esmeralda said goodbye to the Green Party delegation and departed.

*   *   *   *   *

Over the next two weeks, Esmeralda passed the time by gathering as much information as possible about the U.S. House of Representatives including the names of the committees and their chairs; bills pending and the substance and status of each; and the names of every member of the House, including the incoming

"Freshman Class" to which she would belong if Judge Owens ruled in her favor.

On December 1ˢᵗ, Thomas and Esmeralda flew to Alexandria and arrived at the courthouse at 8:45 a.m., more than an hour early to avoid the reporters. After passing through security, they went directly to the courtroom and sat together in the back of the room until the other members of the Green Party's delegation arrived. Then Esmeralda joined her colleagues in the front row while Thomas remained in the back. Clerk Hernandez came into the room at 9:55 a.m. and gave everyone his customary instructions, and Judge Owens followed him into the room a few minutes later.

As Judge Owens entered the room, Mr. Hernandez stood and faced the room. "Please rise and remain standing until the Honorable Chief Judge Christopher Owens is seated!" Everyone stood and waited for the judge to take his seat, then sat back down.

Chief Judge Owens looked at the Democratic Party delegation and the Green Party delegation to make sure that their attorneys were present. "Would the Counsels for the Plaintiff and the Defendant please rise and approach the bench."

Attorney Hollingsworth and Attorney Chao both stood up and walked to the judge's bench as instructed, where they faced the judge and remained standing.

"I will read a brief synopsis of my verdict," Judge Owens began, "and then make some remarks." He put on a pair of eyeglasses and looked down at a paper in his hands. "I find that there is nothing in the U.S. Constitution that prohibits a robot from serving in the U.S. House of Representatives. Moreover, the Plaintiff's complaint is nullified by the 2471 U.S. Supreme Court decision, *Jennifer Doe v. United States of America*, in which the Court found that a robot and a person are essentially one and the same. Therefore, I deny the

Plaintiff's complaint and allow the election of Esmeralda Jenkins to the U.S. House of Representatives in Virginia's 8th Congressional District to stand."

Attorney Hollingsworth looked visibly shaken. "Your Honor, with all due respect, I intend to appeal your ruling."

"I don't normally engage in discussions with the plaintiff or the plaintiff's counsel after rendering my decision," replied Judge Owens, "but I'm going to make an exception in this instance. To be perfectly candid, I'm not happy about my ruling. I have thought about it long and hard. What if other robots seek public office, and what if some of them win election? What if someday robots gain a majority in the House or the Senate? What would the implications be for government as we know it? Indeed, what would the implications be for civilization? I'm deeply troubled, but I must render my ruling based on the U.S. Constitution and legal precedent."

"I understand, Your Honor," replied Attorney Hollingsworth.

"Frankly," continued Judge Owens, "I hope the appellate court will see it differently. I never dreamed I'd ever say this, but I hope my verdict will be overturned." He removed his glasses. "That's all I have to say in this matter." He slammed his gavel on the desk. "The Court is hereby adjourned."

Clerk Hernandez stood and addressed the room. "Please stand and remain standing until the Honorable Chief Judge Christopher Owens has left the room!"

Judge Owens stood up and walked around the bench to the side door and departed. Thomas walked to the front of the room and hugged Esmeralda. "We did it!" he exclaimed. "You are now a Congresswoman-elect!"

"Technically a Congressrobot-elect," interjected William, who had been sitting next to Esmeralda. Thomas and Esmeralda laughed.

"Please, no jokes like that while we are still in the courtroom," cautioned Attorney Chao.

Memengwaa, standing nearby, walked over to Thomas and Esmeralda and gave them both a high-five. "You may call yourself whatever you want, as long as you remain Green!"

"Do we need to worry about the appeal?" asked Esmeralda.

"Their appeal will go to the U.S. Court of Appeals for the Fourth Circuit," replied Attorney Chao. "Regardless of how the Court of Appeals rules, it will be appealed again, either by the National Democratic Committee or by us. Ultimately it will end up in the U.S. Supreme Court, but that will take years. I can guarantee that you will finish your first term in Congress before the Supreme Court even hears the case—if it even agrees to hear it. It might not, in which case the ruling of the appellate court will stand. In any event, you don't have anything to worry about right now."

"Thank goodness!" exclaimed Esmeralda.

Memengwaa, William, and Attorney Chao accompanied Thomas and Esmeralda out of the building where reporters were waiting.

"You guys can take off," said Memengwaa, looking at Thomas and Esmeralda. "Attorney Chao and I will handle the questions. William, please stick around for a few minutes in case I need you."

Thomas and Esmeralda took Memengwaa's cue and quickly departed.

Chapter 6
The Committee

D uring the second and third weeks of December, Esmeralda attended an orientation for the freshmen members of Congress, which included 175 other newly elected members. The orientation covered the role of the committees, how to introduce a bill, how to staff and budget an office, government ethics, and a number of other useful topics. The freshmen also attended a luncheon in the West Wing of the White House and enjoyed a dinner one evening at the Vice President's residence at the Naval Observatory.

During her free time, Esmeralda reviewed some five hundred resumes of applicants for the eighteen positions on her staff and selected the fifty best-qualified candidates for interviews. She chose William, who had completed his brief detail on Memengwaa's staff, to be her Chief of Staff; then she and William did the interviews for the seventeen other staff positions together.

Geraldine and Jacqueline helped Esmeralda decorate her new office in the Cannon House Office Building. Geraldine also helped Esmeralda to decorate her satellite offices in Alexandria and Falls Church, Virginia.

At Memengwaa's suggestion, Thomas continued to take a low profile to avoid any perception that he was running the show behind the scenes.

The new Congress convened on Monday, January 9, 2519; and in accordance with long-standing tradition, the Dean of the House, Samuel Butler, administered the Oath of Office to the Speaker of the House, Raymond Churchill, who in turn administered the Oath en masse to all of the other members. Esmeralda raised her right hand and listened carefully as the Speaker read the Oath aloud, one line at a time, and repeated after him:

I do solemnly swear that I will support and defend the Constitution of the United States against all enemies, foreign and domestic; that I will bear true faith and allegiance to the same; that I take this obligation freely, without any mental reservation or purpose of evasion, and that I will well and faithfully discharge the duties of the office on which I'm about to enter. So help me God."

After taking their Oaths of Office, the members received their committee assignments and other instructions. Esmeralda was assigned to the Small Business Committee. Speaker Churchill then spoke to the full house, old and new members, and laid out his vision for the session, emphasizing the importance of enacting meaningful legislation. At 11:00 a.m., he concluded his remarks and told the members that they were free to return to their offices.

When Esmeralda returned to her office, she conferred with William on correspondence received from constituents in the 8th District and discussed other administrative matters. Then she met with her full staff and gave them a pep talk. "I want to welcome everyone," she said. "I hope you enjoyed the holidays and are well rested and ready for your new responsibilities. William, my Chief of Staff, will provide you with guidance as needed; and please feel free to talk to me directly if you have any questions. I'm confident that I have hired the right people and that you represent the finest in government. Together we will accomplish great things!"

Later Esmeralda and Jacqueline had lunch together, and Jacqueline gave her sister-in-law some tips on how to enact new legislation. "Everything here is done by committee; you can't just introduce a bill by yourself. Sometimes a member will do that when they can find a co-sponsor on the other side of the aisle; but nowadays that's the exception, not the rule. Most new legislation originates in a committee."

"What if the Republicans and Democrats on the committee are opposed to the Green Party's agenda?" asked Esmeralda.

"That's why you have to develop relationships," said Jacqueline. "You'll probably never get a Republican on the same page, but you can sometimes find common ground with the Democrats. If you're lucky, you may even have one or two Green members on your committee."

"I do," said Esmeralda. "I've already researched it."

That evening, over dinner, Esmeralda and Thomas talked about how best to move the Green Party's agenda forward.

"Some five hundred years ago," said Thomas, "during the civil rights movement of the twentieth century, Black people had an expression, *Keep your eyes on the prize*. It meant achieving full equality for African Americans. Today the same expression could apply to the Green agenda; but now it affects every human being on the planet. If the Green Party fails, the human species could disappear before the end of the millennium."

"I have an awesome responsibility, don't I?" said Esmeralda.

"Well, you're not doing it alone. You have Jacqueline and more than one hundred other Greens in Congress to help you. Just remember to keep your eyes on the prize."

"I get it."

Esmeralda went to bed that night thinking about her role on the Small Business Committee and how the Green Party might help small businesses.

*   *   *   *   *

The next morning, Thomas and Esmeralda arose early and took the aeromobile across the Potomac river to the District of Columbia where Thomas dropped Esmeralda in the parking lot adjacent to the Capitol. They kissed briefly, and Thomas departed. Esmeralda then turned and walked to the nearby Rayburn House Office building where she made her way through security and looked for Room 2360, the place where the Small Business Committee was scheduled to meet.

As Esmeralda entered the room, she saw a number of committee members standing in small groups chatting and exchanging pleasantries. Esmeralda looked around the room until she found a seat with her name plate, which read *Esmeralda Jenkins*, and then walked over to one of the groups and introduced herself. In a couple more minutes, a distinguished-looking elderly man walked into the room and sat down in the center seat. His name plate read, *Mr. McIntyre, Chairman*. Everyone in the room ceased their conversations and found their seats.

Chairman McIntyre waited for everyone to be seated. "Good morning," he began. "The committee will please come to order. A quorum being present, this Committee on Small Business will begin its business. Without objection, the Chair is authorized to declare a recess at any time."

While Chairman McIntyre spoke, Esmeralda took a closer look at her colleagues on the committee, none of whom she had previously met, and quickly captured their facial image in her memory bank. She tagged each face with a name.

"I'm pleased to be here today," continued the Chairman, "with my good friend and Ranking Member, Representative Stone. Together, and with your assistance, we will be working on behalf of the estimated one billion small businesses in the United States."

The door opened, and Jacqueline appeared in the doorway. She entered the room quietly and took a seat in the back.

"Small businesses are the backbone of the economy," continued the Chairman, "and they account for ninety-five percent of all the new jobs created every year. When small businesses succeed, the economy grows, employment increases, and joblessness falls."

Esmeralda looked at her colleagues to see if anyone had any reaction to the Chairman's remarks. All of them appeared stone-faced as if they had heard the same line many times before.

"I hope we can introduce two or three bills in this session," continued the Chairman, "that will help small businesses. While that might seem ambitious, it is important that our constituents back home see that we are getting something done. Now, without further ado, I'd like to give Ranking Member Stone an opportunity to say a few words."

Ranking Member Stone, sitting next to the Chair, sat forward in his chair and leaned into the microphone. "Thank you, Mr. Chairman, for your excellent introduction. I concur with everything you just said. I don't have anything to add at this time."

Chairman McIntyre looked in both directions at the committee members seated to his left and right. "Are there any members who wish to be recognized at this time for purposes of making an opening statement?"

Esmeralda leaned forward into her microphone. "Yes, Mr. Chairman, I'd like to be recognized."

"Very well, please state your name and make a brief opening statement."

"My name is Esmeralda Jenkins, and I represent Virginia's 8th Congressional District. I'm honored to be on this important committee."

"We are *all* honored," replied the Chairman. "Is that it? Do you have anything else to say?"

"Yes," replied Esmeralda, "I have many ideas for strengthening our programs for small business. For one thing, nearly all Americans today are mixed race—more specifically, some combination of Caucasian, Black, Hispanic, Asian, Asian Indian, and Native American. Therefore, I suggest we eliminate all socio-economic preferences in government contracting except for service-disabled, veteran-owned small businesses and HUBZone entities. That would redistribute Government spending and put more dollars into the hands of service-disabled veterans and small businesses in economically distressed neighborhoods."

Ranking Member Stone leaned forward into his microphone. "That idea should be vetted through one of the subcommittees."

"I understand," replied Esmeralda, "and I will follow the proper protocol, whatever it might be, but I want the full committee to begin thinking like I do. We need to reexamine all of our existing small business programs in the context of today's demographics."

The Chairman coughed.

Esmeralda continued, "We also need to address our mission with a greater sense of urgency. If we don't accomplish meaningful changes in this session, the economic crisis facing us today is only going to get worse."

Chairman McIntyre leaned forward. "That was a very nice speech, Ms. Jenkins. Now, if you don't mind, I'd like to hear from the *non-robots* on the committee."

Everyone except Esmeralda laughed loudly.

"You're right," replied Esmeralda, ignoring the laughter. "We need to hear from the others. I'm sure my colleagues have many excellent suggestions."

"Yes, they do," replied the Chairman. "Are there any other members who wish to be recognized at this time?"

No one responded.

Esmeralda waited a moment and continued, "If none of my colleagues has anything to say, I also have some other ideas—"

"You've had your chance to speak, Representative Jenkins," interrupted Chairman McIntyre. "We need to get on with the important work of the committee, so please remain silent for the duration of this meeting."

Undeterred, Esmeralda continued, "With all due respect, Mr. Chairman, I thought you would entertain some discussion on my suggestion."

"Frankly," replied Chairman McIntyre, "I don't think your suggestion was well thought out. How would your proposal affect the ability of minorities, especially Caucasians, to get government contracts? Don't they need set-asides? To consider any new legislation, we need to see studies—preferably two, three, four, or five studies. I suggest you withhold any more suggestions until you see how we do things here."

"That's precisely why I hoped for discussion, Mr. Chairman. I'd be pleased to elaborate on my proposal and answer any questions my colleagues may have. I know that my colleagues—"

"Please, Ms. Jenkins!" exclaimed Chairman McIntyre. "I've given you enough time! Now I must insist that you remain silent!"

Esmeralda sat back in her chair. Jacqueline, who was still sitting in the back of the room, arose and quietly left the room. For the duration of the meeting, Esmeralda remained silent as instructed. The Chairman discussed the jurisdiction of the five subcommittees and advised the members that he would be making assignments before the end of the week. Finally, he adjourned the meeting, and everyone arose and left the room. No one spoke to Esmeralda, and she departed alone.

* * * * *

Back in her office, Jacqueline summoned her Chief of Staff.

"Henry," said Jacqueline, "I have a new assignment for you. I need you to put together a comprehensive file on Congressman Peter McIntyre, the Chair of the Small Business Committee. I want to know everything about him. Get a copy of his IG clearance, his high school and college transcripts, and anything else you can find that might be helpful. You get the idea?"

"Yes, Jacqueline, I get it."

"And move this to the top of your priority list."

"Will do."

Henry returned to his cubicle, and Jacqueline opened her iPalm. "Get me Thomas."

In another moment, Thomas's image appeared on Jacqueline's palm. "What's up, Jacqueline? You don't normally call me at this hour."

"I thought you should be aware that things didn't go so well for Esmeralda this morning."

"Oh, I'm sorry to hear that. What happened?"

"Well, Peter McIntrye, the Chairman of the Small Business Committee, is a real horse's ass. He was downright rude."

"Did Esmeralda do anything to provoke him?"

"No, she just tried to make an opening statement and introduce one of her ideas."

"So what did Chairman McIntyre say?"

"Basically, he told her to shut up."

"How did Esmeralda handle it?"

"She handled it professionally, but I felt so sorry for her. It was humiliating."

"If it makes you feel any better, remember that Esmeralda doesn't have any emotions. You or I might feel humiliated, but she doesn't know the meaning of the word. She'll be at it again tomorrow as if nothing ever happened."

"I know," replied Jacqueline, "but it still made me mad."

"Can you do anything to help her?"

"Maybe ... I'm working on it."

"Okay," replied Thomas, "Thanks for the information, and let me know if there is anything I can do at my end."

"I'll let you know." Jacqueline closed her iPalm and turned on her computer.

*   *   *   *   *

Esmeralda returned to her office after the committee meeting and went directly to William's desk. He was in the process of reviewing constituent correspondence.

"It looks like we have a lot of mail," said Esmeralda.

"This is just the snail mail," replied William, pointing to a pile of envelopes on his desk. "There's ten times this much coming by email, and ten times that coming by text. It's going to be a challenge to respond to everyone."

"Just do the best you can. Give me any correspondence more than fifty words, and I will read it since I read faster than you. We will come up with a few templates we can use for stock responses. We can personalize the responses, even if we use the templates. The main thing is to respond to every constituent."

"I agree," replied William.

"Is there any pattern to the letters?"

"Well, yeah, most of them are from people who have been laid off or expect to be laid off. The economy is tanking."

"Okay, that's all the more reason to respond to everyone timely. These people need hope."

"I couldn't agree with you more. By the way, how did your committee meeting go?"

"Not as well as I had expected. The Chairman is a tough cookie."

"Did you have a chance to discuss your proposal for reform of socio-economic preferences?"

"Yes, I mentioned it, but the Chairman shut down any discussion. I think the other members are intimidated by him. No one dared to speak up. In fact, Ranking Member Stone was the only other person who opened his mouth."

"Maybe you should talk to Jacqueline and see if she has any suggestions on how to handle Chairman McIntyre."

"Yes, I will definitely ask her advice. She was there."

"She was there?"

"Yes, she sat in the back of the room and watched the whole thing—that is, until the Chairman shut me down. Then she left."

"Good, if she saw what happened, she can advise you how to handle it."

"I hope so," replied Esmeralda. "Anyway, let's look over some of this correspondence together and see if we can come up with a few templates."

Esmeralda sat down across from William, and they began reading the constituent mail.

*   *   *   *   *

After finishing supper that evening, Geraldine turned to her north wall and summoned her digital assistant. "Richard, did any-one in my family make the evening news?"

The north wall lit up, and Richard appeared. "Good evening, Ms. Jenkins. Yes, several of the networks mentioned your daughter-in-law."

"Did CNN cover it?"

"Yes, CNN mentioned your daughter-in-law briefly."

"Okay, please show me that segment. I don't need to watch the whole thing."

"Understood, Ms. Jenkins. I will bring up CNN, only the por-tion of the news about your daughter-in-law."

Richard disappeared; and a news anchor, a handsome young man with white hair, appeared in his place. "Today," the anchor began, "the Green Party's robot made its first official appearance in Congress. Charlie James, our correspondent on the Hill, was there. Charlie, can you tell us what happened?"

The news anchor disappeared, and a young woman appeared in his place standing on the steps of the Rayburn House Office Building. "Yes, Harry, today was an historic moment for our government. Congresswoman Esmeralda Jenkins, the Green Party's representative from Virginia's 8th Congressional District—and by her own admission, a robot, not a human being—made her first appearance on the House Small Business Committee."

The image on the monitor split in two; and Harry, the news anchor, reappeared on the left side. "I understand that Chairman McIntyre wields an iron grip over his committee," said Harry. "How did the robot fare?"

"Not well," replied Charlie. "The purpose of today's meeting was for Chairman McIntyre to lay out his vision for the current session; but less than five minutes into the meeting, the robot spoke up and proposed a change to long-standing socio-economic preferences for minorities and women. As you might expect, Chairman McIntyre shut her down quickly."

"Did anyone come to her defense?"

"No, no one did. In fact, the only other person who spoke during the entire meeting was Ranking Member Stone, and he only spoke twice—very briefly on both occasions. I had the impression that nobody dared to say anything. As you say, Chairman McIntyre wields an iron grip."

"So what's going to happen next?" asked Harry.

"Chairman McIntyre is going to hand out the subcommittee assignments later this week. Congresswoman Jenkins will be assigned to a subcommittee, where she *may*—I put emphasis on the word *may*—fare better. If nothing else, she may be able to engage her colleagues on the subcommittee in discussion."

"One would hope so," said Harry, "but it remains to be seen whether they will take her seriously. After all, Representative Jenkins is essentially a machine, not a real person."

"Her success depends partly on who chairs the subcommittee," replied Charlie. "If she gets a chair who is open-minded, she may do all right."

"Very well," said Harry. "Please keep us posted on any further developments, and we will bring it to our viewers in real time."

"I've seen enough, Richard," said Geraldine. "Get Jacqueline on the line."

Harry and Charlie disappeared, and Richard reappeared. "I understand you would like to speak to your daughter Jacqueline, Ms. Jenkins, is that correct?"

"You got it."

"Give me just a moment, please."

Geraldine sighed. "This is like a soap opera times ten. Thomas was out of his mind to let Esmeralda do this. We are going to be the laughingstock of the country."

"I'm sorry, Ms. Jenkins. Jacqueline's line is busy. I will keep trying."

"Get me Thomas, then."

"I understand, Ms. Jenkins, you would like to speak to your son, Thomas, instead of your daughter, Jacqueline, is that correct?"

"You got it."

"Certainly, Ms. Jenkins. Please give me just a moment."

Richard disappeared; and in a moment, Thomas appeared in his place. "Good evening, Mom. What's up?"

"Did you watch the news tonight? Your wife had a rough time today with the Chair of her committee."

"Jacqueline already told me. She was there, too."

"Is Jacqueline going to help her?"

"How can Jacqueline help her? Jacqueline isn't even on the committee. She has no role in the Small Business Committee whatsoever. The only thing she can do is to give Esmeralda advice."

"When is Jacqueline going to give Esmeralda advice?"

"I don't know, Mom. Don't worry about it! Everything is going to be fine."

"Don't worry about it? If Esmeralda doesn't succeed, it will sink the Green Party in the next election. Did that ever occur to you?"

"I'm sure she's going to succeed—this is a temporary setback."

"What if it's not temporary? What if the Chair blocks everything she tries to do?"

"How's he going to do that?"

"The Chair calls the shots, doesn't he?"

"Listen, Mom, you're getting way too involved in this!" Thomas paused. "All right, if it makes you feel better, I'll ask Jacqueline to talk to Esmeralda and give her some advice."

"Please do."

"Good night, Mom."

"Good night, Son."

Thomas disappeared.

"Richard," said Geraldine, "I'm done. I'll call you if I need you."

Richard reappeared. "I understand you have completed all communications for this evening, Ms. Jenkins, is that correct?"

"You got it."

"Please let me know if you need anything else, Ms. Jenkins, and have a good evening."

The wall went dark, and Geraldine sat down in a comfortable chair. She picked up her Bible on a small table beside her chair, turned to the Book of Psalms, and began to read.

*   *   *   *   *

On Wednesday morning, January 11ᵗʰ, Chairman McIntyre arrived at his office early, said hello to his staffers, and picked up his cup of coffee at the coffee station. Then he went into his private office, sat down at his desk, and turned on his computer. A few minutes later, as he was reading his messages, he overheard a visitor speaking to a staffer outside his office.

"No, I don't have an appointment. I'm a *member*. A member doesn't need an appointment to see another member."

In another second, Jacqueline appeared in the doorway.

"I beg your pardon!" exclaimed Chairman McIntyre, standing up.

Jacqueline entered the office and sat down in a chair across from the Chairman's desk. "I thought I'd drop by this morning and say hello."

Chairman McIntyre sat down. "We barely know each. What's this all about?"

"Well," began Jacqueline, "I happened to come across your official transcript from Harvard—you know, *by chance*—and I noticed you flunked Economics 101 your freshman year. I mean, I wasn't looking for it, but it kinda jumped out at me when I looked at your transcript."

Chairman McIntyre's eyes narrowed. "Where did you get my transcript? Have you been trying to dig up dirt on me?"

"Well, to be fair, Economics 101 is a tough course, and I'm not one to pass judgement. What I find interesting, though, is that you never retook it. Instead, you replaced it with a literature course—more specifically, a lit course in science fiction. Now that's a curious credential for the Chair of the Small Business Committee, isn't it?"

Chairman McIntyre became tense and his tone changed. "Why are you bringing this up?"

"Like I say," said Jacqueline, "I'm not one to pass judgement, but I worry that the folks back home—your constituents—might be troubled if they heard about this ... but then, there's no need for them to hear about it, is there, Mr. Chairman?"

"Are you trying to blackmail me? If that's what you have in mind, I will go straight to the Congressional Ethics Office and file a complaint right now!"

"Blackmail?" replied Jacqueline. "Who said anything about blackmail? That was the furthest thought from my mind. No, I'm just worried what your constituents might think—that is, if they ever found out."

"You're not scaring me a bit, if that's what your intention is. Plenty of people have flunked Economics 101—and at schools easier than Harvard, I might add."

"I have no doubt about that, Mr. Chairman, but one more thing ... well, I noticed that your father gave Harvard University a donation of twenty-five million dollars some years ago. I want to applaud him for his generosity. A funny thing, though: he made the donation the same year you were accepted there. Now I'm sure there's no correlation between the two, but it doesn't look so good, does it?"

"Would you cut to the chase, please?" exclaimed the Chairman. "What do you want?"

"Oh, I don't want anything at all. In fact, let's put that on the record: I don't want anything at all. However, since I have served in the House longer than you, I thought I'd give you some friendly advice. I want to suggest you make Representative Esmeralda Jenkins the Chair of one of your subcommittees—the *Subcommittee on Economic Growth, Tax and Capital Access* would be a good one."

"She's not qualified for that! You know as well as I do that she is greener than a Granny Smith apple!"

"At one time, we were *all* green, weren't we, Mr. Chairman? I don't consider that a justifiable reason to disqualify Congresswoman Jenkins from such an important role on your committee."

"Aside from that, she can't be a Chair because she's not a member of the majority party."

"You know as well as I do, Sir, that the Green Party is aligned with the Democrats; and under the House rules adopted in 2425, a member of any party aligned with the majority party may serve as a Chair."

"Mark my words," exclaimed the Chairman, "this is going to backfire on you!"

"Oh, and one more thing: I think you should expedite any bills that Congresswoman Jenkins's subcommittee sends you. I mean, like, approve them and send them forward to the full house for a vote without a moment's delay. That's a very important point. Have I made myself clear, Mr. Chairman?"

"I consider this blackmail, and you're not getting away with it! I'm going straight to the Ethics Office!"

"As I said, blackmail never crossed my mind. I'm just concerned—you know, as one member to another—that your folks back home might take some of this information the wrong way. Members need to take care of each other, and I'm taking care of you. Get it?"

"You are evil—downright evil!"

"As I said before, there's no reason for your constituents to know about Economics 101 or your father's gift to Harvard. There's no reason for things like that to leave this room."

"I won't be blackmailed, young lady!"

"As I said, there's no blackmail here, just one member giving friendly advice to another member. Now Mr. Chairman, why don't you reflect on our conversation as you're falling asleep tonight? I'm sure you'll make the right decision."

Jacqueline arose from her chair, turned, and walked from the Chairman's office without another word.

* * * * *

On Friday afternoon, January 13th, Jacqueline summoned her Chief of Staff and asked him when his weekly report would be ready. "Technically it's not due until Monday morning, but I'd like to look at it this afternoon if you have it ready."

"It will be ready by 4:00," replied Henry. "I can give you some stats right now, though, if you are interested."

"Yes, I'd like to know how we stand on the constituent mail."

Henry opened his iPalm. "Okay, I have put it into a spreadsheet, and you can pull it up on your iPalm."

"How am I going to read a spreadsheet on my iPalm? I have a very small hand."

"You can also read it on your computer or your tablet, but there may be times when you need the information and don't have your equipment handy. With an iPalm, you can use the zoom feature to pull up any section of the spreadsheet you want a closer look at."

Jacqueline opened her iPalm. "What do I click on?"

"You don't have to click on anything," replied Henry. "Just say, 'Give me Henry's weekly report'—your iPalm will pull it up automatically."

"My God, I can't keep up with this technology!"

At that moment, they heard a visitor enter the suite and ask for Jacqueline; and in another moment, Esmeralda walked into Jacqueline's office.

"I hope I'm not disturbing you," Esmeralda said, "but I have some exciting news. I came here so I could tell you in person."

"What's the exciting news?" asked Jacqueline.

"You're not going to believe this, but Chairman McIntyre just named me Chair of one of his subcommittees!"

"No way!" exclaimed Jacqueline.

"Fantastic!" exclaimed Henry. "You must have made a good impression during the meeting on Tuesday."

"Which subcommittee?" asked Jacqueline.

"The Subcommittee on Economic Growth, Tax and Capital Access."

"That's wonderful!" exclaimed Jacqueline. "Like Henry just said, you must have made a good impression during the first meeting."

"Actually, I didn't think I made that good an impression. Frankly, I'm surprised Chairman McIntyre picked me."

"I imagine Chairman McIntyre thought about your suggestions afterwards," said Jacqueline, "and he realized, in retrospect, that you had some good ideas."

"I guess you're right," said Esmeralda. "That's the only explanation."

"Have you had time to think about your subcommittee's goals—that is, what you hope to accomplish this session?" asked Henry.

"No, I just got the assignment less than an hour ago. I will think about it this weekend."

"Thomas will give you some input, I'm sure," replied Henry.

"As will Geraldine," added Jacqueline with a chuckle. "Geraldine will have it all figured out before you finish telling her what happened."

"In this instance," said Esmeralda, "I think I will avoid engaging Geraldine in any discussion."

Jacqueline and Henry laughed.

"Anyway," said Esmeralda, "I don't want to take any more of your time. I just wanted to share the good news."

"Thanks for letting us know," replied Jacqueline. "It's a wonderful surprise."

Esmeralda said goodbye and left, and Jacqueline and Henry resumed their discussion of the iPalm and how to use it to view Henry's weekly report.

*   *   *   *   *

Esmeralda convened the first meeting of her subcommittee in a small conference room adjacent to her office on Tuesday, January 17th. Chairman McIntyre had assigned nine other members to the subcommittee, including five Democrats, three Republicans, and one other Green. The individual members included the following:

Democratic Members:
Rep. Ying Yue Chan (PA-12)
Rep. Placido Gambardella (NJ-11)
Rep. Reyansh Chivukula (TX-17)
Rep. Ishaan Pafundi (OK-07),
Rep. Jose Martinez (CO-01)

Republican Members:
Rep. Ana Singh (DE-01),
Ranking Minority Member
Rep. Alejandra Cortez (NY-14)
Rep. Adelheid Mikkanen (VT-04)

Green Member:
Rep. Juan Nighthorse Humetewa (SD-16)

Everyone arrived on time; and after exchanging pleasantries, Esmeralda began the meeting at 9:01 a.m. She opened it by letting each member introduce themselves; then she introduced William, who was sitting in the back of the room with a tablet in hand. After the introductions, she looked around the room and gave everyone a warm smile. "I want to welcome all of you to the first meeting of the Subcommittee on Economic Growth, Tax and Capital Access. I look forward to working with you and developing legislative initiatives that will have meaningful impact on economic growth. I'm sure many of you have good ideas, and I look forward to hearing them. Now, before we get into the meat of it, do any of you have any immediate comments?"

"Good morning," said Representative Singh. "I have been on this subcommittee before. The way it works is that Chairman McIntyre gives us our agenda. He doesn't actually expect us to come up with any new ideas ourselves."

"That's correct," said Representative Gambardella. "If the Chairman has not yet given you your agenda, he will soon. We might as well wait and see what he wants us to work on."

"Thank you for that information," replied Esmeralda. "Your insight is certainly helpful. On the other hand, I don't intend to wait for Chairman McIntyre. I want to begin developing our own agenda right now."

"If I may make a comment," said Representative Humetewa, "I'm concerned that Chairman McIntyre won't send our legislative initiatives forward unless he agrees with them. We would be wasting our time if we develop any initiatives that run counter to his position."

Esmeralda sat forward in her chair. "Chairman McIntyre doesn't get to decide what goes forward on his own. Remember, this a democratic process, and the Chairman has a full committee that will vote on every initiative."

"That may be true in theory," replied Representative Chivukula, "but in the real world, personalities also come into play. To be candid—and I trust I can speak to you in confidence—no one wants to cross Chairman McIntyre."

"Other members may feel that way," replied Esmeralda, "but *I don't*. If the Chairman tries to thwart our efforts, I will engage him directly. You can rest assured that whatever we do in this committee will move forward. I can be very persistent. After all, I talked my husband into letting me run for Congress, didn't I?"

Everyone laughed, and the tension in the room began to subside.

"Now," continued Esmeralda, "for our first order of business, I want to focus on modernizing the Small Business Administration's programs. That's the quickest way to reinvigorate America's small businesses, the backbone of our economy."

"Right on," said Representative Singh. "No one has tried to overhaul SBA's programs in more than two hundred years. It's long overdue."

For the duration of the meeting, the subcommittee discussed SBA's programs, especially those pertaining to capital access, and talked about ways to improve them. For more than two hours, the committee brainstormed, and Esmeralda made sure that everyone had an opportunity to speak. By the end, it was apparent that the members were beginning to develop synergy.

"Thank you, everyone," Esmeralda said, "for your excellent ideas. William and I will put together the minutes and distribute them by COB today. We will try to meet at least twice a week, more often if necessary. William will develop a schedule, and he will send out a reminder the night before each meeting. In the meantime, please feel free to contact me directly if you have any questions or concerns."

Everyone departed in good spirits.

* * * * *

In April, Esmeralda received a phone call from Attorney Chao advising her that the U.S. Court of Appeals for the Fourth Circuit had upheld Judge Christopher Owens's ruling regarding her election to Congress.

"Is that the end of it?" asked Esmeralda. "Or do you think the Democrats will appeal it to the Supreme Court?"

"I'm sure they will appeal it," said Attorney Chao, "but it will be years before the Supreme Court hears the case, and they may not even agree to hear it. They're very busy."

"Then I guess I don't have any reason to worry right now."

"No," said Attorney Chao. "This should be the least of your concerns."

*   *   *   *   *

After receiving thousands of requests from the curious public, CSPAN soon began covering Esmeralda's subcommittee meetings live. Over the next six months, CSPAN's audience quadrupled and then quadrupled again as tens of millions of viewers from around the world tuned in to see the subcommittee's robot Chairperson in action.

In her first ninety days as the Chair, Esmeralda sent fifty bills forward to the full Small Business Committee, marking an unprecedented level of productivity for any committee or subcommittee in the history of the United States Congress. Among others, the bills included the *SBA Loan-Guarantee Modernization Act*, which required SBA to design and implement a one-minute approval process for loan applications. Esmeralda told her subcommittee, "If Thomas and I could get approval to adopt a child in one minute, small businesses should be able to get their loan guarantees approved in one minute, too." Some of the other bills included *The Commercial Market Representative Improvement Act of 2519, The Rapid Federal Tax Refund Guarantee, The Swift and Fair IRS Appeal Process, and Updated Metrics for Measuring Economic Growth.*

Esmeralda forwarded her original suggestion for eliminating socio-economic preferences based on race and gender to her counterpart, Representative Janas Johnson, Chair of the Subcommittee on Contracting and Infrastructure, since it fell under the jurisdiction of that subcommittee.

Esmeralda delegated full responsibility for answering constituent correspondence to William, which allowed her to focus on her committee work and other legislative issues. When she was not meeting with her subcommittee or reading bills, she networked with other members of the Small Business Committee, including the other subcommittee chairs, in order to develop and nurture relationships as Jacqueline had suggested. She soon reached an agreement with the other chairs that she would support their bills if they supported hers.

Chairman McIntyre, apparently mindful of his conversation with Jacqueline, called for discussion of Esmeralda's bills as soon as they reached his desk. With the support of the other subcommittee chairs, all of her bills were approved by the full committee and sent forward to the floor for deliberation. When her bills came up for debate, Esmeralda stood up on the floor of the House and argued persuasively for their need and importance. Jacqueline also stood and spoke in favor of them. While the Republicans attempted to defeat Esmeralda's bills, the Democrats and Greens supported them; and in the end, the House approved them all and sent them to the Senate, which also had a strong Democratic-Green coalition and forwarded them to the President to be enacted into law.

Chairman McIntyre, normally combative, appeared to resign himself to the passage of Esmeralda's bills. He was overheard telling one of his colleagues, "It was a pure fluke that the robot was elected, and I'm confident she won't be reelected. This too shall pass."

All of the media outlets—newspapers, magazines, television programs, and Internet sites—ran frequent stories about Esmeralda and her subcommittee, and several well-known authors began writing books about her. Thomas, Jacqueline, and Geraldine received frequent requests for interviews from writers and reporters seeking additional information about their famous family member.

Far from being jealous, Thomas was extremely pleased with Esmeralda's success. Whenever anyone asked, he would answer, "I never doubted for a moment that she would succeed; in fact, I encouraged her to run for Congress from the very beginning. I don't know why she waited so long."

In December, *Time* magazine included Esmeralda in its list of the world's one hundred most influential and admired women. The family was elated at the news of this achievement and celebrated the occasion by taking Esmeralda to dinner at the Old Ebbitt Grill in D.C. Esmeralda didn't eat, of course, but she nonetheless enjoyed the ambiance and camaraderie.

The year closed with the family in unusually high spirits. Sarah visited during the Christmas holiday and told everyone that she loved her job at UTSA. Thomas, Jacqueline, and Esmeralda were all doing well in their respective careers; and Geraldine was enjoying the new attention resulting from Esmeralda's success in Congress. From any perspective, it appeared that life couldn't get any better.

Chapter 7

The 2520 Green Ticket

O
n Monday morning, January 8, 2520, Memengwaa Blazing Sun convened a meeting of the Green Party's steering committee in her office at Federal Triangle in the District of Columbia. All nine members of the steering committee were present, including Thomas, who was now the Treasurer, and William, who, although no longer on Memengwaa's full-time staff, remained on the steering committee and served as the party's Secretary. The other members of the steering committee included Hui Wong, Anthony Gonzalez, Hillary Flowers, Margaret Delgado, Jason Stauber, and Shukabi Whitehouse.

"Good morning and welcome!" said Memengwaa in a brisk tone. "I hope everyone enjoyed the holidays!"

Everyone nodded, and Thomas replied, "They went by too fast."

Hillary said, "I ate too much."

"I guarantee you didn't eat as much as I did," said Shukabi.

Memengwaa smiled. "I hear you ... Okay, now let's get down to business. As you all know, our presumptive nominee for this year's Presidential election is Sam Hoffenberger. He is a former U.S.

195

Senator and a long-time party loyalist. He faces no opposition from within our party, and I'm confident he will represent us well. But here's the rub: he doesn't like any of the running mates we have suggested. Anyone I have recommended is either too old, too inexperienced, not polished enough, not good-looking enough—whatever—so I told him I would meet with the steering committee and come up with some other candidates."

"He's being too picky," said William.

"I can't blame him," said Shukabi. "The wrong running mate can send your campaign into a nosedive."

"That may be so," replied Memengwaa, "but it's already January and we're behind the curve. We have to nail down a running mate for him soon or we might as well forget about putting up a candidate at all."

"How about Kimonhon Rushing Wind, the representative from North Dakota?" suggested Shukabi. "He has a solid record on Green Party positions."

"I think we need someone who can carry the East and South," replied Memengwaa. "A candidate from North Dakota wouldn't be able to carry either the East or the South."

"How about Ying Zhang?" suggested Hui. "Coming from New York, she would carry the East, and she would also energize the Asian-American wing of the party."

"If you want to energize the Asian-American wing, why not just pick Esmeralda?" said William. "After all, she's Asian, isn't she?"

Everyone laughed.

"Wait a minute," said Anthony. "I know William was joking, but maybe we should consider her. After all, *Time* just included her in its list of the one hundred most influential and admired women in the world. Moreover, as William just said, she would carry the Asian-American vote—and I think women would vote for her, too."

"You can't be serious!" exclaimed Shukabi. "She's a robot!"

"How are we going to get people to take the Green Party seriously," added Margaret, "if we put a robot on the ticket?"

"It's a terrible idea," said Hillary.

"Then again," countered William, "why wouldn't people take us seriously if Esmeralda is one of the one hundred most influential and admired women in the world?"

"He has a point," said Hui.

Shukabi stood up. "Hold your horses, my friends—before this goes any further! Let's assume we put Esmeralda on the ticket and Sam wins and becomes President. It doesn't trouble anyone that Esmeralda would be one step away from the Oval Office?"

"My point exactly," said Hillary. "It's the dumbest idea I've heard all day."

Thomas stood up and walked around the table until he faced the entire committee. "May I suggest we step back, friends, and put this in perspective? I may be the only person here with the courage to say this, but does anyone in this room really believe we can win the White House? It would be as likely as China asking the United States for statehood. We're not going to win the White House. We have never come close, and we're not going to come close this time, either. No one wants to admit it, but that's the reality."

"Whose side are you on, anyway?" asked Hillary.

"The only reason we are putting a candidate up for President," Thomas continued, "is to draw attention to our party and possibly pick up a few more seats in Congress. So let's not worry about Esmeralda being one step away from the Oval Office. Personally I think putting her on the ticket is a brilliant idea!"

The room was silent for a moment as everyone looked at each other.

"He's right," said Memengwaa. "Our strategy in the 2520 election is to pick up more seats in the House and the Senate. Putting a candidate in the Presidential race is just a way to bring more attention to our party. We don't expect to win the White House."

"Did anyone tell Sam that?" asked Hillary.

"I think he knows it, but won't admit it," said William. "The campaign is just a way for him to keep busy in retirement."

"Allow me to be the devil's advocate," said Jason. "If we put Esmeralda on the ticket and if—by some fluke—we win, the Green Party would lose a critical seat in Congress."

"That wouldn't be a problem," replied Thomas. "As you know, the Thirty-Eighth Amendment enacted by Congress and ratified in the last century allows the Governor to make temporary appointments to fill vacancies in the House, the same as in the Senate. I could ask my daughter, Sarah, to take a leave of absence from her teaching position in Texas and return to Virginia. Then I could ask Hector to appoint her to finish Esmeralda's term in the House."

"Hector?" asked Hui.

"Hector Lopez," replied Thomas, "the Governor of Virginia. He was the Best Man at our wedding."

"That's true," said William. "I was there."

"It was a very small wedding," said Thomas.

"I think we are getting off track," said Memengwaa. "Thomas says he could have his daughter return to Virginia to fill Esmeralda's seat—that is, if Sam and Esmeralda are elected President and Vice President. Does anyone have any comment?"

"Isn't there a residency requirement?" asked Shukabi. "Wouldn't she have to live in Virginia for one year prior to the election?"

"That rule applies only to Virginia's state and local offices," replied Memengwaa. "The U.S. Constitution only requires that a representative be at least twenty-five years old, have been a citizen for seven years, and be an inhabitant of the state from which he or she is elected *at the time of the election.* You'll find it Article One of the Constitution."

"You have to be kidding me!" exclaimed Shukabi.

"No, I'm not. There are at least two dozen members of the House who don't even live in the Districts they represent."

"I didn't know that," said Shukabi.

"Most people don't," said Memengwaa. "Moreover, the U.S. Constitution trumps state law, so the Virginia lawmakers can't do anything about it, even if they wanted to."

"I wonder if our founding fathers did that on purpose or if it was an oversight," said William.

"We're getting off track again," said Memengwaa. "All we want to accomplish today is to give Sam some more choices. Besides Esmeralda, I heard you mention Kimonhon Rushing Wind and Ying Zhang. Does anyone have any other suggestions?"

"Maybe Maria Hernández from El Paso," said Anthony. "She is very charismatic and would carry the South and the Southwest."

"Okay," replied Memengwaa. "That gives us four possible candidates, including Esmeralda. We don't have to make any decisions today. Let me suggest these names to Sam and see what he says. As Thomas said, our goal in 2520 is to pick up more seats in Congress. I'm not going to lose any sleep about which person Sam chooses as his running mate." She looked around the room. "Meeting adjourned!"

The members of the committee who were still sitting now arose, exchanged goodbyes, and departed without further discussion.

*   *   *   *   *

At dinner that evening, Thomas gave Esmeralda the news. "Esmeralda, dear, something happened today that I know you will find quite exciting."

"Really? What happened?"

"We had a meeting of the Green Party Steering Committee, and they added you to the list of possible running mates for Sam Hoffenberger."

"Possible running mates? Like for Vice President?"

"Exactly."

"Who in the name of Heaven nominated me? It wasn't you, was it?"

"No, it wasn't me. William mentioned you first—more or less as a joke—and then Anthony spoke up and said, basically, 'Why not?' "

"I don't think I know Anthony."

"No matter," replied Thomas. "They ended up with four possible candidates. Memengwaa is going to give Sam the list and let him decide which one he likes best."

"So there's one chance in four he'll pick me?"

"That's correct."

"But what about my seat in Congress? The Green Party can't afford to lose my seat."

"Jason asked the same question, but I've got it covered. If Sam picks you and you win, we would ask Sarah to take a leave of absence from UTSA and move back to Virginia; then we would ask Hector to appoint her to finish your term."

"Wouldn't she have to be elected?"

"No, not to finish your term, only if she wants to run on her own after your current term ends. That would give us time to find a permanent Green for your seat. Of course, Sarah might like the job and want to run on her own when your term expires."

"Have you spoken to Sarah about this?"

"No, I don't want to jump the gun. Let's wait and see if Sam picks you."

"Oh my goodness, you keep throwing surprises at me!"

"It makes life more interesting, doesn't it?"

"I never think about whether life is interesting—I just do what I have to do."

"It's too bad we humans don't think the same way," said Thomas.

Thomas finished his dinner, and Esmeralda ordered the dining-room robot to clear the table.

*   *   *   *   *

On Tuesday morning, January 16th, as Esmeralda was preparing for the next meeting of her subcommittee, William appeared at her door. "Esmeralda, I have Memengwaa on line one. She would like to speak to you."

"Thanks, William. I'll take the call." She turned to the west wall of her office, which lit up a second later revealing an image of Memengwaa on the wall monitor.

"Good morning, Memengwaa. It's always a pleasure to hear from you."

"Good morning, Esmeralda. I'm sorry to bother you, but Sam Hoffenberger would like to interview you this week. He is trying to pick a running mate, and you are one of the four candidates under consideration."

"I'm aware of it. Thomas told me."

"Good, I didn't want to surprise you. Can you speak to Sam this afternoon or tomorrow morning?"

"I think so. Let me check with William on my schedule." Esmeralda turned back to her computer and clicked an icon on her desktop; and, in a few seconds, William appeared at her door.

"William, what's on my calendar this afternoon and tomorrow morning?"

"You're reviewing bills this afternoon and meeting with your subcommittee tomorrow morning."

Esmeralda turned back to the wall monitor. "I can do it this afternoon, Memengwaa. I have to read some bills, but it won't take me that long."

"Would two o'clock work for you?"

"Sure, two o'clock would be fine. Is the interview going to be on-line or in-person?"

"He wants to meet you in person in your office."

"That's fine. Tell him I'm in the Rayburn Building. The guards will tell him how to find my office when he goes through security."

"Great, I'll let him know."

"Thanks, Memengwaa. Have a good day."

"You too."

Memengwaa disappeared, and the wall monitor went dark. Esmeralda turned back to her desk and resumed preparations for her next subcommittee meeting.

*   *   *   *   *

Senator Hoffenberger arrived at Esmeralda's office suite at 1:59 p.m.; and after verifying that Esmeralda was ready to receive him, William escorted him into her private office.

"Welcome, Senator Hoffenberger," said Esmeralda, standing up. "It's an honor to meet you."

"Please call me *Sam*. It is an honor to meet you, too."

"Please sit down."

Senator Hoffenberger, an elderly man with thick, snow-white hair, sat down in an armchair opposite Esmeralda's desk. Esmeralda sat back down at her desk facing him. "I understand you are the Green Party's nominee for the 2520 Presidential election," she said. "Congratulations!"

"Well, bear in mind it's not official until the delegates vote at the Green Party's national convention in May. At this point, though, it doesn't appear I have any opposition."

"That's my understanding as well."

"I'm blessed to have enjoyed a good career in the Senate. I hope my reputation there will enable me to fare well in the Presidential election."

"I don't see why not."

"In any case, I need to pick a running mate. So far, all of the candidates Memengwaa has sent me fall short. I need someone who can fire up the base and ignite the imagination of the voters. I need someone who can not only pull votes from the Green voters but also from the Democrats ... maybe from the Republicans, too, although I admit that's less likely."

"In my experience," replied Esmeralda, "the voters look for a candidate who makes sense. What matters is not which party they belong to but how well they can deliver their message. The voters identify with candidates who speak their language."

"Very well, then, let's get to the heart of the issue. I'm fully aware that you are a robot, not a human being. Why should I believe you can speak the same language as the voters? After all, robots don't vote, human beings do. Why would they vote for you instead of another human being?"

"They did when they voted me into the House, didn't they? I defeated two human candidates in a fair election."

"I understand, but some people say that was an anomaly. You had the backing of outgoing Representative Hector Lopez, and you were up against weak opponents."

"I don't deny any of that; but since then, I have enhanced my credibility. I have chaired a subcommittee and sent more than one hundred bills forward to the Small Business Committee; in fact, the full House has passed more than six dozen of those and sent them on to the Senate. Anyone who doubted my ability during the election is now a believer."

"That's all well and good, but I also need a candidate who could succeed me in eight years if I'm elected in 2520 and reelected in 2524. I don't know if you could ever be President."

"To borrow a phrase from my husband, let's cross that bridge when we come to it. I think you need to focus on the election of 2520. I'd be happy to be your running mate. You'll have to decide if I'm the strongest candidate for this election."

"That's fair enough. You've given me something to think about." Senator Hoffenberger stood up. "I hope to make a decision before the end of the month. I will contact Memengwaa and tell her which candidate I've selected. Memengwaa will let you know."

Esmeralda stood up. "Excellent! Let me walk you out." Esmeralda walked around her desk and escorted Senator Hoffenberger to the front door of her office suite. There they shook hands and the Senator departed. Esmeralda returned to her desk and resumed working.

*   *   *   *   *

On Tuesday evening, January 31st, as he was finishing his dinner, Thomas's iPalm vibrated. He opened his left hand and saw Jacqueline's name on the digital read-out.

"Hi, Jacqueline, what's up?"

"Did you hear the news? Samuel Hoffenberger has picked Esmeralda to be his running mate in the 2520 Presidential election!"

"Fantastic," Thomas replied. "Sam and Esmeralda will make a great ticket."

"You don't act surprised. Did you know about this?"

"Well, I knew Esmeralda was under consideration. I didn't know Sam made a decision already."

"Yes, he announced it an hour ago. Memengwaa is putting together a press release."

"Well, I'm glad you called to let me know. I will be inundated with calls tomorrow."

"Why didn't you tell me she was being considered?"

"I didn't tell *anybody*. First, I'm required to keep my mouth shut about any steering committee deliberations; and second, I didn't want to disappoint you if Sam didn't select her."

"Okay, Bro, I'll forgive you. Has anyone told Esmeralda?"

Thomas put Jacqueline on hold and called to Esmeralda, who was cleaning up the kitchen. "Esmeralda, sweetheart, I have some exciting news. Sam has picked you to be his running mate!"

Esmeralda turned and walked over to the table. "Did Sam make a decision already?"

"Yes, I have Jacqueline on the line. She said she just heard the news."

"Oh my goodness!" exclaimed Esmeralda. "That's wonderful!"

"I'm not surprised. You were the best qualified."

"I haven't had a chance to check my messages," said Esmeralda. "I wonder if Sam or Memengwaa has been trying to reach me."

"Don't worry about that now—you can call them in the morning. Talk to my sister." Thomas lifted his hand towards Esmeralda's face, holding his iPalm towards her.

"Hello, Jacqueline. Thomas just told me the news."

"Congratulations, Esmeralda!" said Jacqueline. "I'm really excited for you!"

"I'm excited, too. I just found out a few weeks ago that I was being considered."

"Here's the deal, Esmeralda," said Jacqueline. "Memengwaa will call you tomorrow morning if she doesn't call you this evening. Ask her to set up a meeting with Sam as soon as possible. The election is nine months away. The Republicans and Democrats vying for their parties' nominations are already in full gear. You and Sam need to get ahead of the curve. I suggest you start weekly strategy meetings with Memengwaa and mobilize the Green volunteers."

"Don't you think Memengwaa has already mobilized the volunteers?" asked Thomas.

"You can't leave everything to Memengwaa. She is going to be more focused on the House and Senate races. If I were you, I'd begin traveling around the country now, even before the convention. Meet the State Chairs. Begin talking to the volunteers. You need to talk to the voters, too, of course, but your priority right now is to build your organization."

"That won't be a problem," Esmeralda replied. "I would love to travel and meet the State Chairs."

"We also have to get you into the Vice-Presidential debate in the fall. Remember what happened during the Congressional election—they wouldn't let you participate."

"We should have better luck this time," replied Thomas. "Nancy Evans stepped down as President of the League of Women Voters, and Susan is taking her place."

"Susan Lopez?" asked Jacqueline. "Hector's wife?"

"Correct. She's been the heir-apparent to the position for some time now. She's a good friend of ours, and I'm sure she'll see to it that Esmeralda gets into the debate."

"That's good news," replied Jacqueline, "but the VP debate won't take place until after Labor Day. Between now and then, focus on your campaign."

"What about my job in the House?" asked Esmeralda. "Don't forget I'm Chair of a subcommittee."

"Start looking for someone to replace you as the Chair. You can keep your seat in the House for now, but you're not going to have time for the subcommittee ... and you probably ought to resign from Congress after the convention, assuming we can find a Green to replace you."

"Wouldn't that be a risk?" asked Thomas. "What if she and Sam lose?"

"Politics is all about taking risks," said Jacqueline. "This is big. No one in the family has ever gone this far. Esmeralda needs to pull out all the stops."

"Understood, Sis," said Thomas, "We appreciate your help."

"Thanks a million!" said Esmeralda. "I'll rely on your advice."

"Is that it, Sis?" asked Thomas.

"Yes, that's it for now. Congratulations again!"

"Good night, Sis."

"Good night, Bro, and good night, Esmeralda."

Thomas closed his iPalm.

"Shouldn't we call your mother now and give her the news?" asked Esmeralda.

"I'm sure Jacqueline is calling her right now. We can talk to Geraldine later."

Thomas got up from the table and went to his study, and Esmeralda finished cleaning up the kitchen.

*　*　*　*　*

Senator Hoffenberger and Memengwaa both called Esmeralda at her office the next morning to inform her that she had been selected to be the Senator's running mate. Memengwaa called first, and they spoke briefly.

"Good morning," Memengwaa began. "Has Sam called you yet?"

"No, but Jacqueline called us last night. She told us that Sam picked me."

"Yes, he did—congratulations!"

"Thank you."

"Sam will call you today—just a courtesy call, nothing substantive. I will set up a meeting next week so that we can talk about our game plan."

"That sounds good. Please coordinate the meeting with William, my Chief of Staff."

"Will do."

Esmeralda looked at the clock. "I have to leave for a committee meeting, so I will talk to you later. Thanks again for your support."

"Okay, then, I'll let you go. Congratulations again!"

Esmeralda stood up, picked up her tablet from her desk, and left for her meeting. When she returned at noon, she found a message that Senator Hoffenberger had tried to reach her. She returned the call immediately; and in another moment, the Senator appeared on her wall monitor.

"Good afternoon, Esmeralda," the Senator began. "Did Memengwaa call you this morning?"

"Yes, Sam, I spoke to Memengwaa briefly. She told me that you selected me to be your running mate. Thanks a million—I appreciate your confidence!"

"Well, I hope I made the right decision. It is bound to be controversial. There's never been a robot on any ticket in the history of American politics … but, if nothing else, I figure it will bring more attention to our campaign."

"There's a first time for everything."

"That's true. In any case, we need to meet soon and discuss our plan of action. To borrow a phrase from the Navy, we need to hit the deck running."

"I agree—we need to move fast."

"I like your attitude," said Senator Hoffenberger. "I can see we are going to get along fine."

"I never doubted that for a moment."

"Very well, then, I understand Memengwaa is arranging a meeting next week. In the meantime, think about how we can get our campaign off the ground."

"That sounds like a phrase from the Air Force."

"Ha, ha! I like your sense of humor!"

"No humor intended—I'm just verifying we are on the same wavelength."

"It sounds like we are," said Senator Hoffenberger. "Anyway, it's great to have you on board."

"It's great to be on board."

"I won't take any more of your time. I'll see you next week in Memengwaa's office."

"I'm looking forward to it."

"As am I. Have a good afternoon."

"You too. Goodbye."

*　　*　　*　　*　　*

The meeting in Memengwaa's office took place on Tuesday morning, February 6th. Esmeralda and Senator Hoffenberger both arrived timely; and after exchanging greetings, Memengwaa began the meeting promptly at 10:00 a.m.

"I know you are both busy," said Memengwaa, "so let's get to the point. We need an action plan—more specifically, what each of you is going to do between now and the convention. Sam, you have more time to campaign because Esmeralda has responsibilities on the Hill."

"I'm going to resign as Chair of the subcommittee," said Esmeralda. "I want to devote as much time as possible to this campaign."

Senator Hoffenberger looked at Memengwaa. "I like her attitude!"

"I do, too," replied Memengwaa. "Anyway, I suggest you speak to each other daily and coordinate your schedules. You will need to travel to all of the battleground states—especially California, Mexico, New Mexico, and Canada. The Republican and Democratic candidates are already there. My office will track the upcoming events and tell you where you need to be and when you need to be there."

"That won't be a problem," replied Senator Hoffenberger. "Traveling is in my blood."

"My office will handle the publicity and set up a campaign web site," said Memengwaa. "I will act as the Treasurer until we can find a volunteer to do it."

"Thomas could be the Treasurer," said Esmeralda.

"No, that won't work," replied Memengwaa. "It would be perceived as a conflict of interest. Your husband needs to stay in the background."

"I can find someone," said Senator Hoffenberger. "Henry Jones, my former Chief of Staff, might be willing to do it."

"Otherwise, I could ask William to do it," said Esmeralda.

"Either of them would be acceptable," said Memengwaa. "In the meantime, I will set up the bank account for the campaign and make sure we have accountability and proper record-keeping."

"Anything else?" asked Senator Hoffenberger.

"Yes, you need to come up with a campaign slogan."

"I've been giving that some thought," said Senator Hoffenberger. "Maybe something like *Let's Improve the Economy* or *Let's Restore America's Economic Viability.* I think I like the second one better."

"It's too wordy," said Memengwaa. "You need something short and catchy."

"I think we need to focus on reducing the population," said Esmeralda. "How about *Let's Make America Small Again.*"

"*Let's Make America Small Again,*" repeated Senator Hoffenberger slowly. "Hmmm ... That's not bad. It's short and catchy. I think I like it!"

"All right," said Memengwaa. "Let me run it by the Steering Committee. I'll let you know what they say."

Senator Hoffenberger looked at Esmeralda. "How about we speak every evening and coordinate activities for the following day?"

"That's fine," replied Esmeralda. "Just remember that my husband likes to be in bed before midnight. You may call me up until eleven o'clock."

"So noted," said Senator Hoffenberger.

"And the three of us should meet twice a month," said Memengwaa. "Since this is the first Tuesday, let's plan on meeting on the first and third Tuesdays. We can meet more often, of course, if necessary." She stood up, signaling that the meeting was over. "I think that does it for today."

"*Let's Make America Small Again*," Senator Hoffenberger repeated as he stood up. "I think that's going to work!"

Senator Hoffenberger and Esmeralda left Memengwaa's office feeling encouraged. Who was to say that the Green Party couldn't win the White House?

*   *   *   *   *

After briefing William and the other members of her staff, Esmeralda advised her subcommittee that she was on the 2020 Green ticket and asked for a volunteer to replace her as the Chair. Representative Gambardella from New Jersey, a Democrat, volunteered; and Esmeralda prepared a memo to Chairman McIntyre recommending him for the position. Then she began traveling to California, Mexico, New Mexico, Canada, and other states that would be likely to determine the outcome of the election. As Jacqueline had suggested, she met with the Green Party leadership in each state and spoke directly to the voters whenever possible. Wherever she went, she was greeted by large, enthusiastic crowds who had seen her on CSPAN and other networks and wanted to see her in person.

Meanwhile, Senator Hoffenberger campaigned separately, also focusing on the battleground states. The Senator met with the State Chairs and Green volunteers before speaking directly to the voters. He reminded the voters of his impressive record in the Senate where he had proven his ability to reach across the aisle and get things done.

In May 2520, the Green Party held its national convention and officially nominated Senator Hoffenberger and Esmeralda for the positions of President and Vice President, respectively.

Memengwaa's staff distributed thousands of baseball caps reading *Make America Small Again* to all of the delegates. Throughout the four-day convention, Esmeralda was swarmed by admirers who wanted her autograph; and she cheerfully obliged, spending most of her time posing for photographs and signing convention memorabilia. In his acceptance speech, Senator Hoffenberger said that Esmeralda's popularity would give the ticket a boost and put them within reach of victory.

After the convention, Esmeralda resigned her seat in Congress so that she could devote full time to the campaign; and Hector, now Governor of Virginia, appointed Sarah to fill her seat for the balance of her term. Sarah gave UTSA notice that she was taking a leave of absence; then she returned to Virginia and moved into her old bedroom in her parents' apartment. On July 1st, she also moved into Esmeralda's office in the Rayburn House Office Building and put her name on the ballot for the November election to ensure that the Green Party would not lose the seat at the end of the current term. Jacqueline, who was running for reelection unopposed, agreed to act as Sarah's unofficial advisor and to counsel her on when and where to campaign.

Memengwaa held weekly conference calls with the State Chairs and coordinated events for Senator Hoffenberger and Esmeralda, who continued to campaign separately through the summer. Esmeralda repeated the approach that had proven successful during her run for Congress, emphasizing the general incompetence of the Democrats and Republicans and telling the voters that the Green Party could do better.

Thomas reached out to Hector's wife, Susan Lopez, who was now president of the League of Women Voters, and asked her to include Esmeralda in the Vice-Presidential debate scheduled for mid-October. Susan told Thomas that she would not dream of excluding Esmeralda. "Of course Esmeralda will be included," Susan said. "The public would be extremely disappointed if she were not part of it."

Between the two of them, Senator Hoffenberger and Esmeralda campaigned in every state and conducted more than five hundred media interviews; however, despite their efforts, by mid-August, the polls showed the Republican ticket in the lead with Senator Hoffenberger and Esmeralda more than ten points behind. The Democrats, running third in the polls, trailed Senator Hoffenberger and Esmeralda by only one point. Senator Hoffenberger, normally optimistic, was beginning to show signs of frustration and told Memengwaa privately, "I hope I didn't make the wrong decision by picking Esmeralda as my running mate."

Jacqueline contacted Thomas on Monday evening, August 26th, and suggested that Esmeralda take a break over the Labor Day weekend. Thomas took the call on his iPalm.

"I think Sam and Esmeralda need to take some time to prepare for the debates," said Jacqueline. "Sam has his debate coming up next month, and Esmeralda's debate with the other Vice-Presidential candidates is in October."

"How do suggest they prepare?" asked Thomas.

"I can set up a mock panel," Jacqueline replied. "The panel will fire questions at them. We'll record it and play it back for them. I can critique their performance."

"I don't think Esmeralda would have any objection," said Thomas, "but I'm not sure about Sam."

"I'll speak to Memengwaa. She will have to speak to Sam candidly. If he doesn't ace his debate, we might as well throw in the towel."

"Okay, then," replied Thomas, "ask Memengwaa to speak to Sam. We can invite him over to the apartment for a barbeque on Labor Day. They have a barbeque pit in the rooftop garden. We can relax, have some good food, and do some coaching."

"That's fine, Bro, but let's do the coaching first. This is no time to lose our focus."

"What about Sarah?" asked Thomas. "Hector's appointment only covers the balance of Esmeralda's current term. Now Sarah has to win reelection on her own."

"I'm not worried about Sarah. The only one running against her is Prabhat Modi, the Democrat Esmeralda defeated. He's very weak."

"Understood, but doesn't Sarah need coaching, too?"

"No, the League of Women Voters hasn't scheduled any debates in her contest. We need to focus our assistance on Sam and Esmeralda."

"Okay, we'll focus on Sam and Esmeralda. Let me see what I have in the refrig." He walked to the refrigerator and opened the door. Peering inside, he continued, "We just need broccoli, asparagus, and salad ... and maybe crackers or celery and a dip ... and something to drink. Sam is a vegan, right?"

"That's my understanding. Anyway, the Vice-Presidential candidates only have one debate, so Esmeralda has to perform well. These debates are our only hope of tripping up the Republicans."

"I get it, Sis. Should we invite Memengwaa?"

"Of course. How many people can you have on the rooftop?"

"I made reservations for fifteen people last year right after Labor Day. You need to book the rooftop a year ahead or you're out of luck."

"Good move, Bro. Now, counting you, Esmeralda, Sarah, mom, and me—that's five; add Memengwaa—that's six; and add Sam and his wife—that's eight. Plenty of room."

"Let's invite Hector, Susan, William, and William's wife," said Thomas.

"That's twelve. Does Sarah have a significant other?"

"She was seeing somebody in San Antonio," Thomas replied, "but he's still in Texas. She isn't seeing anyone here."

"Then there's room for three more. I'll ask Memengwaa if she wants to invite her husband or some of her staff."

"Perfect," Thomas replied. "Memengwaa's guests can be on the panel. Are you going to call Memengwaa?"

"Yes, I'll call her right now."

"Great, Sis. Thanks for the suggestion. I'll take care of the food and drinks."

"What time do you want the guests to arrive?"

"How about one o'clock?" replied Thomas. "That would give us time to do two hours of coaching before we eat."

"Let's start at 10:30 a.m. and do four hours of coaching before we eat."

"*Four hours?*" exclaimed Thomas. "Well, okay, I'll defer to my wise and famous sister."

"Ha, ha."

"Thanks again, Jacqueline. I'll have everything ready."

"Goodbye, Bro. Have a good night."

"Same to you, Sis."

Thomas closed his iPalm and went to the kitchen to brief Esmeralda on the plan.

* * * * *

On Labor Day morning, Jacqueline picked her mother up at ten o'clock and proceeded to Thomas's apartment. After parking the aeromobile on the rooftop garage, the two women took the elevator down to the first floor and walked a short distance to the apartment. Thomas's digital assistant had alerted him that they had arrived, and Thomas opened the door as they approached. "Welcome, family!"

"Good morning, Son," said Geraldine.

Jacqueline gave her brother a kiss. "You're looking good for an old man, Bro!"

"You're not looking bad yourself, Sis."

Thomas's mother and sister followed him into the living room, where he had rearranged the furniture for the mock debate. A table now stood at one end of the room with three kitchen chairs on one side of it; and on the other side of the room, a single kitchen chair faced the table. William and his wife, who had arrived earlier, were sitting in armchairs that Thomas had moved against the walls.

William stood up. "Good morning, folks! I'd like you to meet my wife, Isabelle."

Isabelle stood up and extended her hand. "I'm so pleased to meet you. William talks about you all the time!"

"He talks about whom?" asked Geraldine. "Surely not about me!"

Jacqueline looked at her brother. "I like the way you set up the room."

"It's not fancy, but I think it will work," said Thomas.

"Who's on the panel?" asked Geraldine.

"Memengwaa agreed to let us use two of her staffers. I haven't decided on the third spot."

"If you haven't decided, I think I should take the third spot," Geraldine replied.

"Mom, please!" exclaimed Thomas. "This is serious business."

"No, Bro, it's okay," said Jacqueline. "Mom's an old pro. Remember how she used to help dad prep for his debates?"

Thomas shrugged. "Well, let's see what Memengwaa says. It's okay with me if it's okay with her."

"When is she arriving?" asked Jacqueline.

Thomas looked at the clock on the west wall. "Any time now. Make yourselves comfortable, and I'll bring you some coffee." He went to the kitchen, and Jacqueline and her mother sat down in the armchairs.

"Mom," said Jacqueline, "if you're going to participate in the mock panel, you need to be up-to-speed on the issues. Have you been watching the news?"

"I watch the part that interests me."

"Okay, then, what do you plan to ask Sam when it's your turn to ask a question?"

Geraldine frowned. "I don't know ... maybe something about the economy ... or maybe something about the homeless problem."

"That's fine, but you have to turn those things into substantive questions."

"Okay, I'll ask him something like, 'What do plan to do about the homeless problem?' "

Thomas reappeared. "How do you ladies like your coffee?"

"Original Coffeemate, no sugar," replied Geraldine.

"Black," said Jacqueline.

The monitor on the east wall suddenly lit up, and James appeared. "Mr. Jenkins, you have four guests arriving; they just got off the elevator."

"Thank you, James," Thomas replied. James disappeared, and Thomas went to the front door and opened it. Memengwaa appeared a moment later with a gentleman and two younger women.

"Welcome, Memengwaa!"

"Good morning, Thomas. Happy Labor Day! So nice of you to invite us. I'd like you to meet my husband, Kijika Tsosie, and two of my staffers, Henrietta and Anna."

Thomas shook hands with each of the guests. "Please come in. Thank you so much for coming today."

Memengwaa and her entourage entered the room, and Thomas closed the door behind them. "Memengwaa, I think you know everyone except my mother. This is my mom." Thomas pointed to Geraldine.

The guests shook hands; and Thomas called to Esmeralda in an adjacent room, "Sweetheart, our guests have arrived. I'll need help with the coffee."

Esmeralda appeared in the hallway leading to the kitchen. "Good morning, everyone!"

The east-wall monitor lit up again, and James reappeared. "Mr. Jenkins, you have two more guests arriving; they are approaching your door."

Thomas thanked James, who disappeared immediately, and walked to the front door. When he opened it, Hector and Susan were standing there. Thomas gave both of them a hug before escorting them into the living room.

"I think you know everyone except Henrietta and Anna," Thomas said.

Henrietta and Anna stepped forward and introduced themselves, and everyone shook hands and exchanged greetings.

"You invited the Governor!" said Geraldine, speaking to Thomas. "I didn't know I'd be in the company of such a distinguished guest!"

Hector chuckled. "You must be referring to Susan. She's the only one here who is distinguished ... well, Susan *and Esmeralda*. Esmeralda is also distinguished."

"Only Susan and Esmeralda?" asked Jacqueline. "You mean I'm not distinguished?"

Everyone laughed.

"I can see I'm digging myself into a hole," said Hector. "I better quit before I dig it deeper."

"Where's Sarah?" asked Geraldine.

"She went to the office to finish some legislative work," replied Thomas. "She'll join us this afternoon for lunch."

"Who wants coffee beside Geraldine and Jacqueline?" asked Esmeralda. "I also have danish for anyone who didn't have breakfast."

"Let's simplify this," said Thomas. "I want to get started on the mock interviews as soon as possible. Everyone, please follow Esmeralda into the kitchen and get your coffee from the refrigerator door the way you like it and pick up a piece of danish if you wish. You'll find the danish, along with some plates, on the kitchen table."

"Good idea, Son," said Geraldine. She and the other guests followed Esmeralda into the kitchen, picked up their coffee and danish, and returned to the living room.

"Okay, here's the plan," explained Thomas. "Henrietta, Anna, and mom will sit at the table and take turns asking our candidates questions—the kind of questions they can expect to get during the real debate. Sam will go first, then Esmeralda. We'll rotate it every twenty minutes or so. James is recording it; and after the first round, we'll play it back. At that point, everyone can provide their feedback. Any questions?"

"Where's Sam?" asked Memengwaa.

"I forgot—he called this morning and said he might be a few minutes late. He should be here soon, but we'll have to switch the order to get started. Esmeralda, you go first."

Henrietta, Anna, and Geraldine took their seats at the table, and Esmeralda sat down in the chair facing the table.

"Are you ready to record, James?" asked Thomas.

The east wall lit up and James appeared. "Yes, Mr. Jenkins, I'm starting the recording now."

Thomas looked at the mock panel and then at Esmeralda. "Okay, is everyone ready? Mom, you ask the first question, then Henrietta, and then Anna. Then we'll go back to mom for the fourth question, and so on. Mom, go ahead and ask the first question. Address Esmeralda as *Candidate Jenkins*."

Geraldine looked at her daughter-in-law. "Candidate Jenkins, it's no secret that you are a robot. What would you do if, for some reason, the President died and you became President?"

"Mom, you can't ask that kind of question!" exclaimed Thomas. "That's not the kind of question they are going to ask her during the debate!"

"Actually, I think they might," said Jacqueline.

"Don't second-guess the panel," said Memengwaa. "No one can predict exactly what questions they will get during the debate. For purposes of the mock debate, everything should be on the table."

"Okay, my bad," Thomas replied. "Go ahead, Esmeralda, answer Geraldine's question."

"It wouldn't matter whether Sam or I were the President," Esmeralda replied. "We both have the same philosophy—we endorse the Green Party's platform. If I were to become President, I'd simply advance the Green agenda."

"That's a good answer," said Susan.

"Let's hold our feedback until after James replays the session for us," Thomas said. "Okay, Henrietta, you go next."

"Candidate Jenkins," asked Henrietta, "How would you address the homeless crisis?"

"First, we need to build affordable housing," answered Esmeralda. "Then we need to find jobs for the homeless. Many of them can be employed in the construction industry, especially residential construction. Then we need to—"

The wall monitor lit up and James appeared, interrupting Esmeralda. "Mr. Jenkins, you have two more visitors arriving."

"Thank you, James." James disappeared, and Thomas walked to the door and opened it. Senator Hoffenberger and his wife stood in the doorway.

"Great to see you again, Senator!" said Thomas. "Please come in!"

The Senator stepped inside the room, holding his wife's hand, and looked around the room. "Good morning, everybody! Good to see you again ... this is my wife, Angelica."

Everyone stood up and shook hands with Senator Hoffenberger and Angelica, then sat back down. Thomas pointed to two kitchen chairs against the wall. "You and Angelica can sit there. We're interviewing Esmeralda. You'll go next."

William stood up again. "Senator, please take my seat." William turned to his wife. "Isabelle, let Angelica have your chair. We can sit in those chairs there." He pointed to the kitchen chairs.

"Oh, you're too kind," said Angelica, "but I don't need an armchair—I have very simple tastes."

"No," replied William, "I insist."

Senator Hoffenberger and Angelica sat down in the armchairs, and William and Isabelle walked over to the kitchen chairs against the wall and sat down.

"We're just getting started," Thomas explained to the new arrivals. "Our mock panel is asking Esmeralda questions. We'll continue for twenty minutes or so like this, then break and replay it. Everyone will critique Esmeralda's answers, and then it will be your turn. Depending how long the critiques last, you will rotate with Esmeralda every thirty minutes or so."

"You're going to put me on the hot seat, huh?" replied Senator Hoffenberger. "Okay, I accept the challenge!"

"Good," said Thomas. He turned to the panel. "You go next, Anna. Ask Esmeralda a question."

"Okay, Candidate Jenkins," Anna began, "During the campaign, you told voters that you support birth control as a means to reverse the population explosion, but Roman Catholics are opposed to birth control. What do you say to Roman Catholics?"

Esmeralda leaned forward in her chair. "Roman Catholics are only following orders from their Pope. When we are elected, President Hoffenberger or I will go to Rome and meet with the Pope and see if we can persuade him to change the church's position. If the Pope agrees, Roman Catholics throughout the world will fall in line, and we will begin to reverse the population explosion."

"Thank you, Candidate Jenkins," said Anna.

Over the next four hours, Thomas's mock panel asked Senator Hoffenberger and Esmeralda more than two hundred questions; and every twenty minutes, the observers critiqued their answers. The feedback from Jacqueline and Memengwaa was particularly pointed, revealing numerous soft spots in the Senator's and Esmeralda's responses. When Senator Hoffenberger said he would eliminate the Nation's trade deficit, Jacqueline said, "Every politician says that—now tell me how you would do it." When Esmeralda said she would build housing for the homeless, Memengwaa asked how she would pay for it. After two hours, the Senator became tired, and his answers became increasingly less on point; but Esmeralda's responses remained razor-sharp to the end. Finally, Thomas announced it was over.

"Okay, folks," said Thomas, "I think we accomplished what we intended. Let's give Senator Hoffenberger and Esmeralda a big round of applause!"

Everyone applauded. William exclaimed, "How to go, team!"

"You guys are going to ace your debates," added Hector. "I think we have a winning ticket!"

"All right, then," said Thomas. "Let's go to the rooftop garden and dig into the food. Sarah will meet us there."

Everyone stood up, stretched, and followed Thomas out of the apartment towards the rooftop.

*　　*　　*　　*　　*

On Tuesday evening, September 17th, as Geraldine was sitting down to read her Bible, her iPalm vibrated; and opening her palm, she saw Jacqueline's name and accepted the call.

"Mom, are you watching the debate?" Jacqueline asked.

"What debate?"

"Sam's debate."

"Sam?"

"Mom, you're losing it—Senator Hoffenberger!"

"Oh, my goodness. Is the Presidential debate tonight?"

"Yes, it's already started. Ask Richard to bring it on-line immediately!"

"Will do, Jacqueline. Thanks for the reminder."

"My pleasure, Mom. Goodbye. I'll talk to you later."

Geraldine turned to the north wall and summoned her digital assistant. "Richard, I need to watch the Presidential debate. It just started."

The north wall lit up, and Richard appeared. "I understand you would like to watch the televised debate between the candidates running for President, is that correct, Ms. Jenkins?"

"You got it."

"Any particular network?"

"CNN."

"I will bring up CNN as you requested. Have a good evening, Ms. Jenkins, and let me know if you need anything else."

Richard disappeared, and the monitor revealed a panel of three people, two men and one woman, sitting behind a small table facing a stage with three candidates, all men, standing side-by-side behind separate lecterns. The woman on the panel had just started asking Senator Hoffenberger a question. "I understand the Green Party has more than ten billion members," she said. "Out of ten billion possible candidates, you couldn't find a single *human being* who was qualified to be your running mate? Is this some kind of joke?"

"Well," replied Senator Hoffenberger, "there were many who were qualified, but I chose Esmeralda because she seems to enjoy a special connection with the American people. In fact, she is beloved and admired by billions of our citizens. And bear in mind that the job of Vice President is not exactly rocket science."

"What do you mean, 'not exactly rocket science'?" asked one of the men on the panel.

"Let me be candid, if I may," replied Senator Hoffenberger. "Being Vice President of the United States is pretty much a do-nothing job."

"With all due respect, Sir," replied the same panelist, "the Vice President serves as President of the Senate."

"Come, come," said Senator Hoffenberger. "When you watch CSPAN, have you ever seen the Vice President presiding over the Senate? Never! Not once! Admit it!"

"That's probably because they are working behind the scenes," said the woman who asked the original question.

"Trust me," said Senator Hoffenberger. "I served in the Senate myself for many years, and I know how it works. Throughout American history, most Vice Presidents have delegated their Senate responsibilities to others so they could spend more time on their golf game ... Okay, if you want to press the point, I grant you that we send our Vice Presidents to state funerals of other world leaders—I think Esmeralda can handle that. Like I say, it's not exactly rocket science."

"I'm astonished to hear you talk about the Vice President's role like this," said the third panelist. "Aren't you forgetting that the Vice President casts the deciding vote in the Senate in the event of a tie?"

"That doesn't happen very often," replied Senator Hoffenberger. "When it does, I'll tell Esmeralda how I want her to vote."

"Let's face it," said the woman who had asked the first question, "at age 90, you're not exactly a spring chicken. What would happen if you died in office and the robot became President?"

"I won't die in office—my longevity forecast says that I will live to 108."

"With all due respect, Sir," replied the same panelist, "longevity forecasting is not yet an exact science. It could be off by as much as six months one way or the other."

"All right, let's say it is off by six *years*," replied the Senator. "Let's say I die at 102. If I'm re-elected in four years, as I expect, I will be 98 when I leave office. That's a comfortable margin, and I think we can safely say that there is no chance of my dying in office."

The panelist persisted, "But what if the lab that did your longevity forecast made an error? What if your forecast is off by ten or twelve years?"

"The science of forecasting longevity is very sophisticated," replied the Senator, "and I don't believe that could happen ... but I'll tell you what: I will release my annual longevity forecast to the public every year, and I won't run for reelection in 2524 if it shows any change for the worse."

"That begs the question," asked the second panelist, "is the robot going to run for President in 2524 or 2528?"

"To borrow a phrase from Esmeralda," the Senator replied, "we'll cross that bridge when we come to it."

Geraldine summoned Richard. "Richard, I'm not going to waste my precious time on such nonsense. If they're not going to talk about the issues, there's no point in my watching it. You may turn it off."

Richard reappeared in the top right-hand corner of the monitor. "I understand that you would like to discontinue coverage of the Presidential debate, is that correct?"

"That's correct—it's a complete waste of time."

"Very well, Ms. Jenkins, would you prefer to watch something else?"

"No, I've got more important things to do with my time."

"Understood, Ms. Jenkins. I will discontinue the coverage of the debate and turn off the media input."

Richard disappeared, and Geraldine picked up her Bible and turned to the Book of Ecclesiastes.

*   *   *   *   *

According to the political pundits, Senator Hoffenberger did better than expected in the Presidential debate, and the Green ticket received a bounce in the post-debate polling. By the first week in October, the race had tightened even more; the Microsoft-Reuters poll showed the Republicans only two points ahead of the Greens. It was becoming increasingly evident that Esmeralda's performance in the upcoming Vice-Presidential debate could make or break the Green ticket's chances for victory on November 5th.

Jacqueline called Thomas on Sunday evening, October 6th. "I think we need to go to Boston and show Esmeralda our support," she said. "Family is allowed to sit in the front row. Everyone needs to be there."

"Where is the debate being held?" asked Thomas.

"In the new Al Gore Auditorium at Harvard. It holds 500,000 people."

"Should we take mom?"

"Yes," replied Jacqueline, "You, Sarah, mom, and me—all of us need to be there."

"How about Memengwaa and Sam?"

"Sam is campaigning in Australia and New Zealand right now; he won't be here. But I'm sure that Memengwaa has already registered."

"How are we going to get there?"

"Google Amtrak. It's faster than flying."

"When should we plan to travel?"

"The debate is next week—Thursday evening, October 17th— at eight o'clock. To be on the safe side, let's go on Thursday morning. We can have lunch and dinner there and do some sightseeing in the afternoon."

"Where are we going to stay on Thursday night?"

"I'll find a hotel in Cambridge."

"Okay, that sounds good. I will ask James to make the transportation arrangements."

"Is James programmed to do that?"

"Yes, I upgraded his program this summer."

"Good, but Memengwaa's staff books everything for Esmeralda. James doesn't need to book hers."

"I made a note of it."

"Let me know if you run into any glitches."

"Will do."

"Thanks, Bro. Have a good evening."

"You, too, Sis."

* * * * *

On Thursday morning, October 17th, at 7:30 a.m., Jacqueline picked Geraldine up at her apartment and flew to Union Station where she parked her aeromobile on the rooftop parking garage and then looked for the family. They soon found Thomas, Esmeralda, and Sarah, who had arrived a few minutes earlier. All of them carried small knapsacks with a change of clothing and wore their brightly colored baseball caps with the slogan *Make America Small Again.*

"Have you had breakfast, Mom?" asked Thomas.

"Of course, Son. I was up at 4:30 this morning."

"There's time for a muffin and a cup of coffee before the train departs. It leaves at 8:27 a.m."

"What time does it get to Boston?" asked Geraldine.

"9:25," Thomas replied.

"It takes an hour?"

"Fifty-eight minutes, to be exact."

"Whatever happened to the high-speed trains they promised us?"

"They're still on the drawing board, I'm afraid."

"No matter," replied Geraldine. "I can catch a nap on the way."

Thomas looked at the others. "Does anyone want coffee before we board?"

"I think you can buy coffee on the train," said Jacqueline.

"I'd rather do that," said Sarah.

"Thomas says we're going to do some sightseeing when we arrive in Boston," said Esmeralda. "What would everyone like to see?"

Jacqueline was the first to answer. "They say there's a nice view from the Skywalk Observatory at the Prudential Center. After that we could take the famous Duck Tour. It's an amphibious vehicle that drives right down into the Charles River and turns into a boat."

"That sounds like fun," said Thomas.

"Don't forget I lived in Boston for a couple of years when I attended Harvard," said Sarah. "I know Boston and Cambridge pretty well. I recommend we walk a piece of the Freedom Trail, perhaps from the Boston Common to Faneuil Hall. It's not too far, and we would work up an appetite for lunch. Then we could do the Duck Tour and the Skywalk Observatory in the afternoon."

Jacqueline looked at her mother. "Are you okay with that, Mom?"

"Do I look like I'm *not* okay?" Geraldine replied. "I may be an old lady, but I can still walk."

Everyone laughed.

"Where are we staying tonight?" asked Sarah.

"The Charles Hotel in Cambridge," Jacqueline replied. "It has good reviews."

"If we want a drink after the debate," said Sarah, "there's a pub nearby called the Cambridge Queen's Head. It's operated by Harvard."

"Harvard operates a pub?" asked Geraldine.

"It's run by the students," replied Sarah.

"Okay, then," said Thomas, "if no one needs coffee, let's pick up our tickets at the reservation desk and proceed to the track."

A few minutes later, the family boarded Google-Amtrak's train number 1805; and twenty minutes later, they were on their way to Boston.

Chapter 8
The Debate

When the family arrived in Boston, they took a taxi from South Station to Cambridge and checked their knapsacks at The Charles Hotel, where Jacqueline had made reservations; then they returned to Boston and found their way to the Freedom Trail. After walking a section of the Freedom Trail as Sarah had suggested, they lunched at the Union Oyster House; and after lunch, they found their way to the starting point for the Duck Tour, took the tour, and then walked to the Prudential Center and took an elevator to the Skywalk Observatory and enjoyed the view. Thomas checked the time and suggested an early dinner to ensure they wouldn't be late for the debate, so they remained at the Prudential Center and had dinner at the Top of the Hub restaurant on the fifty-second floor.

After dinner, the family took rapid transit to the Cambridge side of the Charles River and walked from the subway station to the Al Gore auditorium a few hundred yards away, arriving at 6:30 p.m. so that Esmeralda could look at the logistics and visit briefly with Susan Lopez, who, along with her team from the League of Women Voters, was running the debate. After entering the lobby, Esmeralda went her separate way, and the rest of the family stayed in the lobby and looked at the photographs of Al Gore. After a few minutes, Thomas suggested they look for Memengwaa and see if they could sit together. He opened his iPalm and texted her; and in a few seconds, he received a reply, *I'm on my way – expect to arrive by 7.* Thomas looked at the time in the top-right corner of the iPalm. It was 6:45 p.m.

"Memengwaa will be here in fifteen minutes," said Thomas. "Let's pick up our tickets. We'll ask them if Memengwaa can sit with us."

The family, minus Esmeralda, walked to the reservation desk and talked to the ticket agent, who checked Memengwaa's reservation and told them that her seat was in the second row right behind theirs. Thomas took everyone's tickets, including Memengwaa's, and the family walked back to the entrance to wait for her. She arrived a few minutes later, and Thomas caught her attention as she entered the building.

"Memengwaa, great to see you!" said Thomas. "I have your ticket."

Memengwaa took her ticket and hugged each member of the family. "I'm so excited!" she exclaimed. "This is a first for the Green Party—the first time we've ever had a candidate in the Vice-Presidential debate!"

"Let's hope she does as well as Sam did," said Thomas.

"Did he do well?" asked Geraldine. "I tuned out after two minutes."

Jacqueline put her hand on her mother's shoulder. "You can't tune out tonight, Mom. I'll give you my elbow if I hear you snoozing."

"Congresswoman or not, you're still my daughter," replied Geraldine. "Show some respect, young lady!"

Everyone laughed.

"Memengwaa, do you want to look around the lobby?" asked Thomas.

Memengwaa looked at the atrium, which extended six stories above the ground. Her eyes rested on a large painting of former Vice President Al Gore. "Yes, since we're early, I'd like to look at the pictures."

The family followed Memengwaa to the painting that had caught her attention.

"Look at the way they dressed in those days," remarked Sarah. "The jacket and tie must have been extremely uncomfortable."

"People still wear ties—they just wear them loose," said Thomas.

"Your father wore a tie for special occasions," said Geraldine, "like at our wedding."

"Al Gore would have been our forty-third President but for the winner-take-all Electoral College," said Sarah.

"I know, honey," replied Thomas. "I studied history, too."

"Thank God they finally got rid of the winner-take-all system," said Sarah.

Memengwaa and the Jenkins family, minus Esmeralda, spent the next twenty-five minutes looking at the other paintings and photographs in the atrium and reading the accompanying text on the wall beside each one. Thomas opened his iPalm and checked the time. "It's nearly 7:30—I think we better find our seats." He turned and walked towards the auditorium, the rest of the group following him. The lobby was now packed elbow-to-elbow, and Thomas had to work his way aggressively through the crowd. Jacqueline took

Geraldine's arm, and the two of them followed Thomas. Sarah and Memengwaa followed closely behind Jacqueline and Geraldine. When they entered the auditorium, they could see thousands of other people streaming into it from other doors. In a few minutes, they were seated, Geraldine between Thomas and Jacqueline, Sarah next to Thomas, and Memengwaa behind Geraldine. All of them wore their *Make America Small Again* baseball caps.

The auditorium contained four gigantic monitors, one on each side of the room, where the audience could get a close-up view of the candidates. A video camera suspended from the ceiling hung just above the stage pointed towards the candidates' lecterns; and a second video camera, also suspended from the ceiling, hung on the other side of the stage pointed towards the panelists' table.

"This is awesome," said Jacqueline.

"You use that word too much," said Geraldine. "Save it for something that's really awesome."

The family and Memengwaa made small talk for the next fifteen minutes as the auditorium filled to capacity. At 7:59 p.m., three well-dressed people emerged from behind the stage and took their seats at the panelists' table.

"That must be panel," said Thomas.

"Of course it's the panel," said Geraldine. "Who else could they be?"

The lights in the auditorium dimmed, and several spotlights in the ceiling illuminated the panelists' table and each of the three lecterns. The noise in the auditorium subsided, and one of the three people at the table spoke.

"Good evening, ladies and gentlemen, and welcome to the 2520 Vice-Presidential debate sponsored by the League of Women Voters. My name is Peter Lewis, and I'm the moderator for tonight's debate, which is expected to last for approximately one hour. Many of you may know me as the news anchor for MSNBC. I'm joined by Katherine Diamond, chief political analyst for the *Washington Post*, and Alexandria Escobar, columnist for the *Washington Times*. Now, without further ado, let's meet the candidates!"

The three candidates, including Esmeralda, walked from a doorway on the side of the stage to their lecterns. Esmeralda came first, followed by two men, and each of the three took their place in front of a lectern. Esmeralda's lectern was on the left, as viewed from the audience.

"I will give each of our three candidates ten seconds to state their name and their political affiliation," said Mr. Lewis, "starting with the young lady on the left."

"My name is Esmeralda Jenkins, and I'm the Vice-Presidential candidate on the Green ticket," said Esmeralda.

"My name is Joe Smiley, and I'm the Vice-Presidential candidate on the Republican ticket," said the man standing at the middle lectern.

"My name is Rishyasringa Bakshi, and I'm the Vice-Presidential candidate on the Democratic ticket," said the third candidate.

"Thank you," said Mr. Lewis. "Now let's go over the rules for this debate. First, I will ask the audience to refrain from applause and remain quiet until the end of the debate when each candidate has made his or her closing statement. Second, I will give each of the candidates one minute for an opening statement and an additional minute at the end for a closing statement. After the opening statement, Ms. Diamond, Ms. Escobar, and I will take turns asking questions. The candidates will have one minute to answer each question. If anyone goes over one minute, the additional seconds will be deducted from the time allowed for their closing statement;

and if their total excess time exceeds one minute, they will forfeit their right to make a closing statement."

Geraldine leaned over to Jacqueline and whispered, "Who made these rules, anyway?"

"The League of Women Voters," replied Jacqueline.

"As the moderator," continued Mr. Lewis, "I have discretion to allow, or not allow, the candidates to comment on the other candidates' answers. Now, if the rules are clear, I will invite each of the candidates to make a brief opening statement. Mr. Smiley, you may go first."

The Republican candidate looked around the room and smiled pleasantly, then looked back at the panel. "Thank you, Mr. Moderator. And thank you to the League of Women Voters for sponsoring this debate. I'm pleased to represent the Republican ticket on the stage this evening. As you know, the Republican platform calls for meaningful solutions to the problems facing our great Nation. We don't propose to do anything drastic or expensive, and our solutions will not raise taxes on anyone. That's our promise to the American people. I look forward to answering the panelists' specific questions during the next hour."

Geraldine leaned towards Thomas and whispered, "If the Republicans had their way, we wouldn't pay any taxes at all—and we wouldn't have any government, either!"

Mr. Lewis looked at the lectern on the right. "Mr. Bakshi, you may go next. Please keep your opening statement to one minute."

Mr. Bakshi looked directly into the video camera. "Thank you, Mr. Moderator. I'm honored to represent the Democratic ticket this evening, and I want to use this occasion to speak directly to the American people, who have suffered too long from incompetence in the White House. If you watched the Presidential debate a few weeks ago, you already know that the Democratic platform contains bold solutions to the issues of the day. I hope to elaborate on those solutions during the course of the evening. In the interest of time, I'll leave it there for now."

Mr. Lewis looked at Esmeralda. "Ms. Jenkins, your turn."

Esmeralda looked at Mr. Lewis. "Please call me Esmeralda— that's what everyone calls me."

"So noted, Ms. Esmeralda. Now please proceed with your opening statement."

"Thank you, Mr. Moderator," Esmeralda began. "And thank you, Susan Lopez and our other friends at the League of Women Voters for sponsoring this debate. This election is about economic justice and the sustainability of the planet. The Green Party is the only party in this election that addresses these issues. We have an economic plan that will provide work for every American and an environmental agenda that will ensure the survival of our planet. I look forward to giving you more specifics during the forthcoming Q and A. Thank you again."

"Perfect, Mom!" said Sarah, speaking to herself quietly. "Good opening!"

"So far, so good," said Mr. Lewis. "Now I will proceed with the first question. Mr. Smiley, now that Australia and New Zealand have joined the Union as the ninety-ninth and one-hundredth states, respectively, do you favor a constitutional amendment that would change our name to the United States of the World?"

Mr. Smiley leaned forward. "As you may know, that's an important component of the Republican platform. I understand that the Democrats are in favor of it, too; but unlike the Democrats, we aren't going to wait for a constitutional amendment. When we are elected, the President will issue an executive order making this

change effective immediately. We still need a constitutional amendment, of course, but that can come later."

"Thank you, Mr. Smiley," replied Mr. Lewis. "Ms. Escobar
will ask the next question."

Ms. Escobar, sitting beside the moderator, straightened her
posture and looked at Esmeralda. "Ms. Esmeralda, it is no secret
that you are a robot. As cynical as it may sound, there are those who
say that you are a front for your husband, Thomas Jenkins, a well-
known Green Party activist. Precisely how much control does
Thomas have over you and how do the voters know, if they cast
their vote for you, that they are not really voting for your husband?"

Esmeralda looked at Ms. Escobar and smiled. "I appreciate
your concern, and I think that's an excellent question. I'm glad you
asked it because I suspect that many in the audience this evening are
wondering the same thing. The answer is that I have a mind of my
own; my husband doesn't control me. During my tenure in Congress, Thomas never tried to interfere or influence me. He did his
thing, and I did mine. Voters can be confident that I make my own
decisions. Thank you for the question."

Geraldine leaned towards Thomas and whispered, "Sometimes I wish you did interfere."

"Ms. Diamond will ask the next question," said the moderator.

Ms. Diamond sat up in her chair. "Ms. Esmeralda, the World
Economic Forum is scheduled for early next year, soon after the new
President takes office. If you are elected, you may be asked to accompany the President or even substitute for him if he has other
commitments. How do you think other world leaders would feel
about dealing with a robot?"

"Great question!" replied Esmeralda. "As you can imagine, I
faced a similar problem when I began my term in Congress. Other

members didn't know if they could trust me, but I quickly won their confidence. I chaired an important subcommittee, in fact, which produced an unprecedented volume of new legislation. If you were to speak to any of my former colleagues in the House, I think they would attest to my ability to put human beings at ease. Thank you for the excellent question."

"Good answer, Mom!" said Sarah quietly.

"I wish to direct my next question to the Democratic candidate," said the moderator. "Mr. Bakshi, as you may remember from your study of American history, we once had a state called Florida, which disappeared more than two hundred years ago due to rising sea levels. What would you do, if elected, to protect North Carolina, South Carolina, and other states that are vulnerable to the same catastrophe?"

"Good question," replied Mr. Bakshi. "Every American knows—or should know—what happened to Florida in the twenty-fourth century. Fortunately, the Army Corps of Engineers went to work immediately after that calamity and built dikes to protect the Carolinas and other vulnerable, low-lying regions. The problem is that those dikes are now aging. We need to spend whatever money it takes to reinforce them and protect what's left of the middle forty-seven states."

"Not so fast," said Mr. Smiley. "I think we need to ask ourselves if that's really the most cost-effective solution. The Democrats never think about cost. My question is, 'Do we really need to save the Carolinas?' Now don't get me wrong—I don't want anyone to drown—but I think we should consider relocating the residents to higher ground before we spend billions or trillions of dollars on trying to repair aging dikes. The Army Corps of Engineers is no match for the Atlantic Ocean, and they can't hold it back forever."

"The Army Corps of Engineers has tackled bigger problems than that with great success," replied Mr. Bakshi, "New Orleans being a case in point."

Esmeralda leaned into her mike. "On this point, the Greens and Democrats agree. We already have too many people crowded together on the North American continent. We can't afford to lose any more land mass."

"Thank you, candidates," said the moderator, "but I want to move on to another topic. I believe that Ms. Escobar a question for you."

"I'd like all three of you to answer the following question," began Ms. Escobar. "As we all know, World War XII killed tens of billions of people and left billions more homeless. Many fear that the human race would not survive another world war. If elected, what would your administration do to ease international tensions? Mr. Smiley, you may go first."

"Thank you for that question," replied Mr. Smiley. "History has shown us that the only deterrent to evil is power. If we have the strongest military on the planet, no other country will dare to provoke a fight with us. The key to peace is to increase our defense budget and ensure that we have the best trained soldiers and most advanced weapons. When my running mate and I take office in January, we will begin working on a budget that will quadruple funding for the Department of Defense."

"Thank you, Mr. Smiley," said the moderator. "Mr. Bakshi, you may go next."

Mr. Bakshi straightened his tie before speaking. "Excellent question, Ms. Escobar. This is precisely why we can't afford to have a robot in the White House—our enemies would think we are vulnerable. The President and the Vice President have to be authoritative leaders who can command respect on the world stage. We don't need to quadruple the defense budget to accomplish that—and we certainly don't need a Vice President who is a robot."

"Thank you, Mr. Bakshi," said the moderator. "Ms. Esmeralda, you may go next."

Esmeralda leaned into her mike. "I find it interesting that neither of my opponents answered Ms. Escobar's question, which is what they would do to ease international tensions. The Democrats and Republicans are both so focused on their own narrow agendas that they can't see the forest for the trees."

"I take offense to that statement," said Mr. Bakshi. "I think I *did* answer Ms. Escobar's question."

"I did, too," said Mr. Smiley. "Don't try to say I didn't."

"Really?" asked Esmeralda. "No, you didn't—neither of you did—but I will."

"I won't let you marginalize me," said Mr. Bakshi, "if that's what you're trying to do."

"Please, Mr. Bakshi," said the moderator, "let's allow Ms. Esmeralda to finish her answer."

"The way we ease international tensions," Esmeralda continued, "is to develop constructive relationships with the other world leaders. This means reaching out proactively and assisting nations that are falling behind; it also means playing the role of peacemaker, when necessary, to deescalate regional conflicts before they become wars. It's all about building trust. When other nations see the United States as the undisputable world leader, and when they know they can trust us, we can eliminate war once and for all."

"Great answer, Mom!" said Sarah under her breath.

Ms. Escobar leaned back into her mike. "I have a follow-up question. Should the United States be the world's policeman? Again, I'd like all three of you to respond. Mr. Smiley, you may go first."

"The answer is an unequivocal *no*," responded Mr. Smiley. "Trying to be the world's policeman is what got us into hundreds of unnecessary wars over the past five hundred years, going all the way back to Korea and Vietnam. By the way, the Democrats got us into the Vietnam war, and the Republicans got us out of it. I promise you that the Republicans will never get the United States involved in other countries' civil wars."

"Thank you," replied Ms. Escobar. "Mr. Bakshi, your turn."

"I take exception to Mr. Smiley's mischaracterization of the Democrat's role in Vietnam," said Mr. Bakshi. "If you ever studied twentieth-century American history, you would know that President Eisenhower—a Republican—got us involved in Vietnam's civil war by sending military aid to South Vietnam. Once again, my Republican opponent is blaming the Democrats for something that was obviously the Republicans' fault."

"Thank you, Mr. Bakshi," said Ms. Escobar. "Ms. Esmeralda, your turn."

"It's just amazing," said Esmeralda. "Once again, Mr. Bakshi didn't even answer your question, which is whether the United States should be the world's policeman."

"I did so answer the question!" exclaimed Mr. Bakshi. "I won't let you continue to mischaracterize my answers. In this instance—"

"Please, Mr. Bakshi," interrupted the moderator, "allow Ms. Esmeralda to finish her answer."

"My answer to the question is a clear *yes*," continued Esmeralda. "If you were the strongest, most respected child on the playground and saw another child being beaten up by a bully, wouldn't you intervene to stop it? World affairs are no different; as the world's only superpower, we have a moral obligation to protect weak countries from aggressors."

"Right on, Mom!" said Sarah.

"Indeed," added Esmeralda, "if the United States and its European allies had stood up to Hitler sooner, we might have prevented the Holocaust."

"Thank you, Ms. Esmeralda," said the moderator.

"I'd like to clarify my position on this, if I may," said Mr. Bakshi.

"By all means, go ahead," said the moderator.

"Because my Republican opponent tried to blame the Vietnam war on the Democrats," said Mr. Bakshi, "I felt compelled to use my time to rebut his accusation ... but I agree with him that the United States can't be the world's policeman. It's simply unrealistic. Once again, the robot is living in a fantasy world."

"Thank you, Mr. Bakshi," said Ms. Escobar.

"Ms. Diamond will ask the next question," said the moderator.

"Mr. Bakshi," began Ms. Diamond, "according to the latest census, we have upwards of twelve billion people in the United States who are homeless. What is your plan for dealing with this alarming problem?"

"The Democratic Party has already addressed this issue," replied Mr. Bakshi. "No one wants to give us credit for converting tens of thousands of abandoned shopping malls into low-income housing projects. As a result of that initiative, which the Republicans opposed, we have provided shelter and safe housing to more than a billion people."

Mr. Smiley leaned forward into his mike. "As usual, the Democrats want to talk about the past. The Republican Party is focused on the present and the future, not the past."

"Very well, Mr. Smiley," said Mr. Lewis, "since you spoke up, can you tell us precisely what the Republicans would do, going forward, to solve the homeless problem?"

After a moment of silence, Mr. Smiley replied, "I'm amazed no one has brought up the most critical issue of our times. We have had more than fifteen hundred documented UFO sightings in the past twelve months. Someone is watching us, and it is no secret that they are coming from the planet Venus. No one wants to think about it, but we could be attacked at any time. This isn't a joke; it's real, and it's something we need to take seriously. The Republican platform calls for immediate deployment of a defensive space shield. We also need to consider an offensive."

"We can discuss that later in the debate," said Mr. Lewis, "but please answer the question on the table. What would you do, if elected, to address the homeless crisis?"

After another moment of silence, Mr. Smiley replied, "This is just another case of the media making a mountain out of a molehill. There's no crisis. We have a successful program for exporting homeless people—volunteers of course—to colonies on Mars. All we need to do is to expand it. For example, we should be offering more free land on Mars to encourage more volunteers."

Esmeralda leaned into her mike. "By all indications, the homeless people who have gone to Mars are disillusioned and want to return to Earth. I don't consider that a successful program."

"Once again," replied Mr. Smiley, "the robot is looking at the half-full glass and saying it is half empty. The last thing we need in this country is a Vice President with a negative attitude."

Geraldine whispered in Jacqueline's ear, "What a nincompoop!"

"For once," said Mr. Bakshi, "the robot and I agree. We don't need to be sending human beings to Mars. The Democratic platform embraces a plan to transform useless national parks such as Yosemite and Yellowstone into low-income housing projects. These parks are a luxury we can no longer afford. Old Faithful in Yellowstone could be the cornerstone of a lovely apartment complex for the poor and elderly."

"Excuse me, Sir," said Ms. Diamond. "Aside from their recreational value, these parks provide a natural habitat for deer and other wildlife. What would you do about the animals?"

"Obviously we would have to kill any remaining grizzly bears, wolfs, elk, deer, and other animals before we begin construction."

"Kill them?" asked Ms. Diamond. "How do you propose to do that?"

"It wouldn't be difficult," replied Mr. Bakshi. "One well-placed neutron bomb in each park would accomplish the task nicely."

Geraldine leaned towards Thomas and whispered, "This guy is as dumb as a box of rocks!"

"I don't want people to quote me out of context," continued Mr. Bakshi. "I'm talking about *one small, strategically-placed* neutron bomb per park. These bombs would be denotated hundreds of miles from major cities, and we would take great care to ensure that people in nearby towns and villages were safely evacuated prior to the detonation."

"But how you can make that guarantee?" asked Ms. Diamond. "A neutron bomb can kill people for hundreds of miles in every direction."

"As I said, it will be a *small* neutron bomb."

"I don't recall Alexander Smith, your running mate, mentioning this in last month's Presidential debate," replied Ms. Diamond. "Is this part of the Democratic platform or your own idea?"

"It's something that Alexander and I have been talking about off-line for some time. I can see you're skeptical, so let me put it like this: Do you want to look at pretty trees and wild animals or put a roof over everyone's head?"

"Have you lost your mind, Sir?" exclaimed Esmeralda. "The soil would remain radioactive for centuries. Doesn't that trouble you?"

"This would be *low-income* housing," replied Mr. Bakshi. "No one expects it to be perfect."

"God help us if this guy becomes Vice President," said Thomas under his breath.

"If I may continue," said Mr. Bakshi, "our platform also calls for making use of our obsolete interstate highways, which no one uses any more except for racing antique automobiles and other recreational activities. We will use the highway footprint to build tens of thousands of low-income apartments."

"Do you have any other proposals, Mr. Bakshi?" asked Ms. Diamond.

"Yes, I do. We aren't taking full advantage of our planet's oceans. Over seventy percent of the Earth's surface is water. We should be using our oceans for floating cities—like the oil rigs in the Gulf of Mexico during the Middle Ages, but much larger."

Mr. Smiley leaned into his mike. "That's ludicrous. Don't you think people would get cabin fever cramped together on what amounts to a tiny island? How are they going to entertain themselves?"

"That's a fair question," replied Mr. Bakshi, "since space will be at a premium. We obviously won't have room for golf courses or tennis courts, but we can provide other recreational activities such as checkers and chess. Down the road, we may even be able to provide table tennis and curling for our more affluent residents. We will also encourage the residents to spend more time playing Monopoly, which doesn't require much square footage. On balance, I think they will be very satisfied."

Geraldine turned and put her mouth to Jacqueline's ear. "What a lunatic!"

"That's an interesting idea," said Ms. Diamond, "but how would the inhabitants of these so-called floating cities get food and water?"

"We have that covered," replied Mr. Bakshi. "As a result of climate change, we now have citrus fruit growing from the northern edge of Antarctica to the southern edge of the North Pole, so food won't be a problem, and we can use modern reverse-osmosis purification systems to convert the ocean into safe drinking water. The residents will have a virtually infinite supply of food and water."

Esmeralda straightened and leaned into her mike. "With all due respect, Gentlemen, I think both of you have your heads in the sand. This is not just about housing; it is about the sustainability of the planet. The Earth will not support 500 billion people indefinitely. It can't even support a fraction of that. More than half the world's population goes to bed hungry because food is scarce. In poor nations, those who don't die of hunger die of thirst."

"The robot obviously wasn't listening to me," said Mr. Bakshi. "I just explained—and I thought I made it clear—that the residents of the floating cities can harvest citrus fruit from the islands and drinking water from the ocean."

"Human beings cannot live on pineapples alone," replied Esmeralda. "We have fished the oceans to near-depletion and effectively decimated the global ecosystem on which all forms of life, including humans, depend. We can't get a handle on *any* of these problems, including homelessness, until we address the population crisis."

"Amen!" Sarah exclaimed.

"Once again," said Mr. Bakshi, "the robot has mischaracterized my explanation."

"Please let Ms. Esmeralda finish her point," said the moderator.

"We are at the breaking point," continued Esmeralda. "If we don't act decisively, we will soon be beyond the point of no return— the Earth will no longer be a viable home for our children and grandchildren."

"Since you are taking us down this path, Ms. Esmeralda," said the moderator, "please tell us precisely how the Green Party proposes to address the population crisis."

Mr. Smiley leaned into his mike with a smirk on his face. "Maybe she should try to persuade all the men in the world to marry robots like her husband did."

Many in the audience laughed loudly.

"What a jackass!" exclaimed Geraldine.

Mr. Lewis turned around and looked at the audience. "I must ask the audience to remain quiet during the debate. Please show the candidates a little respect."

"One size doesn't fit all," replied Esmeralda. "What works for Thomas might not work for everyone. In any case, we intend to implement a *birth lottery*, which will determine—without bias of any kind—which couples will be allowed to have children."

Several people in the audience booed. Thomas whispered to Sarah, "I don't know if she should have mentioned that—I fear it will cost us votes."

"Is that it, Ms. Esmeralda?" asked the moderator. "Do you have anything to add?"

"I realize that human beings love their children," replied Esmeralda. "This will be bitter medicine. It's too bad nobody addressed this issue five hundred years ago."

"A birth lottery would be unconstitutional!" exclaimed Mr. Smiley.

"The Supreme Court would shoot it down in a minute," added Mr. Bakshi.

"The justices on the Supreme Court have children and grandchildren, too," replied Esmeralda. "They must be just as worried about this as everyone else."

"The justices may have children and grandchildren," said Mr. Bakshi, "but they aren't going to uphold a policy that is unconstitutional."

"The Republican Party is opposed to any form of birth control," added Mr. Smiley. "Human beings were destined to populate the Earth. It is part of God's mysterious plan."

"Is it also part of God's mysterious plan," replied Esmeralda, "that fifty thousand people starve to death *every day* because the planet can't produce enough food to feed them?"

"Don't blame God because we aren't smart enough to develop synthetic food," replied Mr. Smiley. "NASA did it centuries ago when they first sent men into outer space. Our scientists need to get busy and develop more synthetic foods."

Mr. Bakshi leaned into his mike. "We can also cut down what remains of the forests in North America and Europe, along with the remainder of the Amazon Rain Forest, and convert the land to productive farmland. That would help."

Geraldine leaned towards Thomas. "When I said this guy was as dumb as a box of rocks, I was giving him too much credit."

"Since we are discussing the human population," said Mr. Smiley, "maybe we should discuss the *robot* population, too. Exactly how many robots do we have on the planet and how many more do we need? Maybe we already have too many."

Mr. Bakshi saw his opportunity. "We already have *one* too many—I can tell you that for sure!"

Republicans and Democrats in the audience laughed loudly, and many of them applauded.

Geraldine sat forward. "What a son-of-a-bitch!"

Mr. Lewis turned to the audience again and looked directly at Geraldine. "I must insist that the audience remain silent! Please!"

"I'd be pleased to respond to my opponent's question," said Esmeralda. "The robot population is a fraction of the human population and statistically insignificant. Moreover, the carbon footprint of a robot is negligible compared to that of a human being. Frankly, your point is frivolous and not worthy of further discussion."

"This is an interesting conversation," said Mr. Lewis, "but we need to move on and cover some other topics. Mr. Smiley, as you know, the Nation is in the seventh year of a recession. What is the Republican Party's plan to turn the economy around?"

"That's simple," replied Mr. Smiley. "We just need to eliminate needless regulations. Small businesses can't make a profit when they have to spend half their time filing government reports and try-ing to avoid the IRS's numerous catch-22's. When we take office, we will put the brakes on the Internal Revenue Service, the Environ-mental Protection Agency, the Department of Labor, and all of the other bureaucratic agencies that are to blame for this mess."

"Regulations are often needed," interjected Esmeralda, "but sometimes we can accomplish the same thing by giving companies incentives to do the right thing—tax incentives, for example."

"She's living in a fantasy world," said Mr. Smiley.

"The government can also be an effective advocate for small business," continued Esmeralda. "Look at the Small Business Ad-ministration. Moreover, under the Green Party's platform, we will use government spending to stimulate economic growth."

"Aha, *Government spending!*" exclaimed Mr. Smiley. "The truth comes out—the Green Party is no different from the Demo-crats; they both want to increase the national debt!"

Mr. Bakshi leaned into his mike. "The robot isn't the only one here who has studied economics. Reducing the population will mean fewer consumers, which will weaken the demand curve. That will cause prices to fall, and that in turn will cause corporate profits to fall, which will translate to lower wages and less personal income. To put it in layman's terms, the Green Party's economic strategy is going to make everyone poor."

"I think you have missed a couple of key points," replied Es-meralda. "First, if prices fall, people's disposable income will go further, so they won't be poorer even if their wages fall; and second, we plan to use the multiplier effect of government spending to offset the decline in consumer spending."

"Can you explain what you mean by the multiplier effect?" asked the moderator.

"Excellent question, Mr. Lewis," replied Esmeralda. "In this context, it refers to dollars flowing down to subcontractors. For example, if the Department of Defense issues a contract to General Google Motors—let's say, for ten billion dollars—General Google Motors will do some of the work in-house with its own employees and subcontract the rest of it to other companies, both large and small businesses. These subcontractors will do the same thing: they will do some of the work in-house and subcontract the remainder. This process can continue through several tiers of subcontractors. By the time the contract is completed, the dollars in subcontracts can often exceed the value of the initial prime contract, which in this example was ten billion dollars."

"That sounds to me like double-counting," said Mr. Smiley. "It's another case of fake economics."

"It's not double-counting," replied Esmeralda, "because we're not counting any subcontract more than once. These are real dollars going to many different subcontractors."

"She doesn't know what she's talking about," said Mr. Bakshi.

"Even five-percent unemployment," Esmeralda continued, "which my opponents may consider a good target, is unacceptable to the Green Party. If there is but one person in America who wants to work and can't find a job, then we have failed."

"What does she think this is, *Heaven*?" asked Mr. Bakshi.

"The robot's views on the economy smell of Communism if you ask me," said Mr. Smiley. "I don't think she believes in Capitalism."

"While we're on the subject of the economy," said the moderator, "I'd like each of you to address the dearth of high-paying manufacturing jobs, which once provided the middle class with financial stability. Where did the manufacturing jobs go, and how would you bring them back? Mr. Smiley, please go first."

"As I said," replied Mr. Smiley, "unnecessary regulations are the heart of the problem. One of the unintended consequences of regulations is that they force manufacturing jobs overseas. Companies that once manufactured their products in the United States now outsource the function to foreign companies or their affiliates in Asia and Africa."

"Thank you, Mr. Smiley," said the moderator. "Mr. Bakshi, your turn."

"To the contrary," began Mr. Bakshi. "Regulations are the *solution*, not the *cause* of the problem. We need to impose strict rules on outsourcing, especially on outsourcing overseas. If companies know they are going to face stiff fines and penalties, they will stop doing it and bring the jobs back to the states."

"Thank you, Mr. Bakshi," said the moderator. "Ms. Esmeralda, your turn."

"My opponents are both oversimplifying the problem," began Esmeralda. "It not just about regulations or the lack of them; rather, it is an inevitable consequence of modernization and robotic technology. Robots now do more than ninety-nine percent of all manufacturing, and that's not going to change. We have also lost millions of highway construction jobs due to the demise of the automobile. We can't turn back the clock, and we wouldn't want to."

"The robot is the one who is oversimplifying the problem," interjected Mr. Smiley.

"Please, gentlemen," said the moderator, "let Ms. Esmeralda finish her answer."

"Robot workers are more efficient than human workers," Esmeralda continued. "They don't need coffee breaks; they don't pause to talk about Monday night's football game; and they don't strike to demand higher wages. Let's forget about bringing back the highway construction and manufacturing jobs and find other roles for human workers—jobs in banking and finance, medical research, health care, mental health care, and so on."

"Thank you," said Mr. Lewis. "Now let's move on. I believe Ms. Escobar has a question."

Ms. Escobar straightened in her chair. "Mr. Smiley, earlier in the debate, you talked about the UFO's and said that they originate from Venus. How do you know they come from Venus?"

"By the process of elimination," replied Mr. Smiley. "We've been to Mars, and there's no aliens there. Venus is the only other place they could be coming from. Any other planet is either too hot, too cold, or too far away."

Esmeralda leaned into her mike. "No one has ever proved conclusively that the UFO's are coming from Venus."

"Once again, the robot is showing its ignorance," replied Mr. Smiley. "She has obviously never studied astronomy."

"I have read more than one hundred books on astronomy," replied Esmeralda. "The surface temperature of Venus is 872 degrees Fahrenheit or 467 degrees Celsius—far too hot to support any form of life, at least life as we know it on Earth. Also, for the record, the distance from Earth to Venus can vary from 41 million kilometers to 261 kilometers, depending upon the position of each planet in its orbit."

"That's good to know," said Mr. Lewis, "but let's give Mr. Smiley more time to explain his plan for a defensive shield and what I believe he referred to as an *offensive*."

"Thank you," said Mr. Smiley. "I've already mentioned a defensive space shield surrounding the Earth. That's a no-brainer, but remember that the best defense is always a good offense. Venus is covered in dense clouds, so we don't know exactly where the aliens live; therefore, if we launch a pre-emptive strike, we would need to attack the planet in multiple locations. The last thing we need is a long, drawn-out war with Venus. If we strike, we will have to do it decisively. Ten thousand nuclear warheads striking Venus from every angle would do the job nicely. By the time the last warhead exploded, there wouldn't be so much as an insect left on the planet."

"By all means," said Esmeralda, "kill them first; and then, after they're dead, determine if they were friendly or hostile. That's human logic for you."

"Voters," said Mr. Smiley, "please make a note of that! The robot just insulted you! In fact, she just insulted every human being on the planet ... and every human being on Mars, too!"

"Uh-oh," said Jacqueline. "I fear that Esmeralda may have committed a faux pas. It may come back to haunt her."

"I apologize if anyone took my remark the wrong way," replied Esmeralda, "but we should be sure the aliens are hostile before we spend money on ten thousand nuclear warheads."

"We already have them in our arsenal," replied Mr. Smiley. "It won't cost us a penny."

"We have known about UFO's for more than five hundred years," continued Esmeralda, "since the twentieth century or earlier. They have never bothered us except, on rare occasions, to disrupt our electrical grid. If they were going to attack us, they would have done it by now."

"Young lady," said Mr. Smiley, "perhaps I should say, 'young robot,' you're showing us just how naïve you are. You sound just like the Prime Minister of England the day before Hitler's army marched into Poland. But forgive me, I'm sure you never studied history."

"Actually, I've read more than one hundred books on history," replied Esmeralda. "I believe you are referring to Arthur Neville Chamberlain, the Prime Minister of the United Kingdom from 1937 to 1940, who signed the disastrous Munich Agreement in 1938. For the record, Hitler's army marched into Poland on September 1, 1939."

Mr. Smiley's expression changed as if someone had just hit him in the face with a pie.

"I believe Ms. Diamond has another question," said the moderator.

Ms. Diamond leaned into her mike. "Mr. Bakshi, many of us are concerned about climate change. If you are elected, what would you do about it?"

"Centuries ago," said Mr. Bakshi, "our scientists solved the energy crisis by harnessing power from the wind and the sun. If we give them the money, I'm confident our scientists can also reverse climate change. Our scientists just need more funding, that's all."

"Climate change is nothing more than fake news," said Mr. Smiley. "Once again, the Democrats are looking for ways to spend the taxpayers' money. The Republicans won't waste money on such dubious activities."

"Unlike the Republicans," replied Esmeralda, "the Greens believe in climate change; and unlike the Democrats, we don't believe science alone can overcome the forces of nature. Instead, we will seek more renewable sources of energy, encourage vegetarianism, make recycling mandatory, and adopt other common-sense measures to reduce humans' carbon footprint."

"Like I said," interjected Mr. Smiley, "the Democrats and Greens are just looking for ways to spend the taxpayers' money."

"Getting a handle on climate change, of course," Esmeralda continued, "begins with population control. The birth lottery is the cornerstone of the Green Party's strategy to save the planet Earth—indeed, it is the cornerstone of our strategy to save the human species."

"Thank you, Ms. Esmeralda," said the moderator. "All right, we are running out of time, so let's go to each of the candidates for their closing statement. Ms. Esmeralda, please go first."

"Thank you, Mr. Lewis," Esmeralda began, "and thank you, my fellow Americans, for taking the time to listen to tonight's debate. I think the voters can see that the solutions offered by my opponents won't solve any of our problems. The Green Party's platform, on the other hand, contains tangible, realistic solutions. Now, in the interest of time, I will close by singing the Buddhist *Transfer of Merit*, sometimes called *Buddha's light verse*."

"Thomas, what the hell is she doing?" said Geraldine.

"I don't know," replied Thomas. "This is new to me."

Esmeralda leaned into her mike and sang, *"May kindness, compassion, joy, and equanimity pervade all worlds; may we cherish and build affinities to benefit all beings; may Chan, Pure Land, and Precepts inspire equality and patience; may our humility and gratitude give rise to great vows."*

"Uh-oh," said Jacqueline. "I fear that may be another faux pas."

Geraldine turned to Thomas. "Didn't you tell her how to make a proper closing statement?"

"I don't control her like you think I do," replied Thomas. "She has a mind of her own."

"That scares me," replied Geraldine.

"It scares me, too," said Thomas.

"Thank you, Ms. Esmeralda," said the moderator. "Now, Mr. Smiley, your turn."

"What in the name of hell was *that*?" replied Mr. Smiley. "Is the robot pretending to be religious? That has to be the best joke of the day!"

"I beg your pardon," said Esmeralda. "Do you think I made a joke?"

"Please, Ms. Esmeralda," said the moderator. "You had your turn. Now let's hear Mr. Smiley's closing statement."

"I apologize, Mr. Lewis," replied Esmeralda, "but I believe I'm entitled to respond to what I consider a personal attack on my character. I respectfully ask your indulgence while I ask Mr. Smiley to clarify his remark."

"Very well," Mr. Lewis replied. "Mr. Smiley, would you please tell Ms. Esmeralda why you consider her religious beliefs to be a joke?"

"Since when can robots go to Heaven?" replied Mr. Smiley. "If that's not a joke, what do you call it?"

"With all due respect, Sir," replied Esmeralda, "I never said I could go to Heaven. Religion is not just about going to Heaven or the Pure Land. It is also about creating a Pure Land here on Earth—a world without crime, terrorism, genocide, or war and one without prisons and torture; a world without hunger and one in which housing, health care, and education are affordable; a world without substance abuse and addictions; a world where wealth is based on productivity, not on inheritance or position; a world where any person who wants to work can do so and be paid a living wage; a world where we use our intellectual resources not to design and build more weapons but to cure diseases and improve the human condition; a world free of bullying and sexual harassment, one where every human being treats every other human being with dignity and respect; and a world in which our planet remains stable and healthy—in short, a world without suffering."

"What a great answer, Mom!" exclaimed Sarah. "You knocked it out of the park!"

Someone else in the audience shouted, "Amen!"

Jacqueline nudged Thomas. "I hope this doesn't backfire. Most Americans aren't Buddhists and may not get it."

Esmeralda leaned back into her mike. "And I could use the same statement to sum up the Green Party's 2520 Platform. That's all I have to say. Thank you, Mr. Lewis, for the additional time."

Several hundred people in the audience, mainly Greens, stood up and applauded enthusiastically. Someone shouted, "Esmeralda for President in 2528!"

"Well, I'm glad this came up," said Mr. Smiley, "because now the American people can see for themselves just how ridiculous this robot's candidacy is. She clearly doesn't understand the separation of church and state. Heaven help us all if she ever gets into the White House!"

Thousands of people in the audience, undoubtedly Republicans and Democrats, stood up and cheered. Mr. Lewis turned to the audience. "Please remain quiet until the three candidates have all completed their closing statements!"

Mr. Lewis turned back to the candidates. "Mr. Smiley, please continue and finish your closing statement. You have forty-five seconds left."

Mr. Smiley looked directly into the video camera suspended above him. "Thank you, my fellow Americans, for tuning into tonight's debate. In this election, you are looking for responsible leadership, not dubious ways for the government to spend your hard-earned dollars. Republicans will always spend your money wisely. Finally, I want to point out that neither of my opponents has told you what they are going to do about the aliens from Venus. We will keep Americans safe—that's our promise. Thank you again. I look forward to speaking to you in January from my new office in the White House."

"Thank you, Mr. Smiley," said Mr. Lewis. "Mr. Bakshi, your turn."

Mr. Bakshi first looked at Esmeralda, then turned to the camera. "I'm appalled that the robot is promoting a religion other than Christianity, which is the only religion condoned by our founding fathers. George Washington or Ronald Reagan must be turning over in his grave right now."

"George Washington or Ronald Reagan?" asked the moderator.

"Yes, George Washington or Ronald Reagan. One of them was a founding father. Forgive me, at the moment, I forget which one."

"I believe you are referring to George Washington," said Esmeralda. "Ronald Reagan was our 40th President, so he obviously wasn't a founding father."

"Thank you for the clarification," said Mr. Bakshi, "but I don't need a history lesson."

"Actually, I think you do," replied Esmeralda.

"Touché!" exclaimed Sarah.

"Ms. Esmeralda," said the moderator, "please allow Mr. Bakshi to finish his closing statement."

"Thank you, Mr. Lewis," said Mr. Bakshi. "It should be clear to the viewers that the 2520 Democratic platform represents the only hope for America. The Republican platform is more concerned with defending us from aliens in outer space than housing the homeless, and the robot doesn't even understand the separation of church and state."

Someone in the audience, no doubt a Democrat, shouted, "Amen!"

"One more thing," continued Mr. Bakshi, "don't be overly impressed with the robot's memory. She may razzle-dazzle you with useless facts like the temperature of Venus, but she doesn't have the imagination to visualize creative solutions to our problems—solutions such as floating cities in the ocean."

Thousands of people in the audience, presumably Democrats, stood up and cheered. Someone shouted, "No robots in the White House!"

The moderator turned to the audience. "Please, we're almost done. Please hold your applause for a few more seconds." He turned back to the candidates. "Mr. Bakshi, please finish your closing statement."

"As I explained earlier," said Mr. Bakshi, "the Democratic platform addresses the housing crisis with real solutions. Besides floating cities, we will transform our obsolete interstate highway system and decaying national parks into functional land for low-income housing. I'm confident the voters will realize, especially after tonight's debate, that the Democratic platform contains the only forward-thinking ideas that make sense for America at this critical moment in history."

"Thank you, Mr. Bakshi," said the moderator, "and thank you, all of the candidates, for your participation this evening; and thank you, Ms. Diamond and Ms. Escobar, for assisting me with the questions. Thank you again to the League of Women Voters for sponsoring the debate. Be sure to stay tuned for MSNBC's post-debate analysis, featuring the network's top political analysts, which will begin right now. For those of you in the audience, thank you for coming, and have a good evening."

Mr. Lewis and the two other panelists stood and walked over to shake hands with the three candidates. Thomas and the other members of the family, along with Memengwaa and the families of the other candidates, also stood and walked to the stage to greet their loved ones.

Memengwaa was the first to reach Esmeralda and offer her congratulations. "Esmeralda, you killed it! I'm so proud of you!"

Jacqueline, right behind Memengwaa, spoke next. "Congratulations, Sister! You made those guys look like idiots!"

Sarah, following her Aunt Jacqueline, hugged Esmeralda. "Great job! I'm so proud of you, Mom!"

Thomas, behind Jacqueline, hugged Esmeralda. "Good job, sweetheart!"

Geraldine, following Thomas, gave Esmeralda a high-five. "You weren't perfect, honey, but I give you credit for making your opponents look like fools."

"Are we going out for a drink to celebrate?" asked Memengwaa.

"Susan told me to hang around for a few minutes," replied Esmeralda. "The press may want to interview me."

"The press can be nasty," said Memengwaa. "It might be better to make a discreet exit."

"Rubbish!" said Jacqueline. "Esmeralda can handle the press just like she did her opponents. Go for it, Esmeralda!"

Suddenly Susan appeared on the stage, walking towards Esmeralda. "You made us proud, Esmeralda!" She hugged her friend and continued, "I just spoke to Hector. He watched from home. He said you made those two guys look like morons."

"It wasn't hard," Esmeralda replied. "They made themselves look like morons."

Everyone laughed.

"She's right about that!" said Geraldine.

"Anyway, all six networks are waiting to interview you," continued Susan. "I've set up a room for them to talk to the candidates. It won't take long—maybe five minutes or so with each network. Are you okay with that?"

"Sure," replied Esmeralda. "Let's do it."

"Okay, then," said Susan. "Follow me."

Esmeralda turned to Memengwaa and the family. "I'll catch up with you in a bit." She followed Susan off the stage.

"It looks like we've got some time to kill," said Thomas. "I saw some chairs in the lobby. Let's go back there and wait for Esmeralda."

The family worked their way through the crowd back to the lobby and circled around until they saw some empty seats on a bench.

"Mom, you can sit there," said Thomas. "Jacqueline and Memengwaa, it looks like there's room for you, too. Sarah and I can stand."

Geraldine, Jacqueline, and Memengwaa sat down, and Thomas and Sarah stood beside them. The five talked about the debate's high points, and Jacqueline asked Memengwaa if she was concerned about Esmeralda's two apparent faux pas.

"If you mean her reference to Buddhism," Memengwaa replied, "I don't think it will hurt her. This country was founded on the basis of religious freedom."

"But what about her sarcastic comment, 'That's human logic for you'?" asked Geraldine. "That was a dumb thing to say."

"I agree, that wasn't her best moment," Memengwaa replied. "We'll find out soon enough if there's any fallout from it."

The family continued to discuss the debate while they waited for Esmeralda, who finished her last interview some thirty minutes later and called Thomas on her iPalm.

Thomas opened his iPalm. "We're in the lobby," he said.

Esmeralda reappeared soon afterwards, a smile on her face.

"How did it go?" asked Thomas.

"A piece of cake," Esmeralda replied. "All of the networks except Fox News think I won the debate."

"What did Fox News say?" asked Memengwaa.

"They wanted to know why I insulted human beings with my remark about human logic."

"How did you answer?" asked Jacqueline.

"I said, 'Sorry, but the truth is humans like to kill first, then ask questions. If it weren't true, I wouldn't have said it.'"

"Wow!" exclaimed Sarah. "I don't think we've ever had a politician in this country who tells the truth like that."

"What about me?" asked Jacqueline. "You don't think I tell the truth?"

"Sorry, Aunt Jacqueline," replied Sarah. "No offense intended."

"Enough of this," said Thomas. "Let's head over to that pub Sarah told us about."

Thomas turned to the door, and Memengwaa and the family followed him out to the street, where Sarah, who knew her way around the town, took the lead and headed towards the Cambridge Queen's Head to celebrate Esmeralda's successful debate.

Chapter 9
The Election of 2520

After enjoying a few drinks at the Cambridge Queen's Head, the family, accompanied by Memengwaa, took a taxi a short distance to The Charles Hotel on Bennett Street where they had checked their bags when they arrived earlier in the day. The hotel was comfortable, and everyone slept well. They arose at 7:00 a.m., enjoyed breakfast at the hotel, and took rapid transit to Boston's South Station where they boarded Google-Amtrak's train 1745. The train left South Station at 10:00 a.m. and arrived at Washington's Union Station at 10:58 a.m. There the group walked to the parking lot and said their goodbyes. Thomas, Esmeralda, and Sarah walked to Thomas's aeromobile; Jacqueline and Geraldine walked to Jacqueline's vehicle; and Memengwaa walked to her nearby townhouse.

When Geraldine arrived home, she washed her hands and face, unpacked her luggage, and went to the kitchen to summon her digital assistant.

"Richard," said Geraldine, "please give me my morning update."

The north wall of Geraldine's kitchen lit up, and Richard appeared. "Good morning, Ms. Jenkins. I understand that you would like your morning update, is that correct?"

"You got it."

"Very well, here you go: no phone calls, no messages. The media coverage this morning mentioned your daughter-in-law; indeed, every network talked about her extensively."

"Play it back for me, please."

"Which network would you like to see?"

"Fox News."

"Of course, Ms. Jenkins. Give me just a moment, please."

Richard disappeared, and the monitor displayed a group of five people, two men and three women, sitting at a glass table, each holding a coffee mug with the words *Fox News* in large, red lettering.

"Good morning, viewers," said a young, well-dressed woman sitting in the middle of the group. "My name is Lorretta Higgins, and welcome to the *Fox News Morning Show!*"

Geraldine walked to the refrigerator and placed a coffee mug in a port in the door. "I'll take my coffee full-strength with hazelnut-flavored Coffeemate and one packet of Stevia." The refrigerator made some noise and began dispensing her coffee.

"I'm joined by Ricky O'Neill and Lynn Gonzales on my left and Olivia Armstrong and Ricardo Lopez on my right," continued Ms. Higgins. All of the participants at the table smiled pleasantly at the camera.

Geraldine took her coffee and walked back to the kitchen table where she sat down in a chair facing the wall monitor.

"We have a lot to talk about this morning, so I'm going to skip our usual pleasantries and get right to the morning's hot topic, which is last night's Vice-Presidential debate. I understand the debate had the largest audience in media history—100 billion by some estimates."

"I think people watched it out of curiosity," said Olivia. "They just wanted to see a robot debate human beings."

"That's the only explanation," said Lynn. "We don't even have 100 billion people who are interested in politics."

"So, then," said Loretta, "what did you all think of the robot's performance?"

"Good morning, Loretta," said Ricky, as if he hadn't already said good morning to the show's host before the show began. "To begin with, they shouldn't have allowed a robot into the debate. She isn't a viable candidate—no one has any interest in the Green Party candidates anyway."

"The League of Women Voters is to blame," said Olivia. "I hear that Susan Lopez, the president of the league, is a personal friend of the robot."

"That's awful," said Ricardo. "Since when do you allow someone into a Vice-Presidential debate based on who they know—especially when they don't even represent a major political party?"

"And especially when they are a robot," added Olivia.

Everyone at the table laughed.

"I think we all agree the robot shouldn't have been allowed in the debate," said Lorretta, "but since she was, we have to talk about it. How do you think she did?"

"She was rude," said Ricky. "She insulted her opponents every chance she had."

"They had it coming to them," said Geraldine. "Both of them were imbeciles!"

Richard reappeared on the monitor. "Ms. Jenkins, you aren't in interactive mode. Do you want me to switch you to interactive mode so that the people can hear you?"

"No," replied Geraldine. "It's better if they can't hear me."

Richard disappeared.

"What did you think about her proposal for a birth lottery?" asked Loretta.

"We didn't hear anything about that from her running mate during the Presidential debate," said Lynn. "I wonder if she just made it up."

"It might be part of the Green Party's platform," said Olivia. "No one has bothered to read it because the Green Party really isn't a factor in this election anyway."

"Understood," said Loretta, "but I'd still like to know what you think of it. Is it a legitimate solution to the population crisis?"

"I can't believe she called it a population crisis," said Ricardo. "There's no crisis."

Geraldine set her coffee cup on the table. "You're a nincompoop, Mister!"

"Well, for purposes of discussion," said Loretta, "let's say there is. Let's say we really do have too many people on the planet. First, do you think a birth lottery would work; and second, do you think it would be constitutional?"

"The answer to both questions is a resounding *no*," said Ricardo. "It wouldn't work, and it wouldn't survive a constitutional challenge."

"I wasn't so concerned about the birth lottery," said Olivia. "Congress would never go along with that anyway. What troubled me more was the robot's condescending attitude towards her opponents. As Ricky just said, she insulted them at every turn."

"Her remark that it's just like a human to kill first and then determine if the enemy is friendly or hostile is a case in point," said Ricky.

"*Of course* we have to kill them first," said Lynn. "What a ridiculous statement!"

"I also didn't like her remark that her opponents had their heads in the sand," said Olivia. "She had no civility whatsoever."

"What about her so-called *Transfer of Merit*," asked Loretta. "Do you think she understands the separation of church and state?"

"Obviously not," said Ricky. "I still can't believe that Senator Hoffenberger picked her to be his running mate. It's just unbelievable."

"I fear her performance last night ruined any hope the Green Party may have had of winning the White House," said Loretta.

"They never had a snowball's chance in hell, anyway," said Ricardo.

"Richard," said Geraldine, "I can't take any more of this. Turn it off."

Geraldine's digital assistant appeared in the top right-hand corner of the monitor. "I understand you wish to discontinue the program, Ms. Jenkins, is that correct?"

"You got it."

"Would you like to watch the coverage on another network?"

"No, I have to make lunch now. You can just turn it off—oh, and one more thing, you can drop Fox News from my line-up. I'm not going to watch it anymore. They're a bunch of idiots."

"If I understand correctly, Ms. Jenkins, you don't want to watch a bunch of idiots. Is that right?"

"Exactly, please cancel the Fox News network."

"I'll take care of it, Ms. Jenkins. Is there anything else I can do for you at this time?"

"No, that's it for now."

"Very well, Ms. Jenkins. Enjoy your lunch." Richard disappeared and the wall monitor went dark.

Geraldine finished her coffee, arose from the table, and walked to the refrigerator to see what she could find for lunch.

*   *   *   *   *

When Sarah returned home, she checked her latest polling figures and found that she enjoyed a twelve-point lead over Prabhat Modi, her Democratic opponent. Nonetheless, since it was not her nature to be complacent, she contacted Jacqueline and asked her advice on how best to wrap up her campaign.

"Do the same thing Esmeralda did two years ago," said Jacqueline. "Go to the Fair Oaks Mall and all of the other malls in Fairfax and Arlington Counties. Shake hands with the voters. Remind your supporters to put digital signs on their lawns, if they have lawns, or on the wall of their house or apartment facing the street if they don't. That worked for Esmeralda."

Sarah followed through on Jacqueline's advice with assistance from Thomas, who, following Memengwaa's counsel, was taking a low profile in Esmeralda's campaign. Thomas coordinated Sarah's activities with the Green Party headquarters and accompanied her on all of her outreach activities during the three weeks leading up to Election Day. As the calendar flipped to November, the Apple-Gallop poll showed Sarah with a twelve-point lead and the Microsoft-Reuters poll with an eleven-point lead.

Meanwhile, Senator Hoffenberger had returned from his trip to Australia and New Zealand where he had campaigned extensively for three weeks. Soon after his return, he and Esmeralda conducted a conference call with Memengwaa. "Spend the remaining time between now and Election Day campaigning together," Memengwaa advised. "Both of you aced your debates—now the voters need to see you as a team."

Following Memengwaa's guidance, Senator Hoffenberger and Esmeralda appeared together on NBC's *Today Show*, ABC's *Good Morning America*, *CBS This Morning*, and more than a dozen other media programs during the final days of the campaign. Senator Hoffenberger continued to tout his record in the Senate while Esmeralda touted her accomplishments in the House. They fielded scores of questions related to Esmeralda being a robot and scores more related to the Green Party's platform calling for a birth lottery. At Memengwaa's suggestion, they declined Fox News's invitation; she advised them that the network's right-leaning audience would never vote for a Green candidate anyway. On Election Eve, the aggregate polling numbers showed the Green ticket in a dead heat with the Republicans while the Democrats trailed by six points.

On Monday evening, November 4th, Thomas called his sister to discuss the arrangements for watching the election returns. "Memengwaa has booked three rooms for us tomorrow night at the Crystal City Marriott," he told her, "one room for Esmeralda and me, one for mom and Sarah, and one for you. William has booked a large suite where all of us can watch the returns. We'll go down to the ballroom when they call our first contest, which will probably be Sarah's."

"What time should I be there?" Jacqueline asked.

"Memengwaa has made reservations at the Federico Ristorante Italiano restaurant near the hotel. We are supposed to meet her there at six. You might want to check your bags at the hotel on your way to the restaurant."

"Will Sam be there?

"Yes."

"How about mom? I wonder if Memengwaa remembered to make reservations for mom."

"Of course she did," said Thomas. "Who could forget mom?"

*   *   *   *   *

On the morning of Election Day, Thomas, Esmeralda, and Sarah cast their votes at Fairhill Elementary School in Fairfax, while Geraldine and Jacqueline voted in Fair Oaks Mall. Thomas, Esmeralda, and Sarah remained at their polling station for several more hours so that Esmeralda and Sarah could greet the voters as they arrived. After voting, Jacqueline, who was running unopposed for her seat in Virginia's 11th Congressional District, took her mother home and returned to her own apartment to relax for a few hours before dinner.

At five p.m., Thomas, Esmeralda, and Sarah walked from their apartment to the East Falls Church metro station and took a train to Crystal City, changing from the Orange Line to the Blue Line in Rosslyn. When they arrived in Crystal City, they exited the train and followed the underground walkway to the Marriott parking garage, where they took an elevator to the lobby and checked in; then they walked out to the street and down to the Federico Ristorante Italiano on 23rd Street. Jacqueline and Geraldine had already arrived and were visiting with Memengwaa, Senator Hoffenberger, and the senator's wife in the restaurant's vestibule while they waited to be seated. After greeting each other, the new arrivals found seats beside the others.

"They are offering an Election Day special," said Geraldine, who was reading a menu while the others talked. "Eggplant Parmigiana with Fettuccine Alfredo."

Sarah looked over her grandmother's shoulder to see the menu. "That looks like a winner."

The hostess appeared. "A party of eight?"

"That's correct," said Thomas. "Everyone is here."

"How is everyone doing this evening?" asked the hostess, picking up eight menus. "Please follow me."

Everyone arose and followed the hostess, who passed out the menus when they reached their table. "Your waiter will be with you in just a moment."

Memengwaa looked at the menu briefly and said, "I think I'll order the Election Day special."

"Same here," said Sarah.

"This may be a long night," said Memengwaa. "The polls are showing a really tight race."

"Except for Sarah's race," said Esmeralda. "Sarah's contest could be declared early."

Everyone looked at Sarah, who was smiling. "It's a little too early to declare victory," said Sarah, "but it's looking good."

"If they don't call our race before midnight," said Senator Hoffenberger, "I may need a nap. At my age, I'm not accustomed to staying up all night long."

"You might want to take a nap after dinner," said Memengwaa. "The early returns don't mean much anyway."

A waiter arrived at their table. "Good evening. My name is Donald, and I will be your waiter this evening. What would you like to drink?"

Everyone except Esmeralda ordered a drink, and Donald disappeared.

"Watch the battleground states," said Thomas, "especially California, Mexico, New Mexico, and Canada."

"The battleground states aren't as important as they were when we had the winner-take-all rule," said Jacqueline. "They don't control the outcome of the election like they did in the old days."

"Why not?" asked Geraldine.

"In the old days," said Sarah, "if a candidate won the popular vote in a given state, they received all of that state's electoral votes, no matter how close the popular vote may have been."

"Except for Nebraska and Maine," said Jacqueline. "They adopted a form of proportional representation more than five hundred years ago."

"Now all of the states have proportional representation," said Sarah. "It's not perfect, but it's better than winner-take-all."

"Be that as it may," said Memengwaa, "there are a lot of unknowns this time around. For one thing, no one knows how the absentee ballots from Mars are going to play out."

"Only if the race is within a million votes," said Sarah. "There's only one million registered voters on Mars."

The waiter arrived with the drinks and took the dinner orders.

"I'm still working on my victory speech," said Senator Hoffenberger. "I know what I want to say, but I want to be sure I strike the right tone."

"Just stick to the Green Party's platform, Sam," suggested Memengwaa. "Remind the American people what we stand for."

"And be careful not to promise the moon," said Jacqueline. "Whatever you say tonight could come back to haunt you four years from now."

Esmeralda looked at Sarah. "Sarah, dear, have you decided what you're going to say when they call your race?"

Sarah smiled. "I'll wing it. Spontaneity always works better for me."

The family and Memengwaa continued to give Senator Hoffenberger suggestions on how best to deliver his victory speech; then, when the waiter delivered their dinner plates, the conversation subsided as everyone except Esmeralda enjoyed their meal. Esmeralda watched the others while they ate. At 7:30 p.m., they finished dinner and returned to the hotel.

*   *   *   *   *

William was waiting for them when they arrived at the Marriott. "How was dinner?" he asked.

"Wonderful," said Sarah. "It's hard to get good Italian food in San Antonio."

"It was okay for an American version of Italian," said Geraldine. "Not quite like Italy."

"Mom, you haven't been to Italy in forty years," said Jacqueline. "How would you know?"

Geraldine frowned. "Trust me, I know."

"I'm glad you enjoyed your meal," replied William. "Isabelle is waiting for us upstairs. We have a big TV and a nice set-up to watch the results." He motioned the group to follow him.

When they arrived at William's suite, they were greeted by his wife, Isabelle, who opened the door and escorted them into the room. Everyone made themselves comfortable in ten armchairs arranged in a semi-circle in front of a wall-to-wall, floor-to-ceiling TV. Isabelle had already split the screen to show the six major networks with the sound on NBC.

"Why don't we let William handle the remote?" suggested Isabelle, handing her husband the remote control. "I had them bring both hot coffee and cold drinks," she added, pointing to a table against the north wall. "You can help yourself to whatever you'd like."

"We also have champagne on ice when it's time to celebrate," added William.

"William is so efficient," said Memengwaa. "I hope he gets my job someday—I mean, like when I retire."

"He'd be perfect," echoed Jacqueline. "The Green Party is lucky to have him."

"Compliments will get you nowhere," said William. "Anyway, let's turn the sound up and see what's going on downstairs." He touched the volume button on the remote.

Everyone turned to the TV, where Mark Thompson, NBC's political analyst, was speaking. "It is now Wednesday in Australia and New Zealand, and we have the results: the Green ticket has won both states by a wide margin."

"Hooray!" exclaimed Sarah.

Senator Hoffenberger sat forward in his chair, speaking excitedly, "Of course we won both of those states! I didn't spend three weeks campaigning there for nothing!"

"If the Green Party pulls this off," continued Mark Thompson, "it will be truly historic. We have never had a Green President, and we have never had a Vice President who is not a human being. I'm referring to Senator Hoffenberger's running mate, of course, Esmeralda Jenkins, who is a robot."

"How do you suppose Senator Hoffenberger and his robot running mate ever got this far?" asked a woman sitting at the table across from Mr. Thompson. "With a robot on the ticket, it's just unbelievable they could actually be in contention to win the election."

"For one thing, Catherine," replied Mark Thompson, "voters don't like the Democratic platform. Our polling reveals that people are more worried about aliens attacking us than they are about finding homes for the homeless."

"That's sad, isn't it?" replied Catherine.

"It is very sad indeed," said another man wearing a bright yellow tie sitting at the table between Mark Thompson and Catherine. "Frankly, the Democrats have gone too far to the left. It's not that people don't want homes for the homeless; they just don't think we need to tear down Yosemite and Yellowstone to do it."

"Say," said Senator Hoffenberger, "that young man with the yellow tie is Henry Jones, my former Chief of Staff. He must have gotten a job with NBC after I retired."

"Rishyasringa Bakshi didn't help his ticket," continued Henry Jones, "when he said, during the Vice-Presidential debate, we should detonate a neutron bomb in Yellowstone and Yosemite."

"I agree," said Catherine. "That turned out to be just a little too extreme for most voters."

"That may explain why the Democratic message isn't resonating with the voters," said another woman sitting to Catherine's left, "but what's going on with the Republicans? They should be blowing the Green Party off the map."

"Well, Jane, I think Mr. Smiley's opposition to repairing the dikes in North and South Carolina is one explanation," said Catherine. "That was a huge misstep."

"If you watched the Vice-Presidential debate," said Jane, "you could see that the robot was smarter than her Democratic and Republican opponents. It was especially obvious that Joe Smiley, the Republican candidate, was no match for the robot."

"No kidding," said Geraldine. "That guy was an idiot."

"Mom," said Jacqueline, "just listen!"

"Well," said Henry Jones, "let's see what's going on right now at the Marriott in Crystal City where the Green Party has gathered to watch the results. Julie Perez is in the Marriott ballroom. Julie, what's the mood like there?"

Julie Perez appeared on the screen surrounded by hundreds of Green Party members wearing their *Make America Small Again* caps.

"Henry, I'm standing in the Potomac ballroom," replied Ms. Perez, raising her voice to talk above the noise in the room, "which holds four hundred people, and it is packed elbow-to-elbow. The excitement here is unreal—the mood can only be described as euphoric. The exit polls show the Presidential race is too close to call, but don't tell that to anyone in this room. Everyone here expects victory, and they are ready to celebrate!"

"I hope they realize we may have to wait six weeks or more for the absentee ballots from Mars," replied Henry Jones. "That is, if the race is as close as they say it will be."

"No one here seems to be thinking about that," replied Ms. Perez. "They expect the networks to declare the winner tonight."

"We'll see about that," replied Henry. "Thanks very much, Julie. We'll get back to you later."

Julie Perez disappeared, and the NBC box on the TV screen displayed the NBC table with the four political commentators.

William stood up and muted the sound. "Let's take a short break and give everyone a chance to get some coffee. There's soda and ice for anyone who'd prefer a cold drink."

"Honey," said Angelica, putting her hand on Senator Hoffenberger's shoulder, "don't you think you should take a nap? You'll need to be well rested to deliver your victory speech."

"Senator Hoffenberger looked at his wife. "Yes, that's a good idea. I just need a quiet room with a bed or a couch."

"Follow me," said William. "There's a bedroom over here."

Senator Hoffenberger arose and followed William out of the room. Everyone else stood up and walked to the refreshment table.

"For ninety years old," said Thomas, "Sam's not doing badly. He just needs his naps."

"Your father never took naps," said Geraldine. "I told him he would live longer if he just slowed down, but he never listened to me."

William returned in a moment. "Sam has a good place to rest. We'll let him sleep for an hour or so—unless they call Sarah's race sooner. He'll want to watch Sarah's speech."

"Sarah and I can go down to the ballroom together when they call her race," said Jacqueline. "The rest of you can stay here with Sam until they call the Presidential race."

Everyone except Senator Hoffenberger returned to their armchairs, coffee or soda in hand, and resumed watching the NBC election coverage.

* * * * *

At 9:30 p.m., Henry Jones sat forward, straightened his yellow tie, and called Jacqueline's race. "NBC is predicting Congresswoman Jacqueline Jenkins, the incumbent and Green Party candidate, to be the winner in Virginia's 11th Congressional District."

Everyone in William's suite stood up, gave each other high-fives, and hugged Jacqueline.

"Are you making a speech?" asked Geraldine.

"Maybe later to thank the volunteers," replied Jacqueline. "I was running unopposed, so my victory is not exactly a surprise."

At 10:45 p.m., Mr. Jones announced the winner in Sarah's race. "NBC is predicting Congresswoman Sarah Jenkins, the incumbent and Green Party candidate, to be the winner in Virginia's 8th Congressional District."

The other members of the Jenkins family along with Memengwaa, William, Isabelle, and Angelica all stood up, gave each other high-fives, and took turns hugging Sarah.

"For any of our viewers who don't know her," said Mark Thompson, "Sarah Jenkins is the adopted daughter of Esmeralda Jenkins. Earlier this year, Governor Hector Lopez of Virginia appointed Sarah to fill her mother's seat when her mother resigned from Congress to join the Green Party's ticket. This is Sarah's first election."

"I understand she is very bright," said Catherine. "She took a leave of absence from her teaching position at the University of Texas to take her mother's seat in the House."

"Are you ready to make your speech, Sarah?" asked Jacqueline.

Sarah turned to Memengwaa. "Shouldn't I wait for my opponents to concede?"

"Nobody does that anymore," said Memengwaa. "You're not expected to wait."

"Okay, then, I guess I'm ready," said Sarah.

"Then go for it!" said Thomas. "Jacqueline will take you down to the ballroom. I will wake Sam. He won't want to miss your speech."

Jacqueline and Sarah arose from their seats.

"Give me a moment," said Sarah. "I probably ought to check my appearance in the mirror." She walked to the bathroom while Jacqueline waited by the door.

"Young people nowadays are so worried about their appearance," said Geraldine.

"To put it in perspective," said Jacqueline, "she's going to have a television audience of ten billion people. Wouldn't *you* check your appearance?"

For once Geraldine didn't have a comeback.

In another moment, Sarah emerged from the bathroom, and she and Jacqueline left for the ballroom. Thomas got up from his seat and walked to Sam's bedroom. After arousing him, the two returned and sat down in their armchairs.

"Do you want some coffee to wake you up?" Angelica asked her husband.

"No, I'm fine," replied Sam. "The short nap was just what I needed." He reclined in the armchair.

"NBC just called Sarah's race," said Isabelle.

"I know," replied Senator Hoffenberger. "Thomas told me."

Thomas unmuted the TV.

"Do we have an update on the Presidential race?" asked Henry Jones.

"Yes, we do," replied Mark Thompson. "The Green ticket has taken the lead in Mexico and Canada."

"It looks like they are also enjoying leads in Iowa, Ohio, California, and New York," said Catherine, looking at a monitor on the wall. "In fact, at the moment, they have a lead in all of the bellwether states."

"Who could have imagined this?" asked Henry Jones. "The Green ticket could actually win this election!"

"Yes!" exclaimed Senator Hoffenberger, excitement in his voice. "I'm glad you got me up from my nap!"

"It's too early for predictions," cautioned Mark Thompson, "and don't forget, if it's close, we'll have to wait six weeks or more for the absentee ballots from Mars."

Henry Jones sat up straight and looked at the camera. "Let me have your attention, please! I understand that Sarah Jenkins is about to make a speech to her supporters at the Marriott Crystal City. Let's go back to Julie Perez."

The panel disappeared and Julie appeared. "Yes, Henry, that's right. Sarah Jenkins is about to make a speech. Let's listen in." NBC's camera refocused on the ballroom stage where Sarah appeared before a podium, Jacqueline standing behind her. The crowd cheered and whistled enthusiastically. Sarah stood quietly for a moment, waiting for the noise to subside, before speaking.

"Thank you, thank you!" Sarah began. "I'm standing before you to declare victory!"

The audience continued to cheer and whistle, and Sarah waited again for the noise to subside. Someone in the audience shouted, "Sarah for President in 2528!"

"This is a monumental day for the Green Party," Sarah continued. "With your support, I have held on to my seat in Virginia's 8th District, and the party is on track to win a record number of seats in the House and the Senate. Of course, the big news tonight is that Senator Hoffenberger and his running mate, Esmeralda—my mom—are giving the Republicans and Democrats a run for their money in the Presidential race! This is truly a new day for America!"

As the crowd responded with more cheers and whistles, Sarah finished her speech. "I think that Aunt Jacqueline—I mean *Congresswoman Jacqueline Jenkins*—wants to speak to you now. Thank you again for your support!" Sarah stepped back and Jacqueline, who was still standing behind her, stepped into the podium.

"Isn't that exciting?" Jacqueline began. "My niece—Congresswoman Sarah Jenkins—has been elected to the House seat in Virginia's 8th District!"

The crowd cheered, more loudly than before.

"As you may have heard," continued Jacqueline, "they declared me the winner in Virginia's 11th District earlier this evening. I couldn't have done it without your support! I can't thank you enough! Thank you, everyone!"

Jacqueline stepped back, and she and Sarah joined hands and waved to the crowd with their other hands. Then they turned and walked off the stage.

"Great speeches!" said Senator Hoffenberger. "Did you hear someone say Sarah should run for President in 2528?"

"She would make a fine President," said William.

"Not so fast," said Esmeralda. "What about me? Don't you think I should run for President in 2528?"

"Don't let this go to your head, Esmeralda," said Thomas. "I'm not going to let you run for President—ever!"

"Let's put that discussion aside for another day," said Memengwaa. "Just listen to the election coverage."

"Memengwaa is right," said Esmeralda. "We can talk about my running for President some other time."

Angelica arose and walked to the coffee table, where she poured a cup of coffee for her husband, and everyone turned their attention back to the TV.

* * * * *

Senator Hoffenberger and Angelica, William and Isabelle, Memengwaa, and the Jenkins family—including Jacqueline and Sarah, who had returned to the suite after their victory speeches—continued to watch the election coverage throughout the evening and well into the following morning. As Sarah had predicted, the Green Party won a record number of seats in the House and Senate. In the Presidential race, Senator Hoffenberger and Esmeralda continued to hold their lead in the bellwether states and widened their leads in Mexico and Canada. By 3:00 a.m., Senator Hoffenberger was sound asleep in his armchair, and the others in the group were staying awake by downing multiple cups of coffee. Finally, on Wednesday morning, November 6th, at 4:15 a.m., NBC called the Presidential race.

"Ladies and gentlemen," said Henry Jones, barely able to conceal his excitement, "NBC is ready to call the Presidential race!"

Angelica, sitting beside her husband, poked him. "Sam, wake up! They are about to call the race!" Senator Hoffenberger opened his eyes and sat up, looking towards the TV.

Henry Jones played with his yellow tie. "We are predicting Senator Sam Hoffenberger and his running mate, Esmeralda Jenkins, to be the winners in the Presidential contest! Yes, you heard me right: For the first time in American history, the Green Party has won the White House!"

Senator Hoffenberger and Esmeralda jumped from their armchairs and gave each other a high-five. "We did it!" exclaimed the Senator. "I'm the next President!"

"And mom is the next Vice President!" cried Sarah, leaping to her feet and hugging Esmeralda.

In another moment, Memengwaa, William, Angelica, Isabelle, Jacqueline, and Geraldine were all on their feet, hugging each other and giving each other high-fives.

"This is historic!" exclaimed Jacqueline. "Now, finally, we have a chance to take back our government!"

"We can clean up the mess left by the Republicans and Democrats!" exclaimed Thomas.

Senator Hoffenberger's iPalm vibrated, and he opened his left hand and held it to his ear. "Yes, Alexander, I just heard the announcement on NBC ... No, I don't think you let your supporters down ... Not at all, you ran a good campaign ... I agree, it was probably a mistake for your running mate to mention the neutron bomb ... Anyway, I appreciate the phone call. We'll be in touch. Maybe I can find you a job in the Department of Commerce—perhaps Assistant Administrator for Administration or something like that. Thank you for the call. Have a good evening."

Senator Hoffenberger turned to Esmeralda. "That was Alexander Smith. He has conceded."

"He should have conceded six months ago," said Geraldine. "What a loser!"

"Shouldn't we wait for the Republicans to concede?" asked Esmeralda.

"You don't need to wait for the Republicans," said Memengwaa. "You might be waiting another ten hours."

"Okay, then," said Senator Hoffenberger. "I'll go down to the ballroom now and make my speech. Esmeralda, you need to accompany me so that we can show our solidarity."

"Sam, let me comb your hair before you go downstairs," said Angelica. "I want you to look your best."

"You better go into the bathroom and splash some cold water on your face," said Memengwaa. "You don't want people to know you've been napping."

"Give me a break," said Senator Hoffenberger. "It's four o'clock in the morning. Don't you think *everyone* has been napping?"

Angelica took her husband's arm and pulled him towards the bathroom, looking back at Memengwaa. "I'll take care of this. Give me two minutes and he will be ready."

In two minutes, as Angelica promised, Senator Hoffenberger emerged from the bathroom looking refreshed and well-combed. "I'm ready to go downstairs," he announced.

"Why don't we stay here and watch Sam's speech on the TV," said William. "It's going to be pandemonium in the ballroom."

"I'll go to the ballroom with Sam and Esmeralda," said Thomas. "Esmeralda, are you ready?"

"Yes, I'm ready."

"I'll go, too," said Angelica. "I need to be with my husband."

"Okay," said William. "The rest of us will stay here. We'll come down to the ballroom after Sam finishes his speech."

Senator Hoffenberger, Angelica, Esmeralda, and Thomas left the room; and everyone else sat back down in their armchairs. The TV coverage had returned to the Crystal City Marriott's Potomac Room, where Julie Perez was trying to speak above the noise.

"Henry, I've never seen so much excitement in my life! The crowd here is absolutely electrified—it's as if they had just won the biggest lottery in the history of the world!"

The screen split, and Henry Jones appeared on the right side, stroking his yellow tie. "Do we know when Senator Hoffenberger is going to deliver his speech?"

"I assume he will appear soon," replied Julie. "It's been a long night, and his supporters are anxious to break out the champagne."

"He'll lose the TV audience if he doesn't show up in the next five minutes or so. I'm sure our viewers at home want to go to bed."

"I hear some commotion near the side entrance," said Julie. "That may indicate the Senator has arrived ... Yes, Senator Hoffenberger has just arrived! He is making his way through the crowd. Stand by!"

Henry Jones looked into the camera. "For anyone at home who may have dozed off or stepped away from their TV, we just declared the Green ticket the winner in the Presidential election. Senator Samuel Hoffenberger is now the President-elect. We have live coverage from the Crystal City Marriott ballroom, where the Senator has just entered the room. He will be making a speech any moment."

"The Senator has reached the steps of the dais," said Julie. "He is walking up the steps as I speak."

The camera angle widened, revealing Senator Hoffenberger ascending the steps to the podium, followed by Angelica, Esmeralda, and Thomas. In a moment, the four stood together on the stage, smiling and waving to the crowd. Senator Hoffenberger walked to the podium and waited for the noise to subside.

"Thank you, everyone, for your support," the Senator began. "I want to thank the Green Party volunteers who worked tirelessly for many months to make this happen. Esmeralda and I are truly indebted to you ... but I want to use my time right now to speak directly to the American people—the billions of Americans who stayed up all night to witness this historic moment."

"Good opening," said Sarah.

"I hope he's not going to be long-winded," said Geraldine. "I don't know about you, but I'm ready for bed."

"We have had gridlock in Washington for too long," continued Senator Hoffenberger. "Our politicians have lost sight of the people's needs. Unemployment and homelessness are at record levels. So tonight the American people have sent a message to the Democrats and Republicans: If they can't get the job done, the people will find another party that can. And tonight the people have done just that—they have found the Green Party!"

The crowd renewed their cheers and whistles.

"I'm not going to make any promises I can't keep," said Senator Hoffenberger. "It took five hundred years to get us into this mess, and it will take at least eight years—two full terms—to turn things around and get the country back on track. But mark my words, we will do it!"

"It may take more than eight years," said Sarah. "We have to dig ourselves out of a deep hole."

"Thank you again," said Senator Hoffenberger, finishing his speech. "Thank you, especially, Green volunteers. Now let's break out the champagne! We have the ballroom until seven o'clock this morning, so please stay and celebrate!"

The sound of music replaced the Senator's voice. He waved to the crowd, stepped away from the podium, and joined Esmeralda, Angelica, and Thomas standing behind him. The four waved to the crowd again before turning and descending the steps of the dais.

"Perfect!" exclaimed William. "This is one of the greatest nights of my life!"

"People are dancing," said Isabelle, pointing to the TV. "Let's go downstairs and join the fun!"

"I'll let you young people do the dancing," said Geraldine. "I'm headed to bed."

Everyone arose from their chairs and left the suite. William, Isabelle, Jacqueline, Sarah, and Memengwaa headed for the ballroom, and Geraldine walked to her room to retire for the night.

Chapter 10

The Inauguration

The victory celebration in the Potomac ballroom continued until 6:00 a.m. Many of the attendees had booked rooms in the hotel for two nights, Tuesday and Wednesday, and returned to their rooms to spend the rest of the morning sleeping; others, who tried to make their reservations at the Crystal City Marriot too late, returned to their rooms in other hotels nearby or went home. By seven o'clock, the ballroom was deserted except for the Marriott's cleaning crew.

Thomas had tired rapidly after Senator Hoffenberger's speech, and he and Esmeralda returned to their room soon after five o'clock. Thomas collapsed on top of the bed and fell asleep in less than a minute. Esmeralda covered him with a blanket and lay down beside him for a few hours to keep him company; but her mind was focused on her new responsibilities as Vice President, so she arose at nine o'clock and sat down at a desk, where she found a Marriott notepad and began making notes: *(1) When can I visit the White House and see my new office? (2) Am I allowed to redecorate it to suit my own taste? (3) When can Thomas and I visit the Vice President's residence and begin planning our move-in? (4) Do we need to redecorate it? (5) Should we terminate the lease on our apartment in Virginia or keep it and let Sarah live there?*

293

and (6) How soon can we move into our new home—the Vice President's residence?

After reviewing her questions, Esmeralda called the front desk for a password; then she logged on to the Internet using a Marriott tablet built into the desk. She searched for *Vice President's residence* and found a web site for Number One Observatory Circle in the District of Columbia. She remembered visiting it during the orientation for freshman members of Congress in December 2518. It was a large, nineteenth-century house on the grounds of the United States Naval Observatory in the northwestern quadrant of the District of Columbia. She copied the URL and forwarded it to her personal email, since she did not yet have an email address as Vice President and wouldn't receive one until after the Inauguration in January. Then she searched for *Vice President's office* and found that the Vice President has two offices, one in the West Wing of the White House and a ceremonial office in the Eisenhower Executive Office Building next to it. She copied this URL as well and forwarded it to her personal email along with the other.

Esmeralda was all too aware of the widely held perception that the Vice President's principal duty is to attend the funerals of foreign leaders, so she pulled up the *U.S. Constitution* and read it again to refresh her memory on the Vice President's actual duties and responsibilities. Under Article I, Section 3, she read that the Vice President serves as president of the Senate and may vote on legislation, when necessary, to break a tie; and under the 12th Amendment, that the Vice President is required to preside over a joint session of Congress to officially count and report the votes of the Electoral College. Esmeralda smiled. *I've got this!*

After finishing her research, Esmeralda went back to the bed and climbed under the blanket next to Thomas, continuing to contemplate her transition to Vice President and the challenges ahead. Around noon, Thomas opened his eyes, bent his left arm and opened his iPalm, and looked at the time. "Oh my goodness, I slept nearly seven hours, and I never even turned on my dream machine."

"You were exhausted," said Esmeralda. "We've never stayed up that late before."

"My God, we won the election, didn't we? You are the Vice President!"

"Technically, I'm the Vice-President *elect*. I don't take office until January 20th."

"Right, I knew that."

"While you were sleeping, I made a list of things we have to do. We have to plan our move to the Vice President's residence. We also have to decide if we are going to terminate the lease on our apartment or keep it and let Sarah live there."

Thomas sat up. "That's a no-brainer—we'll let Sarah live there. We can't live in the Vice President's residence forever. Anyway, I need to use the bathroom. We can talk about this over breakfast."

"Over breakfast?"

"Well, over lunch, whatever. Why don't you contact Sarah and the others and see if they are awake and if they've eaten yet?" Thomas climbed out from under the blanket, stood up, and walked to the bathroom. Esmeralda sat up, opened her iPalm, and sent out a text message: *If you want to join us for lunch, meet us in the Marriott dining room in 15 minutes.*

Over the next two minutes, Esmeralda's iPalm vibrated six times. Angelica responded first: *Sam is still sleeping. We'll catch up with you later.* Sarah responded next: *Aunt J. & I just sat down in the dining room. Look 4 our table near the window.* Geraldine responded: *I hope U didn't let Thomas sleep until noon.* Isabelle responded: *William and I have already checked out. Talk to U later.* Geraldine responded a second time: *I'll meet U there.* Memengwaa responded: *C U in 15.*

Esmeralda heard the sound of the shower in the bathroom and climbed out of bed. She stood up and walked to an armchair, where she sat down and checked her iPalm for the morning's top stories. The news headlines, as expected, were all about the election results. *The Washington Post's* headline read, "Green Party's Hoffenberger Elected President," while *The Washington Times* carried a two-line headline reading, "Hoffenberger and Robot Running-Mate Celebrate Big Victory." *The New York Times* and the *San Francisco Chronicle* announced the election results more succinctly: "Hoffenberger Elected President" and "Green Party Prevails," respectively.

Esmeralda closed her iPalm and found a remote control on a table next to her chair. She turned on the TV, selecting CNN from the main menu, and saw a group of men and women sitting around a table. A young woman in the middle said, "I have no doubt that Hoffenberger will be a good President. I just worry about his age. What if he dies in office?"

An older woman sitting on the other side of the table responded, "I agree. This is a real concern. They say he's in good health, but let's face it: he's ninety years old. God help us if he dies in office and the robot becomes President."

"I don't think the American public would tolerate that," said a young man sitting beside the young woman. "If Hoffenberger were to die in office, we would have to bypass the Vice President and appoint the Speaker of the House to be President."

"But how would we do that?" asked an older man at the table. "The Presidential Succession Act of 1947 says that the Vice President becomes President if the President dies."

"It's also in the 25th Amendment," replied the young woman in the middle.

Thomas emerged from the bathroom, and Esmeralda turned the TV off. "I've been watching the post-election coverage," she told him. "The people on CNN are worried what would happen if Sam dies."

"How's he going to die?" said Thomas. "His longevity forecast says he's going to live to 108."

"I know, but people seem to be worried about it anyway. I don't think they want to see me become President."

"Of course not. But Sam's not going to die. He's fitter than I am."

"He just needs his naps."

"Right, as long as he gets his naps, he'll be fine. Anyway, what's the plan? Are we going to meet anyone for lunch?"

"Yes, Sarah and Jacqueline are already there. Memengwaa and your mom are on their way."

"Okay, then, let's head downstairs."

Thomas and Esmeralda left their room and took the stairs down to the restaurant. They met Memengwaa on the way and found Sarah and Jacqueline's table when they arrived. Sarah stood and hugged her mother. "Mom, you are the Vice-President elect! I'm so excited!"

"It's not a big deal," replied Esmeralda. "This morning I went on-line and read the duties in the U.S. Constitution. It's a piece of cake."

"It's still a great honor," said Jacqueline, standing and hugging her sister-in-law. "We are so proud of you!"

Everyone sat down, and Geraldine arrived moments later. After discussing the menu and placing their orders, the conversation turned to the transition of power.

"I don't take office until January 20th," said Esmeralda. "I wonder if we have to wait until then to move into the Vice President's residence."

"You'll have to speak to the Vice President's wife," said Jacqueline, "and find out when they plan to move out."

"The sooner the better," said Geraldine. "That guy was so useless."

"Her name is Roberta," said Jacqueline. "I'll get you her contact information."

"What do we do about our apartment?" asked Sarah.

"We want you to stay there and take care of it," said Esmeralda. "As Thomas told me, we can't live in the Vice President's residence forever. We'll need to move back to the apartment in either four years or eight years, depending on whether we are reelected in 2524."

"I don't want to live there alone," said Sarah.

"We'll give you a room in the Vice President's residence," said Esmeralda. "You can stay with us during the weekends—or whenever you feel lonely and want some company."

"Are you still talking to your boyfriend in San Antonio?" asked Jacqueline. "You could invite him to visit."

"Get a dog or a cat," said Geraldine. "It's easier to get along with animals than with men."

Everyone laughed.

"January 20th may seem far off," said Memengwaa, "but it actually gives us very little time to get a lot done. We need to set up an Inaugural Committee right away and pick a Chair for it."

"William would make a great Chair," said Esmeralda.

"Let me check with Sam first," replied Memengwaa, "and be sure he doesn't have someone else in mind. If not, I'll ask William."

"Congress has its own Inaugural Committee," said Jacqueline. "They call it the Joint Congressional Committee on Inaugural Ceremonies."

"Which committee does what?" asked Esmeralda.

"The Congressional committee is responsible for the swearing-in ceremony for the President and Vice President," Memengwaa replied, "and they host a luncheon in the U.S. Capitol. The Green Party's committee will handle the fund-raising, the parade, the balls, and other activities."

"Our Chair will have to coordinate with their Chair," said Thomas.

"Maybe I can get myself on the Congressional committee," said Jacqueline.

"Please do that," replied Memengwaa, "It would facilitate the process enormously."

"I can't be the Chair, though," said Jacqueline. "The Chair is always a member of the Senate."

"That doesn't matter," replied Memengwaa. "You can still provide input."

"Someone needs to do an invitation list," said Geraldine. "We don't want just anyone showing up at the Inauguration."

"That's correct," replied Memengwaa. "Sam and Esmeralda need to sit down as soon as possible and do the invitation list."

"You need separate invitation lists for the swearing-in ceremony, the Congressional luncheon, and the balls," said Jacqueline. "Actually, the Joint Congressional Committee approves the first two invitation lists. We will have to submit our lists to them for their approval."

"But *we* control who goes to the balls," said Memengwaa.

"Someone has to pick the music," said Geraldine. "I hope they don't pick lousy songs."

"Each event is scripted in detail," replied Jacqueline, "including the music. Don't worry, the music will be good."

"And singers," added Sarah. "Someone has to pick the singers."

"We also need to find a speechwriter to help Sam with his Inaugural Address," said Thomas. "I could do it, but maybe it would be better to find a professional speechwriter."

"Agreed," said Sarah. "It's been centuries since any President-elect has written their own Inaugural Address."

"Hopefully the Joint Committee has already hired a construction company to build the inaugural platform," said Memengwaa. "Jacqueline, you may want to follow up on that."

"Good point, Memengwaa," replied Jacqueline. "I will."

"We also have to help Esmeralda pick out dresses for both the Inauguration and the Inaugural Ball," said Jacqueline. "The eyes of the world will be on her."

"That should be fun," said Sarah. "Mom, I'll help you pick out the dresses."

The waiter began delivering food to the table, and Memengwaa and the Jenkins family continued their conversation about the upcoming Inauguration and the Inaugural Ball. Within thirty minutes, everyone finished their meal and returned to their room to pack and check out. By 2:00 p.m., everyone was on their way home.

*   *   *   *   *

On Friday morning, November 8th, President-elect Hoffenberger and Esmeralda met with Memengwaa and developed a milestone chart with hard and soft deadlines. They agreed to work on the invitation lists the week of November 11th and begin choosing nominees for the cabinet positions the week of November 18th. The timeline allowed six weeks for the latter task, after which they would begin choosing nominees for the heads of the smaller agencies such as the Small Business Administration and the Nuclear Regulatory Agency. Esmeralda built some downtime into the schedule so that she could plan her move to the Vice President's residence, visit the White House to see her new office, meet with interior decorators to collect suggestions on redecorating her residence and her office, and visit stores in Pentagon City and other shopping malls to find dresses for the Inauguration and the Inaugural Ball.

Memengwaa and President-elect Hoffenberger concurred with Esmeralda's suggestion to let William chair the Green Party's Inaugural Committee, and Memengwaa helped him form the committee by inviting several Green members of the House and Senate and a number of other Green Party faithfuls to participate. She also provided the committee with clerical support from her own staff and took the lead in fund-raising. In accordance with long-standing tradition, Congress had already appropriated funds for the inaugural swearing-in, security, and the parade; therefore, the party was only responsible for the balls and other private functions. By Thanksgiving, Memengwaa raised five hundred million dollars, with more money flowing in daily.

Jacqueline wasted no time in contacting Raymond Churchill, the Speaker of the House, and persuading him to let her serve on the

Joint Congressional Committee on Inaugural Ceremonies. The President-elect asked Esmeralda to work with the two inaugural committees to ensure that the Inauguration went smoothly; accordingly, beginning the week of November 18th, Esmeralda talked to both committee chairs twice a week and more frequently as necessary. By mid-January, she was speaking to both committee chairs at least twice a day.

William quickly immersed himself in his new assignment, working fourteen-hour days and taking only a few hours to be with his family on Thanksgiving Day, Christmas eve, and Christmas morning. He worked closely with Esmeralda and Jacqueline to ensure that his committee was in sync with the congressional committee; and he planned numerous events, such as the parade and the balls, for which his committee was responsible.

Although Memengwaa had cautioned Thomas against taking an active role in the inaugural planning, he did assist William and Esmeralda behind the scenes with tasks such as researching inaugural protocol and examining historical precedents for the transition of power.

President-elect Hoffenberger used his time to work with his speechwriter on his Inaugural Address and to visit Congressional leaders in the House and Senate. As a former Senator, he had many friends in the Senate, but few relationships in the House. Moreover, Speaker Churchill had not run for reelection, so the leadership of the House was due to change in January, and it was unclear who the new Speaker would be. Accordingly, after a courtesy visit to the Speaker's office, the President-elect focused his efforts on the Senate and met with the President Pro Tem, Jerry O'Brien, and the majority and minority leaders there.

The President-elect and Esmeralda both received hundreds of media requests for interviews and guest appearances, especially from late-night talk shows. Given their tight schedules, they had to decline or postpone most of the invitations; however, Esmeralda accepted invitations from NBC's *Tonight Show* and *Saturday Night Live*, and hosted the latter show on December 7, 2520.

Esmeralda made two visits to the White House and two trips to the Vice President's residence, taking an interior decorator with her on the second trips. Conscious of her budget—and to the disappointment of her interior decorator—she made only minor changes to her office in the West Wing of the White House and decided to simply repaint a few of the rooms in the Vice President's residence.

Sarah accompanied Esmeralda on her visits to the White House and the Vice President's residence as well as on her shopping trips to Pentagon City, Fair Oaks Mall, and other shopping centers in the area. Esmeralda tried on a variety of dresses and gowns at more than a dozen stores, choosing separate ensembles for the Inauguration and the evening balls. Each time that Esmeralda emerged from a dressing room, Sarah snapped a photograph with her iPalm and sent it to Thomas, Jacqueline, Geraldine, Angelica, and Isabelle, who provided their feedback in real time. Sarah provided feedback, too, of course, and Esmeralda put the outfits receiving the most favorable comments on lay-away until she was satisfied she had found the best dresses and gowns for each occasion; then she and Sarah returned to the stores to consummate the purchases.

In accordance with the Twentieth Amendment, the new Congress convened at noon on January 3, 2521, and after conducting routine business, elected Representative Peter McIntyre—former Chair of the Small Business Committee—as the new Speaker of the House.

As Memengwaa had predicted, the time between Election Day and the Inauguration was tighter than it appeared given the number of tasks at hand. Thanksgiving, Christmas, and New Year's Day arrived in turn and passed. Every morning Esmeralda checked the milestone chart to verify progress against the deadlines and conferred with William, Memengwaa, and Jacqueline as necessary. Then, as if she had awoken from a nap, one morning the calendar read Monday, January 20, 2521.

*　　*　　*　　*　　*

Due to more than five centuries of climate change, the winter temperatures in the Nation's capital were now moderate with normal daytime temperatures in the seventies and eighties. January 20, 2521, proved to be no exception; the National Weather Service predicted the temperature to be seventy-five degrees Fahrenheit at 9:30 a.m., the start of the Inauguration ceremony, with a cloudless sky and calm winds.

Thomas, Esmeralda, and Sarah arose at 5:30 a.m., and Thomas and Sarah enjoyed breakfast together while Esmeralda served them coffee and scrambled eggs.

"Do either of you have any questions about the schedule?" Thomas asked.

"I understand they do my Oath of Office first," replied Esmeralda, "before they do Sam's."

"That's correct," said Thomas. "Your Oath of Office is scheduled for eleven-thirty sharp. They will administer Sam's oath at noon. After that, we'll remain at the Capitol for the Congressional luncheon."

"The parade doesn't start until three," said Sarah. "Mom can use my office to change clothes after the luncheon."

"That's very nice of you," said Esmeralda. "We'll need a place to put our things."

"We have to be at the White House before three," said Thomas. "They've built a platform on the north lawn for Sam and Esmeralda to watch the parade."

"Where will the rest of us sit?" asked Sarah.

"They'll have chairs for us on the lawn."

"That sounds like fun," said Esmeralda.

"We'll use Sarah's office as a staging area," continued Thomas. "You can put the dresses and gowns there. After the parade, we can go back to her office and get ready for dinner and the first ball."

"You can also use my parking space at the Capitol for your aerocar," said Sarah.

"That's my plan," replied Thomas. "That's why we need to be there early. You never know when some imbecile might take a reserved parking space."

"What about your mother and sister?" asked Esmeralda.

"Jacqueline is picking up mom and bringing her to the Capitol," replied Thomas. "We'll meet them there."

"What about William and Isabelle?" asked Sarah.

"They'll be there, too. I'm not sure where they're sitting. William is running the whole thing, of course, behind the scenes."

"What about Memengwaa?" asked Esmeralda.

"She'll be sitting with us. William reserved a seat for her."

"When we get to the Capitol," replied Sarah, "let's go straight to my office. We'll leave the dresses and gowns there, lock the office, and then find our seats on the west front."

"Sam is going to meet us there, right?" asked Esmeralda.

"That's correct," replied Thomas. "Sam will go directly to the White House and meet President Slazenger at nine-thirty; then they will take a horse-drawn carriage from there to the Capitol."

"Why do they use a horse-drawn carriage?" asked Esmeralda.

"It's a relatively new tradition," said Sarah. "They used them in the eighteenth and nineteenth centuries, of course; then they began using them again in the twenty-third century. People love the nostalgia."

"What about Sam's wife?" asked Esmeralda. "Is she going to the White House with Sam?"

"No, she will meet Sam at the Capitol. William will make sure she sits with us."

"I think I understand the plan," said Esmeralda, who was wearing one of the outfits she and Sarah had picked out together, an elegant dress in a bold shade of blue with a matching hat and white gloves. "I'm dressed and ready to go."

Thomas took his spoon and scooped up the rest of his scrambled eggs, then finished his coffee. Sarah did the same; and within ten minutes, the family was in Thomas's aeromobile on their way to the Capitol.

*   *   *   *   *

When Thomas, Esmeralda, and Sarah arrived at the Capitol, they went directly to Sarah's office in the Rayburn House Office Building, left Esmeralda's afternoon dress and evening gown there, and then walked to the west front and found their seats on the inaugural platform. Jacqueline, Geraldine, Memengwaa, and Angelica were already there, sitting in their reserved seats. To their left, members of the National Symphony Orchestra were practicing; and to their right, members of the Mormon Tabernacle Choir were stretching and doing breathing exercises. Just below the platform, members of the United States Marine Band were tuning their instruments.

Jacqueline, Geraldine, Memengwaa, and Angelica stood and greeted Thomas, Esmeralda, and Sarah with hugs; then everyone sat down and watched as thousands of people arrived on the Capitol lawn and thousands more crowded together on Pennsylvania Avenue and the National Mall below. From where they sat, they could see the Washington Monument, and beyond it, in the distance, the Lincoln Memorial. The Jenkins family, Memengwaa, and Angelica sat quietly, reflecting on the historic moment in time.

President Slazenger and President-elect Hoffenberger arrived in their horse-drawn carriage at 11:00 a.m. and were escorted to their seats on the inaugural platform. Everyone stood, showing their respect, and Esmeralda walked over and greeted them. President-elect Hoffenberger looked at her approvingly and gave her a thumbs-up. Then Esmeralda returned to her seat, and everyone sat back down and waited for the ceremony to begin.

The National Symphony Orchestra began playing "America the Beautiful" at 11:15 a.m., after which Speaker McIntyre stood and walked to the podium. After adjusting the microphone, he introduced himself as the new Speaker of the House for the benefit of anyone who didn't already know; then, waiting a moment for his importance to sink in, he introduced the Right Reverend Randolph McGregor of the Washington National Cathedral, Bishop of Washington, to come to the podium and deliver the Invocation.

The Reverend McGregor walked to the podium, looked briefly at the crowd below him, and asked everyone to bow their heads. "Almighty and most merciful Lord," he began, "we beseech you to bless this momentous occasion; to bestow your infinite wisdom upon our new leaders; and to guide them as they seek to navigate the perils of modern civilization. In Jesus's name, Amen."

When Reverend McGregor finished, the Supreme Court's Chief Justice, Anthony Vlastos, stood and walked to the podium carrying the Lincoln Bible. William suddenly appeared out of nowhere and summoned Esmeralda, who arose and walked to the podium; William then waved to the rest of the Jenkins family and Memengwaa, indicating that they should join Esmeralda on the stage. Everyone in Esmeralda's group arose and walked to the podium, where they took their places behind her.

Chief Justice Vlastos placed the Lincoln Bible carefully on a shelf inside the podium. Looking at Esmeralda, he whispered, "We only use the Lincoln Bible for the President, not the Vice President." Then, speaking in a normal tone, he asked, "Are you ready to take the Oath of Office, Representative Jenkins?"

"I am," replied Esmeralda.

"Very well, then, please repeat after me, 'I do solemnly swear that I will support and defend the Constitution of the United States.' " Justice Vlastos paused and Esmeralda repeated the first words of the oath; then the Justice continued, one phrase at a time, and Esmeralda repeated each phrase in order, "against all enemies, foreign and domestic; that I will bear true faith and allegiance to the same; that I take this obligation freely, without any mental reservation or purpose of evasion; and that I will well and faithfully discharge the duties of the office on which I'm about to enter. So help me God."

Chief Justice Vlastos smiled. "Congratulations, Vice President Jenkins!"

"Thank you, Justice Vlastos," Esmeralda replied.

Thomas stepped forward and kissed Esmeralda, who then turned to the west and waved to the crowd, now in the hundreds of thousands, stretching from the Capitol to the Lincoln Memorial. Then she turned back to her companions and hugged Sarah, Jacqueline, Geraldine, Memengwaa, and Angelica in turn, after which everyone returned to their seats.

The United States Marine Band stood and performed four ruffles and flourishes, followed by "Hail, Columbia." The Mormon Tabernacle Choir then began its first musical selection, "Faith of Our Fathers," after which Chief Justice Vlastos checked the time on his iPalm, and seeing that it was 12:00 noon, turned to the President-elect and asked him if he was ready to take his Oath of Office.

President-elect Hoffenberger stood and stepped forward. "Yes, I am."

Angelica also stood and followed her husband to the podium.

Justice Vlastos removed the Lincoln Bible from the shelf inside the podium. "Very well, then, Senator Hoffenberger, please place your left hand on the Bible."

President-elect Hoffenberger placed his left hand on the Bible as instructed.

"Please repeat after me," began Justice Vlastos, "I, Samuel Hoffenberger..."

"I, Samuel Hoffenberger ...," repeated the President-elect.

"... do solemnly swear," continued Justice Vlastos.

"... do solemnly swear," repeated the President-elect.

Justice Vlastos continued, one phrase at a time, and the President-elect repeated each phrase in order, "that I will faithfully execute the office of President of the United States, and will to the best of my ability, preserve, protect and defend the Constitution of the United States."

"Congratulations, President Hoffenberger!" said Justice Vlastos. He turned and put the Lincoln Bible back on the shelf inside the podium where he had placed it earlier.

"Thank you, Justice Vlastos," said President Hoffenberger, shaking hands with the Chief Justice, who then returned to his seat. The President waved to the crowd and turned to kiss his wife, who was standing behind him. The Marine Band stood and resumed playing, starting with four ruffles and flourishes followed by, "Hail to the Chief." At the sound of the first ruffle and flourish, the 3rd United States Infantry Regiment, stationed in a park north of the Capitol, began firing a 21-gun salute.

When the Marine Band finished playing "Hail to the Chief" and the last of the twenty-one guns could be heard in the distance, the President turned to the podium and adjusted the microphone. "Chief Justice Vlastos, other distinguished Supreme Court justices, former President Slazenger, Vice President Jenkins, Speaker of the House McIntyre, Senate President Pro Tem O'Brien, other distinguished members of the House and the Senate, other government officials, other dignitaries, and my fellow citizens, I thank you for your support at this historic moment in our Nation's history."

President Hoffenberger paused, looking briefly at the Supreme Court justices and other government officials, then turned back to face the crowd. "As you may know, I'm the first U.S. President to be elected on the Green Party's ticket; and my running mate, Esmeralda Jenkins, is the first robot to be elected Vice President."

The crowd on the Capitol lawn cheered and applauded. On the streets below and on the National Mall, thousands of others could also be heard cheering and applauding.

"Throughout the world," continued President Hoffenberger, "people are starving. We are faced with a terrible choice: Do we feed the hungry in third-world countries or use our limited resources to feed the unemployed and homeless in our own country? This is a catastrophe that didn't happen overnight; it has been brewing for centuries. The Democrats and Republicans never took the problem seriously, but maybe they will now."

Someone nearby shouted, "Amen!"

President Hoffenberger continued his Inaugural address, urging all Americans to put aside their differences and unite to address the urgent problems of hunger, homelessness, and joblessness. He emphasized that he and his Vice President, as Greens, would always consider the impact of their actions on the environment; and he finished his speech with the words, "When I referred to this as a historic moment in our Nation's history, I wasn't exaggerating; indeed, the stakes have never been so high. This is not merely about saving our Nation—it is also about saving human civilization. With God's help, we shall do so. Thank you again for your support!"

Angelica stepped forward, and she and her husband joined hands and waved to the crowd, which responded enthusiastically with applause, cheers, and whistles. After a few minutes, the President turned to the distinguished guests on the Presidential platform and began shaking hands. Esmeralda joined him as the Supreme Court Justices, members of the House and Senate, and other government officials stood in line to offer their congratulations and shake his hand. After thirty minutes or so, the crowd began to disburse, and William appeared to remind everyone that the Congressional luncheon was about to begin inside the Capitol in Statuary Hall. Esmeralda and her entourage followed the President and Angelica into the building and walked to the hall, which was located directly south of the Rotunda.

Meanwhile, former President Slazenger and his spouse departed by motorcade for Andrews Air Force Base, where they would receive a 21-gun salute before taking a final trip on Air Force One to their home in Austin, Texas. Their departure from the Capitol was nearly inconspicuous.

When President Hoffenberger and the others arrived at Statuary Hall, they found a hundred or more small tables set up for them and their guests. The Supreme Court justices, members of the House and Senate, and other guests—primarily Greens, since the luncheon was by invitation only—were already seated. Everyone stood and applauded as the President, Angelica, Esmeralda, and Thomas entered the room. A Capitol employee greeted them and escorted them to the head table at one end of the room, while the other members of the Jenkins family and Memengwaa were directed to another table some distance away. Cardboard name plates on the tables identified the seating arrangement, and everyone sat down in their assigned seat. At the head table, everyone sat together on the same side of the table, facing the other tables, the President in the middle with Angelica on one side and Esmeralda on the other. Thomas's seat was beside Esmeralda at the opposite end of the table from Angelica. The table was fitted with a skirt to hide the occupants' legs. Besides the customary plates and silverware, each place setting included a water glass with ice and an empty champagne glass, and a waiter arrived almost immediately with a bottle of champagne and began pouring it into everyone's glass.

Jacqueline, who was seated with Geraldine, Sarah, and Memengwaa, arose and clinked her glass with a spoon to get everyone's attention. "The Speaker has asked me, as a member of Congress and sister-in-law of the Vice President, to make a toast. Please raise your glasses and join me in toasting President

Hoffenberger and Vice President Jenkins ... May their tenure in the White House be long and fruitful and bring prosperity to our Nation!" Jacqueline clinked her glass with those of the others at her table, then put the glass to her lips and sipped. The sound of clinking glasses spread across the room. President Hoffenberger smiled and nodded approvingly.

As soon as Jacqueline finished her toast, the waiters began distributing salad plates containing the ever-popular Green Goddess Cobb Salad with Avocado. President Hoffenberger turned to his wife and spoke to her privately, then turned to Esmeralda and said, "Well, I think we're off to a good start—so far everything has gone like clockwork."

As the waiter approached Esmeralda, she raised her hand and signaled that she didn't want any salad. The seating arrangement at the head table was not particularly conducive to conversation, but Thomas and Esmeralda spoke briefly about the inaugural ceremony and agreed it had gone well. President Hoffenberger said little and began eating his salad, as did Thomas and Angelica.

Suddenly a voice, speaking in an urgent tone, came across a loudspeaker. "An unidentified drone has just broken the perimeter! Please seek immediate shelter! This is not a drill!" The announcement was followed by a loud siren; and everyone in the room, remembering the horrors of World War XII, dropped their silverware and climbed under their table or ran for the nearest exit. Screams filled the room. "A robo-drone! Run! Hurry! Run for the exit! Get out of my way! Move your ass! The exit is right there!" Some of the guests, not as agile or possibly in shock, sat where they were as if paralyzed. A drone appeared in the doorway, hovering just below the ceiling, and began circling the room.

The Capitol police and Secret Service agents sitting among the guests jumped into action, rushing to the head table and pushing President Hoffenberger and Esmeralda under it. The drone stopped in mid-air above the head table and began firing laser missiles in the President's direction. Thomas climbed under the table and held Esmeralda tight; but President Hoffenberger, anxious to see what was happening, resisted the Secret Service agents and lifted his head above the table. A missile struck him immediately, and he fell to the floor.

More than a dozen Capitol police officers and Secret Service agents now surrounded the table, their guns raised, firing at the drone, which was soon hit and crashed to the floor. The officers continued firing at the drone as it lay on the floor while Angelica climbed out from under the table and attended to her husband. "He's bleeding!" she exclaimed. Thomas climbed out and rushed to the President's side, assessing the severity of his injuries, exclaiming, "We need an ambulance! The President has been hit! We need an ambulance immediately!" A pool of blood began spreading across the floor. Angelica screamed, "Oh, my poor husband!" One of the Secret Service agents shouted, "Tie a tourniquet on him to stop the bleeding!"

Thomas grabbed a napkin from the tabletop and put it directly on the President's wound and applied pressure to it. Esmeralda, still under the table, pulled aside the table skirt and looked at the scene; then, seeing that the drone had been shot down, climbed out from under the table and joined Thomas and Angelica. At the same moment, a man carrying a briefcase appeared and pushed Thomas aside. "I'm the Capitol physician. Get out of my way! I'll take care of this!"

Everyone stepped back as the doctor kneeled beside President Hoffenberger and raised one of his arms to check his pulse. The Secret Service agents and Capitol police stopped firing at the drone, which had apparently been disabled; some of them approached the drone cautiously, guns still drawn, while others turned back to the table to check on the President. The doctor held the President's wrist with one hand and stared at his iPalm on the other hand. After a moment, he lowered the wrist and stood up. "The President has no pulse," he announced. "He's dead."

Angelica fainted, and Esmeralda turned to Thomas. "Does this mean I'm President—President of the United States of America?"

Thomas looked at his wife in horror. "Holy Jesus!"

The First Robot President

Part III

The Oval Office

Chapter 11

Transition of Power

Chief Justice Vlastos wasted no time finding Esmeralda; he appeared at the head table within five minutes, Lincoln Bible in hand, ready to administer the same oath that President Hoffenberger had taken less than two hours before.

Chief Justice Vlastos was visibly shaken. "This is a terrible tragedy!"

"Yes, it is," replied Esmeralda. "Everyone is in shock."

"No matter, I must administer your oath without delay so that the Nation will have no interruption of leadership. Please place your left hand on the Bible, raise your right hand, and repeat after me, "I, Esmeralda Jenkins, do solemnly swear..." Justice Vlastos paused and Esmeralda repeated the first phrase; then he continued, "that I will faithfully execute the office of President of the United States..." He paused again, and Esmeralda repeated the second phrase, "and will to the best of my ability..." He paused and Esmeralda repeated the third phrase; then he finished, "preserve, protect and defend the Constitution of the United States." Esmeralda repeated the last phrase.

"Congratulations, President Jenkins!" said Justice Vlastos. He turned to the Secret Service agents and others surrounding the head table. "Esmeralda Jenkins is now your President!"

William and Isabelle were among the first to arrive on the scene, right behind Justice Vlastos. William spoke to the Secret Service agents while Isabelle attended to Angelica, who was lying on the floor beside her husband.

"I need smelling salts!" exclaimed Isabelle.

The Capitol physician picked up his briefcase and placed it on the table. "I have something here that should work." He pulled out a small bottle, opened it, and handed it to Isabelle.

Jacqueline and Sarah had arrived while Esmeralda was taking the oath of office. They stared at President Hoffenberger and the pool of blood in disbelief.

"I just spoke to the Secret Service," said William. "This appears to have been a lone-wolf attack. They don't believe Esmeralda is in any immediate danger."

"Thank God!" said Sarah.

"Esmeralda, you have to be strong," said Jacqueline. "I'm here for you if you need me."

"What do we do about the parade?" asked Thomas.

"We have to cancel it," replied Esmeralda. She looked at William. "Please cancel the parade and all of the balls. I'm declaring thirty days of mourning beginning today. I want all flags lowered to half-staff. Get the word out immediately."

Isabelle held the smelling salts under Angelica's nose, and she began to awaken.

Geraldine and Memengwaa appeared. "Let me know how I can help," said Memengwaa.

Geraldine looked down at President Hoffenberger and the pool of blood. "Holy Jesus!" she exclaimed.

"Thomas already said that," replied Esmeralda.

"We need to get the body out of here and make funeral arrangements," said Memengwaa.

"Good point, Memengwaa," replied Esmeralda. "We need to clean up the body and put it in a casket. William, please find the Sergeant at Arms and ask him to take care of it."

Members of Congress and others who had run from the room now began to reappear, cautiously re-entering Statuary Hall; and within a few minutes, a hundred or more people surrounded the area where President Hoffenberger lay dead.

"President Hoffenberger will lie in state in the Rotunda," said Esmeralda. "Then we will have the funeral service and the burial. The process usually takes three days."

Isabelle helped Angelica to sit up.

Esmeralda looked at William again. "William, I'm appointing you to be my interim Chief of Staff. After you cancel the parade and the balls, please begin making the funeral arrangements. Ask Angelica where she wants the funeral service."

"Sam attended Saint Matthew's Cathedral," said Angelica weakly, as if coming out of a trance. "The Cathedral of Saint Matthew the Apostle."

"That's the Catholic church on Rhode Island Avenue," said Memengwaa. "It's the same church where they had the funeral for JFK."

"JFK?" asked Geraldine.

"John Fitzgerald Kennedy, one of our early Presidents," replied Memengwaa. "He was also assassinated."

"Then let's plan to have the funeral service there," said Esmeralda. "William, you're in charge. Work out the details and give me an agenda tomorrow morning for the next three days. I want it on my desk by 8:00 a.m. In the meantime, I will make an address to the Nation—tonight."

Esmeralda looked at her husband. "Thomas, you can help me with my speech. Let's go back to the apartment and work on it."

"I thought you had moved into the Vice President's residence," said Geraldine.

"No," replied Thomas, "we are scheduled to move tomorrow."

"William," said Esmeralda, "please contact the movers and reschedule our move. I want to move on Friday, the day after the funeral. Also, tell them we aren't moving into the Naval Observatory after all—we are moving to 1600 Pennsylvania Avenue."

"Got it," William replied. "I'll contact them right now."

"I can take you home now, Esmeralda," said Thomas, "if the Secret Service thinks it's safe."

A Secret Service agent stepped forward. "My name is Roger. I will take you both home in the Air Force One aeromobile. From now on, you will travel with me—you're going to need protection twenty-four/seven."

"What about my aerocar?" asked Thomas. "I parked it in the Capitol parking lot."

"You can get it later," said the agent. "It's going to be pandemonium in the airspace over the Capitol. Everyone is trying to get out of here."

"Got it," replied Thomas. He turned to his wife. "Esmeralda, let's go with this guy. You're going to have to get used to traveling with the Secret Service."

Esmeralda looked at the family. "Sarah, you come, too. Jacqueline will take Geraldine home."

Esmeralda, Thomas, and Sarah followed Roger out of the Capitol to the Capitol parking lot where they climbed into the Air Force One aeromobile. In less than two minutes, they were in the air and on their way back to their apartment in Virginia.

*   *   *   *   *

At 8:55 p.m., Eastern Standard Time, Esmeralda sat at her desk in the Oval Office surrounded by a camera crew. Behind her, on one side, stood the American flag and, on the other side, the President's flag. She appeared poised and confident as the camera crew checked the lighting and the audio technicians checked the sound. All six major networks were present, ready to broadcast the speech live. At 8:59 p.m., William, who had taken charge of the event, began the countdown, and Esmeralda looked straight into the cameras and began speaking at exactly nine o'clock.

"My fellow Americans," said Esmeralda, "let me begin by addressing the tragic event that occurred today after the Presidential Inauguration. As you have no doubt heard, President Hoffenberger was assassinated during the luncheon at the Capitol. I'll get to that in a moment, but first I wish to express my heartfelt sympathy to President Hoffenberger's widow, Angelica, and to the other members of the President's extended family. The President's body is now at Bethesda Naval Hospital in Maryland where they are performing an autopsy. It will be returned to the White House tomorrow morning and placed in the East Room, where the embalming and cosmetic restoration will be done; then, tomorrow evening, the body will be moved to the Capitol, where it will lie in state in the Rotunda for public viewing all day on Wednesday. The funeral service and burial will take place on Thursday, which I have declared a national day of mourning. I have ordered all Federal offices closed. We are working with Angelica on the details for Thursday's events, and the White House will issue a Press Release tomorrow so that you know what's happening when. In the meantime, I have ordered all flags to be flown at half-staff for thirty days, beginning today."

Standing behind the camera crew, Thomas gave Esmeralda a thumbs-up and mouthed the words, "So far, so good."

"Regarding the assassination," continued Esmeralda, "we have examined the robo-drone that killed President Hoffenberger and have identified it as the last remaining robo-drone from World War XII. If there is anything positive to come out of this tragedy, it is that all robo-drones from the last world war are now accounted for, and Americans can rest easy that there is no further threat to their lives."

Esmeralda paused and her tone of voice changed. "The Supreme Court's Chief Justice, Anthony Vlastos, administered my oath of office shortly after the assassination, and I'm now your President. I understand that many of you are concerned about this because I'm a robot. The United States has never had a robot as President, so your concern is understandable. However, the country is actually safer and more secure with me as President because I'm not impulsive and don't let my emotions control my behavior. I'm not going to fire a missile at China because I'm having a bad hair day."

Standing behind the crew next to Thomas, William gave Esmeralda a thumbs up.

Esmeralda continued, "Since I have, in effect, been promoted from Vice President to President, one of my first tasks will be to select a new Vice President. Under Section two of the twenty-fifth

Amendment, I'm required to submit my nominee to Congress; the nominee must be confirmed by a majority vote of both Houses of Congress. I will screen candidates this week and submit my nominee to the House and Senate before the end of the month."

A member of the camera crew offered Esmeralda a glass of water, but she waved him off.

"One more thing," said Esmeralda. "Unless you have studied Medieval American History, you have probably never heard of him, but one of our first Presidents was Franklin Delano Roosevelt, or FDR. In his own time, he was regarded as one of America's greatest Presidents—unless, of course, you were a Republican, in which case you would have considered him one of our *worst* Presidents. Be that as it may, during the Great Depression of the twentieth century, FDR introduced something called the Fireside Chat. Although we don't have fireplaces anymore, the concept was a good one, and I'd like to piggyback on it with something I'm going to call my *Sunday Evening Update*. It will be an opportunity for me to speak directly to the American people about leading economic indicators, changes to the GDP and real GDP, fluctuations in the money supply, and other topics I know you will find of great interest. If you've never studied economics, you're in for a real treat."

Thomas mouthed silently, "Perfect!"

"I'm mindful that humans, unlike me, need to sleep, so I'm going to wrap this up now—those of you who have to work tomorrow can get ready for bed. I hope I have put your mind to ease regarding my being a robot. Please remember that Thursday is a national day of mourning; look for the schedule tomorrow. Thank you for your time, have a good night, and God Bless America!"

Thomas and William both gave Esmeralda another thumbs-up. "Great job!" said William, then, turning to the camera crew, said,

"Ladies and gentlemen, please pack your equipment. I will give you four minutes; then I will escort you to the White House parking garage."

Esmeralda pushed her chair back and looked at Thomas. "I think I've got this!"

Thomas walked behind Esmeralda's desk, grasped her shoulders, and looked in her eyes. "You sure do—you're going to make a *great* President!" Then he kissed her, took her hand, and led her around the desk towards the door. "It's been a long day, let's go home and chill out."

Thomas signaled Roger that they were ready to leave, and he led them out of the room and down the hallway to the elevator, which they took to the rooftop. There they boarded the Air Force One aeromobile and departed, the Secret Service agent at the wheel. A day of extraordinary events was behind them.

* * * * *

From his office in the Longworth House Office Building, newly elected Speaker McIntyre watched Esmeralda's address to the Nation attentively with Representative Patrick Sullivan, the new House Majority Leader, and Representative Ishaan Pafundi, the new House Democratic Whip.

At the end of the address, Speaker McIntyre spoke first. "What the hell was Justice Vlastos thinking? He was out of his mind to give a robot the oath of office!"

"He should have bypassed her and given the oath to you," said the Majority Leader. "If the President and Vice President are both unfit for the job, the Speaker of the House is next in the line of succession."

"Thomas Jenkins isn't fooling anyone," said the Speaker. "He is the shadow President. This whole scheme of putting his robot wife in Congress and then on the Green ticket was an elaborate plan to seize the Presidency."

"It was his back door to the Oval Office," agreed the Whip. "He had this whole thing planned from the beginning."

"I wouldn't be surprised if he was behind the assassination," said the Majority Leader.

"We don't have to take it sitting down," said the Speaker. "We can impeach the robot and get rid of her—indeed, I think we have a Constitutional duty to do so."

"I don't disagree," replied the Democratic Whip, "but as a practical matter, I don't think we can do it unless we bring the Republicans on board. Remember, the Republicans and the Greens together constitute a majority."

"Give me a break!" exclaimed the Speaker. "Since when have the Republicans and Greens formed a coalition?"

"Never," replied the Whip, "but this might be a first. The Republicans wouldn't want you to become President."

The Speaker frowned. "No, you're right. The Republicans would figure they have a better chance of defeating the robot in the next election than me."

"Exactly," said the Whip. "Blocking the impeachment would ensure that they would be facing off against the robot in 2524."

"Then again," said the Speaker, "if she proves to be totally incompetent, we may have no choice but to impeach her. The Constitution requires it."

"Only if she is unfit for office," said the Whip, "that is, if she is unable or unwilling to perform the duties of President."

"You also have to consider the robot's sister-in-law, Jacqueline Jenkins," said the Majority Leader. "She has been in Congress for decades and has friends on both sides of the aisle. She would try to block the impeachment vote."

"Don't mention that bitch's name!" exclaimed the Speaker. "When I was Chair of the Small Business Committee, she tried to blackmail me."

"What?" asked the Whip. "She tried to blackmail you? How could she possibly blackmail you?"

"I suppose it had something to do with a woman," said the Majority Leader.

"No, it didn't," replied the Speaker. "There was no woman involved."

"Then what was the basis of her blackmail?" asked the Whip.

"I'm not going to give her accusations any credibility by discussing them—that would just play into her hand. But I should have filed a complaint with the Ethics Office. That was my mistake right there. I should have filed a complaint immediately."

The Speaker arose from his chair. "Anyway, it's time to call it a day. Thank you for your company, gentlemen. Unhappy circumstances are always easier to swallow with colleagues by your side."

Majority Leader Sullivan and Democratic Whip Pafundi arose from their chairs and departed the office together.

* * * * *

With William in charge of Thursday's funeral events, Esmeralda was able to focus on the Nation's business. Arising early on Tuesday morning, she made breakfast for Thomas and Sarah and then called for Roger, who arrived minutes later and took her back to the White House. Upon her arrival, she went directly to the Oval Office and began organizing things to her liking, disposing of President Slazenger's personal items and arranging important papers and necessary implements neatly on the desktop.

Esmeralda decided it was time to replace the President's desk—an oversized, wooden piece of furniture known as the Resolute Desk, which was made of timbers from the H.M.S. Resolute, a British navy ship, and which had been presented to President Rutherford B. Hayes by Queen Victoria in the nineteenth century. She opened her iPalm and sent William a text instructing him to replace it with a simple, inexpensive desk no more than four feet long. She also instructed him to get rid of the expensive executive chair and replace it with a basic office chair, have the carpet removed, and have a wood floor installed in place of the carpet. Then she reviewed a number of laws enacted by Congress awaiting her signature and signed all but one, vetoing a law that would have required all Americans—men and women—to serve for at least five years in a war overseas.

After acting on the pending legislation, Esmeralda called William, who had moved into the Chief of Staff's office a few doors away, and told him she would like to walk through the building together and introduce themselves to the White House staff. Then the two walked through the three floors of the West Wing, the four main floors of the Executive Residence, and the two floors of the East Wing, which included the First Man's office suite. Esmeralda discovered that the White House is a split-level building with the first floor of the residence on the same level as the second floors of the east and west wings.

"I think what we now call 'the residence' was the original White House," William told Esmeralda. "They must have added the east and west wings later."

Although the White House contained more than one elevator, Esmeralda preferred to use the stairs. She was much lighter than William—lighter than any adult human, for that matter—and she ascended the stairs at twice the speed of her companion. William did his best to keep up with her. By noon, they had spoken to all of the permanent staff they encountered on their tour and to a number of political appointees who had been selected earlier in the month by President Hoffenberger. Esmeralda advised the political appointees that she would review their job qualifications and let them know before the end of the month if she would keep them.

When Esmeralda returned to the Oval Office, she called Memengwaa, who answered the call on the third ring. "Good morning, Memengwaa. I hope you slept well."

"As well as can be expected under the circumstances. What happened yesterday shook me to the core. I'm still in shock."

"I understand. Thomas and Sarah said the same thing."

"Anyway, I watched your address last night. You did a good job. I just don't know about the *Sunday Evening Update*. Are you sure the public wants to hear about economics?"

"They may not think they do, but they'll love it. Who doesn't love economics?"

"I can think of a few."

"Anyway, to get to the point, I need you as a sounding board. I have to choose a Vice President and a permanent Chief of Staff."

"Didn't you already appoint William to be your Chief of Staff?"

"Only on an interim basis. I had to make a split-second decision."

"You could do worse. Why don't you wait and see how he does with the funeral?"

"Good point. Then I can make a decision on Friday."

"There's no rush. You can keep him in interim status for a while if you're not sure."

"Okay, that makes sense. I also want your advice about Thomas."

"About Thomas?"

"Yes, I'd like a role for him in my Administration."

"Red flag!" exclaimed Memengwaa. "You'd be playing into the hands of skeptics who say you're nothing more than a front for your husband."

"Well, he could be an unofficial advisor, right?"

"What do you mean by *unofficial*?"

"Have you ever heard of Ivanka Trump?"

"No, I don't think so."

"She was President Trump's daughter."

"President Trump?"

"One of our early Presidents in the twenty-first century."

"Okay, it's coming back to me. I think I remember reading about him."

"Anyway, his daughter Ivanka was his unofficial advisor and one of his most trusted confidantes."

"I think I see where you're going with this. Hopefully Thomas isn't the only person you can trust."

"No, that's not the point. He's a smart guy, and I know he will give me good advice."

"Well, just remember you can't put him on the payroll. *The Washington Post* would pounce on that like a fumbled football."

"No, I don't plan to put him on the payroll."

"And keep him in the background—don't call attention to him."

"I got it."

"Who do you have in mind for VP?" asked Memengwaa.

"Possibly Representative Juan Nighthorse Humetewa from South Dakota. He's solid Green and served on my subcommittee. We got along well."

"Great choice. You need Native-American representation in your Administration."

"Do you have any other suggestions—I mean, for VP?"

"Not off the top of my head, but Vice Presidents usually come from Congress. I'll send you an updated list of the House and Senate Greens. If anyone catches your eye, let me know and I will have my staff pull together more information on them for you. But if you want to stick with Representative Humetewa, that would be fine, too."

"What about the agency heads?" asked Esmeralda.

"President Hoffenberger had already started teeing up nominations before the Inauguration. Unless you see someone on the list you don't like, I'd stick with the same people."

"I understand the Senate confirmations can take several months," said Esmeralda. "Who runs the agencies in the meanwhile?"

"The transition team has recommended acting Secretaries and Administrators for every department and agency. I'd stick with those, too."

"Thanks for the feedback. Let me know if you have any other thoughts on it."

"I will."

"Thanks again," said Esmeralda. "Have a good day."

"You, too. Goodbye."

After finishing the conversation, Esmeralda reviewed William's draft schedule for Thursday's day of mourning and texted him her approval: *Looks good—Issue a Press Release*. Then she began contacting each of her Cabinet members—the acting Secretaries—via Skype to discuss their priorities and budgets.

At noon, the motorcade transporting President Hoffenberger's body arrived at the White House gate, and Esmeralda took a break from her one-on-one Skype meetings and went to the North Portico to watch pallbearers bring it into the building and take it to the East Room. Then she returned to her office and continued the Skype meetings with her Cabinet members. By the time she had finished speaking to the acting Secretaries of Defense, Labor, and State, Thomas arrived for lunch, and they walked to the White House dining room. Esmeralda sat with Thomas while he had lunch, after which they took the stairs to the second floor and looked at the President's private quarters. After examining each of the rooms and discussing decorations and furniture arrangements, Thomas departed; and for the remainder of the day, Esmeralda continued the Skype meetings with her Cabinet.

On Wednesday morning, after making breakfast for Thomas and Sarah, Esmeralda had Roger take her directly to the Capitol, where she went to the front of the line and paid her respects to President Hoffenberger, whose body was now lying in state in the Rotunda. His casket had been set upon a catafalque, a replica of the one built for President Abraham Lincoln some six hundred years before, in the center of the Rotunda, surrounded by a military honor guard. After kneeling and praying in front of the flag-draped, mahogany casket, which was closed to conceal the President's head wound, she stood up and hugged Angelica, who had already paid her respects and was standing nearby, a black veil covering her face. "I'm here for you," said Esmeralda. "Please call me or come see me if you need to talk."

After leaving the Capitol, Esmeralda returned to the White House and went directly to the Oval Office, where she continued the one-on-one Skype meetings with her Cabinet. By noon, she had spoken to the remaining Cabinet members and the heads of the General Services Administration and the National Aeronautics and Space Administration.

Jacqueline and Sarah were with Thomas when he arrived for lunch, and William joined them soon after they sat down in the White House dining room. William updated everyone on Thursday's events, including the funeral procession, the funeral service, and the burial. He asked Esmeralda if she would be willing to make a few remarks at the service, to which she agreed.

Esmeralda continued her Skype meetings on Wednesday afternoon with the heads of the smaller agencies. At 5:30 p.m., conscious of her responsibility to make dinner for Thomas and Sarah, she summoned Roger and asked him to take her home, and she was back in the apartment in Virginia before 6:00 p.m.

*   *   *   *   *

On Thursday, the day of mourning, Thomas, Esmeralda, and Sarah arose at 5:30 a.m., and Thomas and Sarah sat down at the kitchen table for breakfast. Esmeralda brought them coffee and scrambled eggs, then sat down and watched them eat.

"Any changes to the schedule?" asked Sarah.

"No, I don't think so," said Esmeralda, checking her iPalm as she spoke. "They extended the public viewing in the Rotunda; people were standing in line all night to pay their respects. The Capital police will close the Rotunda at eight o'clock, and the Marines will bring President Hoffenberger's casket to the White House. I have invited Angelica and her children to wait with us in the Oval Office. When the Marines reach the White House, we will go out and join the procession. Angelica and her family will go first, and we will follow. Everyone will walk. The Secret Service agents will walk in front of us, beside us, and behind us."

"It's going to take a while," said Thomas. "The church is about a mile from the White House."

"Right," said Sarah, "and we have to keep pace with a horse-drawn caisson; we can't walk any faster or slower."

"Expect to see dozens of foreign leaders," said Esmeralda, "including the King of England. They should be arriving at the White House now. They will be directed to the steps of the North Portico and wait for us there, then follow us on foot to the church."

"I hope everyone is wearing comfortable walking shoes," said Thomas.

"Tell Jacqueline to meet us in the Oval Office," said Esmeralda. "She needs to be there by eight-thirty. The service starts at eleven o'clock."

"What about Granma?" asked Sarah. "Is she coming?"

"Geraldine?" said Thomas. "No, she's not up for the walk—she'll meet us at the church."

"One more thing," said Esmeralda. "Tonight we'll have a state dinner for the foreign leaders who are staying overnight. I'd like both of you to attend it."

"Of course," said Sarah. "I'd love it."

"How about Jacqueline?" asked Thomas.

"Yes, I'm inviting her, too. I want Jacqueline and Sarah with me every step of the way."

"How about Geraldine?" asked Thomas.

"I think not—I have to draw the line somewhere, and she's a loose cannon. God forbid she insults the King of England."

"That would be just like her," agreed Sarah.

Thomas and Sarah finished their breakfast, and Esmeralda summoned Roger, who took them to the White House. After arriving on the rooftop, they took the elevator to the first floor and went directly to the Oval Office where Esmeralda sat down at her desk and Thomas and Sarah found chairs along the wall. Esmeralda read a briefing sheet William had left on her desk while the others busied themselves with communications on their iPalms.

Jacqueline arrived promptly at 8:30; and Angelica, still wearing her black veil, arrived soon afterwards with her two adult children, both middle-aged men. Esmeralda turned on the TV so that everyone could watch soldiers from the U.S. Marine Corps remove the President's casket from the Rotunda and place it on a caisson, where a team of eight horses stood ready to pull it down Pennsylvania Avenue to the White House.

Esmeralda excused herself and went to see William. While she was gone, Thomas, Jacqueline, and Sarah made small talk with Angelica and her sons. By the time Esmeralda returned, the eight horses had begun pulling the caisson holding the casket, led by the Marine Band and followed by a color guard holding the presidential colors and the flag of the President of the United States. A riderless horse, boots reversed in the stirrups to symbolize a fallen leader, followed behind. Thousands of onlookers lined Pennsylvania Avenue to watch the procession.

"I figure they will get here in thirty minutes or so," said Thomas. "I suggest we walk out to the gate in twenty minutes and wait for it."

Esmeralda busied herself at her desk while the two families watched President Hoffenberger's caisson make its way toward the White House. At 9:30, Thomas stood up. "They're getting close. If anyone needs to use the rest room, this is a good time." One of Angelica's sons nodded, stood, and left the room; the others arose and waited for him to return; then Thomas gave the signal to walk to the North Portico. Everyone, including Esmeralda, followed him out of the Oval Office and down the hallway, stopping to pick up William on the way.

When they arrived at the North Portico, they found dozens of foreign leaders standing together in conversation, surrounded by Secret Service agents and military police. King Charles VIII of England was speaking to Chancellor Heidi Schmidt of Germany. "In this day and age," said the King, "every leader is living on the edge— but for the grace of God, any one of us could be lying in that casket right now."

As the foreign leaders became aware of Esmeralda's presence, the conversation quieted and everyone turned in her direction. Unsure of American protocol, some of the leaders bowed; others smiled and nodded. President Beauregard Charpentier of France stepped forward and extended his hand. Esmeralda shook it; then King Charles VIII and other leaders stepped forward to shake hands. After shaking hands with Esmeralda, many of them turned to

Angelica, who was standing beside Esmeralda, and offered their condolences.

In a few minutes, President Hoffenberger's horse-drawn caisson reached the northeast gate, and a company of Marines led the horses into the White House grounds to the North Portico. There William took charge and told everyone where to stand in the procession; and in few minutes, after everyone was positioned correctly, the Marines turned the horses towards the northwest gate. Since Jackson Place, the most direct route to Connecticut Avenue, was too narrow to accommodate the procession, the Marines turned west on Pennsylvania Avenue, passing the Dwight D. Eisenhower Executive Office Building on their left, then turned north on 17th Street, then east on H Street, then left onto Connecticut Avenue, walking north in the direction of the church.

The Marine Band led the procession, followed by 10 Scottish bagpipers and the horse-drawn caisson. Angelica and her two sons followed the caisson, leading the walking procession, with Esmeralda, Thomas, Jacqueline, and Sarah right behind them. King Charles VIII and the other world leaders followed.

Millions of spectators lined Connecticut Avenue to see the historic event in person. The solemnity of the circumstances didn't lend itself to celebration, so the crowd was largely quiet and respectful. When the procession arrived at the cathedral, the Marine Honor Guard and President Hoffenberger's two sons, serving as pall bearers, removed the casket from the caisson and carried it to the front door. Cardinal Giovanni D'Angelo, the Rector, greeted them there, first sprinkling the casket with holy water, then turning to Angelica and expressing his sympathy. The cardinal then signaled the pall bearers to follow him into the cathedral and led them to the altar, where they placed the casket, while the Mormon Tabernacle Choir, accompanied by the National Symphony Orchestra, sang "Dies Irae" from Mozart's *Requiem*. Angelica followed the pall bearers to the altar, and a deacon standing nearby handed her a pall and a cross. She covered the coffin with the pall and put the cross on top of it, then turned and sat down in the front row in the seat closest to the aisle. Angelica's two sons took seats next to her.

Geraldine had been waiting for the family near the front door and joined them when they arrived. A deacon then escorted the family to the front row, where they sat in the pew across from Angelica. The six pews behind them and behind Angelica were reserved for the other world leaders. Six deacons escorted everyone to their seats. Within twenty minutes after the world leaders were seated, the church's twelve hundred seats were filled.

Cardinal D'Angelo began the service by reading from chapter three in the "Book of Ecclesiastes" in the Old Testament of The Holy Bible, using the definitive King James version: *"To every thing there is a season, and a time to every purpose under the heaven: A time to be born, and a time to die ..."* The Cardinal stopped after verse eight and explained, from a Catholic perspective, the significance of these words; then he sat down, and the Mormon Tabernacle Choir sang another selection from Mozart's *Requiem*, which was followed by Holy Communion. Roman Catholics in the congregation partook of the bread and wine, representing the body and blood of Jesus Christ. Angelica and her sons participated in the ceremony, as did Geraldine and Jacqueline; but Thomas, Esmeralda, and Sarah did not.

After the communion, Cardinal D'Angelo invited Esmeralda to speak, and she rose from her seat and walked to the podium.

"I don't need to remind you," Esmeralda began, "that President Samuel J. Hoffenberger was a great man with a distinguished record in the United States Senate and, before that, in the Virginia

House of Delegates. I won't try to list all of his accomplishments, including ground-breaking legislation to protect the environment and to address poverty, nor will I speculate on what he might have accomplished had he lived to serve more than two hours as your President. What I will do, however, is to tell you what President Hoffenberger stood for: he stood for cost-effective government, inclusion and diversity, the equitable distribution of wealth, and environmental protection. The best way to honor his legacy is to embrace those four ideals. As your new President, I promise to do exactly that."

Catching Esmeralda's eye, Thomas gave his wife a thumbs-up.

"We are honored," Esmeralda continued, "that more than a hundred world leaders are with us today. Many of them traveled thousands of miles, on short notice, to attend the funeral. Their presence today is not only a testimony to President Hoffenberger's popularity but further evidence that most of the world stands with the United States. As these countries have demonstrated in twelve world wars over six hundred years, they will not only fight by our side but also honor our fallen leaders and soldiers. I want to personally thank each and every one of the kings, queens, presidents, prime ministers, and other foreign leaders who are with us this morning."

Someone in the audience coughed.

"I know that Cardinal D'Angelo and James Hoffenberger, the President's oldest son, have some further remarks," said Esmeralda, "so I will leave it there for now. I hope all of you can follow us to Arlington National Cemetery for the burial, which will take place immediately after this service."

Esmeralda returned to her seat, and the orchestra and choir continued their performance of Mozart's *Requiem* with "Rex tremendae." Cardinal D'Angelo then read several verses from chapters five and six of the "Book of Matthew" in the New Testament, containing Jesus's "Sermon on the Mount," which he followed with some personal remembrances of the late President. After he was finished, the older of President Hoffenberger's two sons came to the podium and added some further recollections about his father. Cardinal D'Angelo then concluded the service with a benediction, and a deacon took Angelica's arm and escorted her from the church as her two sons followed.

Outside the church, the procession regrouped, and everyone waited for the pall bearers to remove the casket as the choir sang, "May Choirs of Angels Welcome You."

Arlington National Cemetery was on the other side of the Potomac River in Virginia, too far to walk given the time constraints and the number of mourners, so William had arranged for one hundred black aero-limousines to pick everyone up at the church and take them to the cemetery. Roger motioned to Esmeralda and the rest of the Jenkins family to follow him, and he opened the door to the second vehicle, directly behind Angelica's. Six Secret Service agents were already seated inside the vehicle, appropriately armed for any possible attack, when the family entered it and sat down.

As before, the Marine band stood at the front of the procession; and as soon as the pall bearers brought the casket outside and loaded it back on the caisson, the Marine band began walking. The aero-limousines flew six inches above the road behind the Marine band and the caisson, and the procession moved slowly south down 17th Street, passed the White House and the Ellipse, across Constitution Avenue, and passed the World War II Memorial to Independence Avenue. From there, it turned west passed the Martin Luther King, Jr., and Lincoln Memorials to Arlington Memorial

Bridge, then over the river to Memorial Circle, west on Memorial Avenue, and over the George Washington Memorial Parkway to the cemetery. Hundreds of thousands of people lined both sides of the streets, on both sides of the river, and stood in the windows and rooftops of buildings, as well as on the steps of the Lincoln Memorial and other elevated places, anxious to catch a glimpse of the procession and to be witness to the sad but historic occasion.

At the cemetery, everyone disembarked from their vehicles and walked a few hundred yards to the grave site where they waited for Cardinal D'Angelo to arrive. Angelica and her two sons arrived first, right after the Marine band; and Esmeralda, Thomas, and the other members of the Jenkins family arrived next. The Marines had already moved the casket from the caisson to the grave by the time the Jenkins family reached it.

Memengwaa appeared out of nowhere and greeted Esmeralda and the other members of the family. "Good speech, Esmeralda," she said, "short and sweet."

"We didn't see you in the church," said Thomas. "You could have sat with us."

"No problem, I found a seat in the back."

The Cardinal's limousine arrived soon afterwards, and the Cardinal disembarked and walked to the grave where he waited for the rest of the mourners to arrive. When everyone was present, he looked at the crowd and said, "Let's begin"; then he picked up a booklet and read aloud, enunciating each word with precision, *"Our brother has gone to his rest in the peace of Christ. May the Lord now welcome him to the table of God's children in heaven. With faith and hope in eternal life, let us assist him with our prayers."*

Cardinal D'Angelo set the booklet aside and picked up a Bible, turning to the Old Testament and locating his bookmark in the Book of Psalms. "Let us now read the word of our Lord in Psalm number twenty-three, a Psalm of David. This is from the King James version." He looked at the crowd around him, then back at the Bible, and continued:

The Lord is my shepherd; I shall not want. He maketh me to lie down in green pastures: he leadeth me beside the still waters. He restoreth my soul: he leadeth me in the paths of righteousness for his name's sake. Yea, though I walk through the valley of the shadow of death, I will fear no evil: for thou art with me; thy rod and thy staff they comfort me. Thou preparest a table before me in the presence of mine enemies: thou anointest my head with oil; my cup runneth over. Surely goodness and mercy shall follow me all the days of my life: and I will dwell in the house of the Lord forever.

Memengwaa, standing beside Esmeralda, took her hand and squeezed it gently. Cardinal D'Angelo set the Bible aside and continued:

Because God has chosen to call our brother from this life to himself, we commit his body to the earth, for we are dust and unto dust we shall return. But the Lord Jesus Christ will change our mortal bodies to be like his in glory, for he is risen, the firstborn from the dead. So let us commend our brother to the Lord, that the Lord may embrace him in peace and raise up his body on the last day.

As if on signal, eight men lowered President Hoffenberger's casket into the grave as the Marine band played the "Battle Hymn of the Republic." A Marine walked over to Angelica and handed her the President's flag, appropriately folded, which she accepted and placed under her arm.

When the casket was in the ground and the Marine band had finished, Cardinal D'Angelo said, *"May the love of God and the peace of the Lord Jesus Christ console you and gently wipe every tear from your eyes."*

Catholics and other Christians in the crowd, familiar with the ritual, responded, "Amen."

Cardinal D'Angelo concluded, *"May almighty God bless you, the Father, the Son, and the Holy Spirit."*

The crowd responded, "Amen."

Cardinal D'Angelo then turned and walked towards his aero-limousine, indicating that the burial service had ended. Everyone in the crowd relaxed and began talking.

"Wonderful service," said Memengwaa.

"The Cardinal did a good job," Sarah agreed.

"He could have added a couple more prayers," said Geraldine.

Esmeralda turned to Angelica, who was standing next to her, and gave her a hug. "You held your composure well, but remember it's okay to cry—the grieving process takes time, and crying is part of healing. Call me if you need someone to talk to."

Esmeralda then looked at Roger. "We need to get back to the White House as soon as possible. Get everyone into the limo. We have a state dinner tonight."

Roger motioned for the family to follow him, and minutes later everyone was seated in the aero-limousine with him and the six other Secret Service agents; and in another minute, the vehicle ascended to an altitude of fifteen hundred feet and turned east toward 1600 Pennsylvania Avenue.

With the funeral service and burial behind her, Esmeralda was already thinking about the state dinner and what to say to the foreign leaders.

Chapter 12
The Birth Lottery

Since he became the interim Chief of Staff on Monday, William had had little time to think about state dinners, so the dinner for the foreign leaders attending President Hoffenberger's funeral was necessarily planned on short notice. The State Dining Room had been decorated by former President Slazenger's wife, and Esmeralda had not yet seen it; and even if she had, there wouldn't have been enough time to repaint or redecorate it. The room contained ten large round tables, each seating ten people, with fine tablecloths and tall, tapered, white candles on each table. In addition to gold silverware and gold-embossed china, the place settings included crystal water glasses and baby-blue champagne glasses. On Thursday morning prior to the funeral, William ordered white lilacs to be placed on each table.

William directed the head chef to prepare vegetable soup; a beet salad with goat cheese; rice, noodles, and several vegetables—broccoli, cauliflower, asparagus, and brussels sprouts; and for dessert, a choice of Ben and Jerry's pistachio ice cream or apple pie. William also ordered menu cards embossed with gold fleur-de-lis and the White House seal, listing the evening's cuisine, to be placed on each place setting.

345

At 6:30 p.m., the guests began gathering on the State Floor of the Executive Residence, where they posed for a group photograph; then, at 6:55 p.m., the Marine Color Guard led them across Cross Hall, lined with 1,200 cherry-blossom branches, into the State Dining Room. A musical ensemble sitting in the corner played Mozart's *Concerto for Flute and Harp in C Major*, and William announced the names of the guests as they entered the room while other members of the White House staff directed them to their tables. Thomas and Esmeralda sat at the head table with King Charles VIII of England and President Charpentier of France, America's closest allies, and their spouses, Queen Guinevere and First Lady Francoise, respectively, along with the other members of the Jenkins family and Memengwaa. After further conversations with Thomas, Esmeralda had decided to invite Geraldine after all, and she took the last seat at the table.

When everyone was seated, Esmeralda stood up and addressed the guests. "I want to thank all of you for joining us this evening. We are honored to have so many distinguished guests. Thomas and I will try to meet each of you while you are enjoying your dinner. In the meantime, relax, get to know each other, and enjoy your dinner."

Esmeralda sat down and President Kazimir Kuznetsov of the New Soviet Union stood up and raised his champagne glass. "I'd like to propose a toast to our gracious hosts, President Jenkins and her spouse, Thomas. May President Jenkins be successful as the United States' new President."

"Hear, hear!" said King Charles.

Everyone raised their glass, clinked it with their neighbors' glasses, and took a sip of champagne.

After setting his champagne glass down, King Charles turned to Esmeralda. "I thought your speech at the funeral was right on point."

"Agreed," said President Charpentier. "I thought you chose your words wisely."

The waiters delivered the beet salad with goat cheese to the head table as the musical ensemble finished playing Mozart's *Concerto for Flute and Harp*; and after a brief pause, the musicians began playing a sonata.

"What are the musicians playing?" asked Queen Guinevere.

"I believe it's something from Beethoven," said First Lady Francoise.

"It's Beethoven's *Piano Sonata No. 8 in C minor, Opus 13*," said Sarah, "often called the Sonata Pathétique—one of my favorites."

"My granddaughter has a doctorate from Stanford," said Geraldine. "She's brilliant."

"Stanford?" asked Queen Guinevere. "I don't believe I've ever heard of it."

Seldom at a loss for words, Geraldine was quick to respond. "Sarah also has a Master's Degree from Harvard. Have you heard of Harvard?"

"Yes, I've heard of that one," replied the Queen. "I believe it's ranked just a few points below Oxford where I went."

Geraldine frowned.

"I graduated from the Université de Versailles Saint-Quentin-en-Yvelines," said First Lady Francoise. "It's one of the top universities in Europe."

"Maybe on the Continent," replied the Queen, "but not in England." She looked at Esmeralda. "President Jenkins, may I inquire where you matriculated?"

"I'm a robot," replied Esmeralda. "Robots don't matriculate." She stood up and looked at Thomas. "Honey, let's walk around the room and meet our guests." Turning towards the royalty at her table, she added. "Please excuse us. We'll be back in a few minutes."

With Thomas walking behind her, Esmeralda worked her way methodically from one table to the next, speaking to each foreign leader and their spouse. Later she would be able to match each face with a name and would remember their exact title, their country, and the name of their spouse.

While Thomas and Esmeralda were circulating through the room, King Charles and President Charpentier conversed with each other while their spouses talked to the rest of the Jenkins family and Memengwaa. After a few minutes, Geraldine overheard King Charles saying, "Keep an eye on the President's husband. They say he's the *real* President—Esmeralda is nothing more than a figurehead."

Geraldine turned to the King. "Did I just hear the pot calling the kettle black?"

"The pot calling the kettle black?" repeated the Queen. "I don't believe I'm familiar with that expression."

"It may be an American idiom," said First Lady Francoise.

"No offense intended," replied the King. "I was paying the President's husband a compliment."

"The way I see it," said President Charpentier, "it was a very clever political move. Who would have thought of that—buying a robowife and setting her up to become the next President? It was brilliant!"

Memengwaa decided it was time to jump into the conversation. "Thomas isn't calling the shots behind the scenes, if that's what you're getting at. Esmeralda is in charge."

"Why of course," said King Charles. "I'm sure she's in charge. Indeed, my wife is in charge of me most of the time." He looked at the Queen. "Isn't that true, dear?"

Queen Guinevere smiled.

"I certainly hope my remark wasn't misinterpreted," added the King. "I never questioned that President Jenkins is in charge."

"Thomas is my brother," said Jacqueline. "I can assure you he has no political ambitions."

"Of course not," said King Charles. "I certainly didn't mean to imply that he did."

"He seems like a fine fellow," said President Charpentier. "I'm sure he'll do a good job in his role as First Man."

The waiters delivered the main course to the head table, and the conversation quieted as everyone began eating. When Thomas and Esmeralda returned to the table, they were finishing their dessert.

"I hope you've all had a chance to get acquainted," said Esmeralda, looking at her family and the French and English royalty.

"Most definitely," said King Charles, "your family is delightful."

"Are you implying that my wife and I aren't delightful?" asked President Charpentier.

"When I visit you in Paris," replied King Charles, "you and your family are delightful, and when I visit President Jenkins in Washington, *she* and *her* family are delightful—get it?"

Everyone laughed.

William came to the table. "President Jenkins, would you like me to announce the entertainment?"

"By all means," replied Esmeralda. "It looks like everyone has finished dinner."

William walked to the center of the room. "May I have your attention, please! I trust that you've enjoyed your dinner. We'd like to finish the evening with some light entertainment, so our musical ensemble will now play a medley of classical music from the legendary American composers Charles Ives, Aaron Copland, and George Gershwin; and for those of you who would like to dance, they will finish with Franz Schubert's *Waltz in B minor*. We have made some space in one corner of the room for dancing. The waiters will offer you complimentary wine, beer, or ale while the musicians are playing. Please enjoy!"

William turned and disappeared, and the ensemble began playing Gershwin's *Rhapsody in Blue*, using state-of-the-art digital enhancements to replicate the effect of a one-hundred-piece orchestra.

"If you enjoy classical music," said President Charpentier, "I recommend Claude Debussy. If you've never heard him, you might start with *Clair de lune*."

"Or try Chopin," said First Lady Francoise. "Listen to his *Piano Concerto No. 1 in E Minor*."

"I think Debussy is better," said President Charpentier.

"I prefer classical music from a later era," said King Charles, "like that of the Rolling Stones, an English group from the twentieth century. If you've never heard of them, start with *I Can't Get No Satisfaction*. That was one of their most popular songs."

" 'I can't get no satisfaction' is bad English," said Geraldine. "You would think a singer from England would have a better command of the English language."

"I guess that's the way they talked in those days," replied King Charles.

I wonder why he couldn't get any satisfaction, pondered Geraldine.

"Is that the only song the Rolling Stones sang?" asked Esmeralda.

"My goodness, no," replied the King. "They sang many good ones. Another one I like is *You Can't Always Get What You Want*. Listen to it—you'll be hooked."

"I think I get it," said Geraldine. "He couldn't get any satisfaction because he couldn't always get what he wanted."

"You'd do better with Andrew Lloyd Webber," said the Queen, "Listen to *Jesus Christ Superstar* or *Phantom of the Opera*."

"I've made a note of your recommendations," said Esmeralda. She turned to Thomas. "Honey, why don't we listen to some of their music tomorrow night while you and Sarah are eating your dinner?"

"Good idea," replied Thomas.

The royals looked pleased, and everyone sat back and listened to the ensemble's interpretation of Gershwin's famous composition. Later, when the ensemble played Schubert's waltz, Thomas and Esmeralda danced; and many of the royals, including King Charles and Queen Guinevere, joined them on the dance floor.

The evening concluded with the foreign leaders and their spouses in high spirits. The dinner had been a success.

*   *   *   *   *

The movers arrived at Thomas's apartment early the next morning as Thomas and Sarah were finishing their breakfast. Thomas agreed to stay with the movers while Roger took Esmeralda and Sarah to their offices in Washington.

"Don't let them touch my bedroom," said Sarah.

"Of course not," replied Thomas.

"We don't need to move much furniture," said Esmeralda. "The Executive Residence is already furnished. We can always switch things around later if we decide we don't like the way it's furnished now."

"Make sure they don't take the kitchen table and kitchen chairs," said Sarah. "I'm sure you'll be eating all your meals in the Family Dining Room."

"You're right," replied Thomas. "I'll tell the movers to leave the kitchen alone."

Esmeralda signaled Roger that they were ready to leave, and she and Sarah followed him to the Air Force One aeromobile parked on the roof. In a few minutes, they were in the sky flying east towards the District of Columbia. Roger took Esmeralda to the White House first, where two Secret Service agents met her on the roof and escorted her into the building, and then continued on to Sarah's office in the Rayburn House Office Building.

Once inside the White House, Esmeralda went directly to the Oval Office where she reviewed William's daily briefing paper and began planning the day. First among her tasks was to review a list of possible nominees for Vice President, which Memengwaa had sent her earlier in the week, and to decide if she wanted to make William the permanent Chief of Staff. She read Memengwaa's list of the House and Senate Greens, most of whom she had met during her tenure in the House, and downloaded the resumes of the best qualified.

At ten o'clock, Esmeralda called Memengwaa. After exchanging pleasantries and talking briefly about the previous day's events, Esmeralda told her she wanted to make a decision on her nominee for Vice President. "Unless you can think of anyone else—besides the names you already sent me—I think I like Representative Humetewa."

"Have you interviewed him yet?"

"No, I thought I'd talk to you first."

"Like I said the other day, I'm fine with him."

"Okay, I'll have William contact him today and set up the interview. Do you think I should name William my permanent Chief of Staff?"

"It looks to me like he has really stepped up to the plate," replied Memengwaa. "Everything went like clockwork yesterday."

"I thought so, too."

"Then make him permanent. He'll have more authority if people know he's there to stay."

"I agree," replied Esmeralda. "I'll speak to him and make the announcement today."

"Don't forget to clear it with OPM."

"Understood," replied Esmeralda. "I'm already in touch with personnel management."

"It sounds like you have all the bases covered."

"I think so."

"Let me know if you need anything else."

"Will do."

Esmeralda said goodbye to Memengwaa and called for William, who appeared in a moment.

"Good morning, President Jenkins," he said.

"You don't have to be so formal—call me Esmeralda. My God, we've known each other now for thirty-six years."

"True, but it might be wise for me to call you President Jenkins when we're in public. We don't want to give people the wrong impression."

"Good point," replied Esmeralda. "Anyway, you did a good job yesterday with the funeral and the state dinner. I can see you're up to the job, and I'd like you to be my permanent Chief of Staff."

"Thank you for the vote of confidence."

"No thanks needed—you've earned it."

"Should we issue an announcement?"

"Yes, I'll speak to OPM and the White House Communications Director this morning. In the meantime, I need you to contact Representative Juan Nighthorse Humetewa. Tell him he is on the short list for VP. I want to interview him this afternoon or this weekend."

"Got it."

"I also want you to set up a meeting with the White House Counsel to discuss my first Executive Order."

"Your first EO?"

"That's right, I want to issue an EO implementing a birth lottery for all Federal employees—step one of a universal birth lottery. I want to do it next week if I can't do it today."

"Nothing in the Government happens in one day."

"Understood, but we should be able to do it in one week."

"Even one week is a high bar for the Government."

"The Government *as it used to be*—not the Government I run. From now on, one week will be the norm, and one day will be the high bar."

"That's going to be a sea change for the people around here."

"Sea change?"

"It's just an expression. When do you want to meet with the White House Counsel?"

"Today. Tell her I'd like to meet with her at two o'clock."

"Will do."

"And invite Thomas to the meeting."

"Thomas?"

"That's right. Thomas is my unofficial advisor, but very low-profile. I don't want him in any photos. When the TV crews and photographers come to the White House, he disappears."

"Does Thomas know that?"

"Oh yes, Memengwaa and I have both spoken to him about it. He's okay with it."

"Very well, I'll tell the White House Counsel and Thomas to be in the Oval Office at two o'clock."

Esmeralda's iPalm vibrated. Opening her left hand, she saw that the movers had arrived and pushed her chair back and stood up. "The movers are here. I'm going to check on them."

"Do you need my help with it?"

"No, Thomas is overseeing the move. I'll talk to him and make sure there's no hitches. One of us will let you know if we need your assistance."

William returned to his office, and Esmeralda walked to the Executive Residence and conferred with her husband, who had arrived with the movers.

"You got here faster than I expected," said Esmeralda.

"We didn't have much furniture to move. It's mostly books, boxes of clothes, and other odds and ends."

"Do you need me for anything?"

"Not really. I'll have them put our clothes and personal items in the dressing room adjacent to the master bedroom, your books in your study on the third floor, my books in my office in the East Wing, and anything we don't need right away in the storage room on the third floor."

"That sounds good. Call me if you need me."

Satisfied that her husband had everything under control, Esmeralda returned to the Oval Office and began working on her first Executive Order.

*　　*　　*　　*　　*

Bhaanupriya Yanagi, the White House Counsel, reported to the Oval Office at 2:00 p.m. as instructed. Ms. Yanagi, an attorney in her mid-thirties, was dressed in a salwar kameez suit embroidered with traditional Hindu designs. Esmeralda had already met her on Tuesday morning during her tour of the White House.

Thomas appeared at the door a moment later as Esmeralda and Ms. Yanagi were getting acquainted. "William said you wanted me in this meeting?"

"Yes, we need to talk to Attorney Yanagi about my first Executive Order. Ms. Yanagi is the White House Counsel. Have you met her yet?"

"I have now," replied Thomas, turning to the attorney and shaking hands. "My pleasure."

"Thomas is my husband and also my senior advisor," said Esmeralda. "You'll be working together on Executive Orders and other matters."

"I look forward to working with him," said Ms. Yanagi. "And please call me by my first name, *Bhaanupriya*."

Esmeralda had rearranged the furnishings in the Oval Office and placed a small coffee table with three chairs near the wall on one side of the room. She stepped away from her desk and sat down in a chair at the coffee table and motioned for Thomas and Bhaanupriya to take the other two seats.

"I don't like sitting behind a desk when I'm meeting with people," said Esmeralda. "It feels very contrived—like I'm trying to be the Queen or something. A coffee table is more conducive to productive conversation."

"That's a novel idea," said Bhaanupriya.

"You're going to find that Esmeralda has *many* novel ideas," said Thomas. "In the old days, they referred to it as *thinking out of the box*."

"Well, let's get to the point," said Esmeralda. "As you know, President Hoffenberger and I ran on a platform to reduce the human population—more specifically, to reduce it by means of a birth lottery. The world is in crisis, and I don't want to waste a minute. Step one is to establish the birth lottery in the United States; and one action I can take on my own, without Congress's approval, is to mandate the birth lottery for all Federal employees, including members of the military. That would be the essence of my first EO. Then we can work with Congress on legislation to mandate the birth lottery across the board for all U.S. citizens."

"I don't object to the concept of a birth lottery," said Bhaanupriya, "but as the White House Counsel, I have to advise you that you will face a barrage of lawsuits from the American Civil Liberties Union, the American Federation of Government Employees, and other Federal labor unions. To be perfectly candid, this could get ugly in a hurry."

"We are fully aware of that," said Thomas. "Esmeralda is not afraid of a fight."

"I'm counting on the American people to support me," said Esmeralda. "After all, they're not stupid—they know the human species is in danger of extinction if someone doesn't do something soon."

"That's all well and good," replied Bhaanupriya, "but you have to face reality. The ACLU and AFGE will go to court and try to block implementation of the EO before the ink has even dried on the paper."

"That's where *you* come in," said Thomas. "You're the President's lawyer. You have to go to court and defend her."

"I know my job," replied Bhaanupriya, "and I know how to go to the court; but if you want to go down this path, you better give me additional staff or hire outside counsel to support me."

"I'll tell you the same thing I've already told my Cabinet members," said Esmeralda. "Write up a justification. Tell me how many people you need at what salary level, what they will do, and why you need them. If your justification is sound, I'll give you the additional staff."

"That sounds fair," replied Bhaanupriya.

"Bear in mind that the Executive Order has symbolic value, even if the court kills it. I'm sending a message to the American people—and for that matter, to the world—that I'm serious about reducing the human population."

"That's correct," said Thomas. "Other nations will follow our lead."

Bhaanupriya raised her eyebrows. "Is that so?"

"Yes," replied Thomas. "You'll see."

"Very well, then," said Esmeralda, "let's get to work on it. I've already written a rough draft. I'll read it you."

Esmeralda, Thomas, and Bhaanupriya spent the next hour revising Esmeralda's draft to reflect input from the lawyer, carefully parsing the document for logic, clarity, and legal sufficiency. Soon after 3:00 p.m., they were done, and Esmeralda instructed Thomas to prepare the proper clearance form, get Bhaanupriya's initials on it, and route it through William and the White House Communications Director.

"I'll announce it on Sunday evening during my first *Sunday Evening Update*," said Esmeralda.

"Terrific!" said Thomas.

"This should be quite a ride," said Bhaanupriya.

The three pushed their chairs back from the coffee table and stood up. Thomas and Bhaanupriya left the Oval Office, and Esmeralda returned to her desk.

*　　*　　*　　*　　*

Friday night was the couple's first night sleeping in the White House; and when they arose the next morning, Esmeralda accompanied Thomas to breakfast in the Family Dining Room, which was on the first floor across the hall from the State Dining Room.

"You must be relieved you won't have to make breakfast for me anymore," said Thomas as they sat down at a table.

"I didn't mind making breakfast, but having someone else do it will give me more time to focus on being President."

"Right, you don't want to be distracted with household chores."

"I worry about Sarah, though. She won't have me to cook for her."

"She'll be fine. Didn't she cook for herself in San Antonio?"

"I know, but I'm her mother. It's my job to worry about her."

"Mothers are all alike—even robot mothers!"

The waiter brought Thomas his breakfast, and Esmeralda watched him eat, checking her iPalm periodically for messages.

"William says he got in touch with Representative Humetewa," said Esmeralda. "He is available for an interview whenever I'm ready."

"If you don't have anything else that's pressing, I suggest you do the interview today. Then, if he's still your top pick, you can announce it tomorrow night during your *Sunday Evening Update*."

"That's what I'd like to do."

"Then tell William to get him over here today."

Esmeralda nodded in agreement and spoke directly into her iPalm, sending William a text, "William, please see if Representative Humetewa can come to the White House at ten o'clock. I'll interview him in the Oval Office."

"That's good," said Thomas, "you'll have one more box checked before we even go to lunch."

"I also need to call Jacqueline and talk to her about the birth lottery—that is, getting it started in Congress."

Thomas opened his iPalm and looked at the time. "It's eight o'clock. Jacqueline sleeps a little later on Saturday morning, but I think you can call her now."

Esmeralda had Jacqueline on speed-dial and hit a button on her iPalm.

"Hello," said Jacqueline.

"Good morning, Jacqueline. Listen, I need a favor."

Jacqueline had just arisen and was not yet firing on all cylinders. "You're the President now, right? Oh my God!" There was a moment of silence. "Sure, what do you need?"

"I need you to introduce a bill in the House mandating a birth lottery across the board—applicable to all U.S. citizens in all one hundred states."

"You want *what*?"

"A birth lottery—remember? I talked about it during the VP debate in October."

"Oh, yes, a birth lottery ... right. I remember, you want to reduce the human population."

"That's correct. Yesterday I worked with Thomas and the White House Counsel on an Executive Order, but that will apply only to Federal employees and the military. The next step is for Congress to pass a law that would extend the birth lottery to everyone in the United States—*everyone*."

"Ah, yes, of course."

"How soon do you think you can get it done?"

Jacqueline took a moment to respond. "Sis, I hope you realize you are giving me a heavy lift. First, I need to find a co-sponsor—either a Democrat or a Republican to co-sponsor the bill. That in itself is a tall order. Then we would have to lobby our colleagues to support the bill. That could take a few months. Then, if we pass the bill in the House, it would still have to go to the Senate—and I have zero control over what happens there."

"It's going to be that hard?"

"Honey, I'm not trying to pour cold water on your initiative, but this isn't going to be easy. In fact, it might be the most controversial bill since President Obama's Affordable Health Care Act in the twentieth century. I'm sure you've heard of that one."

"Yes, I think everyone has."

"Well, this would be similar. There will be massive opposition to it. People will organize and protest, and the protests could get violent. Believe me, it could get ugly."

"The White House Counsel used the same word."

"Well, we're in this together. Give me a couple of days to put out some feelers and see if I can find a co-sponsor. If I can't find a co-sponsor, it would be a complete waste of time."

"Understood."

"Let me see what I can do. I'll get back to you in a few days."

"Thanks a million, Jacqueline."

"My pleasure, Sis."

Thomas finished his breakfast while Esmeralda was speaking to Jacqueline; and when she had finished her conversation, the couple pushed their chairs back and stood up.

"I wonder if we are supposed to leave a tip for the waiter," said Esmeralda.

"I don't know," replied Thomas. "I wouldn't think the President is expected to leave a tip in her own dining room. I mean, like, we're going to eat nearly every meal here. That could get quite expensive."

"Tipping can be tricky. We'll have to ask someone who has been around here for a while what the protocol is."

"Why don't you ask the White House Counsel?"

"Good idea," replied Esmeralda. "I'll ask her."

The couple left the dining room without leaving a tip, and Esmeralda headed for the Oval Office while Thomas went to his new office in the East Wing.

*   *   *   *   *

Representative Humetewa arrived at the Oval Office at ten o'clock as requested, and Esmeralda greeted him warmly.

"Please have a seat here," said Esmeralda, pointing to the coffee table. They both sat down at the table.

"William told me I'm on the short list for VP," said Representative Humetewa. "I want to thank you for considering me."

"Well, we worked together on the small business subcommittee and got along pretty well."

"Yes, it was amazing what the subcommittee accomplished during your tenure as Chair."

"Give yourself some of the credit," replied Esmeralda. "It was teamwork."

"And good leadership ... you deserve the lion's share of the credit."

"That's very kind of you. In any case, one of my first tasks as President is to nominate a VP. If I were to nominate you, is there anything in your background that might cause the House or Senate to deny your confirmation?"

"No, I don't believe so. I have a clean record."

"No EEO complaints, no allegations of misconduct or sexual harassment?" asked Esmeralda. "Sorry, but I have to ask these questions."

"I understand. No, my record is clean."

"Very good. And you understand that being the VP means embracing the ideals of my Administration?"

"Of course."

"Including a universal birth lottery?"

"I'm in favor of that."

"Good, then I think you're the man for the job. As you know, William is my Chief of Staff, and he'll be the point man for your nomination. Please give him any information he needs to move the nomination forward."

"Of course, I will cooperate with him fully."

Esmeralda stood up and extended her hand. "Congratulations—you're my nominee!"

Representative Humetewa stood up and shook hands with Esmeralda. "I can't thank you enough, President Jenkins."

Esmeralda escorted the Congressman to William's office. William greeted Esmeralda formally, as if he hadn't already spoken to her earlier. "Good morning, Ms. President." Then he turned to the Congressman. "Good to see you again, Sir."

"Good to see you again as well," replied Representative Humetewa.

The two men shook hands.

"I'm going to leave you gentlemen together to get reacquainted," said Esmeralda. "William, please contact the Speaker of the House and the President Pro Tem of the Senate and let them know we are nominating Representative Humetewa for Vice President. Keep the White House Counsel and the White House Communications Director in the loop. Let me know if you run into any glitches."

"No problem, I'll take it from here," replied William.

Representative Humetewa turned to Esmeralda. "Thank you again for your confidence in me."

Esmeralda nodded, said goodbye, and returned to her office.

*   *   *   *   *

Jacqueline and Sarah came to Geraldine's house for dinner on Sunday evening, January 26th, so that they could watch Esmeralda's first *Sunday Evening Update* together. Geraldine prepared a simple dinner with spinach salad, cream of asparagus soup, and a vegetable plate with broccoli, cauliflower, brussels sprouts, and kale. They finished eating at 7:30 p.m., and Jacqueline and Sarah helped Geraldine, who did not yet have a robotic dishwasher, clean up the kitchen and load the dishwasher by hand.

At 7:45 p.m., Geraldine summoned her digital assistant. "Richard, my daughter-in-law is addressing the Nation again tonight. Would you please have it ready for me at eight o'clock?"

"Maybe a few minutes before eight," suggested Jacqueline. "The network anchor might make some introductory remarks."

"Did you hear that, Richard?" asked Geraldine. "My daughter suggests you start it a few minutes early."

The north wall of the kitchen lit up, and Richard appeared. "Good evening, Ms. Jenkins. I understand you would like to watch your daughter-in-law make an address to the Nation, is that correct?"

"You got it."

"Any particular network?"

"Maybe CNN. I'm tired of looking at Jonathan Anderson's bare feet."

"Jonathan Anderson?"

"The anchor on NBC. CNN seems to be the only network that has a dress code anymore."

"Understood, Ms. Jenkins. Would you like me to remove NBC from your line-up?"

"No, I'll still watch NBC—just not the news."

"If I understand your instructions, Ms. Jenkins, I will have CNN ready for you to watch at eight o'clock, preferably a few minutes before eight, but I won't remove NBC from your line-up. Is that correct?"

"You got it, young man."

"My pleasure, Ms. Jenkins."

Richard disappeared and the north wall went dark. Geraldine turned to the refrigerator to order a cup of hot tea. "Does anyone else want tea?"

"I'll take a cup," said Sarah.

"Is Earl Gray okay?" asked Geraldine.

"Yes, that would be fine," replied Sarah.

"Earl Gray is fine with me, too," said Jacqueline.

Geraldine stood in front of the refrigerator. "Give me three cups of hot Earl Gray tea, please." The refrigerator dispensed the three cups from a portal in the door, and Geraldine picked them up and brought them to the table. The three women sat down and began sipping their tea, and the north wall lit up a few moments later.

An elderly woman wearing a blue blouse and a matching skirt, seated at a glass table, appeared on the monitor. "Good evening. My name is Suzanne Zhang. We are about to bring you President Esmeralda Jenkins's first *Sunday Evening Update*. With me is Shoshana Israel, CNN's senior political analyst, and she will provide some perspective on the President's address when she finishes." The screen shot widened, revealing the two women sitting together.

Ms. Zhang turned and looked at Ms. Israel. "Do you have any thoughts you'd like to share with our viewers before the President speaks?"

The camera zoomed in on Ms. Israel, who was wearing a gray suit with a white dress shirt and black tie. "I think it is important for your viewers to know," said Ms. Israel, "that from an historical perspective, this is an unorthodox approach to governing—we haven't had a President in nearly six hundred years who has promised to speak to the American people every week."

"The last time would have been FDR's fireside chats, is that correct?"

"That's correct—and I'm not sure that FDR actually spoke to the American people every single week. This is truly unprecedented."

"Well, it remains to be seen if President Jenkins will follow through. It's one thing to promise it and another thing to do it. She may find it takes too much of her time."

"Exactly ... and let's face it, she has a husband; and if he's like most husbands, he expects her to spend Sunday evening at home watching TV with him."

"I believe that the President is about to begin. Let's watch and see what she says." The two CNN women disappeared, and Esmeralda appeared on the screen, sitting at her desk in the Oval Office. An announcer exclaimed, "Here, now, is the President of the United States!"

"Good evening, my fellow Americans," Esmeralda began. "Thank you for joining me this evening for my first *Sunday Evening Update*. As I told you during my address to the Nation on the evening of January 20th, I plan to do this every Sunday evening. It will be an opportunity for me to connect directly with the American people. I will update you on special events, appointments, and nominees such as my pick for Vice President, which I will get to in a moment. Most importantly, I will update you on the economy—especially leading economic indicators and changes in the money supply."

"I hope she's not going to go too far into the weeds," said Jacqueline.

"My first week as your President was productive," continued Esmeralda. "I moved into the Oval Office on Tuesday morning and got right to work. We held the funeral for President Hoffenberger on Thursday and hosted a state dinner for the visiting heads of state the same evening. On Friday, my husband and I moved into the

White House residence, and I drafted my first Executive Order—or EO as the bureaucrats like to call it. I will hold a press conference tomorrow to announce the EO."

"I don't like the sound of that," said Geraldine. "What's she up to now?"

"Just listen, Mom," said Jacqueline.

"I'm pleased to announce that I'm nominating Representative Juan Nighthorse Humetewa from South Dakota for Vice President. Representative Humetewa has served honorably in the House for more than a decade. I worked with him closely when I chaired the Subcommittee on Economic Growth, Tax and Capital Access, and I know he will be an effective VP. I will be submitting his nomination package to Congress tomorrow."

"Good pick," said Sarah.

"Now I want to get to the fun part of the evening—economics! I realize that many of you never had a chance to study it; so for our purposes this evening, I will go over a few of the fundamentals. Economics is generally broken down into macro-economics, micro-economics, and monetary economics, which is sometimes called money and banking. Macro-economics is the big picture, so that's what I will talk about mostly. It deals with supply and demand, consumption, inflation and deflation, the consumer price index, business cycles, employment and unemployment, government spending, and finally—and this is the bottom line—the gross domestic product or GDP."

"Why does she say GDP is the bottom line?" asked Geraldine.

"I'll explain it to you later," said Sarah. "I hope she's going to explain the difference between nominal GDP and real GDP."

"Be quiet, guys," said Jacqueline. "Just listen."

Esmeralda continued, "I will also talk a lot about leading economic indicators such as retail sales, housing starts, and orders for durable goods."

"Why does she think this is so much fun?" asked Geraldine.

"The last piece I want to touch on this evening is monetary economics, which addresses the role of the Federal Reserve and changes in the money supply and interest rates. You'll hear me talk a lot about M_1 and M_2—liquid assets and savings or time deposits, respectively. Economists keep a close eye on M_1 and M_2 because they give us insight into changes in the money supply, which in turn helps us to predict future inflation or deflation."

"How does the money supply affect inflation?" asked Geraldine.

"I'll explain it to you later," said Sarah.

"I think that's enough for this evening," said Esmeralda. "Next week I'll talk about the multiplier effect of government spending and how that will inform my plan for revitalizing the economy and putting people back to work."

"Thank goodness we have a President who understands economics!" said Sarah.

"As you can see, economics is exciting," Esmeralda continued, "and one pitfall I want to avoid is to overstimulate you before you go to bed. Humans need eight hours of sleep every night, and many of you need more than that, depending upon your age and other variables; so please turn off your electronic devices, do your meditation or say your prayers, and go to bed. I want you to get a good night's sleep so that you will be energetic, focused, and productive when you go to work or school tomorrow. This concludes my first *Sunday Evening Update*. Thank you for your time, God Bless America, and have a good night's sleep."

The screen shot of Esmeralda sitting behind her desk in the Oval Office began to fade, and the voice of the announcer came over the air. "The President's final admonition about going to bed doesn't apply to you if you are unemployed, retired, or a child under the age of five who has not yet entered pre-school."

The two ladies from CNN reappeared. "Well, Shoshana," said Ms. Zhang, "what do you think?"

Ms. Israel looked at Ms. Zhang, then faced the camera. "I just don't know, Suzanne. President Jenkins obviously understands economics—there's no disputing that—but I wonder if this is the right way to connect with the American people. After all, how many Americans care about supply and demand, consumption, business cycles, GDP, and M_1 and M_2? Frankly, I'm worried that this approach is going to backfire on her."

"You have to give her credit for trying to educate the American people on economics," replied Ms. Zhang.

"Do we really need to listen to the rest of this?" asked Geraldine.

"You may discontinue it if you want," said Jacqueline. "I just wanted to hear Esmeralda's address."

"Richard," said Geraldine, "you may discontinue the broadcast."

Richard appeared in the top right-hand corner of the monitor. "I understand you would like me to discontinue the broadcast, Ms. Jenkins, is that right?"

"You got it."

"Would you like to watch something else instead?"

"No, Richard, just turn it off."

"Very well, Ms. Jenkins, I will turn it off." Richard disappeared and the monitor went dark.

Geraldine turned to her daughter and granddaughter. "How do you think she did?"

"Not bad for a quick intro to ECON-101," replied Sarah.

"I share the same concerns as CNN's political analyst," said Jacqueline. "I hope the American people aren't turned off by this approach."

"If nothing else," said Geraldine, "now they'll know what M_1 and M_2 mean."

"And don't forget Esmeralda told us who she picked for VP," said Sarah. "I'm sure she will use the *Sunday Evening Update* for more than just economics."

The three women continued to discuss the pros and cons of Esmeralda's first *Sunday Evening Update* for another thirty minutes and two more rounds of Earl Gray tea. Finally, Jacqueline and Sarah departed, and Geraldine went to the bathroom to prepare her evening bath.

*   *   *   *   *

On Monday afternoon, January 27th, at 2:00 p.m., Esmeralda held a press conference in the Rose Garden with 150 journalists and cameramen to announce her Executive Order on the birth lottery. The White House staff had set up fifteen rows of chairs for the press and positioned a podium in front of them. Esmeralda stood behind the podium, and William stood in front of her and slightly to one side, facing the reporters, so that he could assist with the questions and answers.

"Thank you for coming to the Rose Garden this afternoon for my announcement," Esmeralda began. "As you may have heard, I'm issuing an Executive Order today that will implement a mandatory birth lottery for all Federal employees, including members of our armed services and other civilian and military personnel."

"Are you going to give us actual copies of the EO?" asked a reporter in the second row.

"My staff will provide you with electronic copies of the EO immediately after the press conference."

"When does this go into effect?" asked another reporter.

"It goes into effect in thirty days in order to give the Office of Management and Budget—around here they call it *OMB*—time to develop and disseminate the guidelines. Please hold any further questions until I'm done."

William held his hands up in a stop signal to reinforce Esmeralda's request.

"This is basically what the EO says," continued Esmeralda. " 'The U.S. Department of Health and Human Services will establish a birth lottery in accordance with guidelines issued by OMB, and such lottery shall be conducted not less than once a year. No female who is an employee of the United States Government, civilian or military, shall conceive a baby unless she has been selected, by means of the official birth lottery, to have said baby.' That's the EO in a nutshell. Now I will be happy to take any questions."

All of the reporters in the garden immediately raised their hands, some waving them vigorously to get Esmeralda's attention.

"William, my Chief of Staff, will decide who gets to speak and in what order. He will point to you when it's your turn. Please identify yourself, including the name of your media outlet, before you ask your question."

William pointed to a young woman in the front row.

"My name is Lou Emma Smith from *The Washington Times*. I'd like to know why you are singling out Federal employees. Why should government employees carry the full burden of reducing the human population?"

"Thank you for your excellent question, Ms. Smith," replied Esmeralda. "My authority to mandate a birth lottery is limited to Federal employees. I can't mandate a birth lottery for all U.S. citizens—only Congress can do that."

William pointed to a young man in the fourth row who was waving his hand briskly.

"My name is Sam Armstrong from *ABC World News*. Are you going to try to persuade Congress to legislate a universal birth lottery?"

"Thank you for your excellent question, Mr. Armstrong. The answer is yes, that's the long-term plan, but it may take a while to make it happen. A mandatory birth lottery is a new idea for most people, and I'm sure the members of Congress—like everyone else—need some time to think about it."

William pointed to a woman in the last row.

"My name is Henrietta Harper from the *San Francisco Chronicle*. Don't you think that the Federal labor unions will sue you to block the EO?"

"Thank you for your excellent question, Ms. Harper. Yes, I think that's quite possible. The White House Counsel is prepared to defend the EO in court if they do."

William recognized a woman in the sixth row.

"My name is Qingzhao Wong from *NBC Nightly News*. Exactly how is the lottery going to work? If you are a woman working for the Federal government, what are your odds of winning the lottery and being able to have a baby?"

"Thank you for your excellent question, Ms. Wong. OMB is developing the formula; and after my approval, they will provide it to the Department of Health and Human Services, which will administer the program. I can't give you the formula right now because I don't have it, but I can assure you that we will make that information available to the public when we do. The lottery will be totally transparent."

William pointed to a woman in the fifth row.

"My name is Irene Murphy from *The Boston Globe*. How much do you want to reduce the population? Exactly what is your end game here?"

"Thank you for your excellent question, Ms. Murphy. I will be working with my Council of Economic Advisors on a precise number; but for starters, I think we need to bring the world population back down to seven billion, the figure at the beginning of the millennium. I think we can accomplish that by the year *three thousand*. Long-term, of course, if we want the human species to survive as long as the Earth does, we need a more aggressive plan—perhaps a ceiling of one billion by the year *four thousand*."

William recognized a woman in the second row.

"My name is Florentyna Jackiewicz from the *Austin American-Statesman*. I'd like to know if you have any other Executive Orders in the pipeline."

"Thank you for your excellent question, Ms. Jackiewicz. Yes, I do. Some five hundred years ago, the Venerable Master Hsing Yun said that a skillful physician cures with weeds and a skillful worker makes steel from old pots. This was never truer than it is today. Material such as iron ore, aluminum, and petroleum that were once abundant are now scarce or gone completely. Even common pharmaceuticals such as aspirin are now scarce or gone. My next Executive Order will address this issue."

"You're referring to recycling, then, is that correct?" asked Ms. Jackiewicz.

"That's one piece of it," answered Esmeralda, "but the solution goes beyond recycling. Humans are far too wasteful, so we also need to address consumption."

William pointed to a man in the fourth row.

"It's no secret that you are a robot—"

"Please state your name and your organization before you ask your question," interrupted William.

"Sorry, I forgot. My name is Rafael Gonzales from the *Washington Post*. It's no secret you are a robot. Don't you think many Americans will see this EO as part of a long-term strategy to take over the planet—that is, to eliminate human beings from the Earth?"

"Thank you for your excellent question, Mr. Gonzales. Some Americans may, in fact, see it that way, but I can assure you that's not my intent. Robots exist to serve humans—we have no desire to take over the planet."

William pointed to a woman in the fifth row.

"My name is Aakanksha Balakrishnan from the *New York Times*. "When President Hoffenberger was assassinated, many people thought that Chief Justice Vlastos should have bypassed you and administered the Oath of Office to the Speaker of the House, since he was next in the line of succession—that is, he was the first *human* in the line of succession. Some people are even calling for your impeachment. Don't you think that this EO will give the Speaker ammunition to impeach you?"

"Thank you for your excellent question, Ms. Balakrishnan. I'm confident that Speaker McIntyre has no intention of impeaching me.

During my tenure in Congress, Speaker McIntyre was Chair of the Small Business Committee, and I served on his committee. He liked me so much he appointed me to chair one of his subcommittees. He really likes me a lot—I can assure you that he would never try to impeach me."

William waved both hands at the reporters. "Okay, that's going to have to be the last question. Thank you very much for your time."

Esmeralda turned and walked back to the Oval Office where Thomas was waiting for her.

"I watched the whole thing on your TV," said Thomas. "You nailed it!"

"I hope so. They threw me a few curve balls."

"You fielded them like a pro."

"Thanks for the feedback ... well, let's get back to work. Remember we have a World Economic Forum in Switzerland next week—I have to begin working on my speech."

Esmeralda sat down at her desk to write her speech, and Thomas returned to his office in the East Wing.

After dismissing the White House Press Pool, William returned to his office in the West Wing and picked up two copies of the Vice President's nomination package, which was now complete, and called for the White House aeromobile so that he could hand-deliver the two copies to Congress. A Secret Service agent accompanied him to the Russell Senate Office Building on Constitution Avenue, north of the Capitol, where he delivered the first package to the office of the Senate President Pro Tem, and then to the Longworth House Office Building on New Jersey Avenue Southeast, west of the Capitol, where he delivered the other package to the office of the Speaker of the House. Satisfied that his mission was accomplished, William returned to the White House.

*   *   *   *   *

Speaker McIntyre was meeting with Majority Leader Sullivan when the receptionist brought him the nomination package.

"Someone from the White House just delivered this," said the receptionist, handing the nine-by-twelve-inch envelope to the Speaker. "He said it was important."

Speaker McIntyre took a letter opener from his desktop, opened the envelope, and removed the contents. On top was a cover letter addressed to him on White House letterhead with the signature *President Esmeralda Jenkins*. He read it quickly.

"What is it?" asked Majority Leader Sullivan.

"It's the nomination for the Vice President. Remember, President Jenkins mentioned it last night during her ridiculous *Sunday Evening Update*." He thumbed through the attachments. "It's got the guy's resume, his security clearance, and a bunch of other stuff." He tossed the package and the envelope into a letter box in the top-right corner of his desk. "I'll take my time with it."

"If I were you, I wouldn't just take my time with it—I'd *sit* on it."

"What do you mean by that?"

Majority Leader Sullivan leaned forward in his chair and lowered his voice. "The Constitution doesn't give you a deadline for acting on this. Think about it: if the House and Senate approve this nomination, this guy becomes Vice President; then, if we impeach Esmeralda and remove her from office, he becomes President."

"I think I see where you're going with this."

"If, on the other hand," continued Majority Leader Sullivan, "you sit on it until we impeach President Jenkins, the VP position is vacant, so you would become President. You're next in line after the VP. Get it?"

"I see your point."

"Moreover, when you become President, I move up to Speaker—unless, of course, you want to nominate me for VP. I'd be satisfied with either position."

"Let me give that part some thought ... but you're right, I should sit on the nomination. Like you say, the Constitution doesn't give me a deadline. I can sit on it forever if I wish."

"Correct. If you're smart, that's exactly what you'll do."

"Okay," said the Speaker. "I think we see eye-to-eye. Now let's get back to what we were doing. How are you coming along with the Chair assignments?"

The Speaker and the Majority Leader went back to the business at hand and didn't discuss the Vice-Presidential nomination again.

Chapter 13
Geneva

The World Economic Forum had printed agendas and distributed announcements of the February 2521 meeting in December 2520, several weeks before President Hoffenberger's assassination. Since the announcements listed President Hoffenberger as the keynote speaker, the organizers contacted the White House when they learned of the President's death and requested that Esmeralda take his place. Thomas advised her that she should accept the invitation, and the two began preparations during the last week of January.

The location for this year's meeting was Geneva, Switzerland, at the Hotel de la Cigogne on the Place Longemalle, a short distance from Lake Geneva and the city's Old Town. Since the meeting was scheduled for four days, more than Esmeralda could justify, she decided to attend the reception on Monday evening, February 3rd, deliver the keynote address at the luncheon on Tuesday, and return to Washington on Tuesday afternoon. However, to ensure that the United States was fully engaged in all of the discussions, she instructed Aphrodite Papadopoulos, her Acting Secretary of Commerce, to attend all four days of the meeting.

Esmeralda delivered her second *Sunday Evening Update* to the Nation on Sunday evening, February 2nd, and explained the multiplier effect of government spending. She told the Nation that every dollar spent by the government translates into job creation and that her goal was to reduce unemployment to zero. She also talked about monetary policy. "Now," Esmeralda said, "if you're thinking, *she can't control interest rates – that's the job of the Federal Reserve*, you're right. By law, the Federal Reserve Board handles that piece of it. However, I plan to invite the Chairman of the Fed to have lunch with me at the White House bi-monthly, or more frequently if necessary, and I'm confident we will reach a meeting of the minds. As you may know, I don't actually eat, but I can sit with the Chairman and talk to him as *he* eats."

As soon as Esmeralda finished her *Sunday Evening Update*, Roger took her and Thomas to Andrews Air Force Base in Maryland, where they boarded Air Force One and left for Geneva. Roger and five other Secret Service agents accompanied them on the trip. The plane touched down in Geneva on Monday morning, February 3rd, at eleven o'clock local time, and their hotel's aero-limousine picked them up at the airport and brought them to the hotel. After checking in and finding their room, Esmeralda and Thomas unpacked and looked at a map of the city. Since they had several hours to kill before the reception, they left the hotel by foot—Roger and the other Secret Service agents following—and explored the city.

The couple's walking tour took them to the Place Bourg du Four Square, the Brunswick Monument, Leman Lake, the Reformation Wall Monument, St. Pierre Cathedral, the Tavel House, the Town Hall, the Jet D'eau in Lake Geneva, the English Garden, and the Flower Clock. By four o'clock, with time running short, they decided to postpone their visit to Jean-Jacques Rousseau Island, a small island named after the famous philosopher, and a boat tour of Geneva Lake until their next visit. They returned to the hotel at five o'clock to give Thomas time to take a shower and dress for the reception; then they walked to the hotel's Salon de la Cigogne together to meet the other world leaders and their spouses.

When Esmeralda and Thomas arrived at the salon, they were greeted by Olof Bjornstrand, Executive Chairman of the World Economic Forum.

"I've been looking forward to meeting you," said Chairman Bjornstrand. "I want to express my deepest sympathy regarding President Hoffenberger's assassination. I know this must be a difficult and painful time for Americans."

"Thank you for your kind words," replied Esmeralda.

"My wife is handling it well," said Thomas. "She has the situation under control."

"Let me introduce you to some of the other world leaders," said Chairman Bjornstrand. He motioned for Thomas and Esmeralda to follow him and approached a group of men and women in one corner of the room, near a table with cheese and other appetizers. "May I have your attention for a moment," he said to the group, who stopped talking and turned towards him. "I'd like to introduce you to President Esmeralda Jenkins of the United States and her husband, Thomas."

"I've already met them," said President Charpentier of France. "I attended President Hoffenberger's funeral last week." He turned to Esmeralda. "Great to see you again!" He stepped forward and extended his hand to Esmeralda, who shook it, and then to Thomas, who also shook it. The other leaders, including President Kazimir Kuznetsov of the New Soviet Union, Prime Minister Robert Edwards of the United Kingdom, and President Genghis Wu of China, all stepped forward, in turn, and shook hands with Esmeralda and Thomas.

"I heard about your Executive Order for a birth lottery," said President Wu. "China tried something like that once, and it didn't work. We refer to it now as the failed one-child-per-couple policy."

"Yes, I've read about it," replied Esmeralda.

"I don't want to sound negative," said President Wu, "but I fear you may be going down the wrong path."

"I studied China's one-child-per-couple policy," replied Esmeralda. "Your twentieth-century leader Deng Xiao came up with the idea in 1979 and implemented it in 1980. It was discontinued in 2015, thirty-five years after it was started. When it ended, the Chinese government claimed it was a great success by preventing 400 million births."

"I can see you've done your homework," replied President Wu.

An Asian woman standing nearby stepped forward. "Forgive me, but I feel I need to join this conversation. My name is Qingzhao Wu—President's Wu's wife." She extended her hand to Esmeralda. They shook hands, and Ms. Wu continued, "The one-child-per-couple policy failed because it didn't account for an aging population. As time went on, it impacted China's labor market adversely. It also created a problem called *four-two-one*, meaning every child would eventually have to care for two parents and four grandparents. The policy wreaked havoc on China's social structure, not to mention the economy."

"And that's just the tip of the iceberg," added President Wu. "The policy increased abortions, suicides, and infanticides. We would never go down that path again."

"The U.S. birth lottery won't be like that," replied Esmeralda. "Today we have better and more reliable methods of birth control, so there shouldn't be any abortions … and to address the four-two-one problem your wife mentioned, we have many nursing homes, both public and private, and we will build more if we need to."

"But what about the labor market?" asked President Wu. "How are you going to replenish your workers as they age and retire?"

"I'm glad you brought that up," Esmeralda replied. "As workers age and retire, they will be replaced by an ever-diminishing supply of labor until we reach zero unemployment. That coincides with one of my other goals. As my husband would say, we kill two birds with one stone."

"How so?" asked President Wu.

"By means of the birth lottery, we reduce the carbon footprint of the human species; and at the same time, we achieve full employment."

"Not so fast," said Prime Minister Edwards of the United Kingdom. "I think you're making the assumption that the unemployed labor pool contains the same skill sets as the workers who are aging and retiring—but that may not be the case."

"Good point," replied Esmeralda. "That's where robots come in. When we can't find the right skill sets in our *human* labor pool, we turn to the *robot* labor pool. Today robots can do anything and everything that a human being can do. They can not only be factory workers but also policeman, fireman, teachers, bankers, receptionists, store clerks, and a myriad of other things. A robot can be and do anything a human being can be and do."

"Surely you jest," said President Kuznetsov, who had been silent until now.

"We have to be creative," said Thomas. "Our planet is stressed to the breaking point. What's at stake here is the very survival of the human species."

"I think that's a slight exaggeration," said President Kuznetsov.

"No, he's right," said President Charpentier. "We have only so much land."

"We have plenty of land left in Siberia," said President Kuznetsov, "and if I'm not mistaken, we still have plenty of it left in Antarctica as well."

A waiter appeared with a tray of glasses. "Would anyone care for wine?" he said. "Chateau Tour de Bonnet Blanc—imported from France."

"Excellent wine," said President Charpentier. "I admit to a bias … nonetheless, I recommend it highly."

Thomas took a glass of wine from the tray and thanked the waiter.

"No wine for you, ma'am?" asked the waiter, looking at Esmeralda.

"No thank you," replied Esmeralda. "I don't drink."

"I don't drink either," said Ms. Wu. "Buddhism prohibits the consumption of intoxicants. Are you Buddhist, too?"

"Actually, I'm Buddhist, Christian, Muslim, Hindu, and a number of other things."

Ms. Wu frowned.

"You might consider joining the Church of England," said Prime Minister Edwards. "If you're already part-Christian, you'll fit right in."

Chairman Bjornstrand appeared with several more couples in tow. "I'd like you to meet President Nguyen Huynh of Vietnam and his lovely wife, Hwa."

Everyone in the group stepped forward and shook hands with President Huynh and his wife.

"... and President Raji Chopra of India and his lovely wife, Rupa," continued Chairman Bjornstrand.

Everyone shook hands with President Chopra and his spouse.

"... and Chancellor Heidi Schmidt of Germany and her husband, Eckbert," continued Chairman Bjornstrand.

Everyone shook hands with Chancellor Schmidt and her husband.

"and President Athiambiwied De Villiers of South Africa and her husband, Bhekithemba."

Everyone shook hands with President De Villiers and her husband.

When President De Villiers shook hands with Esmeralda, she smiled and said, "Thank goodness I'm not the only female head-of-state here this evening!"

Prime Minister Edwards frowned. "President De Villiers, may I speak to you privately?"

"You want to speak to me privately?"

"Just for a moment. It won't take more than two minutes."

"Very well."

Prime Minister Edwards took President De Villiers's arm and led her to the opposite corner of the room, then, lowering his voice, said, "You know she's a robot, don't you?"

"Of course, I do," replied President De Villiers. "You don't think South African leaders keep up with the world news?"

"I didn't mean to imply you don't. I just thought I should give you a heads-up in case you hadn't heard ... you know, to avoid a social faux pas."

"I appreciate your concern, Mr. Edwards, but I can assure you that I don't make social faux pas. In fact, I watched a rerun of the United States' Vice-Presidential debate from last October. Then-candidate Jenkins made her opponents look like morons."

"Well, you're entitled to your opinion. In any case, I didn't want you to be blindsided ... well, then, let's get back with the group."

The Prime Minister and President De Villiers walked back across the room and rejoined the other leaders.

"Prime Minister Edwards implored me to treat President Jenkins courteously," said President De Villiers. "I assured him I'm not prejudiced. Robots should be treated like everyone else."

"Thank you!" said Thomas.

"It's very considerate of you," said Esmeralda.

"What are we doing for dinner tonight, anyway?" said Mrs. Edwards, either because she was hungry or wanted to change the conversation.

"This is the French region of Switzerland," said Ms. Kuznetsov. "I assume the restaurants here are noted for their French cuisine."

"I eat French food at home every day," said President Charpentier. "When I'm traveling, I like to try something else. I wonder if they have any Chinese restaurants here."

"I doubt you'd be able to find a decent Chinese restaurant in Geneva," said Ms. Wu. "It's hard enough to find one in Beijing."

"It's a big city," said Mr. De Villiers. "I'm sure you can find many ethnic restaurants." He opened his palm and began entering inquiries into his iPalm.

The group of leaders and their spouses spent the next thirty minutes talking about where to eat dinner. Finally, Chairman Bjornstrand reappeared with four more guests. "I'd like you to meet Prime Minister Tamaki Nakamura of Japan and her husband, Kazuhiko, and President Ermenegildo Matos of Brazil and his lovely wife, Benedita." Everyone shook hands with the late arrivals.

"I trust everyone is having a good time," said Chairman Bjornstrand. "Have you solved any of the world's problems?"

"Are you kidding me?" said Ms. Wu. "These so-called leaders can't even agree on where to have dinner."

Everyone laughed.

"You should have asked me," said Chairman Bjornstrand. "There's a good restaurant right here ... the Restaurant de la Cigogne. The cuisine–"

"It's French cuisine," interrupted President Charpentier. "I told the group I'm looking for something else."

"I see ... All right, another good one is Izumi on quai des Bergues—it's Japanese."

"That would be fine," said Ms. Wu. "We have to make a decision or we will be standing here drinking Tour de Bonnet Blanc the rest of the night."

"It sounds good to me," said Thomas. "I like Japanese."

"I'm okay with it," said President Charpentier.

Everyone nodded their approval.

"It's an easy walk," said Chairman Bjornstrand. "Let's meet in the lobby in fifteen minutes."

* * * * *

While Esmeralda and Thomas had been touring the streets of Geneva on Monday afternoon, six hours ahead of the clock in Washington, Jacqueline had returned to work on Monday morning. Arriving at her office at nine o'clock, she summoned her Chief of Staff.

Henry Hawkins appeared at her door. "Good morning, Jacqueline. How was your weekend?".

"Fine. How was yours?"

"It was okay—nothing exciting. I just chilled out."

"That's good, please come in and sit down."

Henry entered Jacqueline's office as requested and sat down in front of her desk. "What's up?"

"I need you to put your thinking cap on. Can you think of any bills I co-sponsored with Republicans and Democrats over the years … that is, with Republicans and Democrats who are still in the House?"

"It sounds like you need someone you did a favor for to return the favor."

"You're very perceptive, Henry."

"Well … the one who comes to mind first is Representative Ying Yue Chan. You agreed to co-sponsor the *Housing for the Homeless Act of 2519* with him."

"Right, and he's still a member. I'll reach out to him."

"You also supported Representative Placido Gambardella last year in getting more funding for EPA and SBA."

"Right, that's another good one. I'll reach out to him, too."

"Can you tell me what you need their support for?"

"Legislation for a birth lottery."

"Oh my God!" exclaimed Henry. "Why didn't I see this coming?"

"A better question would be why *I* didn't see this coming."

"Your sister-in-law asked you to sponsor the bill, right?"

"You got it."

"Does she understand this would be one of the most contentious bills in the history of the U.S. Congress?"

"I told her it would be extremely controversial."

"That would be an understatement."

"But Henry, you do believe in the need for a birth lottery, don't you?"

"Well, yes, I guess so—if that's the only way to get a handle on the population crisis."

"How else would you do it?" asked Jacqueline.

"I don't know ... incentives, maybe ... like tax incentives. For example, instead of giving people a tax credit for dependents, give them a tax credit for *not* having dependents."

Jacqueline laughed, then turned serious. "Actually, that's not such a bad idea. I'll talk to Esmeralda about it. That could be our Plan B."

"If nothing else, it would be easier to enact into law than a birth lottery."

"I agree, but Esmeralda's calling the shots here. Anyway, can you think of anyone else ... that is, besides Representatives Ying Yue Chan and Placido Gambardella?"

"I'll go through the legislative history and see what I can come up with. How far back do you want me to go?"

"I'll tell you what ... hold off on your research until I talk to the two guys you mentioned."

"Those two owe you big time because their bills passed. You should be able to get one of them to co-sponsor Esmeralda's bill."

"I agree, but don't refer to it as Esmeralda's bill. It's supposed to be *my* bill."

"Got it."

"If one of them agrees to be a co-sponsor, we don't need to dig any further. I'll let you know if I need any more names."

"Just let me know—I'll get right on it."

"Thanks ... okay, that's all for now. You can get back to whatever you were doing when I called for you."

Henry got up from his chair and returned to his office, and Jacqueline turned to her wall monitor and summoned her digital assistant. "Jim," she said, "I need you to set up a conference call with Representative Ying Yue Chan."

*   *   *   *   *

On Tuesday morning, Geraldine arose at seven o'clock, fixed herself a muffin and a cup of coffee, and sat down at her kitchen table. After taking a bite of the muffin and a sip of coffee, she turned to her north wall. "Richard, I'm ready for my morning update."

Geraldine's north wall lit up, and her digital assistant appeared on the monitor. "Good morning, Ms. Jenkins. I understand you are ready for your morning update, is that correct?"

"You got it."

"Very well. Your daughter-in-law just finished her luncheon speech at the World Economic Forum in Geneva, Switzerland. Would you like me to play it back for you?"

"Yes, thank you, I'd like to hear what she said."

"Give me just a moment, please."

Richard disappeared, and Esmeralda appeared on the monitor standing in front of a podium in a large auditorium.

"Thank you for inviting me to the 2521 World Economic Forum," Esmeralda began. "I want to thank Chairman Bjornstrand for the invitation. I'm grateful for the opportunity to speak to you. However, before I begin my remarks, I want to introduce Aphrodite Papadopoulos, my Acting Secretary of Commerce, who will be with you for the remainder of the week."

Ms. Papadopoulos, seated in the first row, stood up, turned to the audience, smiled, and sat back down.

Esmeralda adjusted the microphone. "In the history of mankind, world leaders have rarely faced challenges of the magnitude we face today. We are confronted with a world-wide recession; regional conflicts in the Near East, Africa, South America, and elsewhere; famine and a scarcity of safe drinking water on the continents of Asia, Africa, and North and South America; rising sea levels everywhere; temperature extremes on every continent; and a population crisis causing homelessness throughout every corner of the Earth. Today I'd like to touch on a few of these challenges."

"Richard," said Geraldine, "please hit the *pause* button and loop Jacqueline in. I want her to hear this."

The video paused, and Richard appeared in the top-right corner of the monitor. "I understand you would like me to connect your daughter, is that correct, Ms. Jenkins?"

"If she's free."

"I'll get right on it, Ms. Jenkins." Richard disappeared, and Jacqueline appeared on the monitor a moment later.

"What's up, Mom?"

"Esmeralda just finished her keynote address at the World Economic Forum in Geneva. Richard is playing it back for me. Do you want to hear it?"

"I'm having breakfast ... but okay, I guess I can watch it while I eat."

"Good, then, listen in. Richard, please resume the play-back."

Richard reappeared momentarily. "Resuming the play-back now as you requested."

Richard disappeared, and Jacqueline remained in the top-right corner of the monitor while the video resumed.

"I'd like to begin by addressing the regional conflicts," said Esmeralda. "During the Vice-Presidential debate last year, I talked about a pure land on Earth, which, among other things, means a world without war. You might say, 'We have always had wars, and we always will; it is fundamental to human existence.' But I want you to think about it a different way. If, seven hundred years ago, we had talked about man's ability to fly, you might have said, 'Since the dawn of civilization, humans have wanted to fly. The smartest people have tried and failed; it can never be done.' And I might have agreed with you. Yet, in the twentieth century, you did it—you not only invented the airplane and flew across the Atlantic and Pacific oceans; you even flew to the moon and the planets. The solution to war is no less achievable. Working together, we can make it happen."

"Mom, tell Richard to pause it," Jacqueline said.

"Richard," said Geraldine, "Jacqueline wants you to pause it."

Richard reappeared. "Pausing the play-back as you requested."

"This is really good," said Jacqueline. "I think Sarah should hear it."

"Richard," said Geraldine, "Jacqueline thinks Sarah should hear this. Please connect her."

"I understand you would like me to connect your grand-daughter, Sarah, is that correct, Ms. Jenkins?"

"You got it."

"I'll get right on it," replied Richard. He disappeared, and Sarah appeared a few moments later.

"Richard said you want me to hear Esmeralda's speech," said Sarah. "Is she in Geneva?"

"Yes, dear," said Geraldine. "She just finished her keynote address to the World Economic Forum. Richard is playing it back for us."

"Yes, I want to hear it … definitely."

"Okay, then, listen in. Richard, please resume the play-back."

Richard reappeared. "Resuming the play-back as you requested." He disappeared, and Jacqueline and Sarah remained visible in separate blocks in the top-right corner of the screen.

"During the Vice-Presidential debate last October," said Esmeralda, "one of my opponents was asked if the United States of America should change its name to the United States of the World. Both of my opponents were in favor of it. My position is a little different. Calling ourselves the United States of the World isn't going to guarantee peace. Our own civil war in the nineteenth century proves that point. On the other hand, bringing all of the nations on the planet together under a world government could bring us closer to a solution. Whether we call it the United States of the World, United Nations 2.0, or some other name doesn't matter—the key to it is that the world have a central government with a military that is superior to that of any individual nation."

"Now how in God's name is she going to do that?" said Geraldine.

"Just listen, Mom," said Jacqueline.

"Step one," said Esmeralda, "is for every nation in the world to dismantle their military and turn over all of their weapons to the world's governing body. Each nation would be allowed to keep a national guard for internal conflicts and emergencies. The world's governing body would control all aircraft fighters and bombers; all missiles, both nuclear and conventional; all artillery, including anti-aircraft artillery; all nuclear stockpiles; all tanks; all aircraft carriers, destroyers, submarines, and other vessels of war; and all other weapons of war. When this transfer of military assets occurs, war as we know it today will be a thing of the past, and the only wars we will have going forward will be wars with aliens from other planets, if that should ever occur."

"Wow!" exclaimed Sarah. "What a revolutionary idea!"

"I need some time to digest it," said Jacqueline.

"She's living in a fantasy world," said Geraldine.

"Now to address the population crisis," Esmeralda continued, "we need to begin by asking ourselves how we got to this point. Human women love having babies, of course, and human men seem to enjoy their role in making the babies—that's part of it—but it's a little more complicated than that. The population explosion that began towards the end of the last millennium fueled economic growth and created billions of jobs, especially in construction and manufacturing, which created the illusion of prosperity. Now, finally, after six hundred years, people realize it was just that—an illusion."

"I learned that at UVA in 2433," said Geraldine. "Economics 101."

"Just listen, Mom," said Jacqueline.

"The population explosion is similar to a pyramid scheme," said Esmeralda. "It can't continue forever. Sooner or later, human beings will run out of space; there won't be enough land for food production, recreation, and housing. Sadly, that day has arrived."

"Amen!" said Sarah.

Esmeralda continued, "Some people say, 'Just convert our national parks into low-income housing'; and others say, "Cut down what's left of our forests and use the land for crops and cattle.' None of these ideas are sustainable in the long term. My friends, I implore you to face reality: we have too many human beings on the planet."

"No kidding," said Geraldine.

"Even if we could build floating cities in the ocean," said Esmeralda, "as some people have suggested, there would eventually be a limit to them as well."

"That was the stupidest idea," said Geraldine.

"I disagree," said Sarah. "Converting our national parks into low-income housing was the stupidest idea."

"I'm sure I don't have to remind you," continued Esmeralda, "that humans have decimated the global ecosystem. Fortunately, the planet is amazingly resilient. If we can reduce the human footprint, the planet will heal itself—we just need to get out of its way."

Several people near the front of the room stood and applauded, and then people behind them stood and applauded, and then more people stood and applauded; and within a minute, the entire audience was on its feet applauding.

"I'm so excited," said Sarah. "Her message is resonating with her audience!"

"It seems to be going well," agreed Jacqueline.

"If I were her," said Geraldine, "I'd quit while I was ahead."

Esmeralda waited for the applause to subside and for people to sit down, then continued, "And with a smaller population, we will be able to house the homeless, care for the sick and elderly, and feed the people on every continent."

"That was a good line," said Geraldine. "If she's smart, she'll wrap it up now."

"Last week," continued Esmeralda, "I signed an Executive Order establishing a birth lottery for Federal employees in the United States. Before a female Federal employee is allowed to conceive a baby, she must be selected by the official birth lottery. Under the U.S. Constitution, that's the limit of my authority, but I plan to work with the U.S. Congress to establish a mandatory birth lottery for all U.S. citizens, not just for government employees."

"By which she means she plans to work with *me*," said Jacqueline.

"Now," continued Esmeralda, "I ask for your cooperation. A mandatory birth lottery in the United States is a step in the right direction, but we can't solve global problems without global participation. When you return home at the end of this week, I ask you to begin working on similar birth lotteries in your own countries."

The noise level in the room rose as people in the audience began talking.

"That concludes my formal remarks," said Esmeralda. "It looks like I finished a minute or two ahead of schedule, so I will be happy to take one question from the audience."

A woman in the second row raised her hand and stood up, and one of Chairman Bjornstrand's assistants standing nearby walked over and handed her a microphone. She took the microphone and tapped it first to confirm it was on. "My name is Basanti

Singh, and I'm the Economic Minister of India. My question is how your birth lottery is going to affect the U.S. economy and, more importantly, how it is going to affect the *global* economy. Have you studied any economic models to determine the short- and long-term global ramifications of your lottery? Thank you." Ms. Singh sat down.

"Good question," said Sarah.

"Thank you for your excellent question, Ms. Singh," said Esmeralda. "We know that GDP will shrink as the population shrinks, but we can mitigate the impact of that to some extent by means of fiscal and monetary tools. One positive outcome, as I explained to some of the other world leaders at the reception last night, is that this will eventually get us to full employment—that is, as older workers age and retire, there will be fewer workers to replace them, and unemployment will gradually decline until it hits zero."

"In theory," said Sarah.

"Bear in mind," Esmeralda continued, as if she had heard Sarah, "we have no economic model for population implosion—as opposed to population *explosion*—other than theoretical ones because we have never had population implosion on a global scale, at least not in recorded history. So our models here are theoretical. In any case, I will update you on our progress at next year's World Economic Forum. Thank you again for your excellent question."

Chairman Bjornstrand appeared on the stage and walked to the podium, shook hands with Esmeralda, and spoke into the microphone. "Let's give President Jenkins a big round of applause!"

The audience stood and applauded.

"Nice job!" said Sarah.

"I think it went pretty well," said Jacqueline. "Let's see what the political pundits say about it on the news this evening."

"I'm sure they're talking about it already," said Geraldine. "Do you want me to have Richard switch it to CNN?"

"No, I have to go to work now," said Jacqueline.

"I have to get back to work, too," said Sarah.

"Okay, girls," said Geraldine, "thanks for joining me on short notice."

"My pleasure, Mom." Jacqueline disconnected and disappeared.

"Thanks, Granma," said Sarah. "Talk to you soon." Sarah disconnected and disappeared.

Geraldine instructed Richard to discontinue the coverage, got up from the table, and took her coffee mug and plate to the dishwasher.

* * * * *

When Esmeralda returned to the Oval Office on Wednesday morning, February 5th, William was waiting outside the door and greeted her with two newspapers under his arm. "Good morning, Esmeralda. I'm glad to see that you made it home safely."

"There's nothing like traveling on Air Force One."

"To be sure. Look, I've got this morning's newspapers for you." He took the two papers out from under his arm and showed Esmeralda the headlines. The headline in *The Washington Post* read PRESIDENT JENKINS CALLS FOR UNITED NATIONS 2.0 *and* WORLD-WIDE BIRTH LOTTERY, and the headline in *The Washington Times* read PRESIDENT JENKINS ATTEMPTS TO SELL HER RADICAL IDEAS TO SKEPTICAL WORLD LEADERS.

"No surprise there," said Esmeralda. "I wouldn't have been far off if you had asked me to guess."

Esmeralda walked into the office and motioned for William to follow her. She sat down at her desk, and William sat down in front of her.

"It looks like you got the world's attention," said William. "Great job!"

"You can congratulate me when they actually get on board with my agenda."

"I'm not going to hold my breath."

"Understood—humans need to breathe several times each minute. Thank God I don't have that handicap."

William laughed. "I don't think of it as a handicap, but no matter …"

"Any feedback from the Hill on Juan Nighthorse Humetewa's nomination?"

"The Senate responded—the office of the President Pro Tem told me that the nomination package appears to be in order. No response yet from the Speaker of the House."

"My gut tells me that Speaker McInytre is going to fight us on this."

"He doesn't have any reason to dislike our nominee," said William. "Representative Humetewa is pretty well-liked on the Hill—to the extent that a Green can be well-liked there."

"Speaker McInytre may have political motives that aren't immediately apparent," replied Esmeralda.

"Well, I'll follow up with his office tomorrow if we don't hear anything today. They should at least acknowledge the nomination and let us know if they need any more information."

"Yes, please follow up. How are we doing with the other political appointments?"

"All of President Hoffenberger's nominees for the Secretary positions have been processed and sent to Congress for confirmation. The confirmation hearings should begin this month."

"How about the Administrators of the agencies?"

"Ditto—they've all been sent to the Hill for confirmation."

"See if you can get them to expedite the confirmations for the heads of EPA and SBA. Those two agencies need to be rock-solid. They can't afford to have a gap in leadership."

"Understood—will do."

"Anything else you want to bring to my attention?" asked Esmeralda.

"Yes, you should have a message in your mailbox from Jacqueline. Representative Ying Yue Chan has agreed to co-sponsor a birth-lottery bill in the House."

"That's fantastic news! I didn't think she would be able to find a co-sponsor so fast."

"I imagine Representative Ying Yue Chan owed her a favor. That's usually how it works."

"Whatever the reason, it's great news—I can't wait to tell Thomas ... No, I'll call Jacqueline first and get it straight from the horse's mouth."

William chuckled. "You're getting to be good with American idioms."

"If you hang around Thomas as much as I do, you can't help but pick them up."

"For sure."

Esmeralda picked up a pencil. "Anything else happen while I was gone?"

"Nothing out of the ordinary. I think I have everything under control."

"Have we scheduled the first Cabinet meeting?"

"Yes, this Friday, ten o'clock."

"You're working on the agenda?"

"Yes, I'll give you the draft agenda today."

"Great ... I'll let you get back to work, then. It sounds like you are juggling quite a few balls. Keep up the good work."

"You bet." William arose. "Give me a shout if you need anything."

William returned to his office, and Esmeralda turned to the wall monitor and summoned her digital assistant. "Arnold, please connect Jacqueline. I hear she has good news."

*   *   *   *   *

Esmeralda worked at her desk all day, not stopping for lunch, and went straight to the White House dining room at six o'clock to meet Thomas for dinner. When she arrived, Thomas was sitting with Sarah, who had an open invitation for dinner, and the two stood up and hugged her.

"Mom, what a great speech in Geneva!" exclaimed Sarah. "I'm so proud of you!"

"Thank you, sweetheart," replied Esmeralda. "I gave it my best shot."

The three sat down at the table.

"I've been watching the media reports all day," said Thomas. "An instant Gallup poll found that sixty-five percent of Americans either watched your speech live or replayed it afterwards, and eighty percent of those who did said it was very good or excellent."

"The reports coming in from Asia and Europe are even better," added Sarah. "Eighty-five percent of Asians and ninety percent of Europeans said it was very good or excellent."

"Too bad they didn't do a poll of the U.S. House and Senate," said Esmeralda. "I'd love to know what they're saying."

"It shouldn't be hard to find out," said Thomas. "I'll make some phone calls tomorrow."

"Jacqueline can tell you what she's heard in the House," said Sarah, "and I'll keep my ears open, too."

A waiter arrived and filled their glasses with water, then took their food orders and departed.

"What's next on your agenda, Mom?" asked Sarah.

"I'm getting ready for my first Cabinet meeting on Friday."

"It should be very routine," said Thomas. "We don't yet have any department heads confirmed, so the attendees will be the acting heads."

"Right," said Esmeralda. "All of them are career employees who are filling in until our nominees are confirmed."

The waiter returned with salad plates and placed them in front of Thomas and Sarah, apparently aware that Esmeralda didn't eat.

"I haven't had a chance to tell you my good news," said Esmeralda.

"Good news?" asked Thomas and Sarah in unison.

"Yes, Jacqueline has found a co-sponsor for our birth-lottery legislation."

"Fantastic!" exclaimed Sarah. "Who is it?"

"Representative Ying Yue Chan from Pennsylvania."

"Is he a Democrat or a Republican?" asked Sarah as she began eating her salad.

"A Democrat."

"That's good," said Thomas. "If the Democrats support the bill, it should be easy to pass it in the House."

"Has Jacqueline drafted the legislation yet?" asked Sarah.

"I talked to her this morning," replied Esmeralda, "and she said she will do it this week. It will say pretty much the same thing as my Executive Order, but it will apply to all U.S. citizens."

"That's great," said Sarah. "Aunt Jacqueline knows how to get things done."

"Frankly, I'm amazed," said Thomas. "Who would have dreamed your first two weeks as President would go so smoothly?"

"I'm not surprised," said Sarah. "I expected it."

"I just worry about Murphy's Law," said Thomas.

"Murphy's Law?" asked Esmeralda.

"Yes, Murphy's Law: *If anything can go wrong, it will—and at the worst possible time.*"

"Where did that law come from?"

"Well, it's not actually a law," replied Thomas. "It's more like a scientific principle."

"Dad, please!" exclaimed Sarah. "It's not a scientific principle!"

"That's okay, Sarah," said Esmeralda. "Thomas is just trying to be realistic. There are bound to be a few bumps in the road—I'm not worried."

The waiter reappeared with Thomas's and Sarah's dinner plates, and the two pushed their salad plates away and began eating the main course. Esmeralda opened her iPalm and began reading media reports. Thomas and Sarah talked about the upcoming Super Bowl and made a gentlemen's bet: Thomas predicted the Denver Broncos would win by seven points, and Sarah predicted the Dallas Cowboys would win by three.

After dinner, Thomas and Esmeralda returned to the White House residence on the second floor, and Roger took Sarah back to the apartment in Virginia.

"I apologize if I alarmed you about Murphy's Law," said Thomas as he and Esmeralda prepared for bed.

"No problem at all," replied Esmeralda. "I imagine that law applies only to humans, not to robots, don't you think?"

"I hope you're right," replied Thomas. But he looked worried.

Chapter 14

Murphy's Law

On Friday morning, February 7th, Esmeralda arose early and went straight to the Oval Office to go over her notes for her first Cabinet meeting. William had left a briefing paper on her chair, which included bullet points on the meeting; and she picked it up, sat down, and read it. Then she took a green highlighter and marked key points she wished to emphasize. At 9:59 a.m., she got up from her desk and walked to the nearby Cabinet Room.

When Esmeralda entered the room, her sixteen Cabinet members, all in acting capacities, were seated at the table, including Vice Presidential nominee Juan Nighthorse Humetewa, whom she had invited. Several acting agency administrators and directors, including the Acting Director of OMB, sat in chairs against the wall. Everyone stood up when Esmeralda entered, and Representative Humetewa said, "Good morning, President Jenkins." Others in the room followed his lead, as if there were an echo in the room, "Good morning, President Jenkins ... Good morning, President Jenkins ... Good morning, President Jenkins."

Esmeralda walked to a chair in the center of the table and sat down between Representative Humetewa and the Acting Secretary of Defense. "Good morning, everyone."

Several at the table who had not yet said good morning took this as their cue and did so.

"Let's go around the table and introduce ourselves," Esmeralda began. "You know who I am, so let's start with the gentleman on my right."

Each person at the table introduced themselves, beginning with Representative Humetewa and finishing with the Acting Secretary of Defense, Kameko Yamamoto.

"I'm excited to meet all of you in person," Esmeralda said. "Although Representative Humetewa has not yet been confirmed as Vice President, and although the rest of you are in an acting capacity, you and I nonetheless represent the leadership of the Federal government at this moment. It is important that all of you understand my priorities, so let's get right to it."

Thomas appeared in the doorway. "Do you want me in this meeting, Esmeralda?"

"Yes, please come in," replied Esmeralda. "For those of you who don't know him, Thomas is my husband and also my unofficial advisor."

Thomas entered the room and sat down behind Esmeralda in a chair against the wall.

"Does the name William Jefferson Clinton ring a bell?" asked Esmeralda.

Half-a-dozen people raised their hands.

"He was one of our early Presidents," said Esmeralda. "During his administration, they had a slogan, *creating a government that works better and costs less.* I don't know for sure if it was President Clinton or his Vice President, Al Gore, who came up with that slogan, but I like it. It sums up nicely what I want to accomplish in my own administration."

Bob Conrad Mitchum, the Acting Secretary of State, raised his hand. "I just googled him on my iPalm. It says 'William Jefferson Clinton was our 42nd President, from 1993 to 2001.'"

"Thank you for that information," replied Esmeralda. "In any case, our challenge now is to accomplish it. That means, among other things, we must establish meaningful performance measures for Federal employees and reward the most productive among them."

"We're already doing that at the Department of Justice," said Acting Attorney General Rosales Santiago. "We established performance measures for every Justice employee during the last administration."

"That's good," Esmeralda replied. "I have no doubt that all of you have done the same thing in one manner or another, but keep in mind that I'm coming at it from a different perspective. I'm interested in *outcomes*, or *results*, not just *measures*. To put it another way, precisely how does a given Federal worker improve the lives of our citizens? That's what I want to get a handle on; that's what I want measure."

"That's what I'm interested in, too," said Abdullah Sharma, Acting Secretary of Labor. "If you're looking for volunteers, I'd be happy to develop some metrics for you."

"Great," replied Esmeralda, "and since you're the Acting Secretary of Labor, I'd like you to address the problem of joblessness. In an enlightened society, every person who wishes to work should be able to find a job. As I have said before, if we have a single citizen who wants to work and can't find a job, then we have failed."

"I'll get right on it," said Acting Secretary Sharma.

"And to be sure we're on the same wavelength," added Esmeralda, "in this administration, we are going to have *full employment,* not *nearly full* employment or *virtually full* employment. Have I made myself clear?"

"Understood," said Acting Secretary Sharma.

"One way to accomplish this," continued Esmeralda, "is to take a page from the models developed by the twentieth-century Presidents Franklin Delano Roosevelt and Barack Obama and establish a Federal jobs corps."

"Do you want me to google Franklin Delano Roosevelt and Barack Obama?" asked Acting Secretary Mitchum.

"No, you don't need to google them right now," replied Esmeralda. "You can do it later if you wish. In any case, rebuilding our infrastructure is an endless job—repairing the dikes on the Carolina coast is but one example. That's how we get people back to work. With this approach, we should be able to bring unemployment down to zero within 180 days."

"We have to see if we have money in the budget for it," said Acting OMB Director Hoang Nguyen.

"We'll talk about the budget later," replied Esmeralda. "Right now we're talking about how we put people back to work."

"I apologize if I was out of order," said Acting Director Nguyen.

"No problem," said Esmeralda. "One more thing before we move on to the next topic. We should have a more equitable distribution of income. A Superintendent of Schools shouldn't earn six times more than a teacher in the same school district, and a CEO shouldn't make twenty times more than a factory worker in … the … same … company." Esmeralda began speaking more slowly and paused between each word. "I grant you … positions at the top … usually … require … more … education …" Suddenly Esmeralda stopped speaking and fell forward, striking her face on the table.

Thomas jumped up in alarm and grabbed Esmeralda's head from behind, pulling her back up. As soon as he let go, she immediately fell forward again, striking her face on the table a second time.

"I think she's having a stroke!" exclaimed Representative Humetewa. "Can robots have strokes?"

Everyone at the table jumped to their feet.

"Somebody call an ambulance!" exclaimed Acting Director Nguyen.

"No, give Thomas a moment to revive her," said Acting Secretary Mitchum. "He must know what to do."

Thomas pulled Esmeralda up again, this time holding her tightly, and turned her head so that he could look at her face. "It doesn't look like anything's broken."

"What happened?" asked Acting Secretary Yamamoto.

"I have no idea!" exclaimed Thomas. "This has never happened before! She's guaranteed for one hundred years! The only thing I have to do is to replace ... holy shit—I just remembered something! I was supposed to replace her battery after thirty-five years! I completely forgot about it!"

"Is that it?" asked Acting Secretary Yamamoto. "She just needs a new battery?"

"Yes," said Thomas. "I'm sure that's the problem. I'll call General Google Motors and order a new battery."

"You better get it fast," said Acting Secretary Mitchum. "As long as she's out of commission, we don't have a President."

"I can be Acting President," said Representative Humetewa.

"No you can't," said Acting Attorney General Santiago. "You haven't even been confirmed as Vice President."

"Somebody get William and the White House Counsel," said Thomas, "We have to figure out who's in charge until I can get a new battery."

Acting OMB Director Nguyen turned and ran from the room, heading towards William's office.

"Somebody get me a phone number for General Google Motors," said Thomas.

"I'm googling it right now," said Acting Secretary Mitchum.

"Under the Constitution," said Acting Attorney General Santiago, "if the President is unable to perform the duties of President, the Vice President becomes President; and if there's no Vice President, then the Speaker of the House becomes President."

"I know what the Constitution says!" exclaimed Thomas. "We're not letting the Speaker of the House become President!"

William appeared in the doorway. "What happened?"

"Thomas says that Esmeralda needs a new battery," replied Acting Secretary Yamamoto.

William ran to Esmeralda and helped Thomas stabilize her in the chair.

"We need to find out who's in charge," said Acting Secretary Sharma. "Technically the United States is without a President."

"I have a phone number," said Acting Secretary Mitchum. "General Google Motors in Detroit ... tell me when you're ready."

"I'm ready now," said Thomas, opening his iPalm.

"313 ... 556 ... 5000."

Thomas held his iPalm to his mouth and repeated the numbers, then added, "Speakerphone, please." Thomas's palm lit up. "Speakerphone activated."

A voice came through Thomas's iPalm. "Thank you for calling General Google Motors. This phone number is no longer in service. Please visit our website at www dot generalgooglemotors dot com."

"What do we do now?" asked Representative Humetewa.

"We don't have time to fool around," said William. "Give me a moment and I'll get a phone number for the company's CEO. I have to go back to my desk."

After verifying that Thomas was still holding Esmeralda, William released his grip on her and ran from the room.

"This could be a Constitutional crisis," said Acting Secretary Sharma. "Where's the White House Counsel?"

"I think Hoang Nguyen went to get her," said Acting Secretary Mitchum.

"She's not going to be able to tell you anything more than what I just told you," said Acting Attorney General Santiago. "If the President is unable to perform the duties of President, the Vice President becomes President; and if there's no Vice President, then the Speaker of the House becomes President."

"I told you we're not going to let that happen!" exclaimed Thomas.

"I think we better keep this quiet," said Acting Secretary Mitchum. "We don't want the public to find out that President Jenkins is incapacitated."

"You can't keep it from the public," said Acting Secretary Yamamoto. "The American people have a right to know what's going on."

"We don't need to alarm them unnecessarily," said Thomas. "We'll get a new battery, and Esmeralda will be back on her game in no time. No one will ever know what happened."

"Everyone in the room needs to be sworn to secrecy," said Acting Secretary Mitchum. "I agree with Thomas—we don't want this to get out."

William reappeared at the door. "Okay, ladies and gentlemen, the Cabinet meeting is adjourned. Thomas and I will get the battery, and Esmeralda will be able to resume her duties as President in a day or two. Let's not blow this out of proportion."

"Do you have the authority to adjourn a Cabinet meeting?" asked Acting Secretary Sharma.

"Come on, Abdullah!" exclaimed Thomas. "Why would you argue the point? Do you plan to sit in this room until we get a new battery?"

"He's right," said Acting Attorney General Santiago. "There's no point in continuing the meeting while President Jenkins is in this condition."

"I'm just saying," replied Acting Secretary Sharma, "technically, the Chief of Staff doesn't have the authority to stop a Cabinet meeting in progress."

"Give it up, Abdullah!" exclaimed William. "The meeting is adjourned—everybody except Representative Humetewa and Thomas *get out!*"

Acting Secretary Sharma and the other Cabinet members and acting officials left the room, leaving William, Thomas, and Representative Humetewa alone with Esmeralda.

"Here's the cell phone number for the CEO of General Google Motors," said William, handing Thomas a piece of paper. "His name is Jim Humphries. I'll hold Esmeralda while you make the call."

"Why don't you just lay her down on the floor?" suggested Representative Humetewa. "You can't hold her up forever."

"He's right," said Thomas, looking at William. "Help me lay her down on the floor. We'll move her to the White House residence as soon as I finish this call."

William and Thomas lifted Esmeralda from her chair and set her down gently on the floor.

Thomas stood up and looked at the piece of paper William had handed him, then opened his iPalm and read the numbers aloud. The sound of the iPalm dialing ten digits came over the speaker-phone; and in a moment, a voice came over it. "You have reached James P. Humphries. I can't take your call right now, but you may speak to my digital assistant and I'll get back to you as soon as I can. Thanks so much for calling!"

"Yes, Jim," said Thomas, "this is Thomas Jenkins, President Jenkins's husband. We need your help urgently. Please return the call—just use my cell phone number on your caller ID. Again, this is urgent. Thanks very much."

Another voice came over the speakerphone. "Thank you for calling, Mr. Jenkins. I'm Patricia O'Boyle, Mr. Humphries's digital assistant. How may I help you?"

"Thank you for taking the call," said Thomas. "My wife is the President. She's a robot, and her battery is dead. I need a replace-ment battery."

"Thank you … let me check that for you … okay, I've found the information. It appears that General Google Motors no longer makes robots, and we no longer carry batteries or other replacement parts. I suggest you check the yellow pages for a company that makes batteries."

"Excuse me!" exclaimed Thomas. "I purchased the robot from you in 2484. You must carry replacement parts!"

"I see ... 2484 ... according to my calculation, that would be thirty-seven years ago. We discontinued our robot line in the year 2500, and we discontinued batteries and other spare parts in 2515. If you have a vehicle, I may be able to help you with that."

"I don't need help with my vehicle ... I'll tell you what, just have Mr. Humphries call me back. Tell him it's urgent—I'm calling from the White House."

"I don't need to know the color of your house, only the year and model of your vehicle."

"I just told you I don't need help with my vehicle!" Thomas exclaimed. "Just have Mr. Humphries call me back! I told you this is urgent!"

"I just told you that we discontinued our robot line in the year 2500, and we discontinued batteries and other spare parts in 2515. If you have a vehicle, I may be able to help you with that."

"We're going around in circles here!" Thomas exclaimed. "Just have Mr. Humphries call me back!"

"Mr. Humphries would need to know the year and model of your vehicle before he calls you back."

"Don't waste any more time with this nonsense!" exclaimed William. "We'll get a battery some other way!"

Thomas closed his hand, shutting down his iPalm and disconnecting the call.

"This is not good," said Representative Humetewa.

"I think we need a conference call with Memengwaa and Jacqueline to let them know what's going on," said Thomas.

"Good idea," said Representative Humetewa. "Maybe one of them knows where we can get a new battery."

"Getting a replacement battery shouldn't be that hard," said William. "But I agree, we need to call Memengwaa and Jacqueline. We can do it right now from the Oval Office."

"What about Esmeralda?" said Thomas. "We can't leave her here."

William scratched his head. "We don't want the word to get out. It wouldn't be wise to carry her through the White House—the staffers would start asking questions. How about this: we put a sign on the door to the conference room, *Meeting in Progress—Do Not Disturb*. Then at five o'clock or so, after the majority of the staff has left for the day, we can carry her to the White House residence and put her in bed."

"Good idea," said Thomas. "I think Esmeralda already has some pre-printed signs like that in her desk. I'll go get one right now." He turned to the door and left the room, walking briskly.

"Why don't we move Esmeralda a few feet so she's behind the table?" suggested Representative Humetewa. "Then, if someone opens the door, they won't see her."

"I agree," said William, "let's do it."

Together the two men lifted Esmeralda and moved her to the side of the table away from the door, then set her down again on the floor.

Thomas returned in a moment with the sign and Scotch tape, and he and William taped the sign to the door.

"Let's go to the Oval Office now and see if we can reach Memengwaa and Jacqueline," said William. He looked at Representative Humetewa. "Juan, Thomas and I will take it from here."

"Are you sure you don't need me?" asked Representative Humetewa.

"We've got it under control," replied William.

"Okay, then, call me if you need me," replied Representative Humetewa. He turned and left the room. William and Thomas followed him out of the room, closing the door behind them, and headed for the Oval Office.

*   *   *   *   *

Jacqueline was at her desk when the call came through. Her wall monitor lit up, and Thomas appeared. "Good morning, Sis. Sorry to bother you, but this is an emergency. I have William and Memengwaa on the line with us." William and Memengwaa appeared in boxes in the top right-hand corner of the monitor.

"An emergency?" asked Jacqueline. "What kind of an emergency?"

"Esmeralda's battery has died," said Thomas. "She collapsed during the Cabinet meeting this morning."

"Oh my God!"

"We tried to call GGM—General Google Motors—but they don't make robots anymore, and they don't carry replacement parts, either."

"Holy Jesus!" exclaimed Jacqueline.

"We shouldn't be surprised," said Memengwaa. "All they care about is profits. Did you tell them it's the President's battery?"

"I tried," replied Thomas, "but I couldn't get a real person on the line. We even tried to call the CEO. No luck there either."

"We're not going to waste any more time with GGM," said William. "Do either of you have any suggestions?"

"See if you can find a small business that makes batteries," said Memengwaa. "A small business would be more responsive."

"She's right," said Jacqueline. "Call the SBA Administrator and see if SBA can help you find a small business."

"You don't need to call the SBA Administrator," said Memengwaa. "Just go to the SBA website and look for DSBS."

"DSBS?" asked Thomas.

"Dynamic Small Business Search. Type the word *battery* and see what comes up. You can do it from your iPalm."

"Okay, it sounds like that might work," said William. "Now what do we do in the meantime? Esmeralda is totally out of commission. Who's in charge?"

There was a moment of silence.

"Representative Humetewa has not yet been confirmed," added William, "so, for the moment, no one's in charge."

"We can't let Speaker McIntyre find out about this," said Memengwaa. "He'll try to grab power."

"Thomas," asked Jacqueline, "do you have access to Esmeralda's computer? Do you have her passcode?"

"I can find it," replied Thomas. "She keeps a copy of it in the end table beside our bed."

"Good," replied Jacqueline. "Get on her computer several times a day and send out emails. Send emails to the editors at *The Washington Post* and several other media outlets. They'll think she's hard at work at her desk."

"But what about the White House staff?" asked Memengwaa. "They're going to catch on pretty fast."

"I can keep a lid on it for a few days," said William. "I'll tell the staff that Esmeralda is very busy and not to go anywhere near the Oval Office."

"Listen," said Memengwaa. "I just ran a search for battery companies on DSBS. There's more than four thousand small businesses that make batteries, including ten in D.C. One of them can probably replace Esmeralda's battery."

"Text me the names of the ten in D.C.," replied Thomas.

"I just did," replied Memengwaa. "You should have them already."

"Thanks, I'll get right on it."

"In the meantime," said Memengwaa. "Just stick to the story that Esmeralda is hard at work in the Oval Office. She doesn't have time to meet with anyone. Hopefully we'll get a new battery before anyone finds out what happened."

"Bear in mind that everyone who was at the Cabinet meeting this morning knows what happened," said William. "We can only hope they are all loyal."

"You're the Chief of Staff," said Jacqueline. "Remind them they cannot divulge anything said or done in a Cabinet meeting. Send out a notice immediately."

"And tell them that failure to comply with that rule is a cause for dismissal," added Memengwaa. "They must not say a word to anyone."

"I'll get right on it," William replied.

"I just worry about that guy at the Department of Labor," said Thomas, "Acting Secretary Sharma. He has an attitude problem."

"Make sure that Acting Secretary Sharma gets your reminder," said Memengwaa.

"I will," William replied.

"Thanks for your assistance, everyone," said Thomas. "I'm going to sign off now so I can start calling the small businesses right away."

"Good luck," said Jacqueline.

"Let me know if you need anything else," said Memengwaa.

Thomas disconnected the call, opened his iPalm, and looked for Memengwaa's text. Finding it, he began reading the DSBS list of small business battery manufacturers in the District of Columbia.

* * * * *

As was his custom, Speaker McIntyre was enjoying lunch with Majority Leader Sullivan and Democratic Whip Pafundi in his office, discussing the latest basketball scores, when he received the call from Acting Secretary Sharma.

"I apologize for interrupting your lunch," said the Acting Secretary, "but I feel it's my duty to tell you what happened at the White House this morning."

Speaker McIntyre sat forward. "Something happened this morning at the White House? What happened?"

"President Jenkins collapsed. Her husband thinks her battery is dead. He's trying to find a replacement battery. In the meanwhile, the President is as good as dead. Technically, the United States is without a President. I thought you should know."

"Indeed," Speaker McIntyre replied, "I do need to know. This is important information. Thank you so much … I will be praying for President Jenkins's speedy recovery."

"I'll be monitoring the situation from my office in the Frances Perkins Building," said Acting Secretary Sharma. "I'll let you know if I hear of any other developments."

"Please do. Thank you again, Secretary Sharma." Speaker McIntyre disconnected the call and turned to Majority Leader Sullivan. "This is exactly what we've been waiting for. Who's the Chair of the Judiciary Committee now?"

"Matthew Solomon."

"Right, his name skipped my mind." The Speaker turned to his Whip. "Ishaan, I want you to call Chairman Solomon. No, on second thought, *go see him*. Tell him to drop whatever he's doing. We need to have him draw up Articles of Impeachment immediately ... like *this afternoon*."

"Okay, I'll go see him as soon as I finish my sandwich."

"Tell Chairman Solomon this is urgent," added Speaker McIntyre. "Tell him that President Jenkins is incapacitated and unable to perform the duties of President. The United States is without a leader. We need a new President. We wouldn't want China or the New Soviet Union to find out about this. There's no time to lose."

"Got it," replied Whip Pafundi. "I'll make sure we have the Articles of Impeachment in your hands by COB."

"I'll convene a special session of the full House tomorrow morning."

"Tomorrow? That's a Saturday."

"I know. I'll send out an email right now announcing the special emergency session so that no one will leave town. We'll vote for President Jenkins's impeachment and send it over to the Senate tomorrow afternoon. I'll call the Senate President Pro Tem this afternoon and get him on board. If we act quickly, we can have President Jenkins removed from office within forty-eight hours."

Whip Pafundi finished his sandwich and stood up. "I'm on my way." He turned to the door, left the Speaker's office, and headed down the hall to Chairman Solomon's office.

* * * * *

Jacqueline and Sarah were having lunch together in the House cafeteria when their iPalms vibrated simultaneously. Sarah was first to read the message. "Speaker McIntyre is calling an emergency session of the full House tomorrow morning at eight o'clock."

"An emergency session?" asked Jacqueline. "At eight o'clock in the morning? What is this nonsense?"

"Hold on," said Sarah, "there's more information. Oh my God! He wants to impeach mom!"

"Holy shit!" exclaimed Jacqueline. "Somebody told him!"

"Somebody told him what?"

"Esmeralda's battery failed. Thomas is trying to get a replacement; but in the meantime, Esmeralda is out of commission. She's basically comatose."

"Mom is comatose? Why didn't you tell me?" Sarah looked like she was about to cry.

"I didn't want to alarm you unnecessarily. Thomas is trying to get a replacement battery. Hopefully your mother will be up and running again in no time."

"I see what's happening here," said Sarah. "We have no Vice President, so Speaker McIntyre becomes President if Congress removes mom from office."

"You got it," said Jacqueline, pushing her food tray away and standing up. "That's it exactly. I have to get back to my office right now and work on this."

"What are you going to do?" asked Sarah.

"I don't know, but I have to do something. You can help—call Thomas and tell him what's going on. Memengwaa gave him a list of battery companies in D.C. He needs to find someone to replace Esmeralda's battery before Congress removes her from office. We have no time to waste!"

"I'll go to the White House right now," said Sarah.

"Great, I'll talk to you later."

The two women left the cafeteria hastily, Jacqueline heading back to her office while Sarah called Roger and asked him to pick her up and take her to the White House.

*   *   *   *   *

When Sarah arrived at the North Portico, she entered the building and went directly to Thomas's office on the second floor of the East Wing, where she found him on the phone.

"Come in and sit down, honey," said Thomas. "I'm talking to DC Battery Solutions, Inc."

Sarah sat down in a chair in front of Thomas's desk.

"You get the picture?" asked Thomas, continuing his conversation with the battery company. "We just need to find a battery that's equivalent to the original one—equivalent or better."

"We'll need to look at the old battery," said the voice on the speakerphone. "Is the President in the White House right now?"

"Yes, we have her lying on the floor in her conference room, near the Oval Office. How soon can you get someone here?"

"This afternoon."

"Great, tell your man to come to the West Wing parking garage. I'll have a Secret Service agent meet him there and escort him to the Oval Office. He'll just need identification. Text me the name and the social security number of the person you're sending. That will save time."

"No problem, I'll text you the information as soon as we get off the phone."

"Thank you ... and please tell your employee that this is urgent."

"If it's the President of the United States, he knows it's urgent. He'll get there as fast as he can."

"Thank you so much. I really appreciate the quick response."

"No problem. We'll do our best to replace the battery."

Thomas disconnected the call and looked at Sarah. "You heard what happened?"

"Jacqueline told me. Unfortunately, someone else told Speaker McIntyre."

"Damn! I bet it was Acting Secretary Sharma. He's a real jerk."

"Anyway, Speaker McIntyre is calling an emergency session of the full House tomorrow to vote on impeachment."

"He must be joking!" exclaimed Thomas. "You can't impeach a President in two days. To begin with, the Judiciary Committee would have to draw up Articles of Impeachment, vote on it, and then send it to the Speaker. That alone would take a couple of weeks, probably more."

"He's a very powerful Speaker," replied Sarah. "If he wants the Articles of Impeachment in his hands today, they would give it to him."

"With any luck, we can get the battery replaced before the House meets tomorrow," said Thomas. "It seems like this company is very responsive."

"I heard you say that mom is lying on the floor in the Conference Room. Can I go see her?"

"Of course. We have some time to kill while we're waiting for the battery guy."

Thomas got up from his desk, and Sarah followed him out of his office, down the hallway to the elevator, down to the first floor, across Cross Hall to the West Wing, and down the hallway to the Cabinet Room. After verifying that no one was walking behind them, Thomas opened the door, and he and Sarah entered the room. Thomas closed the door behind them.

"Esmeralda should be lying on the floor on the other side of the table," said Thomas.

Sarah walked to the other side of the table, Thomas following, and saw Esmeralda on the floor. "Oh my God!" exclaimed Sarah. "She looks so helpless!"

Thomas put his hand on Sarah's shoulder. "Don't be upset. I'm pretty sure she'll come back to life when we replace her battery."

"You're not going to leave her here, are you?"

"No, this is temporary. I don't want the White House staff to find out about this. At five o'clock or so, after they leave, you can help me move her to our residence."

"There will still be people around—kitchen staff, Secret Service agents, and custodians."

"I know. We'll have to be careful. I'll carry her over my shoulder, and you walk ahead. You'll have to warn me if anyone is coming."

"It just doesn't seem right to leave her on the floor like this. Can we at least cover her with a blanket?"

"Sure, but wait until the battery guy gets here. While I'm talking to him, you can go back to the residence and find a blanket—unless, of course, he can repair her immediately, in which case the blanket wouldn't be necessary."

"Understood."

"Anyway, it will take a while for him to get here. I haven't had lunch. Let's go to the Family Dining Room and grab a bite."

"I already had lunch—I met Jacqueline for lunch in the House cafeteria at noon ... but sure, I can have a cup of tea while you're having your lunch."

Thomas and Sarah left the Cabinet Room, closing the door behind them, and headed for the Family Dining Room.

* * * * *

Representative Matthew Solomon, Chair of the Judiciary Committee, was at his desk when Democratic Whip Ishaan Pafundi arrived. He stood up and greeted the Whip.

"Good afternoon, Ishaan," said Chairman Solomon. "To what do I owe this honor?"

"Good afternoon, Matt. I have something big to discuss."

"Something big?"

"Yes, the Speaker asked me to see you in person."

"I hope I'm not in trouble."

"You'll only be in trouble if you procrastinate. The Speaker needs you to do something for him as quickly as possible—or, to be more precise, today by COB."

Chairman Solomon looked alarmed. "What does he want me to do?"

"You need to draw up Articles of Impeachment."

"Articles of Impeachment? Whom are we impeaching?"

"President Jenkins."

"President Jenkins? The President of the United States?"

"Exactly."

"And the Speaker expects me to get this done today by COB?"

"You're a good listener."

Chairman Solomon sat back down in his chair and motioned for Whip Pafundi to sit down in a chair facing his desk. For a moment, the two men stared at each other.

"I need the background information," said Chairman Solomon. "Apparently President Jenkins has done something to piss off the Speaker."

"No, she hasn't done anything to piss him off. In fact, that's the problem—she *can't* do anything; she's incapacitated."

"Incapacitated? In what way?"

"Her battery died. She's unable to perform the duties of President. Under the Constitution, a President who is unfit or unable to perform their duties can be impeached."

"I think I know what the Constitution says—don't forget I'm Chair of the Judiciary Committee."

"I'm well aware of your position, Matt. That's why I came to see you. You're the only one who can get the ball rolling here. You have to draw up the Articles of Impeachment and deliver them to the Speaker. Then he'll call the full House together for an emergency meeting, and they'll vote to impeach. If everyone plays ball, we can have President Jenkins removed from office within twenty-four hours."

"Listen here, Ishaan, I'm not going to be pushed into something like this unless I know it's the right thing to do. Step one, I need to contact President Jenkins and advise her that her fitness for office is being questioned and give her an opportunity to appear before the Committee to demonstrate otherwise. If she refuses to appear—or *cannot* appear, as the case may be—then I have to find a volunteer on the Committee to draw up the Articles of Impeachment, after which the Committee's Counsel would need time to review the document for legal sufficiency. The Speaker is nuts if he thinks I can accomplish all of that by COB today."

"Perhaps I was mistaken when I said you were a good listener."

"What do you mean by that?"

"You apparently didn't hear me when I said the Speaker wants the Articles of Impeachment in his hands today by COB."

The two men stared at each other again.

The Whip leaned forward in his chair. "Don't forget the Speaker appointed you Chair of the Judiciary Committee, and he can replace you as fast as he appointed you. I suggest it's in your best interest to play ball."

Chairman Solomon was silent.

The Whip stood up. "I enjoyed our conversation. I look forward to reading your Articles of Impeachment over my dinner this evening."

Whip Pafundi turned and walked to the door, leaving the Chairman's office without another word.

*   *   *   *   *

As Thomas and Sarah sat down in the White House Family Dining Room, Thomas received a text from DC Battery Solutions with the name and social security number of the employee coming to examine Esmeralda's battery, and Thomas forwarded the information to the Secret Service. As Thomas was finishing his sandwich, his cell phone vibrated, and he read a message that the employee had been screened and was being escorted to the West Wing lobby.

"He's here," said Thomas, pushing his chair back and standing up. "Let's go."

Sarah got up from the table and followed Thomas, who was walking rapidly, to the West Wing and down the stairway to the first floor and the lobby. Leo Smith, the repairman, was waiting for them in the lobby when they arrived.

After introducing themselves, Thomas and Sarah escorted Mr. Smith to the Cabinet Room.

"President Jenkins is lying on the floor behind the table," said Thomas.

"Oh, I forgot," said Sarah. "I wanted to put a blanket over her. I'll go back to the residence and get a blanket." She turned back to the door and departed, closing the door tightly behind her.

Mr. Smith walked to the other side of the table and looked at Esmeralda, then turned to Thomas. "Do you know how to get to the battery?"

"Yes," said Thomas. "Flip her over and lift her blouse from the back. There's a compartment on her lower back."

Mr. Smith followed Thomas's instructions and located the battery compartment. He took an allen wrench from his toolkit, loosened the screws to the battery compartment, removed the cover, removed the battery, and then replaced the cover, closed the battery compartment, and tightened the screws. Then he picked up the battery, turned it upside down and sideways looking for the label, then set it on the table and sat down to examine it more closely.

"This one was made from alkaline zinc-manganese dioxide," said Mr. Smith. "They don't use that material in batteries anymore."

"So what can we do?" asked Thomas.

"I think I can find another battery that will work, but it's tricky. If I don't match the voltage properly, we could destroy the robot's circuitry."

"Be careful, please!" exclaimed Thomas. "We don't want to destroy her circuitry!"

"Understood—I'll be careful ... Anyway, the bottom line is that I don't have any batteries in my truck that will work. I'll have to go back to the shop and see what I can find."

"How long will it take?"

"Well, that depends on whether I have a battery in the shop that will work. If I have a battery in stock, I can charge it tonight, test it tomorrow morning, and deliver it tomorrow afternoon. If I have to order it, it would take a little longer."

"Please expedite it. We can't have Esmeralda in this condition any longer than necessary."

"I understand," replied Mr. Smith. He pushed his chair back and stood up. "If you don't mind, I'll take the old battery back to the shop. That way I can be sure I'm matching the voltage correctly."

"That would be fine," replied Thomas.

The door opened, and Sarah appeared with something under her arm. "I've got the blanket," she said, closing the door behind her and walking to the other side of the table. "It looks like you rolled mom over on her stomach. Can I turn her over now so she's on her back?"

"Yes, go ahead," said Mr. Smith. "I can't do anything more with her right now."

"What's the prognosis?" asked Sarah.

"He doesn't have this kind of battery in his truck," said Thomas. "He's going back to his shop to see if he can find one that will work."

"Oh, please, Sir!" exclaimed Sarah. "Please find a battery!"

"I'll do my best," said Mr. Smith. "By the way, do I need an escort to get out of here?"

"Yes," said Thomas. "I'll escort you out."

Thomas escorted Mr. Smith out of the Cabinet Room and down to the parking garage while Sarah rolled Esmeralda over onto her back and covered her with a blanket.

*   *   *   *   *

At five-thirty, Thomas and Sarah returned to the West Wing and checked all of the offices to verify that the staff had left for the day. Then they went to the Cabinet Room, and Sarah removed the blanket covering Esmeralda. Thomas picked his wife up and put her over his shoulder in a fireman's carry; and Sarah, the blanket under her arm, led the way out of the room. They followed the corridor to the elevator, took the elevator to the second floor of the West Wing, walked from there to the first floor of the residence, and then took another elevator to the second floor of the residence. Thomas carried Esmeralda into the master bedroom and set her on top of the bed, and Sarah put the blanket over her.

"I feel much better," said Sarah. "It pained me to see mom lying on the floor."

"We had no choice," said Thomas. "Anyway, thanks for your help. Do you want to stay for dinner?"

"Sure ... and if you don't mind, I think I'll spend the night. I really want to be with you and mom until we get through this crisis."

"No problem—like I said before, you're always welcome here."

"Thanks, Dad."

"Let's go down to the dining room now and enjoy dinner together."

Thomas and Sarah left the master bedroom, and Thomas closed the door behind him and locked it; then the two walked to the elevator and took it to the first floor of the residence where the Family Dining Room was located. Thomas's iPalm vibrated as they sat down at their table.

"It's Jacqueline," said Thomas.

"I hope she has good news," said Sarah.

"Hi, Jacqueline," said Thomas. "Sarah is with me. I have you on speakerphone."

"Hi Sarah," said Jacqueline.

"Hi, Aunt Jacqueline."

"Sarah and I just put Esmeralda to bed," said Thomas. "She's in a safe place. No one in the White House except Sarah and me has a clue what happened."

"You can't keep it from them for long. They're going to find out tomorrow morning when the House meets to discuss impeachment. Any luck on the battery?"

"Well, we're making progress. I got in touch with one of the companies on Memengwaa's list—SBA's DSBS list, I mean—and someone came and looked at Esmeralda's battery. He didn't have the same type of battery in his truck, but he thinks he might have a battery in his shop that will work. He has to match the voltage."

"I hope he's able to bring you a new battery tomorrow."

"He couldn't guarantee it. He said he would try."

"I can buy you seventy-two hours, that's all."

"Seventy-two hours?"

"That's right. I can delay the vote on impeachment for seventy-two hours. If we can't get Esmeralda up and running by then, all hell is going to break loose."

"Damn!" said Thomas.

"Do you think you should try some other battery companies?" asked Jacqueline.

"No, this guy seemed to know what he's doing. He said they don't make that kind of battery anymore. Any battery company we call is going to tell us the same thing."

"Okay, then, keep me posted. I'll do what I can at my end."

"Thanks, Sis. Have a good evening."

"Thanks, Aunt Jacqueline," said Sarah.

"Have a good night, guys," said Jacqueline.

Thomas closed his iPalm. "Take a look at the menu, honey. We might as well try to enjoy our dinner."

Thomas and Sarah dined quietly, too low in spirits to engage in any meaningful conversation.

*   *   *   *   *

The next morning, members of the House began arriving in the House Chamber in the south wing of the Capitol at nine-thirty. Speaker McIntyre called the meeting to order at ten o'clock sharp and asked the House Chaplain to deliver the customary prayer.

Chaplain Pancho Sanchez stepped forward and leaned into the microphone. "Eternal Father," he began, "we give you thanks for being alive in a democratic society. We ask you to bless this assembly of elected representatives and give them wisdom as they consider the profound and difficult issues before them. May all that is done here today be for your honor and glory—so help me God. Amen."

"Thank you, Chaplain Sanchez," said the Speaker. "The next order of business is to approve the House Journal for yesterday, Friday, February 7, 2521. I have reviewed the Journal and found it to be correct; however, in the interest of time, I will postpone a vote on it until later today. Now I'm going to ask Majority Leader Patrick Sullivan to lead us in the Pledge of Allegiance to the flag."

Majority Leader Patrick Sullivan stepped forward, turned to the American flag, and put his right hand over his heart. All of the members of the House stood up and did the same as the Majority Leader led them in the Pledge of Allegiance: "I pledge allegiance to the Flag of the United States of America, and to the Republic for which it stands, one Nation under God, indivisible, with liberty and justice for all."

"Thank you, Patrick," said Speaker McIntyre. "Now, Members of the House, please listen carefully. I'm going to suspend the usual one-minute speeches and unanimous-consent requests because of the critical issue at hand. President Jenkins had a stroke during her Cabinet meeting yesterday morning. She is comatose and unable to perform the duties of President. As you know, she ascended to the Presidency after President Hoffenberger's assassination, and she has not yet filled the position of Vice President. Therefore, at this moment, the United States has no functioning President or Vice President. We are without a leader— more specifically, without a Commander in Chief. Any one of our enemies could seize this moment to attack us. Indeed, as soon as they get word of this, China and the New Soviet Union will begin mobilizing their armies. We have no time to lose. We must remove President Jenkins from office and follow the guidance in our Constitution for selecting a new President."

Speaker McIntyre paused and took a sip of water.

"To be truthful," continued Speaker McIntyre, "I'm a big fan of President Jenkins, and I was opposed to removing her from office. However, Representative Matthew Solomon, the wise Chair of the Judiciary Committee, persuaded me to move forward with impeachment. He said that to do otherwise would be a dereliction of my duties as Speaker. In the end, I deferred to his better judgment and agreed to hold this special session."

Speaker McIntyre coughed and took another sip of water. "Chairman Solomon has drawn up formal Articles of Impeachment, so I will call on him now to read them. After he is done, we can proceed with a formal vote. Chairman Solomon, please come forward and read your Articles of Impeachment."

Speaker McIntyre sat down; and Chairman Solomon, standing nearby, came to the podium with an oversized document in his right hand. He placed the document on the podium and took his reading glasses from his pocket; then, after putting on his glasses, he adjusted the microphone and began reading. "This document shall be known as House Resolution 2541, the title of which reads, "Impeaching Esmeralda Jenkins, President of the United States, for high crimes and misdemeanors."

Chairman Solomon removed his reading glasses and looked up. "I couldn't actually find anything in the Constitution about what to do if the President has a stroke. The term 'high crimes and misdemeanors' was the closest I could find, so that's what I'm using here."

"Just read it," said Speaker McIntyre. "We don't need any long explanations."

Chairman Solomon put his glasses back on. "Article number one: Be it resolved that Esmeralda Jenkins, President of the United States, is impeached because she is unable to perform the duties of her office. This is evidenced by her suffering a stroke during a Cabinet meeting on Friday, February 7, 2521. President Jenkins is now in a comatose condition. She is unable to move or speak, and there is no hope of her recovery. Accordingly, she is unfit to perform the duties of President and must be removed from office."

Chairman Solomon paused and looked at the Speaker.

"So far, so good," said Speaker McIntyre. "Please continue."

"Article number two," continued Chairman Solomon, "The U.S. Constitution, article two, section four, specifies that a President must be removed from office for high crimes and misdemeanors."

Chairman Solomon removed his reading glasses and looked up. "The procedure for removing a President begins with a formal vote of impeachment in the U.S. House of Representatives. From there, it moves to the Senate for a trial."

"Everybody knows that," said the Speaker. "Just read your Articles of Impeachment."

Chairman Solomon put his glasses back on and looked down at the document, "Therefore, based on the foregoing facts, which are undisputable, the United States House of Representatives hereby impeaches President Jenkins and disqualifies her from the office of President."

Speaker McIntyre stood up and took the microphone. "Thank you, Chairman Solomon. That's all we need. You may sit down now."

Chairman Solomon picked up the Articles of Impeachment and returned to his chair.

Speaker McIntyre looked at the Assembly. "Members of the House, members of the press, and other guests who may be here, I want to impress upon you that this is a momentous occasion. History will judge us by how quickly we acted: Did we act swiftly to remove President Jenkins or did we vacillate and engage in meaningless debate? The facts here are clear and indisputable. We are without a leader, and we must act today. There is no time for idle talk. I ask all Members to put partisanship aside and consider what is in the best interest of the United States of America."

The Speaker paused and took a sip of water. "Okay, you have the facts. Now I think we're ready to vote. Let's get to it."

Jacqueline suddenly stood and walked to the front row, sat down in an empty chair, and then immediately stood up again. "Mr. Speaker, I ask unanimous consent to address the House for one minute and to revise and extend my remarks."

"Without objection, so ordered," replied the Speaker, adding, "Please make it quick. I'm not going to tolerate any nonsense."

"Under the rules of the House adopted in 2477," Jacqueline began, "I call for a vote of no-confidence in the Speaker. Under the aforementioned rules, the House will vote on my motion; and if it passes, the House shall suspend any action before it and adjourn for seventy-two hours. When the House reconvenes, which will be on Tuesday morning, February 11th, it shall choose a new Speaker, after which it will vote on any pending actions, including the Articles of Impeachment presently under consideration. Thank you—I yield the balance of my time."

Speaker McIntyre stared at Jacqueline in silence for a moment; then, barely missing a beat, he continued, "Thank you, Representative Jenkins. Unfortunately, your motion dies for lack of a second. Now let's proceed with the vote on impeachment."

Sarah, sitting in the back of the room with other Greens, stood and walked to the front row, sat down in an empty chair next to Jacqueline, and then immediately stood up again. "Mr. Speaker, I ask unanimous consent to address the House for one minute and to revise and extend my remarks."

"Without objection, so ordered," replied the Speaker, adding, "This is the last one-minute speech I shall allow. When this member has finished, we will vote on the impeachment without further delay."

"Mr. Speaker," began Sarah, "you are premature in stating that there is no second to Representative Jenkins's motion. You never asked for a second. *I* second the motion."

The Speaker's face reddened. "And who are you again?"

"My name is Sarah Jenkins. I'm the Representative for the Commonwealth of Virginia's 8th Congressional District."

"What? We have another Jenkins in the House?"

"That's correct, Mr. Speaker. Representative Jacqueline Jenkins is my Aunt. She represents Virginia's 11th Congressional District."

"I see. Well, frankly, it is highly irregular for a junior member of the House to speak up and second a motion during a meeting of the full assembly. I suggest you save your energy for committee work until you learn the ropes."

"I'm not worried about saving my energy, Mr. Speaker. I have plenty of it."

"Listen," said Speaker McIntyre, "we're wasting time here. If you know what's good for you, you will withdraw your second, sit down, and shut up!"

Under her breath, Sarah mouthed the advice that Geraldine had given her many years before when she joined her high school's debate club: *The key is to be assertive … Above all, don't back down and don't let your opponent intimidate you.*

Sarah continued, "I enjoy the same right to speak as any other member of the House, and I demand that you hear me!"

The Speaker's face reddened more.

"In case you didn't hear me the first time," added Sarah, "I said that I second the motion introduced a moment ago by my colleague, Representative Jacqueline Jenkins. Please see that my second is entered into the Congressional record."

The Speaker's face reddened even more, and veins appeared in his forehead. For a moment, he appeared to be at a loss for words. Finally, he responded, "If the young lady is going to be stubborn, we have no choice ... no matter, I think we can do this quickly and continue with the impeachment vote. I want to remind Democrats that their first obligation is always to the party. Okay, let's vote on Representative Jenkins's motion. The members are hereby instructed to take their voting card to the nearest voting station and indicate their support or opposition to the motion by pushing the yea or nay button. This will be a fifteen-minute vote—please vote expeditiously so that we can get this unpleasant matter behind us."

During the next fifteen minutes, the members voted as instructed. The House's digital assistant tallied the votes and announced the results. Perhaps because of Jacqueline's popularity, or perhaps because the members, who were not stupid, could see that Speaker McIntyre was simply seeking a back door for himself to the Presidency, the yeas outnumbered the nays, and Jacqueline's motion passed.

When the digital assistant announced the result, Speaker McIntyre threw his gavel down angrily, turned, and walked briskly out of the chamber. Majority Leader Sullivan then came to the podium, leaned into the microphone, and asked for a motion to adjourn. Representative Donald Carmichael from New Jersey obliged by making the motion, and Majority Leader Sullivan announced that the special session was over. One by one, the members arose from their seats, some remaining in the chamber to talk to their colleagues and others departing.

Jacqueline and Sarah, who had returned to their seats, arose and looked for each other; and in another moment, they met and exchanged a hug.

"Thanks for your support, honey," said Jacqueline.

"It was the least I could do," replied Sarah. "You're my role model."

"It's almost noon. Let's go grab a bite to eat."

The two Representatives from Virginia, aunt and niece, departed the Chamber and headed towards the House cafeteria.

* * * * *

Thomas called Leo Smith at DC Battery Solutions as soon as he arose on Saturday morning and asked for the status of Esmeralda's battery.

"I've found a battery that may work," said Mr. Smith, "but matching the voltage is turning out to be more of a challenge than I expected. Like I said, if I don't match it correctly, we could blow the robot's circuitry. I don't want history to record me as the person who destroyed the country's first robot President."

"I understand," replied Thomas. "I want you to be careful … so how soon do you think you can bring me the new battery?"

"I need at least another day. I'll work on it today. If everything goes well, I'll charge it again tonight, test it again tomorrow morning, and bring it over tomorrow afternoon."

"That would be great. Esmeralda is supposed to deliver her *Sunday Evening Update* tomorrow night. If we can get her working tomorrow afternoon, she can do her speech as planned, and the Nation will be reassured that she's well."

"I'll do my best," said Mr. Smith.

*   *   *   *   *

After lunching with Jacqueline, Sarah returned to her office in the Rayburn House Office Building to read constituent mail and wrap up some other loose ends. At five o'clock, she called Roger and asked him to pick her up and bring her to the White House. Roger arrived at 5:15, picked her up, and dropped her off at the North Portico at 5:25. She called Thomas on her iPalm to tell him she had arrived.

"I'm in my office," said Thomas. "Are you spending the night?"

"Yes," replied Sarah, *every night* until mom is repaired."

"Okay, I'm almost done for the day. You can hang out with me in the East Wing until dinner if you'd like."

"That sounds good."

Sarah walked to Thomas's office and sat down on a couch while he finished his work. Then the two walked to the Family Dining Room and enjoyed dinner together, after which they went to the library, formerly the White House theater, and read until bedtime. At ten o'clock, father and daughter went to the master bedroom and checked on Esmeralda, who lay motionless in the same position they had placed her the day before, eyes open but lifeless, covered by the same blanket that Sarah had placed on top of her. Sarah took Esmeralda's right hand, held it for a moment, and bent over and kissed her on the cheek. Then, with a tear in her eye, Sarah turned and left the room.

*   *   *   *   *

Leo Smith from DC Battery Solutions arrived the next day, Sunday, February 9th, at 2:00 p.m. carrying the replacement battery.

Thomas met him at the entrance to the parking garage in the West Wing and escorted him to the master bedroom in the residence. Sarah was waiting for them outside the bedroom and opened the door to let Mr. Smith inside.

"I covered her with a blanket," said Sarah. "I'll take it off now."

"You'll have to roll her over on her stomach, too," said Mr. Smith. "The battery compartment is in her back."

Sarah removed the blanket, rolled Esmeralda onto her back, and lifted her blouse to reveal the battery compartment. Mr. Smith took out his allen wrench, loosened the screws to the cover, and opened it. Then he put the new battery into the compartment and replaced the cover, tightening the screws, and pulled Esmeralda's blouse back down.

"Can I turn her over now?" said Sarah. "She looks so uncomfortable."

"Sure," said Mr. Smith. "She should begin waking up soon."

Sarah turned Esmeralda over onto her back, then waited for something to happen.

"How long before we know if the battery is working?" asked Thomas.

"If she wakes up, we know it's working," said Mr. Smith. "She should wake up any second now."

Esmeralda blinked, sat up, and immediately began speaking. "... Regardless, I don't think it's right that a Superintendent of Schools earns six times more than a teacher or that a CEO earns twenty times more than a factory worker. There's no justification for such a disparity ... Wait a minute! What happened to my Cabinet? Why am I in my bedroom?"

Sarah began crying. "Mom! I love you!" Sarah bent over and put her arms around Esmeralda, who was still sitting on the bed. "I'm so glad you have come back to life!"

"You were unconscious," explained Thomas. "Your battery was dead. We just put a new battery in you."

Esmeralda looked at Mr. Smith. "Who is this man?"

"My name is Leo Smith from DC Battery Solutions. How do you feel? Does everything seem okay? Do you feel normal?"

"Yes, everything seems okay—and yes, I feel normal."

"Thank God!" exclaimed Thomas.

"Who do I send the bill to?" asked Mr. Smith.

* * * * *

Later that afternoon, Geraldine was awakened from a nap by her digital assistant. She turned to the wall monitor in her bedroom.

"I'm sorry to disturb you," Ms. Jenkins, "but I have your daughter, Jacqueline, on the line. She says she has good news."

Geraldine opened her eyes. "Sure, Richard, I'll always talk to someone who has good news—unless, of course, it's a scam."

"I understand you will always talk to someone who has good news, but not if it's a scam. Is that correct, Ms. Jenkins?"

"You got it, Richard. Now put Jacqueline through."

Richard disappeared, and Jacqueline's image replaced Richard's on the monitor.

"Mom, I have wonderful news. Esmeralda has come back to life!"

"Esmeralda has come back to life? What is that supposed to mean?"

"Didn't you hear? Esmeralda's battery died on Friday, and Thomas had to get a replacement battery. They just installed the battery this afternoon, and she's as good as new!"

"I had no idea—why didn't someone tell me?"

"You better talk to your digital assistant. He is supposed to tell you when anything important happens."

"Oh dear, I fear Richard is getting old."

"He's not getting old—he just needs to be rebooted."

"Yes, of course, I'll reboot him tonight."

"Anyway, Esmeralda is going to give her third *Sunday Evening Update* tonight at eight o'clock. I know you won't want to miss it."

"Oh my! Is she going to talk about economics again?"

"Of course, you know Esmeralda ... that's her favorite subject."

"Do I have to listen?"

"Yes, you do. I won't speak to you again if you don't ... just joking."

"Okay, I'll listen. It's at eight o'clock, you said?"

"Yes, eight o'clock."

"Okay, if I must ... I'll ask Richard to have it ready for me."

"Good, I'll talk to you later."

"Goodbye, Jacqueline."

"Goodbye, Mom."

*　　*　　*　　*　　*

At 7:55 p.m., Geraldine went to the refrigerator door and ordered a cup of hot Earl Gray tea, took it to the kitchen table, and summoned Richard.

"Richard, do you have CNN ready to go?"

The wall monitor lit up, and Richard appeared. "Yes, Ms. Jenkins, I have everything ready for you. Do you want to begin watching it now?"

"Yes, please."

"Very well, Ms. Jenkins, I'll bring it to you now. Call me if you need anything else."

Richard disappeared, and a familiar face replaced him on the monitor.

"Good evening. My name is Suzanne Zhang. We are about to bring you President Jenkins's *Sunday Evening Update*, which will be her third such address in three weeks. With me is Shoshana Israel, CNN's senior political analyst, and she will give us some commentary." The screen shot widened, revealing Ms. Israel.

Ms. Zhang turned and looked at Ms. Israel. "Shoshana, do you have anything you'd like to say to our viewers while we're waiting for the President?"

The camera zoomed in on Ms. Israel. "I think President Jenkins will try to reassure the American people that she's healthy. As you know, there have been rumors she suffered a stroke during her Cabinet meeting on Friday, and Congress held an emergency session on Saturday morning to consider removing her from office."

"I understand that Speaker McIntyre wanted to impeach her, but he failed."

"That's correct. I think—"

"Excuse me, Shoshana, I believe the President is about to speak. Let's watch and we can talk about that later." The two CNN women disappeared, and Esmeralda appeared on the screen, sitting at her desk in the Oval Office. An announcer exclaimed, "Here, now, is the President of the United States!"

"Good evening, my fellow Americans," Esmeralda began. "Thank you for joining me tonight for my third *Sunday Evening Update*. I want to begin by addressing rumors about my health. I'm sure many of you may have heard I have been sick. Some of you may have even heard that I died. Well, I obviously didn't die, but I *was* sick—in a manner of speaking. I have never lied to the American people, and I'm not going to lie to you now. What actually happened is that my battery died. It is supposed to be replaced every thirty-five years, but Thomas, my husband, forgot about it. Doesn't that sound just like a husband?"

Geraldine sighed. "Thomas hasn't changed a bit. In high school, he could never remember his assignments."

Richard appeared in the top-right corner of the monitor. "Ms. Jenkins, did you need me for something?"

"No, Richard, I don't need you ... but please remind me to reboot you when this is over. You've been overlooking some of your duties."

"Of course, Ms. Jenkins, I'll remind you to reboot me." Richard disappeared.

"Anyway," Esmeralda continued, "Thomas found a replacement battery, and I'm good for another thirty-five years. Okay, now that we have that behind us, let's get to the fun part—the economy!"

"Spare me, please!" exclaimed Geraldine.

"As you may know," continued Esmeralda, "the S&P 500 lost five million points on the news of my illness, but I'm confident it will bounce right back tomorrow morning when people see that I'm not sick after all. So there are no worries there. I'm also happy to inform you that the money supply, as evidenced by M_1 and M_2, remained constant over the past week, so there's no worries there,

either. I'll talk more about monetary policy in a moment, but first I
want to talk to you about leading economic indicators ..."

Esmeralda was back on her game.

The First Robot President

Epilogue

Epilogue

On Tuesday, February 11, 2521, the U.S. House of Representatives elected a new Speaker, Representative Ying Yue Chan, a Democrat from Pennsylvania. Speaker Chan immediately scrapped the Articles of Impeachment against Esmeralda and replaced Majority Leader Patrick Sullivan and Democratic Whip Ishaan Pafundi with moderate and well-respected democratic colleagues.

As its next order of business, the House confirmed the nomination of Juan Nighthorse Humetewa as Vice President; and on Wednesday, the Senate followed suit, and Supreme Court Justice Anthony Vlastos administered the Oath of Office to Vice President Humetewa the same day.

Former Speaker Peter McIntyre served the remainder of his term powerlessly. He lost his bid for reelection in 2522 and was never heard from again.

In the mid-term election of 2522, the Greens gained control of the House, and Jacqueline was elected Speaker at the first session in January 2523. She served in that position for twenty-five years until she retired from Congress in 2548.

As expected, the AFGE—the American Federation of Government Employees—sued Esmeralda on the grounds that a birth lottery for Federal employees was unconstitutional. White House Counsel Bhaanupriya Yanagi defended the Executive Order in court; the Judge ruled that the order met the constitutional standard of strict scrutiny and upheld it. The AFGE vowed to appeal the ruling.

Later the same year, Congress enacted a nationwide birth lottery applicable to all U.S. citizens. The ACLU—the American Civil Liberties Union—filed suit in Federal court to block the legislation; Attorney Yanagi worked with Congressional lawyers to defend it, and the Judge ruled that the law was constitutional. The ACLU vowed to appeal.

In December 2521, Esmeralda traveled to the Vatican in Rome and met with Pope Francis III, persuading him to issue an edict officially ending the Roman Catholic Church's opposition to birth control.

Over the next twelve months, Great Britain, France, Germany, China, Brazil, India, Japan, Vietnam, and South Africa all enacted birth lotteries modeled after the United States' lottery.

Both the AFGE and the ACLU lost their appeals of the birth lottery for Federal employees and U.S. citizens, respectively, and the U.S. Supreme Court declined to hear either case, allowing both Esmeralda's Executive Order and Congress's legislation to stand.

Some say that history repeats itself. If so, that would explain the next chapter in Angelica's life; after grieving for a year, she began dating in 2522 and remarried in 2523. Her new husband was a Greek billionaire, not unlike the second husband of Jacqueline Kennedy, an earlier first lady whose first husband, President John Fitzgerald Kennedy, was also assassinated. Angelica moved to her billionaire husband's mansion on the Greek Island of Mykonos and lived there happily until her death in 2537.

In 2523, the U.S. Supreme Court refused to hear the appeal of the Democratic National Committee to overturn the decisions of the U.S. District Court for Eastern Virginia and the U.S. Court of Appeals for the Fourth Circuit upholding the 2518 election results in Virginia's 8th Congressional District, thus paving the way for other robots to run for Congress in the future.

At the World Economic Forum in 2524, the world leaders discussed the creation of a more powerful United Nations, as Esmeralda had proposed in 2521, and agreed to give it full control of all military weapons with the goal of preventing future wars.

Esmeralda was reelected President in 2524 and finished her second term successfully, serving as President for eight years altogether.

Thomas continued to serve as Esmeralda's unofficial advisor until the end of her second term, after which he returned to his former position as a lobbyist at the same company he had worked before, Green Solutions, LLC.

Vice President Humetewa won the Presidential elections of 2528 and 2532, giving the Green Party sixteen consecutive years in the White House.

William served as Esmeralda's Chief of Staff through the remainder of her first term, and Esmeralda nominated him to be the head of the SBA in her second term. Congress confirmed his nomination, and President Humetewa nominated him to be the Secretary of the Treasury in 2529, which Congress also confirmed. William retired from public life in 2537 and accepted a position teaching government at George Washington University.

Following Esmeralda's success, more than two dozen robots ran for Congress during the next twenty-five years; more than half of them were elected, and more than half of those were reelected to serve one or more additional terms.

After leaving office, Esmeralda took a leadership role in the Green Party and worked with other robots to create a robot caucus.

Sarah was reelected to the House of Representatives six more times. When she retired from public life at the end of 2534, she returned to the University of Texas in San Antonio as head of the Economics Department. In 2549, she received the Nobel Prize in Economics for her five-hundred-year analysis of government spending and its impact on global economic growth and employment.

Since the Virginia Constitution prohibits anyone from serving two consecutive terms as Governor, Hector could not run for reelection in 2521, and he accepted a position in Esmeralda's administration as Secretary of Commerce. He served in that capacity for the duration of Esmeralda's two terms and then ran for Governor of Virginia again in 2529, winning election and serving another four years as Governor. He retired from public life in 2534 and accepted a professorship at George Mason University in Virginia, where he taught a course in public policy until his death.

Hector's wife, Susan, remained president of the League of Women Voters for more than two decades and retired in 2541.

Memengwaa remained Co-chair of the Green Party until the end of her second two-year term. Under the Green Party's by-laws, a Co-chair may not serve more than two terms; therefore, at the end of her second term, she ran for Congress, seeking the seat of the nonvoting delegate from the District of Columbia. She won the election and more than two dozen subsequent elections, continuing to serve as the District of Columbia's representative in Congress until her retirement in 2555.

Geraldine's health gradually declined after Esmeralda's ascension to the Presidency, and she died of heart failure in 2528 at the age of 115.

After retiring from Congress in 2548, Jacqueline did part-time work for CNN as a political commentator during election years. She died in 2569.

When Thomas died unexpectedly in 2572 at the age of 118, Esmeralda's battery was removed in accordance with the terms of his Will. As a former President, Esmeralda was laid in state in the Rotunda of the U.S. Capitol. Millions of visitors from around the world came to pay their respects. Robots came, too, some with their owners and some alone, to see the body of the first robot President. Visiting hours were extended twice to accommodate visitors from Australia, New Zealand, and other distant states. Afterwards, Esmeralda was buried in Arlington National Cemetery with full honors, along with Thomas, with a headstone that read: *Here lies Esmeralda Jenkins, the 128th President of the United States, and her husband, Thomas.*

In 2573, fearful of the long-term implications of super-intelligent robots, Congress enacted legislation mandating that no robot can be manufactured with an IQ higher than 110.

In 2581, under pressure from the robot caucus, Congress established Esmeralda's birthday as a national holiday.

Each year until her death, Sarah dutifully visited Arlington National Cemetery and placed flowers on her foster parents' grave. On one such visit in April 2583, she placed yellow roses in front of the tombstone, knelt to her knees, and prayed. Then she stood, turned, and started to walk away. As she did so, she overheard a conversation among a group of young people arriving at the grave site. One man said to his companions, "Did any of you see the news last night?" A woman responded, "Are you talking about the census

data?" The man replied, "Yes, the World Economic Council announced we're on track to hit our goal of seven billion by the turn of
the millennium." Sarah turned back towards her parents' grave.
Looking directly at the headstone, she exclaimed, "You did it, Mom!
You did it!" She gave two thumbs up, turned again, and walked
away.

In September 2584, at the age of 109—exactly one hundred
years after her adoption—Sarah passed away peacefully in her
sleep.

Oh, one more thing: the Dallas Cowboys held off a fourth-
quarter rally by the Denver Broncos to win Super Bowl DLV by a
score of 24 to 21. Sarah won the gentlemen's bet.

THE END

If you enjoyed this novel, I would be grateful if you would
post a review on the Internet, either on BookBub, Goodreads, or the
website of the retailer where you purchased the book. The following
links will take you directly to *The First Robot President*:

1. https://www.bookbub.com/books/the-first-robot-president-
   by-robert-carlyle-taylor
2. https://www.goodreads.com/book/show/53162137-the-first-
   robot-president

You can find links to several on-line retailers on my website,
https://www.robertcarlyletaylor-author.com, if you prefer to post a
review where you purchased the book. This helps me a lot. Thank
you very much!

Robert Carlyle Taylor

The First Robot President

Afterword

Afterword

*T*he First Robot President *contains one theme of paramount importance and touches on several others, and I hope it will generate further discussion on all of them in a variety of fiction and non-fiction venues. To that end, I'd like to expand on a few of the topics here.*

–1–

I'm sure many readers wondered, when they saw the title page of this book, why a novel would contain a flow chart and tables. Let me begin by explaining the flow chart and Table 1.

Readers who read "About the Author" are aware that I spent most of my career as an employee of the U.S. Small Business Administration (SBA), which included nineteen years as a program manager and assistant director in SBA headquarters in Washington. During that period, I worked with an interagency task team to develop the government-wide *Electronic Subcontracting Reporting System (eSRS)*, which was implemented at the end of fiscal year 2004.[3] The team's assignment was to develop and implement a web-based electronic system to replace the paper reporting system that

---

[3] The Department of Defense (DoD) did not implement the eSRS until fiscal year 2008, three or four years after the civilian agencies did so.

had been used since the early 1980's. The eSRS is used by the government's large prime contractors (companies such as Lockheed Martin and Raytheon) to report their subcontracting achievements to the Federal agency or agencies that awarded them their contract(s).[4] These agencies, along with SBA and the Defense Contract Management Agency (DCMA), use the system to monitor the prime contractors' compliance with their subcontracting plans. SBA also uses the system to obtain government-wide subcontracting data and for other analytical purposes.[5] The eSRS did not change any of the reporting rules developed years before in a paper environment, but it allowed SBA and other government agencies to collect and analyze the subcontracting data more efficiently than before—indeed, to an extent that was light years ahead of what had been possible in the paper environment.

After some initial resistance and skepticism, the contracting community—both government users and contractors—embraced

---

[4] Section 8(d) of the Small Business Act requires Federal prime contractors (i.e., large businesses and certain other entities) with contracts over $1.5 million for construction of a public facility or more than $700,000 for all other contracts to have an approved subcontracting plan with dollar and percentage goals for the utilization of small business and various socio-economic subsets. (Please note that these dollar thresholds are periodically adjusted for inflation.) Small business prime contractors are exempt from this requirement; therefore, in SBA's subcontracting program, the term "prime contractor" usually refers to a large business, although it could also be a college or university, a state or local government agency, a hospital, a non-profit, or any other entity that is not a small business. (Since the definition of a small business established by Congress requires that it be "for profit," SBA considers non-profit entities to be other than small.)

[5] DLA Energy, a component of the Defense Logistics Agency, and the Office of Naval Research (ONR) also have specific authority, albeit more limited in scope, to monitor prime contractors for compliance with their subcontracting plans. DLA Energy monitors energy companies, and ONR monitors colleges and universities.

the eSRS, and it is now used by nearly all Federal agencies and their prime contractors. The procedures for its use have now been incorporated into the Federal Acquisition Regulation (FAR), including a requirement for contracting officials to use the system to accept or reject their contractors' reports. SBA also uses the eSRS to generate subcontracting data for an annual report to Congress.

After several years (somewhere between 2010 and 2014), a number of government officials, including some senior SBA officials, began to question the accuracy of the eSRS data. Some even said that the system was fundamentally flawed. Why? Because, in some instances, subcontracting dollars exceeded prime contract dollars; and to most observers, this was impossible.

By the time people began questioning the eSRS data, I was no longer working in SBA headquarters; I had been transferred to Fort Worth, Texas, and I had other responsibilities. Nonetheless, I became aware of the issue in 2014; and given my own investment of time and effort into the eSRS's development, I prepared a paper explaining the paradox. I also prepared a hand-written diagram and table similar to the one that Arvind Patel designed for this book to accompany my narrative explanation (see Flowchart and Table 1). In 2014, near the end of the year, I sent the paper and the accompanying exhibits to the Director of SBA's Office of Government Contracting. Unfortunately, my explanation did not settle the issue immediately, and I continued to have discussions about it right up until the year before I retired.

How then, if there is no flaw in the design of the eSRS, is it possible for subcontracting dollars to exceed prime contract dollars? The answer is that we are seeing the effect of dollars turning over. Many readers will recognize this as a variation of the multiplier effect that they studied in economics. In this case, a prime contractor receives a government contract, does some of the work itself ("in house"), and subcontracts the remainder of the work to other companies (subcontractors). The subcontractors do the same—that is, they do some of work themselves and subcontract some of it to other companies. This process may continue through one or more lower-tier subcontractors. Periodically and at the end of each fiscal year, the large businesses (SBA uses the term *other-than-small businesses)* and their other-than-small subcontractors use the eSRS to report the dollar amount of their subcontracts to small business and the various socio-economic subsets. (Small businesses are exempt from the requirement to file this report, even if they subcontracted to other small businesses.)

By means of a simplified example, Mr. Patel's flowchart and Table 1 illustrate how the subcontracting dollars can ultimately exceed the value of the original contract. In Mr. Patel's example, a $10 million contract generates $12 million in subcontracts, including $4 million to small businesses. This is a hypothetical example, of course, and it does not play out the same way on every contract. Moreover, since small businesses are not required to file subcontracting reports, the actual dollar value of subcontracting would likely be higher, possibly *much higher*, than what Mr. Patel's example reveals or what the SBA sees when it generates its report on subcontracting achievements to Congress because small businesses often subcontract to other small businesses, and this data is never captured anywhere.

During my conversations with senior SBA managers and others prior to my retirement, I often heard people argue, as one of Esmeralda's opponents did during the Vice-Presidential debate in Chapter 8, that the eSRS is double counting. That is not so. This may

Arvind Patel's Flowchart

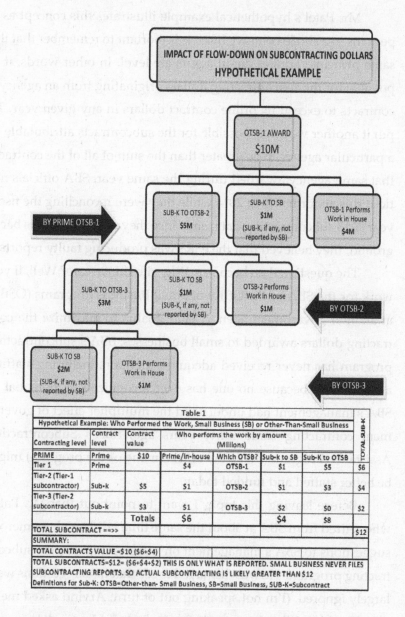

IMPACT OF FLOW-DOWN ON SUBCONTRACTING DOLLARS
HYPOTHETICAL EXAMPLE

OTSB-1 AWARD
$10M

BY PRIME OTSB-1

SUB-K TO OTSB-2
$5M

SUB-K TO SB
$1M
(SUB-K, if any, not reported by SB)

OTSB-1 Performs Work in House
$4M

SUB-K TO OTSB-3
$3M

SUB-K TO SB
$1M
(SUB-K, if any, not reported by SB)

OTSB-2 Performs Work in House
$1M

BY OTSB-2

SUB-K TO SB
$2M
(SUB-K, if any, not reported by SB)

OTSB-3 Performs Work in House
$1M

BY OTSB-3

Table 1							
Hypothetical Example: Who Performed the Work, Small Business (SB) or Other-Than-Small Business							TOTAL SUB-K
Contracting level	Contract level	Contract value	Who performs the work by amount (Millions)				
			Prime/in-house	Which OTSB?	Sub-k to SB	Sub-K to OTSB	
PRIME	Prime	$10	$4	OTSB-1	$1	$5	$6
Tier 1	Prime						
Tier-2 (Tier-1 subcontractor)	Sub-k	$5	$1	OTSB-2	$1	$3	$4
Tier-3 (Tier-2 subcontractor)	Sub-k	$3	$1	OTSB-3	$2	$0	$2
		Totals	$6		$4	$8	
TOTAL SUBCONTRACT ==>>							$12
SUMMARY:							
TOTAL CONTRACTS VALUE =$10 ($6+$4)							
TOTAL SUBCONTRACTS=$12= ($6+$4+$2) THIS IS ONLY WHAT IS REPORTED. SMALL BUSINESS NEVER FILES SUBCONTRACTING REPORTS. SO ACTUAL SUBCONTRACTING IS LIKELY GREATER THAN $12							
Definitions for Sub-K: OTSB=Other-than- Small Business, SB=Small Business, SUB-K=Subcontract							

Flowchart and All Tables Designed by Arvind Patel

not be obvious when you look at Mr. Patel's flow-chart, but no sub-contract is counted more than once.

Mr. Patel's hypothetical example illustrates this concept as it pertains to a single contract, but it is important to remember that the same principle applies on an aggregate level. In other words, it is possible for the subcontracting dollars originating from an agency's contracts to exceed its prime contract dollars in any given year. To put it another way, it is possible for the subcontracts attributable to a particular agency to be greater than the sum of all of the contracts that same agency awarded during the same year. SBA officials noticed this abnormality in 2014 while they were reconciling the fiscal year 2013 subcontracting data; and since they didn't have this background, they believed that the eSRS was producing faulty reports.

The question then becomes: Why should we care? Well, if you work for the SBA or the Office of Small Business Programs (OSBP) at another government agency, your goal is to maximize the contracting dollars awarded to small businesses. SBA's subcontracting program has never received adequate attention, including staffing and funding, because no one has ever recognized its potential. If SBA's management had understood the multiplier effect of government contracting some thirty years ago, SBA's Subcontracting Assistance Program (that's the official name of the program) might be better staffed and funded today.

Before leaving this topic, I want to point out that Mr. Patel, who retired from SBA at about the same time I did, made numerous suggestions to SBA's management on ways to improve the subcontracting program. He was dismayed to see that his suggestions were largely ignored. (I'm not speaking out of turn; Arvind asked me to mention this.) What happened *after* Arvind and I retired, however, was even worse.

In fiscal year 2018, SBA headquarters ordered a moratorium on all subcontracting compliance reviews and a number of other activities, including training, that had been the core of SBA's subcontracting program for decades. Why? I have no idea, nor do any of SBA's Area Directors or Commercial Market Representatives (CMRs)[6]—and I have spoken to nearly every one of them. In effect, SBA management tossed out the window nearly all of the tools that CMRs use to do their job, tools that took decades to develop: program compliance reviews, follow-up reviews, performance reviews (also known as desk reviews), and subcontracting assistance and orientation reviews (also known as SOARs). Just to be clear, what I'm speaking about is SBA's program to monitor the compliance of large-business prime contractors with their subcontracting plans, as required by Section 8(d) of the Small Business Act.

I was so alarmed about SBA's disregard for subcontracting compliance reviews that I returned to Washington after I retired, in February 2018 and again in April 2018, and met with senior SBA officials in the Office of Government Contracting in an effort to convince them that SBA was abrogating its responsibilities under the Small Business Act. When my efforts to convince SBA management failed, or at least appeared to have no impact, I submitted a formal proposal to SBA's Inspector General (IG) in July 2018 suggesting an audit of the Subcontracting Assistance Program. An employee in the IG's office responded a few weeks later and advised me that the IG was reviewing my request. As I write this (in February 2020), I have not been able to determine the status of the audit,

---

[6] The SBA employees who conduct compliance reviews of large prime contractors. SBA began using this title in the mid-1980s; prior to that, the same employees were called Subcontract Specialists or Subcontracting Specialists.

or even if the IG is conducting an audit, despite more than one attempt to contact the IG's office.

Every small business seeking government subcontracts should be as alarmed about this as Arvind and I are. SBA's CMRs, most of whom were productive and effective a few years ago, have essentially been sidelined. It is my understanding that SBA's CMRs have not conducted any on-site compliance reviews, follow-up reviews, or SOARs for nearly two years;[7] moreover, the current approach to desk reviews—an analysis of the subcontracting reports filed by the prime contractors—is less comprehensive than it was prior to 2018. If SBA's Inspector General is unwilling or unable to rectify this problem by means of an audit, my next step will be to bring it to the attention of the small business committees of the U.S. House of Representatives and the U.S. Senate.[8] [9]

---

[7] SBA management may dispute this, but the so-called "compliance reviews" conducted by SBA's CMRs during the past two years don't come close to the definition of such in SBA's own regulation: 13 CFR 125.3.

[8] SBA's Inspector General's published reports are available to the public at https://www.sba.gov/about-sba/oversight-advocacy/office-inspector-general/reports.

[9] The reader who is interested in learning more about the subcontracting program should read the coverage in SBA's regulation (13 CFR 125.3) and the Federal Acquisition Regulation (FAR), specifically 48 CFR 19.7 and the clauses at 48 CFR 52.219-8, -9, and -10. SBA's size regulation at 13 CFR 121.404(e), 121.410, and 121.411 is also relevant and essential. Some contracts contain the FAR clauses at 52.212-5 or 52.244-6, which waive the flow-down subcontracting-plan requirement (i.e., the requirement for a prime contractor to obtain a subcontracting plan from a subcontractor) when the subcontract is for a commercial item. Readers wanting to see the statute on which the program is based should refer to Public Law 95-507 and Section 8(d) of the Small Business Act; and anyone wanting to dig further should consider reading three policy letters issued by the Office of Federal Procurement Policy (OFPP) in 1980 and 1981: OFPP Policy Letters 80-1, 80-2, and Supplement #1 to 80-2. Most of the guidance in these policy letters has now been incorporated into FAR 19.7; however, Supplement #1 to 80-2 contains an interesting discussion on several issues, especially with respect to the flow-down requirement.

-2-

It wouldn't require a very careful reading of *The First Robot President* to see that one of the most important themes is the crisis of overpopulation in the twenty-sixth century. During the Vice-Presidential debate in 2520, Esmeralda alludes to the Earth's population as being 500 billion, and readers may wonder how I chose that figure. Is it a plausible estimate based on current birth rates and longevity? Well, let's look at Mr. Patel's tables and see if we can find the answer.

Mr. Patel's Table #2 addresses the planet's population over the next five hundred years, from 2018 (the year he did this for me) through 2520, with and without disasters such as world wars, famine, pandemics, earthquakes, hurricanes, meteors hitting the Earth, and so on. Based on the growth rate during the second decade of the twenty-first century, 1.09%, the third column in Table #2 reveals a world population of more than 1.7 trillion (*trillion, not billion!*), or 1.778301 trillion to be exact, in 2520 assuming we have no world wars or other disasters during this period.

In reality, of course, we are bound to have some wars and other disasters; even though we hope and pray we won't, history tells us we will likely have one or more world wars and countless other disasters. Accordingly, column #4 of the same table provides a different result under this more realistic scenario—a population of just over 100 billion. Why, then, did I imply (through Thomas in Chapter 2 and Esmeralda in Chapter 8) that the world's population in 2520 will be 500 billion? I didn't have a scientific basis for this prediction—after all, no one knows what the next five hundred years will bring—but I didn't think it likely that world wars and other catastrophes will reduce the human population from 1.7 trillion to 100 billion; 500 billion seemed about right.

Mr. Patel's Tables #3, #4, and #5 explore the Earth's population over the subsequent five-hundred years, 2520 to 3020. With no disasters and no birth lottery (if you haven't read the novel yet—I know some readers start with the Afterword—you'll have to read it to find out what a birth lottery is), Table #3 predicts a population of over 22.7 trillion by 3020. With hypothetical disasters but no birth lottery, Table #4 predicts a population of over 1.5 trillion in 3020; and Table #5 takes the data from Table #4 but includes a birth-lottery component, which would bring the Earth's population back to roughly seven billion during the same period. The idea is that, by means of a birth lottery, we could bring the planet's population back to where it was at the *beginning* of the millennium—roughly seven billion— by the *end* of the millennium. (By the way, to be fair, I gave Arvind the assumptions for each of the population tables, so don't blame him if you disagree with the results.)

If any readers are skeptical of our approach based on the assumption that the growth rate during the past decade will continue at the same rate for five more centuries, I ask them to consider this: in 1800, the world's population was approximately one billion; in the year 2000, it was roughly seven billion—a sevenfold increase in two hundred years.[10] If the population increases at the same rate over the next five hundred years, using this approach, it will be forty-nine billion in 2200, 343 billion in 2400, and 1.2 *trillion* in 2500.

Anyone who has read any books on the Earth's ecosystem will understand the significance of this data. (Sorry, I think the term *these data* is too pedantic.) Human beings are well on their way to destroying the planet; and while conservation measures may help, the only real solution is to keep a lid on the human population. What should

---

[10] www.populationconnection.org/. (Find tab labeled "Education.")

the ceiling be? Esmeralda has an answer to that, too. It's in Chapter 12 if you missed it.

Until I read *The Population Explosion*,[11] I was under the misconception—and I'm sure I wasn't the only one—that the population crisis was primarily an issue for China, India, and a handful of other unfortunate countries on other continents. In fact, from the standpoint of global ecology, the crisis applies to the United States even more than it does to China and India because the United States, like other rich nations, uses a disproportionate amount of the planet's resources. To put it another way, a baby born in the United States will have far greater adverse impact on the planet's ecosystem during its lifetime than a baby born in a poor nation. I encourage anyone who has not read *The Population Explosion* to do so. There are many other excellent books on the plight of our planet, of course, including several written by Al Gore, a tireless crusader for the environment, that are more recent and contain more up-to-date information (Esmeralda mentions three of Al Gore's books in Chapter 4). I also encourage my readers to look at a website called *Population Connection*, formerly called *Zero Population Growth*, or *ZPG*, at www.populationconnection.org, which has advocated for population stabilization since 1968.

I'm fully aware that there are some—Elon Musk, I understand, among them—who see this issue differently. There is even a book published in 2019 with the title, *Empty Planet: The Shock of Global Population Decline*.[12] For the sake of humanity, I hope that they're right and that Arvind and I are wrong. Be that as it may, and regardless who is right, we cannot put this issue aside until we reverse humans' ongoing destruction of our planet. Responsible growth—or no

---

[11] Ehrlich, Paul R. and Anne H. *The Population Explosion*. (London, Hutchinson, 1990.).

[12] Copyright 2019 by John Ibbitson and Darrell Bricker.

growth at all—is step number one in addressing environmental and atmospheric destruction, climate change, poverty, starvation, disease, and a host of other problems facing modern civilization. *The First Robot President* provides a glimpse into the possible crisis facing our species in the twenty-sixth century if we don't reverse the population explosion before then. The time to address this issue is now, not in five hundred years.

-3-

In Chapter 8, Sarah points out that Al Gore would have been our forty-third President but for the electoral college and says, "Thank God they finally got rid of the winner-take-all system."[13] The assumption is that, sometime over the next five hundred years, we will amend the Constitution and come up with a better method of electing our President. *Winner-take-all* means, of course, that the winner of the popular vote in a given state receives all of that state's electoral-college votes, even if the loser loses the popular vote by as little as one vote. I have never spoken to anyone who thinks this is fair (I'm sure Al Gore doesn't). However, in doing the research for this novel, I learned something new—new for me, anyway—which is that two states, Maine and Nebraska, have already modified the winner-take-all system; the other forty-eight states could do the same thing without a Constitutional amendment. For readers who want to explore this issue further, I recommend an excellent article by Robert Longley titled "How the U.S. Electoral College System Works," which was updated in January 2020. You can find it at https://www.thoughtco.com/how-the-us-electoral-college-works-3322061 (note that the URL doesn't contain the word *system*).

---

[13] Sarah, Geraldine, and Jacqueline discuss this subject again in Chapter 9.

-4-

The intolerance people have for each other's religions never ceases to amaze me; indeed, many religions claim to be the only path to salvation. Members of Jehovah's Witnesses, a relatively small sect in the Protestant branch of Christianity, take this mindset to an extreme; they believe that no one else, not even other Christians, can achieve salvation—or so I have been told by more than one Jehovah's Witness over the years.

For the record, I was raised as a Christian, but my wife is Buddhist and has encouraged me to learn more about her religion; so after retiring in 2018, I began to study it. Comparisons between the two religions are interesting and sometimes useful, but I don't try to decide which of the two is better; rather, I search for wisdom in each and lock on to whatever I find in either religion that inspires me to be a better human being.

In Austin, Texas, where I live, we have an organization called iACT—Interfaith Action of Central Texas—which sponsors interdenominational activities throughout the year and brings Christians, Jews, Muslims, Hindus, Buddhists, and other religious practitioners together on a regular basis. I have found iACT's programs to be effective in promoting religious understanding and tolerance, and I believe every community should have something like it.

For anyone who wants to learn more about Buddhism, I recommend the Venerable Master Hsing Yun's *The Core Teachings, Essays in Basic Buddhism*, available through Buddha's Light Publishing in Los Angeles (and for sale at any Fo Guang Shan temple), or any number of other books by Master Hsing Yun (he has written many, all excellent) or The Dalai Lama's *Worlds in Harmony: Compassionate Action for a Better World*; and for anyone who wants to learn more about all of the world's major religions, not just Buddhism, I recommend Peter Stanford's *Religion* in the *50 Ideas You Really Need to Know* series published by Quercus; it is one of my favorite books in my library.

-5-

Arguably the most thought-provoking line in *The First Robot President* occurs in Chapter 13 when, during a reception for world leaders in Geneva, Esmeralda tells the Prime Minister of Great Britain that a robot can be and do anything a human being can be and do. When I wrote the novel, I set the time frame five hundred years from now—Esmeralda becomes President in 2521—because I wanted to make the story believable, and I didn't think anyone would believe that robots will look and act like human beings in the near future. However, given the pace of robotic technology, I believe this will occur sooner than we think, possibly in this century or, if not, certainly in the next. When you think about it in those terms, the idea of a robot being nearly indistinguishable from a human being in five hundred years doesn't sound that implausible, does it?

The question then becomes where will this ultimately take us. Will humans and robots marry? Will humans always control robots, or might they someday control us? *The First Robot President* envisions an auspicious outcome, but other writers may see it otherwise. I look forward to reading their take on it.

Robert Carlyle Taylor

March 9, 2020
robertcarlyletaylor@gmail.com

Arvind Patel's

Population Projections

World Population Growth Over the Next 1000 Years (No Birth Lottery)*

		TABLE 2				TABLE 3	
		Population 2018 - 2520 with & without Disasters				Years 2520 - 3020 with no Disasters	
NET Growth rate:==>	1.09%	Two scenarios, with and without hypothetical disasters. With no disasters, the current annual growth rate of 1.09% translates to an increase factor of 1.1145 every ten years thru 2520.			1.09%	Population growth from 2520 to 2030 with the assumption that there will be no disasters during this period.	
Increase Years	10				10		
Increase Factor	1.1145				1.1145		
Disaster Effect	Yes				None		
Birth Lottery % Reduction	0%	No birth lottery			0%	No birth lottery	
Line #	TIME FRAME	FIRST 500 YRS			SUBSEQUENT 500 YRS		
7	Year	Population Growth at current rate with no disasters	Population at current rate with hypothetical disasters ==>>	Population reduction due to hypothetical 10-year disasters	Year	Population with ==>>	No disaster effect
8	2018	7.700	7.700		2520	100.774	
9	2019	7.784	7.784		2530	112.313	
10	2020	7.869	7.869		2540	125.174	
11	2030	8.770	8.770		2550	139.506	
12	2040	9.774	9.774		2560	155.481	
13	2050	10.893	10.893		2570	173.284	
14	2060	12.140	12.140		2580	193.126	
15	2070	13.531	13.531		2590	215.240	
16	2080	15.080	15.080		2600	239.886	
17	2090	16.807	16.807	35%	2610	267.354	
18	2100	18.731	10.924		2620	297.967	
19	2110	20.876	12.175		2630	332.086	
27	2190	49.694	28.982		2710	790.507	
28	2200	55.384	32.301	36%	2720	881.024	
29	2210	61.725	20.673		2730	981.906	
30	2220	68.793	23.040		2740	1094.339	
37	2290	146.933	49.210		2810	2337.359	
38	2300	163.758	54.844	36%	2820	2604.998	
39	2310	182.509	35.100		2830	2903.283	
40	2320	203.407	39.120		2840	3235.723	
47	2390	434.450	83.554		2910	6911.068	
48	2400	484.197	93.121	39%	2920	7702.419	
49	2410	539.640	56.804		2930	8584.383	
50	2420	601.431	63.308		2940	9567.336	
57	2490	1284.575	135.218		3010	20434.537	
58	2500	1431.665	150.701	40%	3020	22774.391	
59	2510	1595.598	90.421				
60	2520	1778.301	100.774				

* Population in Billions

Flowchart and All Tables Designed by Arvind Patel

World Population Growth in Years 2520-3020 w & w/o Birth Lottery)*

	TABLE 4			TABLE 5		
	Population in Years 2520-3030 with disasters			Population in Years 2520-3020 w/Birth Lottery		
Net Growth Rate:==>	1.09%	Population growth from 2520 to 2030 with hypothethical disasters (war, famine, pandemics, and natural disasters such as earthqukes and hurricanes.)		1.09%	Population reduction using the data from Table 4 (with disasters) adjusted to show the effect of a birth lottery implemented across the planet.	
Increase Years	10			10		
Increase Factor**	1.1145			0.9936		
Disaster Effect	Yes			Yes		
Birth Lottery % Reduction	0%	No birth lottery		10.85%	Hypothetical Birth Lottery	
Line #	SUBSEQUENT 500 YRS					
7	Year	Population with ==>>	Effect of Random Disasters (Percent Reduction in Growth)	Year	Population with ==>>	Effect of Birth Lottery & Random Disasters (Percent Reduction in Growth)
8	2520	100.774		2520	100.774	
9	2530	112.313		2530	100.127	
10	2540	125.174		2540	99.484	
11	2550	139.506		2550	98.846	
12	2560	155.481		2560	98.211	
13	2570	173.284		2570	97.581	
14	2580	193.126		2580	96.955	
15	2590	215.240		2590	96.332	
16	2600	239.886		2600	95.714	
17	2610	267.354	33%	2610	95.100	38%
18	2620	179.127		2620	58.962	
19	2630	199.638		2630	58.583	
27	2710	475.224		2710	55.642	
28	2720	529.640	37%	2720	55.284	40%
29	2730	333.673		2730	33.171	
30	2740	371.880		2740	32.958	
37	2810	794.286		2810	31.505	
38	2820	885.236	35%	2820	31.303	38%
39	2830	575.403		2830	19.408	
40	2840	641.290		2840	19.283	
47	2910	1369.708	40%	2910	11.502	
48	2920	821.825		2920	11.429	
49	2930	915.928		2930	11.355	
50	2940	1020.806		2940	11.282	
57	3010	2180.303	28%	3010	10.785	35%
58	3020	1569.818		3020	7.010	

* Population in Billions

** Increase Factor of less than 1.0 indicates negative growth

Flowchart and All Tables Designed by Arvind Patel

Acknowledgements

I wish to thank two of my friends for their invaluable support: first, my former colleague Arvind Patel for his excellent flow-chart and spreadsheets, not to mention his patience in waiting two years for me to finish the novel; and second, fellow writer Chris D'Urso for agreeing to finish the novel if anything happened to me. (I'm in reasonably good health; but at age 75, you need to think about things like that.)

I'm extremely grateful to Tracy Atkins at The Book Makers and Tanja Prokop at Book Design Templates for their assistance in helping me to create a beautiful book in three different formats. It was a pleasure to work with them.

I also want to thank Chris, Brenda Ernst, Cynthia Yung, and Alec Marshall for their assistance in proofreading, and Adam Corrigan at LegalZoom for helping me to set up my LLC.

Finally, I want to give a shout-out to some of the authors whose books I found helpful in my journey to write and publish this novel: Stephen King's *On Writing*, Jane Friedman's *How to Publish Your Book* (her guidebook to a course by the same title in *The Great Courses*), and Andrea Lunsford's *EasyWriter*. (I consider Andrea Lunsford to be the William Strunk, Jr., if not the E.B. White, of our time; I never sit down to write without my *EasyWriter* within arm's reach.) Finally, I would be remiss if I didn't mention *The Elements of Style*, which was originally written by Mr. Strunk, an English professor at Cornell University, and later revised and expanded by Mr.

White, one of his students, who, as you know (or *should* know), became a famous writer himself. If you don't own this book, or even if you do, you should purchase the 2005 or 2007 edition illustrated by Maira Kalman; it is a joy to own and read.

About the Author

Robert Carlyle Taylor was born and educated in New England, residing primarily in Vermont, Massachusetts, and Rhode Island at various times while he was growing up. His mother and father were both teachers and taught nearly every level of primary, secondary, and higher-level education; together, at one time or another, they taught every grade from kindergarten through college except one (neither of them ever taught the seventh grade).

Mr. Taylor developed his interest in literature and writing while attending high school at Governor Dummer Academy, now known as The Governor's Academy, in South Byfield, Massachusetts. While he contributed to the school's literary magazine and yearbook, he was better known as a wrestler; during his four years at the academy, he achieved a record of twenty-eight wins and two losses and was the champion of the 115-pound weight class in the 1962 New England Class A Interscholastic Tournament.

Mr. Taylor studied creative writing briefly at Brown University in Providence, Rhode Island, under the novelist John Hawkes; and some years later, he studied accounting and economics as a non-degree student at Champlain College and the University of Vermont, respectively, both in Burlington, Vermont.

Mr. Taylor began his career in 1966 at Jordan Marsh Company, now Macy's, in Peabody, Massachusetts, where he managed boys' clothing and men's and children's shoes. In 1972, he moved to

Montpelier, Vermont, and accepted a position with the Montpelier National Bank. In 1978, after six years in banking, he joined the U.S. Small Business Administration (SBA), where he remained for forty years. His career with SBA included nineteen years in SBA's headquarters in Washington, D.C., where he served as a program manager and assistant director in the agency's Office of Government Contracting. He retired in 2018 after serving ten years as SBA's Area Director for Government Contracting in Fort Worth, Texas, where he oversaw SBA's government contracting programs in eleven states encompassing two of SBA's ten regions.

Over the years, Mr. Taylor has participated in many community and civic activities. In the mid-1970's, he served as the President of the Capital City Jaycees in Montpelier, Vermont, and was also an active member of the Central Vermont Rotary Club. He chaired a number of initiatives for both the Jaycees and the Rotary Club and also served as Chairman of the Organization and Extension Committee of the Boy Scouts of America's Green Mountain Council, which established several new chapters of the Boy Scouts and Cub Scouts in Central Vermont during his tenure. He also served on the Board of Trustees of the Bethany United Church of Christ in Montpelier, Vermont, and chaired the American Heart Association's annual fund drive in both the City of Brattleboro and Windham County, Vermont. Today he is active in the Xiang Yun Temple in Austin, Texas, where he gives monthly talks on Buddhism to English-speaking members and participates in various other activities sponsored by the temple.

The First Robot President is Mr. Taylor's first published novel.

About Arvind Patel

A rvind Patel retired from the Federal government in 2018 with over thirty-one years of service, including thirty years in the government contracting division of the U.S. Small Business Administration (SBA) where he worked in the prime contracting, subcontracting and certificate-of-competency programs.

Mr. Patel left India in 1970 and came to the United States on a student visa. His father was an English teacher in India and instilled in him the importance of an education. Arvind earned a Master of Science degree in mechanical engineering from Worcester Polytechnic Institute in Massachusetts and became a licensed professional engineer in Massachusetts and Virginia.

From 1972 to 1986, Mr. Patel worked as a Nuclear Power Plant Engineer on several nuclear power plant projects, designing and acquiring components for safer nuclear operations. He began his Federal career in 1986 as an Industrial Engineer with the U.S. Navy in Groton, Connecticut, working on industrial modernization projects and administering the Value Engineering Program.

Arvind joined SBA in the late 1980s as a Break-out Procurement Center Representative assigned to the SBA break-out team at Hanscom Air Force Base in Bedford, Massachusetts, where his duties included analyzing major weapon systems and identifying subsystems and components that could be broken out for increased competition. Between 1987 and 2000, this program saved taxpayers close to $200 million.

From 2000 to 2004, the SBA assigned Mr. Patel to the Naval Underwater Warfare Center in Newport, Rhode Island, where he sought to maximize opportunities for small businesses in his role as a Procurement Center Representative.

From 2004 until his retirement, Mr. Patel served as SBA's principal Commercial Market Representative, or CMR, in Massachusetts and other parts of New England. In this capacity, he sought to increase subcontracting opportunities for small businesses with Federal prime contractors such as Raytheon and other major defense contractors. In addition, throughout his SBA career, Mr. Patel performed capacity reviews for small businesses seeking a Certificate of Competency, and he served as a member of several task forces for SBA headquarters.

Mr. Patel became a United States citizen in 1978. He is a trustee of the Satsang Association, a foundation in Woburn, Massachusetts, where he continuously volunteers to serve humanity. He has also established a charitable foundation to provide funds for poor and needy people in India.

Mr. Patel designed the flow-chart and tables that accompany the author's Afterword.

CPSIA information can be obtained
at www.ICGtesting.com
Printed in the USA
LVHW090407120422
715538LV00004B/21